T0003450

MY DIRTY CALIFORNIA

Jason Mosberg

Simon & Schuster Paperbacks

New York London Toronto Sydney New Delhi

Simon & Schuster Paperbacks
An Imprint of Simon & Schuster, Inc.
1230 Avenue of the Americas
New York, NY 10020

This book is a work of fiction. Any references to historical events, real people, or real places are used fictitiously. Other names, characters, places, and events are products of the author's imagination, and any resemblance to actual events or places or persons, living or dead, is entirely coincidental.

First Simon & Schuster trade paperback edition August 2023

SIMON & SCHUSTER PAPERBACKS and colophon are registered trademarks of Simon & Schuster, Inc.

For information about special discounts for bulk purchases, please contact Simon & Schuster Special Sales at 1-866-506-1949 or business@simonandschuster.com.

The Simon & Schuster Speakers Bureau can bring authors to your live event. For more information or to book an event, contact the Simon & Schuster Speakers Bureau at 1-866-248-3049 or visit our website at www.simonspeakers.com.

Interior design by Ruth Lee-Mui

Manufactured in China

1 3 5 7 9 10 8 6 4 2

Library of Congress Cataloging-in-Publication Data has been applied for.

ISBN 978-1-9821-7866-6
ISBN 978-1-9821-7868-0 (pbk)
ISBN 978-1-9821-7869-7 (ebook)

For Rika,

my partner in exploring

the great state of

California

Prologue

The podcast *My Dirty California* was scheduled to air in November 2021, but executives at Boxcar Media pulled it at the last second due to two pending lawsuits and an active FBI investigation. The following is a transcript of a clip that leaked from the first episode:

> *I remember reading somewhere the best way to be from California is to be from somewhere else. I'm from Detroit. I moved to LA to get into the film industry, to make movies, and I ended up making narrative podcasts. I never thought I'd do a true-crime podcast, but when I stumbled across Marty Morrel's* My Dirty California *website, I changed my mind. Who is Marty Morrel? I want to resist the impulse to refer to him as a drifter. Marty wasn't drifting or roaming through life. He was studying it and documenting it. It's impossible to make a distinction between my draw to Marty and my draw to his depiction of California. I've been fascinated with California since I moved here. The Golden State's home to nine national parks. If it was a country, it would be the fifth largest economy in the world. In one state, there are twenty thousand square miles of desert and seven hundred miles of Pacific coastline, plus the Sierra Nevada mountains. There's everything from the redwood forest to the Mojave Desert. California's the origin of the film industry, the internet, the personal computer, and the skateboard. People tend to associate Cali with cities like LA, San Diego, and San Francisco, but it's got the highest agriculture output of any state in the US. We've got the biggest trees in the world, the tallest trees in the world, and the oldest trees in the world. I love this state, I really do. Yet, at times, California feels like something hip someone in marketing tried to fit in a*

bottle to sell. California is the kind of place that can make a person who doesn't care about flowers care about wildflowers. But there's a dark history below California's undeniably beautiful surface. A dark history with how its destiny manifested. Japanese internment. The LA riots. The California Alien Land Law of 1913. The Mexican-American War. Facebook. Sometimes I think California never left the gold rush era. Gold was merely substituted with other treasure to chase. Movies. Fame. Waves. Venture capital. Youth. Wine. Love. Spirituality. Technology. I guess I'm part of the everlasting, ever-changing rush. When I first moved to LA, I realized no one here goes bowling. There's too much to do. Marty Morrel did it all. He explored every inch of the city of LA, every crack and crevice of the state of California, and it's all documented in hundreds of videos, thousands of pictures, and scores of essays and journal entries. Even if there hadn't been any crimes, I think I would have wanted to make a podcast about Marty. But there were crimes. I thought murders would be the most disturbing part of this podcast, but that was before I learned about Pandora's House.

Chapter One

Jody

An abnormal day is normal until it isn't.

Jody slices sweet potatoes into chunks that will become sweet potato fries. His father, Joseph Sr., sorts the mail at the kitchen table.

"Should I start cooking the chicken?" The old man sounds like an old man who'd spent forty years smoking cigarettes, but Jody has seen him smoke only the occasional cigar.

"I'm about thirty-five minutes out. Up to you."

Joseph Sr. pulls out a bowl of raw chicken pieces that have been marinating in a special dressing recipe Kraft calls Italian. As he passes by Jody, he says, "You chop 'em like that, you're gon' lose a finger one day."

Jody sighs. He's been using a knife the same way since about the time *Joseph Jr.* became *Jody* by way of *Joey*. This came courtesy of a baby brother who used to throw in extra *d*s where they didn't belong. A brother who called himself *Mardy*. A brother who left at seventeen and hasn't been back in ten years.

A knock on the door echoes from the foyer into the kitchen.

"C'mon'n," says Joseph Sr. "Prolly Cutter. He called earlier about picking up some firewood. Even though his back is holding up better than mine."

The screen door creaks, followed by heavy footsteps through the foyer.

A man steps into the kitchen. But it's not their neighbor Cutter.

It's a drifter-hippie-type fellow with shaggy hair. Pierced ears don't hold any jewelry. A dirty hoop-handled canvas duffel bag rests atop one shoulder. Three patches, whether cosmetic or functional, add an extra layer of scrappiness to an already scrappy-looking bag. Jody knows the man is twenty-seven years old, but his crow's-feet suggest a man in his mid-thirties.

Marty.

His ear-to-ear grin accentuates his pointy chin, and he holds it. Like he's posing for a welcome-home photograph. Stunned, Jody steals a quick glance at the counter. His father stands frozen, like his hands are sitting in cement rather than raw chicken.

Jody breaks the silence. "Marty . . . How . . ." He sets down the knife. Marty drops his hefty duffel to the wood floor. The brothers embrace. The hug helps Jody find the words. "What are you doing here?"

"Felt like visiting."

Joseph Sr. washes his hands with soap and dries them before he extends the right one. Marty chuckles at his father's formality, but he does shake Joseph Sr.'s hand.

"Good to see you, Marty. You look . . . older."

"Well, I got older. You two, you're looking younger." Marty delivers the line with a contagious smile. It reminds Jody of being kids. He fourteen, Marty seven. Whether they played Ping-Pong or soccer or one-on-one basketball or GoldenEye 007, win or lose—whether Jody had let him win or not—Marty wore a sly smile.

"Did you come from LA?" Jody asks.

"Yeah."

Jody leans left, steals a glimpse of the driveway. His dad's maroon Toyota Camry next to his own gray Ford truck. "You fly?"

"Uh, no. My friend was driving 'cross the country. He gave me a ride."

Rory bounds through the doggy door and runs right to Marty. Marty bends and pets the dog.

"Wait, this ain't Sage, is it?"

"Sage died a few years back," says Jody. "We got Rory here three years ago."

"Same breed?"

"Yeah. Mutt," says Jody.

Marty laughs as he strokes the less-exposed fur behind Rory's ears.

"I could've sent the money. That why you're here?"

Marty looks at his father, whose eyes are wide, alive. "What? No. What money?"

Rory seems to sense the tension and runs over to the den and plops onto the sofa.

Joseph Sr. returns to the chicken, starts placing pieces on a griddle. Another knock on the door. Joseph Sr. mutters half under his breath, "Who's this gonna be, your mother?"

Jody's eyes meet Marty's. Reflecting thoughts, memories, fears, and dreams in an echo chamber lost in time. Brothers.

Joseph Sr. shouts out in his gruff nonsmoking smoker voice, "C'mon'n."

The screen door creaks. In walks Cutter, a burly man in his fifties with a frame that looks architecturally designed to chop wood. A guy whose name sounds like a nickname for a goddamn lumberman. And yet, here he is, taking a neighbor's offer for free firewood.

"Hey, Jody. How are you, bud?"

"Good."

"You hear who the Eagles traded? Goddam *Iggles*. They—" Cutter stops when he sees a third man in the kitchen. "Hey, I'm Cutter." He extends a hand.

Marty shakes it. "It's Marty."

"Marty?! *Marty* Marty? Holy shit, it is you. What are you doing here?"

"Just visiting," says Marty.

"Christ, must've been five years. How long you staying?"

"Ten," says Joseph Sr. "It's been ten years."

Jody eyes his dad. Is he trying to come off cold?

"I'll let you guys chat. I'll just grab the firewood."

"It's on the deck. Birch in the back might've rotted, but the rest'll burn good," says Joseph Sr.

Cutter smiles at Marty one more time, then walks out the back of the house.

"Why don't I run to Acme and get some beer for you two to drink? I don't think we have more'n a sixer."

"Dad, that'll be fine," Jody says.

"I don't need more than a beer. As long as it's a Yuengling."

"Still all we drink. Dad, stay here. We'll eat." Jody looks to his brother. "We were just putting together dinner. You hungry?"

"If you've got enough."

"We were making a few meals' worth."

Whole minutes of silence often passed as Jody and his father ate pork chops or barbecue chicken or grilled salmon. And those silences were comfortable. But now, as the three eat, Jody feels every ten-second gap between words.

"What were you doing out there for money?" Joseph Sr. asks, cutting into the latest bout of silence with the fatherly of all fatherly questions.

"Just odds and ends. Enough to make odds and ends meet."

Jody and his father wait for more details that don't come.

"The driveway business still going well?"

Joseph Sr. sighs. "Ups and downs. Was doing well for a few years but a couple Mexican crews popped up. Had to bring my price down a bit to compete. Long as the economy ain't complete shit, folks'll pay to have 'em repaved."

Marty turns to his older brother. "What about you? You still selling those magazines?"

Heat rises into Jody's face and settles in his cheeks. Jody knew his younger brother had thought it was cool he had saved up money mowing lawns and planned to go to Lehigh University as a twenty-four-year-old. He knew his younger brother had thought it was cool that when Jody didn't get the scholarship he hoped he'd get, he had come up with a plan to sell magazine subscriptions on the side to help pay his tuition. But Marty had left before Jody had arrived at school. He left before Jody got obsessed with selling the magazines and began making thousand-person lists of possible customers. Before he started spending fourteen hours a day trying to sell magazines, three hours a day in class, and two hours a day studying, which left a grand total of five hours a day to eat, sleep, and retain half a beer of a social life. He'd been a typical high school student, but his one year of college stood out as atypical. For starters, he was six years older than most members of his class. The guys on his hall stayed busy getting blackout drunk and testing the boundaries of what consent meant. Aside from the age gap, no one else was studying as much as Jody, and on top of studying, he was working a seventy-hour workweek selling magazines door-to-door. By February of his freshman year, Jody experienced a breakdown. *Fatigue*, the doctors called it. His body had rejected his grit. Jody started seeing a therapist. By session number two, she linked the incident with another time in Jody's life. When Jody was sixteen, he was the school's star soccer player as a junior. But the summer before his senior year, he started practicing soccer for six hours a day. His relationships with his friends fizzled out, and he spent little time with his family. And he ended up hurting his knees from overexertion and missing his senior-year season altogether. Like with soccer, in the case of college, an obsessive focus backfired and prevented him from succeeding at the original goal. The doctor diagnosed Jody with obsessive compulsive personality disorder (OCPD), which she explained was different from obsessive compulsive disorder (OCD). The symptoms include an excessive devotion to work that impairs social or family activities, excessive fixation with lists, rigid following of ethical codes, extreme frugality without reason, and hoarding. She started Jody on antianxiety meds he's been taking ever since. Over the course of ten warning that people with his disorder pursue certain career goals to the detriment of personal relationships, and yet here he is at thirty-four without a girlfriend.

After they exchange good nights and Joseph Sr. disappears to his bedroom, Marty's gaze returns to the clock. "He normally go to bed at eight forty-five?"

"No. Sometimes."

Marty chuckles, the laugh evolving into a *hmmm*.

"Give'm a break. It's a lot. You showing up like this. Might've made it easier if you'd called first."

"I thought it would be fun this way."

"Fine. But you gotta see why it'd be hard for him after all these years you haven't visited."

"You guys could've visited me. Planes go both ways last I heard. I at least wrote to you guys. Letters. Postcards. Hundreds of 'em. All them books I sent you. Never got a line back from either of you."

"Sorry, brother. I ain't the letter-writing type."

For a moment, Jody considers taking Marty upstairs to show him the bookshelf in his room. Hundreds of books alphabetized by author. Every time he got a book in the mail from Marty, Jody read it. He added the book to a database. He looked up the author and made a list of every other book that author had ever written. Then he bought a copy of each novel by that author. And he read them all. So when Marty sent Jody an old paperback copy of *Cannery Row*, Jody read it and then read everything Steinbeck wrote, from *Cup of Gold* to *Travels with Charley*.

"You think it's really cool for me to stay here though?"

"Yeah." Jody can't quell his own curiosity. "For how long?"

"I don't know."

"Well, your room's still there."

Marty scoops up his bag, and Jody follows him down the hall and up the stairs. Marty turns on the light and steps inside the room with fading yellow walls, which at their age don't look dissimilar from yellowing white walls.

"He'd've left it the exact way you did. But we had some water damage a couple years ago. Your posters and stuff are in a box in the closet."

The stress-free smile Marty had walked in the door with two hours ago slinks away. The sight of his childhood bedroom seems to bring a rush of memories. The good, the bad, and the complicated.

"Your room still the same?" asks Marty.

Jody shrugs, doesn't offer to show him. He struggles to discard anything, instead organizing his possessions by filling old shoeboxes. At one point, he realized he had way too much stuff. He made an extensive list of what to keep, what to donate, and what to throw out. But making the list was as far as he got.

"You have to work tomorrow?" asks Marty.

"I'm off till the first week of August. Doing a couple soccer camps over the summer. And I've been volunteering over at White Clay Creek a day or two a week. Just helping them maintain the nature trail."

"You want to show me?"

"Sure. We'll take Rory."

Jody and Marty walk along the trail, appreciating the woodland phlox and wild geranium. Rory runs ahead, appreciating the wildflowers his own way. Jody suppresses a belch and fights off a fleeting urge to vomit.

"You all right?" asks Marty.

"Yup," says Jody. A year ago, his dad found Jody throwing up one morning after he'd only had two beers the night before. Over the years, he'd had a harder time drinking without feeling sick the next day, but he never stopped. After calling him "an alcoholic who drinks the least amount of booze ever," his dad said Jody should either quit drinking or go to the doctor. Jody went to a doctor who told him when he drank before bed, it caused the excretion of excess stomach acid overnight, which was making him nauseous. He told Jody not to drink three hours before bed, but he also wanted Jody to see a psychiatrist because he thought the excess stomach acid could be linked to anxiety. The therapist he'd seen a decade earlier, and gotten along with well, had since retired. Jody met with a new psychologist, who wanted to focus on why Jody had continued drinking a beer or two every night if it made him sick. He believed that Jody liked the nausea, that he was always buzzed or hungover, both states functioning to suppress anxiety. Jody thought that was ridiculous and had not gone back or sought a second opinion.

"Does Dad really have a bum knee, or did he just not want to come?" asks Marty.

"He's been having trouble with it. You should cut him some slack. Chill out."

"Chill out? About Dad? I've chilled out about Dad. In high school, I used to daydream about shooting him in the head."

Marty laughs at his own joke, but Jody wonders if he was joking.

"We had different fathers, you and me," Marty adds.

"He was different after Mom died. I admit it."

"*Different* is generous."

Marty was too young at the time to realize silence was the best his father could offer in the wake of his wife's death from breast cancer. And Jody was too young to realize at the time that they weren't experiencing their father's emotional absence the same way. Jody was twenty, and he'd had a *present* father all the way through childhood. But Marty was only thirteen when he lost his mother and his father disappeared into a black hole of silent grief.

They lose sight of Rory as they go around a bend in the trail.

"Did you really have a friend who was driving across the country?"

Marty laughs. "No, I hitched."

"Across the whole country?"

"Truckers do it. For cash."

"Do you got a car out there?"

"No. Well, at times, I shared one with people."

Jody finds the wording strange. They come around another bend, where the trail runs parallel to a creek. Rory jumps in the water. Marty takes off his shoes and socks. He pulls his shirt over his head, revealing an assortment of tattoos covering 70 percent of his chest, back, and arms. Jody looks away. As if it's something he's not supposed to see. Only when he hears the splash of Marty landing in the swimming hole does he return his gaze.

A few moments later, Marty puts the clothes back on over his water-covered, ink-covered skin. Even after they're concealed, Jody can't stop thinking about the tattoos, as if they represent how far the brothers had drifted apart. If there's one thing Jody would never do, it's get a tattoo. He waits until they're hiking again before he asks, "When did you get all those?"

"Different times. Some of 'em I wished I hadn't gotten, and I try to turn them into something else. You like 'em?"

"I don't know. It's whatever you want. I don't really know what you want."

"We're brothers. You can't unknow me."

"I hear you. And partly, it feels like that. Like a month went by and not a decade. But I really *don't* know you, man. I don't know what you're like or what you do."

Another couple of minutes of silence pass before Marty responds. "I've been making this thing. I don't really know what it is yet. It's called *My Dirty California*."

"What are you talking about?"

"It's a website. But it's really just a place I've been doing a . . . project. I didn't even know what it was at first. I wasn't trying to define it. Eventually it kinda became a video log, about my adventures or whatever. A place to store all the pictures I take. And I kept up with it. Posting these videos online."

"So it's a blog."

"No," Marty says. He sounds defensive, as if a blog is uncool. Jody doesn't keep up with what's hip—Instachat, Snapgram, Tickity Tock, tweeting twittering, go-Facebook-fuck yourself. Marty seems uncomfortable, and Jody wonders why he even brought it up in the first place. "It's more a place I can store all these photos and videos and essays till I figure out what to do with the project. Maybe at some point I'll edit them into a documentary or a piece of long-form web video art."

Jody wonders what long-form web video art is. "So anybody can see it?"

"In theory, yeah. Anybody can click on it. But I didn't tell nobody the address, so nobody knows to look for it. No one's seen any of it. But *you* can. Saying, if you want to know me, you should watch 'em. You can even add something if you want. The sign-in password is *mdc*, lowercase."

"Add something?"

"A video about me or us." Marty now appears self-conscious. "No pressure. Never mind."

Jody senses his brother's insecurity but isn't sure what to say. He hears Rory growling ahead. He and Marty jog around the bend, where a hiker has a tight grip on Rory's collar. "Hey, what'r'ya doin'?" asks Jody.

"Dog came up barking at me," the hiker says.

Jody takes Rory and pets him.

"You should really have him on a leash."

"All right, take it easy," Jody says. The hiker speed-walks down the trail.

Marty bends and pets Rory. "Jesus. I see people haven't gotten friendlier around here. I remember being a kid and seeing Trey and Dukes and those other knuckleheads throw rocks at the Amish people when they passed by the Wawa and thinking I just want to get out of here, ya know, go somewhere people are decent."

"You find that place out there?"

"Fuck no. I mean, there's good people in California. But that's not everybody."

• • •

Jody puts beef tips and chicken strips on skewers as Marty chops squash. Outside, Joseph Sr. preps the grill. The three men each working on a bottle of Yuengling. Jody watches his dad come inside holding the propane tank.

"Out," Joseph Sr. says.

Jody takes the tank. "I'll fill it." He heads out the screen door.

Joseph Sr. emerges behind him. "Jody. I'll go."

"It's fine. I don't mind."

Joseph Sr. reaches out for the gas tank, but Jody doesn't hand it to him. "Let me go. It'd be good for you to spend more time with him. I'm worried about him. He doesn't look good to me. He could use you. It's been a long time since he had a brother to talk to."

Jody whistles. Rory comes running from the backyard, excited to go for a drive.

"Don't put that on me. It's been a long time since he's had a father to talk to." Jody gets in his truck with the propane tank and Rory and backs out of the driveway. Ten years ago, neither man had judged the other for Marty's decision to light out for the West Coast. But today, they finally had.

Jody and his dad had words all the time. About which game to watch. Or what to eat for dinner. Or how to get Rory to shut the fuck up. They argued, but as roommates. Bickering. It had been years since they had fought about anything of substance. Jody can't shake the discomfort as he drives to the hardware store. Jody used to feel good about himself for showing Marty the ropes of right and wrong, good and bad, like he was helping his little bro develop a strong moral code. He used to say to Marty, *Do the right thing*, which became *Do right*, then *Do ri*. It became this saying they'd repeat to each other. Something Jody said before dropping Marty off at Little League practice or before Marty got on the school bus. If Marty had gotten in trouble for getting into a fight at recess, their mother would give him a lecture, and Jody would add *Do ri*. But when Jody had his breakdown at twenty-four, the therapist helped him see that folks with his disorder see most actions in life as binary, absolutely right or absolutely wrong. Jody had always operated by a specific code. He drank before he turned twenty-one but waited until he was eighteen because he felt like people should be able to have a beer if they're old enough to die for their country. His doctor had pointed out his need to obsessively categorize everything as right or wrong wasn't the worst inclination. But Jody realized then he should have been there more for Marty. At sixteen, Jody spent all his time with his first serious girlfriend. At seventeen, it was soccer. At twenty-three, it was his desire to go to college. He realized he should have spent more time with his younger brother instead of just popping in as the morality police, instead of just muttering two syllables. He became guilt-ridden with the idea his preachy sentiments had caused Marty to run away to California. And the meaning of the two words *do ri* changed. Instead of an inside-joke–like *oorah*-style bond between brothers, for Jody the words came to symbolize his failure as a big brother and his having pushed Marty three thousand miles away.

Jody waits for his change from the cashier at the hardware store, refilled propane tank in hand. A mom and her two kids walk in the store.

"Hey, Coach!"

Jody nods hello as the family moves past him into the store. *What is that kid's name? Fred or Ben or something.*

The cashier hands Jody his change. "Heard your brother shown up."

"Yeah."

"He was in my class. Marty Morrel was."

"Oh, that's right."

"I remember senior skip day. Some of us went to Dorney Park. Others went to the Jersey Shore for the day. Your brother went to California."

Jody chuckles but doesn't respond.

"Yeah, only Marty'd drop out of high school with one month left. What's he doing back?"

"I really dunno. I'll let you know when the gas needs filling up again."

Jody drives back to the house. He slows as he passes a horse and buggy. He waves to the Amish couple. They wave back. Dusk has conceded to night, and he feels like telling them they ought to be more careful.

Rory runs straight from the truck into the backyard. Jody gets halfway from the truck to the house and stops. He forgot the gas tank. He grabs it from the truck. As he steps from stone to stone, movement draws his eyes to the light in Marty's second-floor bedroom. Jody opens the front door and walks inside. He stops in the foyer.

Fifteen feet in front of him, there's a red streak across the kitchen floor. Jody rushes into the kitchen. His eyes follow the red streak to where it ends. Joseph Sr. lies motionless, facedown on the floor. It appears he was crawling—and leaving a smear of blood behind him—before he was shot in the back of his head. Jody sprints over to his father. "Dad?! DAD!"

Joseph Sr. does not stir. Now Jody lets out an animal-like scream.

"MARTY!"

The house shakes as a body scrambles down the stairwell. Jody leaps to his feet and runs toward the noise. A hooded figure bounds down the stairs and fires a silenced pistol right at Jody. Jody leaps behind the kitchen counter. He army-crawls into the dining room. Makes it to the foyer, where he grabs Joseph Sr.'s shotgun and a box of shells from the closet's top shelf. He hunkers down in the dining room as he loads the shotgun. It takes him a moment. It's been seven years since he touched it, and he'd fired the thing only once, at a range with his dad. Gun loaded, he scrambles into the den. Bullets just miss his head.

Jody hears a barking Rory come in through the doggy door.

Maybe because of Rory's barking, or maybe because he saw Jody with the gun, the figure fires three more shots at the couch where Jody's taking cover and then flees out the back door. Rory runs after him.

Jody gives chase too. As he gets to the back door, to his right he sees Marty on his back in the middle of the living room floor, the tan carpet crimson around him. Jody darts out the back door to see the figure sprinting across the backyard. Rory just behind him. Jody raises his gun and fires. Unscathed, the figure hops the split-rail fence. Jody can't even tell whether he missed left or right. For a second, he considers going after him. Instead, he darts back inside and dials 911 as he rushes to Marty's side.

Marty is alive. His eyes are open. He's breathing. But he also has blood leaking from two gunshot wounds. One in the middle of his stomach, one in his throat.

"Nine-one-one, what's your emergency?"

Jody tries to cover both wounds as he screams into the phone. "This is Joseph Morrel. My dad and brother have been shot. 2513 Oak Cherry Lane. Please hurry."

"Joseph, is the shooter still on the property?"

"The shooter fled. Please hurry."

Jody lets the phone fall to the ground. He puts Marty's respective hands on both of his wounds.

"Hold these tight. I'll be right back."

Jody sprints into the kitchen, where he sees Rory nestled up next to his father. *Maybe he's still alive. Marty looked dead but he is alive. Maybe Dad is still alive too.* He half trips, half slides to his father. Turns him over. Checks his pulse.

"Dad?"

He can't feel a pulse. But his own heart is hammering so fast he can't tell. "Dad? Dad?!"

It's when he looks in his father's eyes he knows he's dead. "No . . . No . . ."

Jody leaves his father's body and sprints back to the living room, where Marty has already let go of his wounds. Marty seems to be slipping in and out of consciousness.

"You're going to be okay. You're going to be okay."

Marty keeps trying to talk, but the gunshot to his throat makes it near impossible. "Nada."

"What?" Jody asks. "Nada?"

"De Nada. De Nada."

"Denada? Nothing? I'm welcome? Marty, what are you saying?"

"De Nada."

"It's okay. Stay calm. You're going to be okay."

Jody tries to keep pressure on the wounds. Marty keeps pointing toward the wall. Jody realizes Marty's pointing to the phone Jody dropped.

"De Nada." Blood gurgles out of Marty's throat every time he tries to talk.

"Stop trying to talk." Jody keeps a hand on each wound and uses a foot to slide the phone to Marty. Marty tries to write on the phone, but he drops it. And now it's out of his reach. Jody can't hand him the phone without taking one of his hands off the wounds.

"De Nada."

"Stop!"

Marty stops trying to talk. His eyelids droop.

"Marty! Stay here! Marty! Hey!"

The sound of an ambulance in the distance draws closer. But now Marty isn't breathing. Jody takes his hand off the stomach wound and checks Marty's pulse. Nothing. He starts doing chest compressions, but the pressure forces even more blood to pour out of the wound in Marty's stomach. Jody'd been certified multiple times to give CPR as a soccer coach, but those instructions didn't include what to do if chest compressions caused more bleeding from a gunshot wound. But what else can he do? Jody keeps trying. He's so focused he doesn't hear two paramedics enter. One has to pull Jody off the body.

Now Jody staggers back, slumps over as the two paramedics try to bring Marty back from no place to this place.

Jody can see both gurneys from the ground where he sits. His hands and clothes are wet with blood, but his face is dry of tears. The coroner talks to a man Jody doesn't recognize. Cutter speaks to a few other neighbors. A slew of officers mill about. Rory keeps running in counterclockwise circles barking. Sheriff Carp gets out of his car and approaches.

"Jody. I'm Sheriff Carp. You coached my younger son last year."

Jody doesn't remember coaching any sheriff's kids.

"I'm really sorry about this. For your loss. Are you able to talk me through some of this?"

Now Jody remembers a mom saying something about her husband being a cop. The kid was a little shit.

"Did you get a good look at this man you told them about?"

Jody shakes his head.

"Anything you can tell us? Was he big?"

"Not big. Not small."

"Okay, good. Did you see his face? What race was he?"

"I didn't see. He had his hood up when he came down the stairs. And he was shooting. I had to get out of the way. When I went outside, he was running. I saw him running."

"Okay. We're going to ask you a few more questions now. And then we'll pick it up again tomorrow morning at the station."

"I'm not sure if you've slept, but I wanted to see if anything had emerged from the blur."

Jody hasn't slept. He doesn't feel tired or awake. Everyone keeps telling him he's in shock. "I've been thinking about it. Picturing it. Him running away. I didn't see him. But I saw him running. The motion."

"Okay?" Sheriff Carp asks.

"I think he had a leg-length discrepancy."

"What do you mean?"

"The way he was running. The mechanics. The way one leg swung outwards. His right leg was longer."

"Sorry if I'm having trouble following you. It's just . . . you can't even tell us what kind of pants he was wearing or how tall he was, but you noticed one leg was longer than the other?"

"It's the motion. And the gait compensation. I coached a kid this season who had a bad discrepancy. We got him wearing a heel lift, but it had already affected his form. You could see an asymmetry in his posture. Pelvic tilt. His hips. Lots of people have a slight difference, like a centimeter. But a two- to three-inch difference is rare."

"Okay, this is good."

Jody can tell Carp thinks it's bullshit.

"What about Marty's phone? We found your dad's. But not Marty's."

"He must've took it. The shooter, I mean."

"Jody, I gotta ask a couple harder questions here. A neighbor heard you scream Marty's name. Like you were angry with him. Did he hurt your dad? And you found him? And then did you retaliate?"

"No. I told you already. I came home and they were both shot and the guy in the hood came barreling down the stairs, shot at me, then went outside."

"Was there tension around Marty showing up? It sounds like from what we're hearing, he left when he was seventeen and hasn't come back till now."

"Yeah, there was tension, but not . . . no. You're asking the wrong questions. Marty didn't do anything."

"What about you though, Jody? Were you angry with Marty? Or your dad? From asking around, it sounds like your dad had put some money aside for Marty."

"This is what you're spending time doing? Accusing me?"

"I'm not accusing you. We're just talking."

"I'm telling you. His right leg is longer by at least two inches. You got any leads? What are you doing to figure this out?"

"We've got everyone working on it."

"Nobody in the whole town saw nothing?"

"Couple knuckleheads were on a mini crime spree later in the night. Rick Bird and his two pals. Guess folks saw them out and about.

Shot at some road signs. Doing doughnuts in the injection molding plant parking lot. They scared some women who were coming out of Mo's at one thirty a.m. Cat callin' or whatever."

"You talk to them?"

"Don't have anything to arrest them on, but we'll get them in for questioning. Left messages on all three of their cells. Just need to track 'em down."

He can't sleep. Jody doesn't even know what time it is. Hours pass. Hours of wanting to cry, his tear ducts not cooperating. When he closes his eyes, he sees blood. And Marty's face as he died. And his dad's face, already dead. The phone won't stop ringing. Family. Friends. More family. Jody stops answering. He turns off the phone.

He can't decide whether to bring a hammer or a box cutter. The police had taken the shotgun as evidence.

Jody rides around town most of the afternoon and evening. He doesn't know him, but he knows what Bird looks like. He doesn't spot him until 9:30 p.m.

From his Ford truck, Jody watches as Rick Bird smokes a cigarette and hits on two women outside a dive bar called Malone's. The two women go inside, leaving Rick Bird alone with his wounded ego and cigarette.

Jody moves from his truck, creeping down the sidewalk. He charges Rick from behind. Thinks about his dead brother and father. And tackles Rick into the pavement. He holds Rick's face into the ground with one hand. Holding up the box cutter with his other hand.

"Was it you? Was it?!"

"I di'n't do shit. Get the fuck off me."

Before the conversation can progress, a huge fellow knocks Jody off Bird. A third man jogging up to the scene kicks Jody in the ribs. The huge fellow punches Jody right in the eye. The two guys who came to Rick Bird's rescue show no sign of letting up until Rick intervenes.

"Hold on. That's Joseph's boy. Get off'm!"

The two men step back from Jody, who rolls onto his back, trying to catch his breath.

"Jody, right?" Rick asks. "Your dad paved our driveway last summer. That shit's fucked up what happened."

"Sheriff Carp told me you're ducking them."

"We were just on one is all. Can't be walking into the station like this. I'm on probation."

Jody tries to picture the killer coming down the stairs, can see only his hood. But he can visualize the guy running across the backyard and hopping the fence. Rick is way too short to be the guy. And the other two men are both overweight. They'd have trouble climbing a split-rail fence without a boost.

"All right, sorry, then." Jody picks himself up and walks to his truck. The view out his left eye shrinking as the blood moves in.

"You gonna tell me about that black eye?"

Jody sits across from Sheriff Carp. He didn't sleep much last night, and he gets the impulse to lie down and sleep on Carp's office couch. "It's nothing."

Carp sighs, phlegm catching in his throat.

"It doesn't seem like it could be a coincidence. We don't lock our doors. I can't remember the last time our town had a shooting let alone a murder. My brother comes home after ten years, and this brutal murder happens, ya know? It's gotta be something he brought home with him."

"I'm not disagreeing with you, Jody. But I called three different departments in LA. The problem is, neither the city of Los Angeles nor the state of California have any record of your brother living there."

"What?"

"He didn't have a driver's license. He wasn't paying taxes. 'Tween that and the fact the body's three thousand miles outside their jurisdiction, I don't think they're keen on helping."

• • •

The house resembles a Tupperware convention. There are a ton of people in the kitchen and five times as many dishes of food as people. Jody slips away and sits on the porch in his dad's favorite rocking chair and pets Rory. Nancy, an ex-girlfriend, waves a sympathetic hello from the yard. Jody pretends he doesn't see her. For the briefest moment, he remembers this one time when they had sex in her hot tub. And he tries to stay there. To remember her panting and coming. To remember how dehydrated they'd gotten. Jody tries to lean into the memory. To be anywhere other than the present. But it won't hold.

"You all right, Joe?"

Jody's uncle Donovan approaches with a glass of J&B scotch. After Jody's mother, Donovan's little sister, passed away, Uncle Don started hanging around Jody and Marty more.

"I'm okay."

"I cried this morning. I'm just letting you know, it's okay if you gotta cry."

Jody has tried. He knows it would make him feel better. But he can't.

Jody glances back to where Nancy was talking with a group in the yard. She's gone now.

"I'm going to come by tomorrow morning, and you and I will figure out the arrangements, okay?"

"Okay."

Jody watches the ceiling fan go in circles. He hasn't been awake the whole night. But he can't seem to stay asleep for more than a few minutes at a time. When he falls asleep, he dreams of his father and brother talking and eating and hiking and arguing. And every time he wakes, the reality that they're dead hits him again. Lying awake, he keeps picturing Marty dying, playing the moment over and over in his head. At least his dad had passed first and didn't witness his son dying.

Giving up on sleep, Jody fires up an old Dell laptop. He types *My Dirty California* into the web browser. Nothing interesting comes back.

Jody types *MyDirtyCalifornia.com* into the browser. A simple website. In black letters it reads:

my
dirty
california

Below, there's a long list of links. Each one labeled with a date. The most recent one reads 6/14/19. Jody scrolls down the web page. Hundreds of entries going all the way back to 2/24/15. Jody clicks on a random entry. It's a video that consists of a slideshow of photographs. Spectacular shots of spectacular trees in a protected area of the White Mountains in Inyo County, California. The trees range from fifteen to fifty feet. It's not their size that makes them stick out but their gnarled, stunted appearance. Marty's recorded voice plays over the slideshow of photographs.

"I went to the Ancient Bristlecone Pine Forest on the way back from Mammoth. I'd never heard of this place till a couple years ago. I saw trees there that are over four thousand years old. The oldest trees in the world."

The trees and landscapes are incredible, but Marty also took innovative shots. Capturing the trees from strange angles. Making them appear at once beautiful and haunting.

"One of the trees is over five thousand years old, but they keep it a secret which tree it is, which I thought was dope. We weren't able to find it. What would it be like to live thousands of years? Everybody's chasing longer lives, and yet we're fucking up the planet and ultimately shortchanging our species' future in the process. If these trees were conscious and had opposable thumbs, they'd probably have tried to live even longer and fucked it up and gone extinct."

As the slideshow flashes more photographs of the Ancient Bristlecone Pine Forest, Jody clicks Back and chooses a different video. This one features Marty talking into the camera.

"I heard about this new meditation technique so I'm going to try it here. It's called mental ginseng. The key is to—"

Jody jumps forward five minutes. Marty has his eyes closed, and he's meditating on camera. Jody chooses a third random entry. This one features another video log of Marty talking into the camera. In this one, Marty's eyes look wonky. The kind of wonky that comes from mixing a six-pack with weed.

"Two weeks ago, I met this waitress who works at Far Bar in Little Tokyo. We talked for a while. I told her I was kinda seeing someone else but that I thought she was cool and that we would get along. I said we should hang out as friends. It seemed to take the pressure off for her. So we went and grabbed lunch as friends and it was fun. We had sex two days later. So then this past weekend, I was at my friend's party and met this other woman. I'd smoked and had a few, and I found myself telling her the same thing. That I was kinda seeing someone off and on, but I'd love to hang out as *friends*. I'd meant it the first time with the Japanese girl. But at this party, I was working a line, playing an angle, strategizing like an analytical cock running around trying to get warm. I think—"

Jody has heard enough. He finds the most recent video, the last one Marty posted on the site. It's a simple sixty-second video log where Marty mentions wanting to go to Eureka and explore Humboldt County.

Jody clicks on the second-to-last video. Another short video of Marty talking into the camera. Here, he mentions being disappointed after staying in Encinitas for a few weeks.

Jody clicks on the third-to-last video. This video cuts back and forth between Marty talking into the camera and photographs he took at a party.

"I went to this ridiculous party in the Hollywood Hills. Not really my scene." Pictures of the house, an infinity pool in the backyard, guests dressed in everything from designer suits to designer swimsuits to T-shirts. "Seemed like everybody was just wandering in circles like zombies asking either what other people did for a living or how they knew the host. Or both. It was Chester Montgomery's house. Guy is a character. Owns an art gallery, known for these legendary parties. I played poker with him and his buddies until three a.m. I'm not that big on poker, but even with all the bluffing, it seemed to be the most honest conversation happening."

Jody presses Back. He's not sure what he thought he'd find. Maybe a simple video that would explain who would want to kill Marty.

At dawn, Jody throws clothes, toiletries, and the laptop into a bag. From his medicine cabinet, he pulls out his antianxiety medicine. He tosses the pills in the bag. But then he takes them out and returns them to the cabinet.

He finds a piece of scrap paper and pen. *Uncle Donovan, please handle burial. I'm sorry. This should cover cost.* He puts a check for eleven thousand dollars written out to Donovan Parker next to the note. For a moment, he tries to picture the funerals. And he knows he should stay. And he knows he won't.

Jody throws the packed bag in the cab of the truck. Rory jumps inside. Jody pulls out an envelope from his pocket. The return address reads: *Marty Morrel, 3353 Hillkirk Road, Los Angeles, CA 90084.*

Jody plugs the address into Google Maps. Thirty-nine hours.

Nine empty to-go Styrofoam coffee cups fill the cup holders and the floor space beneath the passenger seat. Rory sleeps. Jody drives thirty-five miles per hour over the seventy-five-mile-per-hour speed limit. His Ford truck wheezes in protest. Together, a star-filled sky and his high beams reveal miles of straight road ahead. The earth sure looks flat here.

Thirty miles and sixteen minutes later, Jody slams on the brakes and pulls off into the dirt shoulder. He leaps out of the truck. Squats. Too much coffee. Rory sniffs flowers in the moonlight. It's remote territory to reign, but Rory marks it anyway. Finished, Jody slumps backward on his butt. Pants still at his ankles. Practically sitting in his own shit. And his dry face gets the storm it deserves. Sensing the despair of his owner, Rory trots over and nestles up to Jody. The man's best friend had been his dad; now it'll have to be his dog. Jody hugs Rory. And cries. He stops crying. Takes his jeans off. Uses the jeans to wipe his ass. He abandons the pants on the dirt shoulder. Climbs back in the car in his underwear.

Onward. West.

Three more empty coffee cups roll around at the foot of the passenger seat. Twelve in total now. Jody comes into the greater Los Angeles area on the 10 freeway at 1:30 a.m. He pulls off an exit in West Covina.

Jody collapses onto the bed in the motel room, his ass and back and shoulders sore from thirty hours of driving. But he's wide-awake thanks to the half-life of caffeine. After lying on his side for twenty minutes, he pulls out his computer and films a video of himself.

"This is Jody. My first entry. I'm going to use my brother's website to keep track of all this. And in case something happens to me, this will be a place to find what I was able to figure out. I just got to LA. The last four hours took eight hours. Something about Las Vegas traffic on a Sunday. I didn't know that. Never been to California before. Never been too many places out of PA. Anyway, I'm here, so I guess tomorrow I start. Marty shows up in our little town outside Lancaster after not being home for ten years. Two days in, he gets killed. Gotta figure he was in danger, ran away from LA. All I have to go on is the address where Marty was staying in LA. So that's where I'll start tomorrow."

Chapter Two

Pen

Pen pulls her Prius into the Mammoth Mountain Inn parking lot. *Why does he go by Beetle? Is Beetle a code name?*

She scans the lot. Steep snowbanks limit her visibility in every direction. But she does manage to spot one person. A dude in ski goggles and a beanie stands between a red pickup truck and a black SUV.

Which car is his? He's standing between them, but neither car seems to belong to him. Is he going to be a problem?

She waits another few moments and decides, Fuck it.

The Mammoth Mountain Inn is right next to the gondola. She skips the elevator and heads for the stairs. Walking down the third-floor hallway, she spots room 302 just as the elevator opens. Out steps the man with the goggles perched atop his beanie.

Pen heads the opposite direction. Speed-walking down the hall. Glances back. *Is he following me? Yes, he's following me.* Pen runs.

"Penelope?"

Pen darts down the stairs. But melted snow tracked in by skiers and boarders makes this a dicey proposition. Pen slips. Slides down eight steps, ends up on the ground at the bottom. She tries to stand, but the man with the goggles hovers over her.

"I'm Beetle. Are you okay?"

Still grimacing, Pen looks up to see the man has pulled off his hat and goggles. Not a man. A teenager. At least ten years younger than her. Looks between seventeen and nineteen. Maybe twenty.

"*You're* Beetle? Why were you watching me outside?"

"Can't be too careful." Beetle pulls her to her feet. "Are you okay?"

"Didn't even go on the mountain, and I've already had a good fall."

"I had a crazy fall this morning trying to do a triple cork 720."

"I don't know what that is, but it sounds hard. Should we go to your room?"

Pen follows Beetle down the hallway, which looks drab compared to the lobby's rustic chic.

"I'm sorry I couldn't email it to you," says Beetle. "I really don't want a paper trail. Tech companies like to make an example of anyone selling their unreleased software."

"No worries."

Beetle approaches room 303.

"Thought you said 302."

"Like I said, too careful."

The room resembles a temporary crash pad for a teenage snowboarder. Except for all the computer equipment and electronic devices. Pen can identify the external hard drive but that's it.

Beetle goes right to his laptop. He clears an empty pizza box so Pen can sit in the chair next to his. Beetle pulls up the program.

"It's pretty self-explanatory. You can type a word, an expression, or a whole sentence. Or you can record an audio clip. And it will search all video and audio files for a match."

"So it's like Google for audio clips or keywords from video files?"

"It *is* Google. That's where my friend got it. They're experimenting with this as a search engine tool. It'll prob be integrated into your mom's Google within five years."

Beetle hands her a thumb drive. "You got the money?"

"Yeah. But I want to see it work first."

Beetle goes back to the program on his computer. He presses Record, talks into the computer's microphone. "Triple cork 720." He presses Search. Thousands of hits.

"So all these videos contain someone saying that?"

"It's not perfect. It may miss some, might include some false positives, but that's the gist. And it's definitely an improvement on only being able to search transcripts."

Pen opens her bag and pulls out an envelope of cash. Beetle flips through it, counting it either absurdly fast or not really counting it all. "I'm hitting the slopes if you wanna join. Chair fourteen is open for once. Back side's the best side."

"I have to get back to LA. Got a meeting with a production company. I did want to ask you something else."

"Shoot."

"I need to put a message out on the dark web."

"Okay?" Beetle squints with skepticism.

"Is that something you do?"

"Yeah. It's not hard. What's your angle though?"

"I need to get something out there. A message to someone. An SOS. And I can't have it blocked by any government firewalls."

"Not sure I follow. Who's going to be looking for your SOS in the dark?"

Pen ignores his question. "How much would that cost? For you to upload a message to the dark web."

"I'll do it for an extra five hundred."

"Okay." Pen pulls out five more hundred-dollar bills and hands them to Beetle. She tosses him a thumb drive. "Audio clip is on it."

"I'm going to have to listen to it first though."

"Why?"

"I don't mind throwing it out in Onionland, but I gotta know it's not gonna fuck my rep. Asterisks exist on the other side too."

"What are you saying?"

"Even coders have codes. Short answer: no child porn, no terrorism."

Beetle pulls up the audio clip off the thumb drive.

"Dad, it's me, Penelope. I'm hoping you're hearing this message.

I've been getting closer on jumping, but I still haven't succeeded. Let me know where you are and how I can get there. If you can identify the simulation you're in, it may help me get there. You can contact me here without fear of government intervention. Love, Pen."

Beetle looks at Penelope, scouring her face for sarcasm or irony. And not finding any.

When Pen was eight years old, her father came back one night to their apartment on Wilcox Avenue in the heart of Hollywood. He woke her and told her how he'd been drinking at the Pig' n Whistle. He said he'd been flirting with the bartender, and she'd said she had a boyfriend but took his phone number for a rainy day. And then he said he went into the bathroom, and while at a urinal, he dropped his half-full beer bottle. The bottle fell five feet and landed right-side up on the tile floor. Didn't break, didn't spill. He told Pen the bar was special, a historical landmark. And he told Pen the world isn't what people think it is. Two years later, on another night when he had a babysitter watch Pen, he never came home.

"Can you do it?" Pen asks.

Beetle manages to recover. "Uh, yeah, I'll upload it today."

"Thank you. And you'll let me know when he messages me back?"

"Yeah."

Pen waits in the Secret Robot Productions lobby. It had taken her five and a half hours to get back to Los Angeles from Mammoth. She thought her car was going to blow away in the eighty-mile-per-hour crosswinds on 395, so she had to drive slow on that stretch. She had been worried about being three minutes late, but now she's been sitting here in the lobby for twenty minutes.

"Penelope?"

Pen looks up to see a young blond woman whose posture, blouse, earrings, and job suggest she went to an Ivy League school without needing a cent of financial aid.

"Yeah. Pen."

"Nice to meet you. The guys are ready for you. You want something to drink?"

"I'm okay. Thanks."

The assistant holds the conference room door open for Pen. Matt and Jamal stand to meet her. Both have big shoulders and broad smiles.

"Penelope? I'm Matt. Nice to meet you."

"Jamal. Thanks for coming in."

"Of course. Thanks for having me." The leather squeaks when Pen takes a seat in one of the twelve roller chairs.

"How's your day going?" asks Jamal.

"Good. Yeah, good."

Matt leans in. "Well, look, we wanted to have you in for a general meeting, but your agent said you were working on a new idea, and we'd love to hear it. But we did want to say we're huge fans of your short film *The Flying Object.*"

"Oh, thanks."

"What was the budget?" asks Matt.

"Nothing, really. I didn't have a budget. A couple friends helped out but . . ."

"Did one of the bigger houses do the special effects pro bono?" asks Jamal.

"What special effects?"

Matt laughs. Jamal chuckles.

Matt adds, "*Close Encounters* is in my top five. This is the first UFO film since then I was that excited about. I know yours is a short, but that's a credit to you."

"Oh, well, thank you." Pen knows they're talking about the Spielberg film *Close Encounters of the Third Kind*, but she hasn't ever seen it.

Jamal chimes in. "The decision to do a fake doc. Smart. Especially in this market. I always loved *This Is Spinal Tap*. I love the fake documentary as a way into a story."

"I gotta ask. How did you fake it though?" asks Matt.

"Fake it?"

Matt laughs. "I get it. A magician and their tricks. We'll let you keep the secret. Just know we're fans and want to find something to do together."

"Do you want to tell us about your new idea?" asks Jamal.

Pen didn't know she was supposed to pitch a new idea. She thought this was just a general meeting. But she's happy to share what she's been developing. "Sure. Do you mind if I stand?"

"Whatever works," says Matt.

She races through the whole idea in her mind, needing to go over it one more time. After thirty seconds, Pen breaks her silence. "Have you guys heard of Pandora's House?"

Both men shake their heads.

"It's also sometimes called the Fractal House. The Bunker. House of Tunnels. The Underground. But most often, it's referred to as Pandora's House."

"Okay . . ." Matt leans forward, captivated.

"It's an example of an iceberg house."

"What's an iceberg house?" asks Jamal.

"Iceberg houses are houses where you can only see ten percent and ninety percent of the house is below ground."

They nod, intrigued, as Pen keeps going.

"Various rumors exist about Pandora's House. Some people say the architect Zaha Hadid was paid eight figures to design a top secret underground property in Southern California but she had to sign an NDA, and no one knows where it is. Another rumor suggests the Church of Scientology began building a two-hundred-million-dollar bunker but abandoned the project halfway through and sold the property to a couple millennials whose parents had made billions in the dot-com era, and they use the house to throw elaborate weeklong parties. Some say it's where the notorious lizard people live underground. Other people say the house was constructed by the US government as a safe house for the top one percent in the case of an apocalyptic event."

"Has anyone actually seen the house?" asks Matt.

"Lots of people claim to have. It's difficult to know for sure. A man named Charlie Dennis, this accountant who was living in Pasadena, fell off the map, just didn't show up for work one day. Huge missing person case, made national news. He appeared out of nowhere six months later, claiming he had gotten lost in a single house and it took him six months to find his way out. I've tried to interview him, but he's been in a locked psych unit in Santa Barbara for two years."

"I'm getting goose bumps," says Matt.

"Some people say the house is in Beachwood Canyon, right here in LA. I've heard Cypress Park, Glassell Park. Others say it's in Anza-Borrego. Palm Springs. There's evidence online a company was giving tours of the house for fifteen hundred dollars a ticket, but they were shut down by the state of California back in 2016. Regardless of which rumors are true, the common theme is that the house seems to defy the laws of physics. Supposedly, whole rooms remain lit without any windows or source of artificial light. There's an infinite echo, and if you play music, it hums on forever."

"It sounds like a great world for a haunted house movie or show," Matt interjects. "What format are you thinking? Feature? A Blumhouse-style thriller?"

Pen hesitates, realizes they're not on the same page.

Matt keeps going. "We've got to get our boss on board, but this sounds like something we could get you development money to write. Is that what you're looking for, to start with a script? Or there's the route of taking a few grand and filming a proof of concept sizzle reel, ya know, a mood trailer."

"I need money, more so for the research," Pen says.

Jamal and Matt both look to the other to respond.

"Money's money," Matt says. "I mean we'd buy the pitch, and you can use the money for whatever you want."

"I wouldn't be looking to script something. I need money to research the location, and eventually I'll need a crew to document passing through."

"So you're seeing it as a doc?" Matt asks. "About a search for this mythical house? And you think mockumentary?"

"Documentary. Look, I started with an overview about the rumors out there about the house, but I have my own theory. Following *that* theory would be the subject of the documentary."

Matt squints his eyes before nodding. "Okay, what's *your* theory?"

"Well, maybe I should back up. Are you familiar with the simulation hypothesis?"

"The idea we're all living in a simulation," says Matt. "Sure. *The Matrix.*"

"At the rate technology is advancing, how many years do you think it will take before we're able to develop simulations complex enough that the individuals inside don't know they're living in a simulation?"

"Right, I remember hearing about this on a podcast," says Jamal.

"I'm really asking you. How many years?"

"Maybe one hundred years," guesses Matt.

When Pen looks to Jamal, he guesses, "Three hundred years?"

"Okay, so both of you admit it's a real probability we'll eventually create simulations where the people don't know their world isn't real. And at that stage, computers would be able to create a near infinite amount of these simulations. Billions. Let's say millions. If a future will hold millions of simulations where the people don't know their world isn't real, what is the chance *this* world we're living in now is a simulation versus reality?"

"It is pretty mind-blowing to think about," says Matt.

"If we're living in a simulation, there are naturally going to be errors. Anomalies. Little cracks in the programming. There would be multiple places on earth where there's an error in the simulation. Like the green flash. Or *the dress.*"

Pen catches their blank stares. "You know, the dress that was posted online in February 2015. The picture went viral because some people see the dress as black and blue and others see the dress as white and gold. Like ten million people tweeted about it."

Jamal pulls up his phone. Googles *the dress*. Clicks on the picture. "What do you mean? It's black and blue."

Peering over Jamal's shoulder, Matt chimes in, "You're kidding, right? It's white and gold."

Jamal and Matt appear flustered, but they stifle their reaction. As if afraid of being made to look stupid while falling for a magic trick.

"Exactly. So anyway, there are these anomalies. Like Bimini Road. Or the pyramids. There aren't a ton. But there *are* flaws in our simulation, and those *gaps* may be a way to exit this simulation and actually enter an alternative simulation. To jump."

"Jump?" Matt asks.

"Jump simulations. Traverse infinite worlds beyond this one. And I believe Pandora's House is one of these gaps. I want to pass over to another simulation and document it."

Matt fidgets in his chair as Jamal's mouth remains wide open like he's at the dentist.

Matt recovers first. "Pen, this was great. You've given us a lot to ponder. Like I said, we have to get our boss on board, so yeah, we'll uh . . . we'll be in touch."

"Okay, thanks for having me in," Pen says, taking them at their word.

Daniel leads Pen back to his office within the fortress-like home base of the Beacon Talent Agency, or BTA, as it's known in the industry. She had never seen her agent in anything but a suit, and she'd never seen him wearing the same suit. He motions for her to sit.

"Matt and Jamal called."

"Yeah?"

"What exactly did you say?"

"Do you want me to tell you the whole idea?"

Daniel glances at his phone. "No. I have a call in ten."

"What did they say? It sounded to me like they were going to talk to their boss about coming on board."

Daniel scratches his head, which looks less bald than it had a couple of months ago. "Look, I don't want to get too deep into the conspiracies here, okay? I believe you. But I think you're making a mistake to dump everything in a first meeting. Give them a taste. People like mysteries. Intrigue. Foreplay."

"Right . . ." Pen hasn't heard anyone say *foreplay* since her agent used the word as a metaphor the last time she saw him.

"Do you know how many phone calls I get a week with people wanting to know how the hell you faked that UFO video? You've got to give these people what they want."

"What do you mean?"

"I mean if Sundance wants to give you the prize for best narrative short film, don't insist it can only be considered as a doc."

Pen had this fight with the folks at Sundance. She'd had it with Daniel. She felt it would have been disingenuous to accept an award for best narrative short for her documentary short. The film ended up getting so much media attention over which category it should have been in that speculation built that maybe Pen had caused the controversy to give herself more exposure. But Pen hadn't set out to make a documentary as a way to market herself as a filmmaker. She started investigating UFOs only because she suspected their phenomenon could be explained by flying objects slipping in and out of our simulation from other simulations.

"It *was* a documentary."

"Okay, let's not focus on the minutia. I'm trying to get you paid."

"You're trying to get yourself paid."

"Yes. I get paid when you get paid. I want to get us *both* paid. And in order for us to get paid, you can't go into a pitch meeting and . . . Did you tell them you wanted money to take a research crew to another dimension?"

"Dimension? No."

For the first time since Pen arrived, Daniel appears relieved. "Okay. I thought he was exaggerating."

"Not another dimension. A different simulation."

Daniel stares at Pen, relief evaporated. "Wait, what?"

"How many years into the future do you think it will be until we're able to create computer simulations advanced enough the people in these simulations don't know they're in a simulation?"

"Penelope, I've got this call in five minutes. Let's do this another time. I'll get you into more rooms. But you've gotta focus on pitching a specific film or TV project, okay? Do you need your parking validated?"

Taking Sunset Boulevard to Topanga Canyon, Pen speeds home in a race against the setting sun. She pulls onto a dirt road next to the Topanga Creek Bike Station, a mom-and-pop hippie bike shop. They were happy to rent Pen a bungalow on their property for only $900 a month cash since it wasn't permitted as a dwelling. But they were less than happy when she converted it to a makeshift Faraday cage to block electromagnetic waves from entering the bungalow.

Pen walks through the door as an alert goes off on her iPhone. *Sunset, one minute.* She picks up a backpack sitting by the back door. She goes to a bin that holds various mineral deposits and pieces of scrap metal. Iron, onyx, and limestone among others. Pen selects a piece of steel and slips out the back door. The hill outside her bungalow offers a great view of the ocean a mile and a half away. A blob of yellow butter melts into the horizon. Pen makes sure the backpack is on tight. She holds up the piece of steel. And stares at the setting sun. Preparing to *jump*.

At sunset on any given day, the Santa Monica Pier is filled with hundreds of tourists trying to capture the famous green flash. The green flash was one of the first examples Pen's father had shown her as a sign they're living in a simulation. That was when she was eight. Two years later, when he disappeared from her life, Pen believed he had found a gap in their world and had jumped. Miguel Sanchez, the LAPD Missing Persons detective assigned to the case, didn't agree.

Pen holds out the piece of steel. But as the yellow disappears, and the sunset surrenders to the golden hour, no green flash. She trudges back inside. She fills out a log in a composition notebook. *Tried steel, no G.F.*

Pen ignores her groaning stomach and instead downloads her new software. She presses Record and talks into the microphone.

"Pandora's House."

Now, she uses the search form to create a Boolean search. She uploads the audio clip, then types *OR*. She records herself saying "Fractal House." Now she records more audio clips. "House of Pandora." *OR*. "House of Fractals." In the search form, she puts parentheses around the different audio clips she's pasted in there and writes *AND*. Now she records again. "California." *OR*. "Los Angeles." *OR*. "LA."

Content with the Boolean terms, she presses Enter. Her search results in 246 videos. "Beetle, you little snowboarding hacker, you did it."

Pen had long since covered every regular Google search result for "Pandora's House." She'd scoured the Reddit threads and ghosthunter websites that made any mention of it. But regular Google searches don't cover videos and podcasts that don't have transcripts.

The first video in the search results features a sixteen-year-old girl. "I had to do my report today on Pandora's box from Edith Hamilton. It went pretty good I guess, but it was annoying 'cause Freddie kept asking questions and calling it Pandora's *House*. And then I had cheerleading practice after school and the most embarrassing thing happened. I—"

Pen goes back to the search list. The second video features an artist showing off his paintings. "The next piece is a painting I'm calling House of Fractals. I had this fractal T-shirt from when I was a kid that my mom got at this math conference. And the design on the T-shirt was cool, even if—at the time—I was too young to understand what a fractal—"

Pen goes back to the search results, hoping this won't be a list of 246 false positives.

After the eighty-sixth video, she can't ignore her stomach any longer.

Pen eats takeout chow mein while she watches more videos. It's after midnight when she gets to a link for a website called *My Dirty California*. She clicks on the link. It reads 3/25/19 at the top with a video below. Pen presses Play.

The video features a shirtless man with a ton of tattoos talking into the camera. Pen guesses he's about thirty, maybe a couple years older.

"I was supposed to meet this Mexican girl named Renata for breakfast, but she flaked. She just got here, to the US, and didn't have a phone, so it was old-school. You show up or that's it. There's no way to text and say, *Running an hour late*. She was cool. I met her playing soccer, and we were gonna hang last night, but she was going on this haunted house tour. She called it Pandora's House or something. She didn't seem to know much about it. But I looked it up just now and went down the rabbit hole. Some Reddit threads and a couple ghosthunter websites. Not really my scene but some pretty trippy stuff. One dude on Reddit claimed he got into the house and there were essentially an infinite amount of rooms. All underground. That on the outside, it looked like a regular house but on the inside it kept going down. That same guy claimed another guy was lost in there for six months. Again, this ain't usually how I like to spend my time, but it's pretty wild." The shirtless man ends the video.

A few moments ago, Pen's eyelids were giving in to gravity, but now she's wide-awake. She scrolls through the original search results, scanning for other videos from this *My Dirty California* website. She finds another one—this one labeled 4/16/19—and clicks on it. It's another video of the shirtless man, now with a shirt, talking into the camera.

"For some reason, I started thinking about that Mexican girl Renata again. I remember her saying this promoter named Abbott was going to take her to this Pandora's House tour. I poked around a little bit, and I talked to this Abbott guy on the phone, and at first he said he thought he knew who Renata was, and then he changed his story.

I went to go see him, but he wasn't in the office that day, and then he wouldn't call me back. And then I went to the office again, and his coworker said he went to Thailand, one-way ticket. It felt eerie hearing this. When she stood me up for breakfast I didn't think too much of it. There was the wounded male ego. *How could she . . . ?* But beyond that, it wasn't a big deal. Plus I had no way to call her, so I said fuck it, ya know? But now it's got me pretty weirded out. Made me pause about this Pandora's House. She said she was going on a tour that night, and then no one hears from her? Maybe she met someone and they moved to Cincinnati, who knows, but it does got my head spinning a little. I went down the Pandora's House rabbit hole same as before. As much as I said there was in terms of info and conspiracy theories, there isn't *that* much. Anyway, I'll probably fish around some more, try to keep getting in touch with this Abbott guy."

When the video ends, Pen grabs a pen and notebook. She jots down: *My Dirty California, Renata missing, Pandora's House tour, Abbott.*

Pen goes back to the search results. She finds another video from the *My Dirty California* site. But this one features a different man talking into the camera. He looks like the other man, kind of older but his face has fewer wrinkles and so kind of younger. He appears to not have shaved in a few weeks. A beard, but out of neglect, not style.

"Hey this is Jody. Entry number sixty-four. I spent a good portion of the last twenty-four hours looking into a girl named Renata who Marty seemed convinced had disappeared. Marty mentioned her going on this tour of this haunted house called Pandora's House. In the end, I couldn't really find anything out there on this house or on Renata. It seemed like Marty was perplexed by this girl's disappearance, but she might've just stood him up and he was keen to know why. After looking into this, I had to scratch it off the list. I have no reason to think Marty got killed in Lancaster, PA, because of this girl Renata."

The video ends. Pen scribbles: *Marty killed? Someone named Jody looking into Marty's death. Jody thinks death unrelated to Pandora's House.*

Pen goes back to the search results. She scrolls down. Not seeing anymore. She does a keyword search for *MyDirtyCalifornia* within the couple hundred videos from her original Boolean search. No more results.

Now she goes to the *My Dirty California* home page. There are several hundred entries labeled by their date. She scrolls down and finds another clump of links. Atop the second clump, it reads *Jody Morrel*. She selects a random video of Jody's. It's a video of the second man talking into the camera. The older one with fewer wrinkles around his eyes. His beard has grown longer.

"This is Jody Morrel. Entry number ninety-two. I'm starting to think I shouldn't have left my medicine back in PA. For a while, I'd felt like I was working better without it. But now I'm not sleeping much. Shiloh told me Rory's barking was keeping me awake. But now the silence of not having my dog bark keeps me up all night. When I don't sleep, everything gets cloudy. One minute, I see the pieces. Wyatt. The Pontiac. The DMV list. The hitman. Roller. And the next minute, I start doubting it all and think maybe it *was* just a thief or a random act of violence in Lancaster. I've started to wonder if this whole video log hasn't just become a way to look my soul in the mirror. Or maybe it's all a charade, a way to prevent myself from looking my soul in the mirror. I wish I hadn't fucked things up with Shiloh. I think I love her. Shiloh told me I should quit. She says it's easier to press on than it is to mourn, but I don't see how anything could be more difficult than this."

BTA motion picture literary agent Daniel Hudson, wearing AirPods, walks Pen back to his office. Pen sits on the leather couch.

"Everything else good?" Daniel asks.

"Yeah," says Pen.

Daniel waves off Pen, points to his earbuds. "Okay, great. And don't sweat this. Everyone gets fired. There should be a book called that. Like the adult version of *Everyone Poops*. We'll get you on another show ASAP. All right? Okay, be good."

Daniel takes out the AirPods. "What ya got for me?"

Pen stayed up the entire night watching videos from the *My Dirty California* website. She resists the impulse to show Daniel different entries, knowing he'll have a meeting or call in a matter of minutes. She had been told the agency worked in teams, and she signed with a team of three agents. But two months into their client/agent relationship, one of her agents was fired for sexual harassment. Another was one of the victims, and she quit to become a lit manager. Pen's team of three agents became a team of one, Daniel. It seems like Daniel's job is signing clients as opposed to working for clients.

"I think I found a way into the Pandora's House idea," Pen says.

"I thought we talked about this."

"I found this blog. This guy Marty had this thing called *My Dirty California*. Hundreds of these videos. Essays. Pictures."

"Uh-huh." Daniel has started checking emails.

"But he got murdered."

Daniel looks up from his computer. "Murdered?"

"Yeah. He was visiting his brother and dad back in Pennsylvania, and he got killed. His dad did too."

"Really?"

"Yeah. So then the older brother, this guy Jody, he moves to LA to try to figure out who killed his brother. And he starts updating his brother's California project website with his clues."

"I like this. Murder mystery. Whodunit. Personal stakes."

"It gets better. Turns out, Marty was looking for a woman who disappeared the night she was going on a tour of Pandora's House. No one's seen her since. She jumped, Daniel. She left this simulation. Marty figured it out, and the government, or somebody else trying to cover their tracks, they had Marty killed."

"This is cool. Sexy. I can help you sell this."

"Yeah?"

"Yeah. True crime is hot right now. OJ. *Serial*. *Mindhunter*. *Dirty John*. Fucking . . . whatever. Yeah, I could sell this. I think the key is to focus on the brothers though."

"Right, the idea one brother is trying to find out what his dead brother uncovered that got him killed."

"Kind of. Look, I think you're best served to hold back on the angle of the Pandora House. You start talking simulations, and you make people feel uncomfortable. Make their avocado toast taste less good and shit."

"Wait, what?"

"I'm trying to protect your reputation."

"It's not like I'm the only one who holds this view. Elon Musk has said there's a one-in-a-billion chance—"

"One in a billion? C'mon, Pen. That's like saying there's zero chance we're living in a simulation."

"He said there's one-in-a-billion chance we're *not* living in a computer simulation."

"Elon Musk is a quack though."

"Says the guy who drives a Tesla."

"I'm just saying I think you should hold back on the Pandora's House element."

Pen has no interest in holding back on Pandora's House. Her father spent two years looking for the breach before he disappeared. He used to say to Pen with his wide eyes and jolly smile, *The question for you, pumpkin, is when we find the gap, will you have the guts to jump in?* The last few weeks, he became convinced the breach was in a house, specifically a basement. After he disappeared, no one else believed her. Most people thought he skipped town, ran away. Others thought he was killed. Some people thought he was in Palm Springs because he'd gone there three weekends in a row before the night he disappeared. Pen's mother—who lived in St. Louis—told the LAPD he was probably in Vegas, which pissed Pen off, since her mother hadn't spoken to her or her dad in three years. No one believed Pen that her dad found the gap and passed through. She wanted to retrace his steps, and she tried. But her grandmother became her guardian, and Pen had to move to Palmdale. Kids didn't get her there. She had few friends. In eighth grade, she did her geography class presentation on Oxford professor Nick Bostrom's 2003 paper in *Philosophical Quarterly* called "Are You Living in a Computer Simulation?" As she got older, she grew tired of people's eyes glazing over when she tried to talk about the anomalies in the world, the possible gaps, so she began filming videos as a teenager, knowing her words alone would never convince anyone. She graduated high school and went to UCLA film school. There have been tangents, left turns, bum steers, but her search has never changed direction. It always comes back to Pandora's House.

Daniel continues, "Ya know, ground it in reality."

"Reality is merely an illusion, albeit a very persistent one," says Pen.

"This is what I mean, you're going to lose people when you come up with these weird sayings."

"I didn't come up with that saying. Albert Einstein did."

"Look, a guy moving out to LA to figure out what happened to his brother? There's a hook there. Real meat. Amateur investigator. Pen, *that's* a story people will pay you to make a movie about. So where's the story at now? Did the brother find anything?"

"I'm looking into it. The updates online stop pretty abruptly. I think I'm going to go see him."

"Okay, get your thoughts together. Do a little research. Hone in on these brothers. The dead one and the detective one. Put together a pitch, maybe a mood book, and we'll sell the shit out of this."

Chapter Three

Renata

The sun is hot where she came from. The sun is hot on this side too. It has been two days since she jumped from one world to another.

Renata was supposed to cross the border via a 4,300-foot subterranean tunnel that went from Tijuana to the Otay Mesa warehouse district in San Diego. But that had fallen through shortly after her eighteenth birthday. Now, a year later, she crossed just north of Mexicali. They made it safely across, and yet the border town of Calexico was deemed unsafe. So the guide—whose beard and hair are a mix of gray and red, not unlike a coyote's fur—is taking them the extra twelve miles to El Centro, where they'll be safer from US Border Patrol to take a Greyhound bus wherever they want.

A pair of willow trees offers a brief respite from the sun. Of the dozen travelers, half eat snacks from their bags. The other half, out of food, rest their eyes. Renata has only ten ounces of water left. She's sitting on the bank of the New River, a binational waterway, and she's tempted to refill her bottle. However, the Salton Sea–bound water is topped with a layer of white foam. The foam reminds her of taking bubble baths as a kid, which makes her miss her older brother, Gabriel. Three years ago, Gabriel moved to Celaya to work at a Honda auto plant. She has seen him only two times in three years, one of which was their parents' funeral. She forces herself to forget her brother and instead think of her family friend Marco, who she'll see in Los Angeles for the first time in a decade. Since she left four days ago, Renata's been plagued with pangs of sadness. Each time she finds herself missing a person, an activity, or a place, she forces herself to look forward. For everything left behind, she focuses on something positive ahead.

A woman in her sixties holds a baby nearby. Renata makes a funny face, showing her teeth. The baby giggles. Renata and the woman reflect smiles. *My neighbor Debra, who's in her sixties, who makes the best tacos de camarones. New neighbors to meet.* For everything left behind, something ahead.

The guide puts on his wide-brimmed hat and whistles. They move at a steady clip, hugging the river. Renata walks next to an older gentleman named Jorge who plans to join his sister and nephews in Los Angeles. Yesterday, he asked why Renata had left, and she had wanted to say because of *la vacuidad*, but instead, she'd lied and said she had family in LA too.

After her parents died in a fire at the packaging plant where they worked, both sets of grandparents clung to Renata. Grieving their respective lost children, her father's parents leaned into their Christian faith, while her mother's parents leaned into their belief in Santa Muerte. The fulfillment her grandparents and cousins found in their spirituality created a hollowness in her. Or it at least made her aware of a hollowness that already existed. She continued working in the serape shop that made more money selling ice cream than blankets, but she stopped hanging out as often with her family. Without any explanation, her best friend, Sofia, started chilling with a new group of friends in Agua Caliente. The few hobbies she had—playing soccer on the concrete field next to the skate park, baking jericalla with her cousins, and going on Instagram on the computers at Casa de las Ideas—suddenly felt duller. Around this time, a twenty-eight-year-old mechanic named Luis started coming by the shop and bringing Renata gifts and asking if she'd go to dinner with him. He was cute, but he was ten years older and not her type, so she declined each time. One day—whether out of boredom, depression, loneliness, or apathy—she agreed. After dinner, he brought her back to his house in Zona Río. They kissed; she felt nothing. And when she got home, she felt *la vacuidad* more than ever. The next day, she decided to leave, telling herself she should fulfill her parents' dream for her to move to the United States.

They've traveled about a mile since their last break when Renata hears a gasp. She follows other turning heads to the sound of vehicles. A white-and-green United States Border Patrol all-terrain SUV. And a Border Patrol pickup truck. Eighty yards back. They look to the guide, to their leader, but he doesn't offer directions. He flees, wading across the river.

Others follow him into the twenty-foot-wide river. The guide gets halfway across before Renata breaks her fear-induced paralysis and steps into the water.

The older woman grabs her arm. Begs her to take her granddaughter. "Por favor. Por favor."

Renata reaches for the child to take her across the river, but she withdraws her hands. She says she's sorry. Or she at least thinks it. She wades across the river, holding her bag above the shoulder-high water. The guide scrambles up the bank, where he sprints up a hill toward a field.

The SUV and the truck pull up to the river. A Mexican American Border Patrol agent shouts into a megaphone. Telling everyone in Spanish to get down on the ground.

Renata makes it across the river. She glances back as she dashes up the riverbank. The older woman steps into the water to wade across with her baby, but a Border Patrol agent grabs her. Seven total Border Patrol agents are chasing down the fleeing immigrants.

Renata sucks hot, dry air into her lungs as she sprints up a hill. Forty-five yards to her left an obese Mexican man gets tackled by a Border Patrol agent. As Renata comes over the hill, ahead of her there's nothing but a vast dirt plain. Here, with the proximity to the river, there are a variety of plants and weeds growing. But if she keeps going, there's nothing. Dirt and sun. And the occasional cactus. It's run or hide. And if it's hide, it's here. Renata drops to the ground. Into the brush. Staying as low as possible on her back, she pulls up dirt and weeds from all around her and covers herself.

She stays still. She focuses on the clouds in the sky. She hears cries from people getting captured by the officers. Renata lies still, focuses on the air coming in and out of her nostrils. After a few moments, she risks raising her head enough to look back at the river. Nine of the twelve immigrants, including Jorge, have been handcuffed and stand in a line by the cars.

Third and fourth Border Patrol vehicles have pulled up to the scene.

Renata tells herself if they'd seen her drop to the ground, she'd already be in handcuffs.

A Border Patrol agent lets four dogs out of the back of an SUV. The dogs go straight to the river. They swim across and scramble up the banks before dispersing to search the field where Renata is hiding. Renata looks back up at the clouds. Two dogs descend on a young man who was hiding in the field thirty yards to Renata's right. He tries to get up and run. They chase him down, biting at his legs. The young man raises his hands in surrender.

Renata keeps her body as flat as possible. Looks at the clouds. *The hammock in my friend Raul's backyard where we'd watch the clouds. Disneyland.*

Forty-five seconds later, a dog comes over to Renata. First sniffing. Then barking alarm bells. "Shhh. Silencio. It's okay. Silencio."

The dog keeps barking. Renata finds herself thinking about Santa Muerte, thinking about Lita—her mother's mother—coming into her room the day before she left. Renata had told only one friend her plan. Lita had either learned or guessed Renata was leaving. She had said, "Santa Muerte will find you. You cannot run from her."

Renata fishes inside her pocket and finds a plastic package of rice cakes. Staying pressed into the ground, she throws the rice cakes about ten feet away from her. It takes the dog a few moments to rip through the plastic before it chomps on the snack.

Renata closes her eyes as the sound of footsteps grows closer. Two Border Patrol agents approach on foot.

"What do you got there, Sadie?"

"Bad girl, Sadie. Don't eat that shit."

"You're supposed to be looking for beaners, not rice." Both Border Patrol agents laugh.

The dog barks, moving in the direction of Renata.

"No. You're not getting them back!"

"Go look. Go! Search!" says the other guard.

Renata hears the sound of a boot kicking the dog and the whimper of a dog that's been kicked by a boot. The dog scampers off. The two Border Patrol agents walk left from where Renata remains hidden below dirt and weeds. She waits thirty seconds before she opens her eyes. New shapes form in the clouds. Renata watches the shapes, and she smiles. *Gracias. Gracias.*

Renata's anxiety didn't wane as she waited in the dirt and weeds for the Border Patrol agents to leave. Her anxiety didn't wane as she walked the last six miles to El Centro. It didn't wane when she waited in line to buy a ticket. It didn't wane when she boarded the bus. But when she got off in Los Angeles and moved from the bus station onto Seventh Street, her anxiety waned. The sidewalks were full of Black people, brown people, white people. There were homeless people in wheelchairs begging for change. Two older Mexican men were screaming at each other about a scratch-off ticket. And Renata realized no one was looking for her. She was just a brown dot in a giant city of multicolored dots.

Now, she's made it to Koreatown. To the apartment where her family friend lives. She finds apartment 204 and knocks. No answer. She knocks again. She can hear footsteps on the other side. But no one opens the door. She tries knocking again.

"Marco?"

Finally the door opens. On the other side stands a Chinese woman with rosacea. "No Marco."

"Please. I'm looking for Marco. He is unit number 204."

"This unit 204. No Marco. Sorry."

Renata had torn the address from a recent letter from Marco where he reiterated his longtime promise to help Renata when she made it to the United States. Renata shows the address to the Chinese woman. "Please. Are you sure Marco doesn't live here?"

"Live here ten year. No Marco."

The Chinese woman closes the door.

"Espere. Por Favor. Please."

But the Chinese woman doesn't reopen the door. Renata trudges toward the stairwell. She had wavered over whether to run away to America. And along every step of the trip, she had questioned whether she made the right decision. But those internal debates were carried out with the assurance that Marco was in LA. That Marco would help her find a place to stay and a place to work. That Marco would help her get citizenship. Without Marco, without those assurances, there would have been no debate; she would not have come.

A door opens down the hall. A Mexican man emerges, taking out the trash to the chute. He looks older, but she recognizes his big face and small nose. As a child, she had known Marco, and when he moved to California, he told Renata's parents she could come when she got older. After her parents died, he sent her a letter, telling her she was still welcome to come.

"Marco?" she asks.

"Renata? ¿Eres tú?"

She falls into his arms.

Marco switches to English. "You smell absolutely terrible."

Renata laughs.

"You made it though!"

"I did. I was knocking on that door—204."

"I'm 209." Marco takes the piece of paper from her. "El papel se rompió."

"Had to cross a river."

"Your English is good, already sound like a Chicana," Marco says, smiling.

Renata was crushed when her first attempt to come to California didn't work out. And it was tedious to wait eleven months to try again. But in that time, she found a website where she could download TV episodes for free, and she watched all 236 episodes of *Friends* in English without subtitles. Then she watched all 236 episodes with subtitles. She watched the 236 episodes a third time, again without the subtitles. Renata practiced her English with Hector, the man who owns the café next to the serape shop. Hector had worked at a hotel in Imperial Beach for ten years before moving back from San Diego to Camino Verde.

"Come in, come in." Marco leads her into unit 209. "Agave Pequeño is all grown up."

When she was little, Renata often got goose bumps, and Marco said the hair on her arms and legs looked like the spines of an agave plant and he took to calling her Agave Pequeño.

"Thank you for this," says Renata as she looks around the living room of Marco's apartment. It looks much nicer than the tin-roofed house where Marco had lived down the street from her family in Camino Verde.

"Of course. Your father was one of my best friends. I would do anything to help you."

Renata's parents—especially her dad—had made it clear they wanted her to move to the United States when she turned eighteen, and she had made it clear she would never go. But the main reason she'd refused was because she didn't want to leave them. And then they died.

"We can discuss more tomorrow, but I already have a man lined up for you. It will cost three thousand dollars, but you can become a citizen in six months. And you can get a divorce in three years and it's all behind you."

"Thank you." She pauses. "And this man . . . ?"

"You'll meet him once. You won't have to live with him or anything. With papers, you'll get work. And you can pay me a hundred dollars a month for thirty months. I'll give that money to this man. And that's it."

Renata lets all the air out of her lungs in one swoosh. She had worried it would be complicated.

"Are you hungry?"

"Starving. But I'm embarrassed at how dirty I am. Can I shower?"

"Of course. I'll show you your room. You can stay here a few weeks. As long as you need."

Marco shows her into a bedroom. White walls, white sheets, white furniture. The absence of dust. The last four days were dusty.

"Towels in the bathroom."

"Thank you."

"There are some clothes in the drawers in the bathroom. Just a few things for you."

"Thank you so much, Marco." She goes to hug him but stops. "I know. I smell terrible. I'll shower."

Once Marco leaves, Renata closes the bedroom door. She walks into the recently remodeled bathroom. The rain shower has blue tiles with glass walls.

As advertised, the water comes down like rain. Renata washes off all the dirt and grime of her journey. And with it, she tells herself to let fear go. The fear she felt in the village she fled. The fear of those teenage wannabe halcones de Los Zetas who'd chased her as a kid, who'd threatened to chop off her fingers. The fear of getting chikungunya fever. The fear of leaving home. The fear of starting over. The fear of crossing the border. The fear of crossing that river, fear of being found while lying in that dirt.

Let fear go down the drain, she tells herself.

She reaches for a fluffy white towel. She thinks she hears a noise. She turns off the fan. Listens. Nothing.

She opens the bathroom door a crack. Enough to see the bedroom door is closed. Whatever she heard must have been outside her room. Maybe Marco's bedroom door or a cabinet closing.

Now relaxed again, she smiles at the sight of herself in the mirror in the clean white towel. The bathroom has a chest of drawers. She opens the top drawer, looking for the clean clothes Marco suggested she wear.

Inside the highest drawer are pairs of underwear. She picks one up. Not a pair of cotton briefs. But instead a black thong. She holds up another pair. Boy shorts–style purple underwear, but lacy. She flips through the drawer. More lingerie.

She opens the next drawer. A fancy but *short* cocktail dress. She stares at the clothes. *Maybe from an ex-girlfriend? Maybe he didn't even look at them. Or maybe he was trying to be hip.* She closes the drawer, choosing not to wear any of the clothes. Instead, she walks out still wearing the towel.

On the edge of the bed, wearing a robe and only a robe, sits Marco. The noise she heard *was* Marco.

"You scared me."

Marco stands. His gazing eyes threaten. He takes a step toward her in his white robe that matches the white walls and white sheets and white furniture. "Eres hermosa. Very beautiful."

"Marco, please leave."

"I'm going to help you. Everything I said I would do, I will follow through with."

She steps back from him.

"I can help you become a citizen, find work. If I don't, you'll be sent back."

"Please . . ." Was this always part of the invitation? Or had his agenda changed once her parents had died?

"C'm'here." He puts his arms around her. She stands there as he hugs her. Her hands at her sides. His hands reach down, go up under the towel, one hand grasping each cheek. She can feel his sweaty palms and the ends of his fingernails gripping her skin. She pushes him away.

His posture changes. From flared nostrils down to staggered feet. "Don't mess this up. You'll be sent home."

Renata wants to run. And she will run. "Okay."

"Okay? Yes?"

"Yes. My way though. Lie down. De espaldas."

"Okay. However you want." Marco smiles. His teeth as white as the robe, as white as the white walls and white furniture and white bedspread. He sits back on the bed. Lies down. Now Renata scoops up her bag and darts to the door. Marco scrambles to his feet. She tries to slam the bedroom door behind her. It hits Marco, knocks him back but not down.

She crosses the living room, heading for the front door. He's behind her, manages to get a hand on her bag. And he's able to pull her down by pulling the bag down. Like a football horse-collar tackle.

Renata has never punched anyone her whole life, so her soccer instincts take over. Connects with his shoulder. His chest. A third kick goes right into his teeth. Those white teeth. Red with blood now.

His eyes widen, like he's gone from wanting to fuck her to wanting to *fuck* her. As she gets to her feet to run, he grabs her ankle, and she crashes to the ground. As she scrambles to her feet, he reaches for her again. Marco falls to the ground, holding her towel.

But Renata doesn't stop. She's running—naked—with her bag out the door.

Marco chases her down the hallway. A couple of neighbors returning from dinner with doggie bags stop in the hallway, the woman hiding her eyes in horror, the man unable to look away, as a terrorized Renata runs toward them, half covering herself with her bag.

The sight of his neighbors sends Marco ducking back into his apartment.

Renata runs down the stairwell. She emerges from the apartment building onto Normandie Avenue at a full sprint. Still naked. A few people on the street see her and stop and stare.

Renata turns down an alley. She ducks behind a dumpster, pulls out some dirty clothes from her bag. She throws on the clothes and jogs away from Marco's building.

Howling keeps her up all night. She followed a man with a cart into Elysian Park and picked a spot a couple of hundred yards away from him, near Angels Point. She stares at a starless sky for hours. When her eyes follow the howls, she sees the silhouettes of dogs slinking across hillsides. And she thinks about her guide and his reddish-gray beard. As the morning light cuts through the trees, she sees how many tents and makeshift structures surround her. She can count at least fifty. Her stomach whines, pleading for food. *Antojitos on Avenida Popocatépetl. A dumpling restaurant in Arcadia that I read about on a Los Angeles travel blog.*

She walks back down onto Stadium Way. The empty blue and yellow chairs of Dodger Stadium a half mile away. She pulls a flyer from her bag. Neon pink letters spell C-*Hype Promotion*. The glossy flyer features young people partying in a nightclub. The guide had given her the flyer. Had he gotten away? She didn't see if the border agents caught him. On the journey's second day, he had given her the flyer and told her it was a place she could make money, cash he had said, under the table. Where citizenship wouldn't matter. He told her to ask for Abbott. Or was it Abner? At the time, four days ago, when the guide had given it to her, Renata had no interest in the job, but she took the flyer to be nice. Marco was going to help her get citizenship and get a job. But now everything has changed.

Renata walks into a tiny office right on the north side of Venice Boulevard where five different desks are positioned with no seeming order. There are four employees inside the office. Renata eyes a young Latina woman.

"Is Abbott here?"

The Latina woman points out the window, where a young man talks on the phone in a patio area. His collared shirt with the top three buttons undone shows off a shaved chest. Renata goes outside and tries to wait far enough away from Abbott to give him space to finish his call but close enough to let him know she wants to talk to him when he's done.

"Yeah. Tell her to reconsider it though. You get four groups to do bottle service and that's matching fifty covers. Ya know? Okay, Okay. Call me later. Peace."

"Abbott?"

"Yeah?"

"I was told you can get work to me. Under the table."

"I don't know what you're talking about."

"Oh. Okay. Thanks anyway." She starts to walk away but stops. Should she have started in a different way? "Carlos told me to ask for you."

"Where you from?"

"Camino Verde. In Tijuana."

"When did you get here?"

"Two days ago."

"Jesus."

"Do you have work?"

"You can't be talking like that. *Work under the table*'s the first thing you say to me? You gotta be more subtle like."

"I'm sorry."

"I don't have any work for you. But I promote clubs, and those clubs sometimes have young ladies passing out shots, getting men to buy shots. So if you hang out with me when I'm working, maybe you could do that?"

"Yes. I can."

"See how we're being more subtle like?" he asks.

"Yes."

"I can get you gigs. But you gotta kick half back to me."

"Okay."

"You got a place to stay?"

Renata doesn't want to say no.

"There's a motel I know in Lincoln Heights. Cheap rates, and they'll cut it in half if you spend a few hours cleaning rooms each morning."

"That would be great."

"It's on Hanover. Next to the Jack in the Box. I'll introduce you to Gloria. I can take you over there tonight. After work."

"Can I begin work tonight?"

"I work at the clubs most nights, but tonight I got this other thing. I promote this haunted house tour once a month. You can come if you want. On the tour I mean. And I'll take you to the motel after."

"What is it?"

"It's a haunted house. More like *the* haunted house. It's called Pandora's House. You gotta go on a tour, 'cause it's not safe. You could get lost or trapped. It's pretty crazy. It's fun."

"Okay . . ."

"The meetup spot changes every month. It's secret. We're meeting tonight at the Arroyo Seco Stables. Right next to the public golf course in South Pasadena. Be there by ten p.m."

"Okay."

"Yeah, come tonight. We'll hang. You can go on the haunted house tour. And tomorrow night we can start *hanging out* at the club. Making money, okay?"

"Thank you."

After she left Abbott's Mar Vista office, she had walked down Venice Boulevard before the smell of meat, potatoes, and grease grabbed her. Outside the In-N-Out Burger, she has been watching a pair of teenagers try to eat their way through more food than any two people could consume. When they give up and leave their trays, Renata descends on the food like a bird of prey. Scarfs down the leftover scraps. Fries. Hamburger. Bun. Some kind of pink sauce. She chews and swallows at a rabid pace for three minutes before she sees the irate manager coming toward her. A man with a body frame that suggests he's eaten a million hamburgers. Renata runs, knowing the fat man won't try to catch her.

Renata explores the neighborhood, killing time before she has to go to South Pasadena to meet Abbott. Up and down Venice Boulevard, people interact with people. Two men holding hands. A group of three teenage girls carrying skateboards like purses. Patrons waiting in line at a truck serving lobster rolls. Two women in their sixties riding in the bike lane on a bicycle built for two.

She made it here, to the United States of America, all by herself. And now she's here, all by herself.

The lights in a public park draw Renata in from the corner of Barrington and Palms. It's a roller hockey rink, but no one is playing hockey. Instead, a couple dozen teens and twentysomethings play soccer—indoor style. There are a few white people, but the rest of the players are Latino, Middle Eastern, West African, and Asian. One old white man stands nearby with his roller blades and hockey stick, annoyed the rink has been reclaimed by soccer players. A Middle Eastern boy scores a goal, and his team celebrates as others chant, "Farzad, Farzad, Farzad."

Now the teams re-form, one team short a player. A Latino guy points to the short boy standing on the outside of the rink, near Renata. "You wanna play?"

The short boy shakes his head.

"I'll play," says Renata.

Renata takes his half sigh half grunt as a yes.

Three minutes pass, and Renata might as well be running laps. Finally, a player kicks her the ball. She traps it and passes it to a teammate. They see she's not terrible and pass to her more. Renata isn't the best player, but she's playing—speaking the most international of languages.

Later in the game, Renata has a breakaway. Her and the goalie. But it's a street hockey goal, not a regulation soccer goal. Renata fakes like she's going to shoot to the right and shoots to her left. Her fake moves the goalie in the right direction but the ball pings off the post. *Oohs* and *aahs* from the players.

As Renata jogs back, a white player from the other team offers her a high five.

She slaps his hand.

• • •

Renata's exhausted, the right kind. She scoops up her bag and heads for the road. She passes the water fountain where the white guy who gave her a high five—now shirtless, with his tattoos on display—finishes drinking water as she passes him.

"You got skills!"

Renata smiles. "It was fun."

"You play here a lot?"

"My first time."

"I come every Monday. You should come back. People can get agro, but mostly it's chill. What's your name?"

"Renata."

"I'm Marty. Nice to meet you."

"You too."

"Where you from?"

Renata isn't sure whether to lie.

"¿De dónde eres?" he asks.

Renata smiles. But stays in English. "Mexico. I just got here."

"Wow. Welcome. Do you know a lot of people?"

"Not yet. I . . ."

"Do you know *anyone*?" When she hesitates, he asks, "Do you have friends here?"

Renata nods, but Marty seems to see through her lie.

"What are you doing now? Do you want to get some food?"

Renata hesitates. A part of her craves a nice dinner, craves the chance of getting to know someone in her new home. Another part of her doesn't trust him, doesn't trust anyone.

He adds, "I'm kinda seeing someone off and on. I just mean grab dinner as friends. There's this cheap Hawaiian place, Rutt's, right down the road."

When he says *friends*, Renata thinks of the show and pictures them one day living across the hall from each other. Marty doesn't seem like a Ross, Joey, or Chandler.

"Okay."

"Cool. Let's do it."

Mierda. She forgot. "I can't. I'm sorry. I have to go see . . . a haunted house."

"A what?"

Renata laughs, realizes how it sounded. "I'm trying to get work with this man who works for nightclubs. This guy Abbott. And he wants me to go on his haunted house tour with him. He called it Pandora's House." Renata looks at him to see if he's heard of it. Marty shrugs, hasn't.

"Let me get your number and we'll grab dinner another time."

Renata hesitates. Her cell phone broke three weeks ago. She considered buying another one but didn't have the money. Plus, she knew a phone would mean getting voice mails from family and friends when they realize she's gone.

As if sensing rejection, Marty throws up his hands. "Zero pressure. I'll see you at soccer some time."

"It's . . . I don't have a phone."

"Oh . . . Oh. Ummm, let's grab breakfast tomorrow. Are you free?"

"Sure."

"Okay meet me at S and W Diner. It's on Washington in downtown Culver. Right next to this obnoxious brew pub."

"S and W Diner?"

"Yeah. Nine thirty?"

"Okay."

"I'll see you there tomorrow."

"Yes."

Marty starts to walk away but pauses. "Where are you going now?"

"I have to go to Pasadena for the haunted house."

"Do you know how to get there?"

She hesitates long enough that he assumes she doesn't.

"I'm going right by the train station. I'll walk with you."

As they approach the Expo line train station on Bundy, Marty tells her she'll take the Expo line east toward downtown, then the Red line toward Union Station, and then the Gold line toward Azusa, where she'll get off at the South Pasadena stop. He points to a giant freeway overpass. "This place is a concrete jungle. Everybody drives around in their stupid-ass cars. But it's more fun to walk and take the train."

Marty shows her how to buy a TAP card and purchase one fare. It costs $1.00 for the TAP card and $1.75 for the fare, $2.75 total. She searches for coins at the bottom of her bag.

"Do you need a couple dollars?" Marty asks.

Renata feels her face burning. "No, no. I've got it. Thanks." She finds two more quarters and inserts them in the slot.

"Do you want a Clif Bar?" asks Marty, holding up a chocolate chip energy bar. "I've got an extra."

"No, no, gracias, I'm okay. Thank you."

"All right. So, tomorrow?" asks Marty.

"Yes. Nine thirty. S and W Diner."

"Do you like waffles?"

She smiles.

"Me too," he says. "We'll eat some waffles. And eggs."

Marty turns away before turning back. "Nice moves out there tonight."

He smiles. She smiles. And they walk their separate ways.

Renata approaches the stables on foot. A clump of men and women in their twenties and thirties, mostly white, crowd together. They smoke and vape and whisper. They nod hello to Renata, but she stands off to the side. There's a palpable excitement to the crowd. A buzz of anticipation.

A dirty black cat slinks by Renata. *Smelly cat, smelly cat, what are they feeding you?*

Renata fishes through her bag to put on a sweatshirt, and she spots a chocolate chip Clif Bar. Marty must have slipped it in there when she wasn't looking. She smiles, thinking about how sweet he is, as she rips open the packaging and takes a bite.

"You came!"

Renata turns to see Abbott. "Hey!"

"If anybody asks, say you paid Abbott."

"What is this? I don't understand."

"It's a tour of this haunted house. It's like Disneyland for adults. Kinda like an escape room but not. You'll have fun."

"Is it scary?"

"Eerier than scary. You smoke?"

Renata shrugs. She loves smoking weed. *Smoking weed with my friend Flip in the clump of juniper trees behind his house. Going to breakfast tomorrow with Marty.*

Abbott pulls out a plastic baggie of gummies. "This will make it even more fun."

He hands Renata an edible. She hesitates. Pops it. Chews. Swallows.

A few more people have shown up by the time the edible kicks in. She feels a tingling sensation in her cheeks. And realizes she hasn't smiled much in the last two weeks.

A short school bus retrofitted into a party bus pulls up to the curb. Cheers erupt from the others as they climb aboard the bus. The vehicle has the windows covered up so passengers can't see outside.

Renata picks a seat close to the front as Abbott climbs onto the bus.

"Welcome."

Everyone cheers. Renata can't believe how excited everyone is. It reminds her of a time she took a bus with Sofia to Estadio Caliente to see Xolos play Chivas.

"Each of you may have heard different stories about Pandora's House. You've heard about the infinite levels or the horizontal elevators or the weird artificial light with no source. You've heard the rumor that once you go in, you can never come out. You've heard it be called an iceberg house. You've heard about the circle, the portal to another world. Tonight, myths disappear, and *you* will get to see the real house."

More wild cheers. Renata finds their energy odd.

Standing in the aisle, Abbott grabs hold of the seats for balance as the bus starts moving. "This is my eerie tour guide voice."

Everyone laughs. Except Renata, who's thinking about the word *eerie*. That was the second time Abbott had said it.

"Once we get on the freeway, you'll have to turn your phones off and put them in here." Abbott holds up a portable box safe. "The drive to get there is ninety minutes. We may be driving in circles for sixty minutes to throw you off or we may be driving to Joshua Tree or Palm Springs. You will never know. There's no photography. You will not know where we are. The location must be kept secret. Anyone have any questions?"

Everyone raises their hands.

"We'll be there soon enough. And all your questions will be answered and you can see the enigma for yourself."

Renata has heard the word *enigma* before but isn't sure what it means. The collection of words and expressions she knows—like *pivot* and *on a break*—is shaped heavily by watching and rewatching all those episodes of TV.

Renata feels herself getting sleepy. Vision getting blurry. She rubs her temples with the pads of her fingers. Her toes feel strange inside her sneakers. She looks around at the others. No one else seems sleepy or out of it.

Renata keeps waking up, not realizing she was falling asleep. The bus is still moving. Without being able to see out the windows, no one can tell where they are. Colors and noises become too stimulating for Renata. She finds herself wanting to close her eyes to shut everything out. She gives in and closes her eyes. And now she can't open them. She's asleep. Then awake. And then asleep *and* awake. She's asleep for long periods. What feels like years. But even when she's awake, everything remains black. She hears a loud thumping hip-hop beat. And she thinks it's her heart beating. She starts to think she's dead. And then she's not thinking at all.

Renata opens her eyes. Where is she? The room has a strange greenish tinted light. But there's no obvious source. There don't seem to be any windows or lamps. Renata sits up. She's wearing the same clothes she was wearing before. Her head feels light. The walls seem to be made of a green or gray material. She walks to one side. The other.

She thought she was alone but a figure sits up. Another woman.

"You're awake . . ." says the other woman. She's white. In her twenties. Sunken eyes. Thin hair. Peeling skin. Malnourished.

"¿Dónde estamos?"

"What?"

"Where—where are we?"

"I don't know."

"Who are you?"

"I'm Coral."

"Were you on the bus tour?"

"No. What bus tour?"

"For the haunted house."

"I don't know what that is."

Renata's heart thumps in her chest like a jackhammer, and the feeling reminds her of having a nightmare. Is she dreaming? No, she knows she's not. "Where are we? Is this Pandora's House?"

"I don't know."

Renata bangs on the wall.

"What are you doing?"

"LET US OUT!"

"You're wasting your time."

"How long have we been in here?"

"You were asleep, for—I don't know—half a day. At least ten hours."

"Where's Abbott?"

"I don't know Abbott."

"Were you on the bus?"

"When?"

"Tonight."

"I've been here."

"For how long?"

Coral motions to the wall. "I tried to keep track of the nights. The days. But it was hard."

Renata goes to the far wall. There are scratch marks. At least a hundred. Renata's heart rate picks up again.

"What's your name?"

Renata doesn't answer. She's still staring at the hundred some marks on the wall.

"What's your name?" Coral repeats.

"Renata."

Coral leans in. "What'd you say? De Nada?"

"Renata."

Chapter Four

Tiphony

Tiphony is already thinking about gunfire when she walks into her Crenshaw-Imperial apartment and hears gunfire. No matter what she did that day, her mind came back to Jarmon Wade getting shot. She puts down the Taco Plus takeout food in the kitchen and heads into the den, where her husband is playing a first-person-shooter video game.

"Hey."

"Hey, T," says Mike.

"What the fuck?"

Mike pauses the game.

"I told you, you can't be smoking in here. Why would you do that before we go to Pershing Square?"

"Oh. Sorry, I forgot. That's tonight?"

"I don't want you smoking that in here."

"It's legal now."

"I got laws too. I don't want it smelling like this for Gary."

"I knew you were taking him to your mom's, so I thought it was cool."

"So you *did* remember we were going to the rally tonight?"

A smile forms on his lips. At least he knows when to admit defeat. Gotta love him for that. And sometimes she wonders what else there is.

Three minutes later, while bent over the kitchen table, she remembers.

The food is cold but it still tastes good, and cold food after sex feels right.

"Do you still want to go?" she tests him.

"Either way," he fails. "What? What's wrong?"

"It's important. That's what's wrong. But you don't care. You want Gary to be Jarmon Wade in ten years?"

Jarmon was shot and killed seven weeks ago when he emerged from an alley with his skateboard on San Pedro Street not far from Little Tokyo. The story hadn't gotten much national press because Jarmon had a gun. But he hadn't pulled the gun on the police. He had raised his hands, and when the skateboard hit the ground, a cop fired and the bullet tore through Jarmon's heart. Two eyewitnesses swore Jarmon hadn't pulled the gun on the officers, had only raised his hands and inadvertently dropped the board. One witness said the gun fell out of his waistband when he fell. And the other said the cop pulled it out of his waistband and placed it next to the body. The LAPD used the disagreement over this detail to discredit both accounts, and no charges were filed against the officer. Goddamn LAPD. It's like that Brennan dude said, the "to protect and serve" written on LAPD cop cars is in quotes, like they're being sarcastic.

Tiph's gray shirt reads *black lives matter*. She offers and receives nods of solidarity as she and Mike zigzag through the crowd in Pershing Square. Mike seems to walk a half step behind rather than next to her.

A woman with thigh-high boots and sky-high confidence passes them and says to Mike, "Oh shit, hey you."

Who the fuck was that? "Who was that?"

"Tasha."

So *that* was Tasha. An ex of Mike's. Tiph had always wondered what she looked like, and apparently she looks like Rhianna but with bigger tits. Even though Tiph married Mike, she was always confused why so many women were drawn to him. He was always ten pounds shy of being fat and ten dollars short of having ten dollars. But women have always liked him. He even had to get a restraining order against this one crazy lady named Xanny.

They find a nook to post up. Mike drinks from a glass bottle of 7UP and stands with a disposition that suggests he'd rather be playing video games.

Twenty minutes later, Mike finishes his bottle of soda. "Do you wanna go?" He says it like *My bottle of soda is finished so it must be time to go.*

"It's cool. We can stay."

On the far side of Pershing Square, a few Black teenagers have lit something on fire. *Oohs* and *aahs* from a crowd trying to see what's in flames. The crowd pushes in that direction, going *toward* the fire. Mike tries to stand on a nearby bench to see. Tiph's eyes are drawn to her right, where a dozen white men and women enter the park off Olive Street holding signs with messages like *Protect Our Police* and *The Police Matter.*

As they pass Tiph, she can't help herself. "Right now? This is where you're gonna sport that shit?"

A beefy white guy with a goatee takes the invitation for a debate and steps into Tiph's airspace. "They risk their lives every day. To keep us safe. To keep *you* safe."

"*This* isn't about whether we need municipalities and shit. *This* is about stopping young Black men from getting shot by the police."

"I support you. And I also support the police."

"Support the police, then. But right here? Right now? To wave that sign is to diminish what we're trying to say."

The beefy white man with the goatee pokes Tiph in the shoulder. "You don't know what you're talking about."

Tiph touches him back. With a slight shoving motion. "Don't fucking touch me," she warns.

He mimics her open-palmed shove, but she's smaller than him, and the force causes her to take a step back to catch her balance.

Tiph gets her footing and looks up in time to see Mike crack his glass 7UP bottle over the beefy white guy's head. The guy falls to the ground, lost in that ambiguity between awake and unconscious, unambiguously concussed.

Stunned, Tiph turns to Mike just as three other beefy white guys, two of whom also have goatees, pounce on him. A half second later, a fourth white guy, not beefy but with a goatee, jumps in too, making it four against one.

Tiph looks for help, but most of the crowd has shifted to the other side of Pershing Square, where the kids lit the fire. As Mike gets pummeled, Tiph sprints twenty yards to a parked LAPD SUV. "Help! Help!" The car appears empty. The back-left door is open a crack, caught on a seat belt. She opens it; no cops inside—they must have run to the fire. She starts to turn away but spots a riot gun in the partition mount, unlocked. She considers running for the police on the far side of Pershing Square. But she looks back to Mike: the four men might kill him first. And before she can second-guess her plan, she grabs the riot gun that shoots tear gas canisters and she aims the gun at the men on top of Mike. And fires.

Tiphony has to prop her foot on the table to get the right angle. She shoves the old toothbrush in the gap between her skin and the monitor strapped to her ankle.

Gary waddles into the room. Tiph thought waddling would have evolved into regular walking now that he's almost four years old, but Gary hasn't given in to peer pressure (or physics) and has maintained a penguin-like swagger.

"Does it itch?"

"It does."

"What does it feel like?"

"C'm'ere. I'll show you."

When Gary gets close enough, Tiph grabs his foot, causing Gary to flop to the ground on his back. Tiph tickles his ankle. Gary squeals.

When he isn't giving him businesslike speeches about how Gary's destined for greatness, Mike's the kind of fun dad to wrestle on the floor and build forts and make fake fart sounds. Tiph has been trying to fill the void.

Gary manages to squirm out of her grip. "So it tickles?"

"Not really. Here c'm'ere. I'll show you what it actually feels like."

Gary walks back within an arm's length of Tiph. She grabs his ankle. Gary falls to the floor, and Tiph tickles him. Tiph wonders if she could kill a kid by making him laugh too hard but figures she'd hear about it on the news if that was possible.

Gary crawls a few feet away. "You said it doesn't tickle."

"It *doesn't* tickle that bad. I was just tricking you. It's not bad. Just like a watch but on your ankle."

"I don't know what a watch feels like."

"Here, I'll show you."

Gary inches forward. Like a cautious penguin. As he gets within Tiph's grasp, the doorbell rings. Startled, Gary lets out a squeal. Tiph gets up and opens the door. A white hipster dude in his twenties. And his Asian American girlfriend who could be twenty or thirty-seven.

Asian don't crack, Tiph thinks.

"Can I help you?"

The guy smiles. "Hey, we just moved in next door."

His ageless lady smiles. "And thought we'd knock and say hello."

"Oh," says Tiph. "Well, hello."

"Have you lived here awhile?" he asks.

"Ten years."

"Oh, wow. It seems nice. We were over in Culver City. Getting hectic over there. New construction on a new restaurant every day. Trying too hard to be swanky, ya know?"

Tiph stares back. Did LA need two football teams? The city can't seem to find any moderation or consistency. It had two teams, it lost two teams, now it wants two teams again. Which involves building a giant billion-dollar stadium in her neighborhood. Maybe Inglewood's *transitioning*—as white folks liked to call it—was inevitable, but the new stadium accelerated the process. No more 2 percent milk. *White lady* used to mean cocaine around here, but now *white lady* might mean the Lululemonhead who just ran a red light in her Volvo. And once the yogis come in with their mats and downward dogs, it's all downward, dogg. Thirtysomething yuppies flooding in, Caucasian babies of the eighties traded their G.I. Joes for Trader Joe's, overprivileged geriatric millennials grew up looking out for number one, and Inglewood here they come. Fixing and flipping houses that don't need fixing. They already took *bae*, *woke*, *thicc*, and *YOLO*, why not take a city? And now Tiph can't walk to the Laundromat without hearing about the best acai bowl and Billie Eilish playing the Hollywood Bowl. But this isn't just the displeasure of hearing about kombucha, frolf, tech stocks, and the importance of *The Wire*. These cold-brew bros and curly-kale hoes moving in causes rent to increase, causes moms and pops to lose their shops. There's a movement growing to preserve Black businesses and culture in Morningside Park, but Tiph knows it won't be enough. White will win out. In the roulette wheel of life, red or black, always bet on white.

"This seems like a nice neighborhood though. Diverse and chill." The young man doesn't appear at all self-conscious. Trickle-down lack of self-awareness.

The Asian lady friend stares blankly at Tiph's house-arrest monitor. A twinkle of realization in her eye. Now she tries to look everywhere other than Tiph's feet. Tiph's tempted to tell her she's on house arrest because she fired tear gas canisters from a riot gun at four white dudes—and her husband—from twelve feet away.

The Asian lady sees Tiph smiling at her and tugs on her boyfriend's shirt.

"All right, we gotta get back to unpacking," he says.

"Okay now," says Tiph. *Go fuck yourself.*

"Who was that, Mommy?"

"That was gentrification on our doorstep."

"What's genmification?"

"Nothing, baby. Nothing."

• • •

Tiph waits in line to check in at the visitors' area of California State Prison, Los Angeles County. A breeze hits her arms, and she wishes she wore a sweatshirt. Seasonless LA, where trees don't know when to lose their leaves and people don't know when to wear their jackets.

The female clerk doesn't make eye contact with her. "Name?"

"Tiphony Carter. *P-h*. And an *o* not an *a*.

"Carter with an *o*?"

"Tiphony with an *o*."

"O? Oh, *o*. Tiphony?"

"Yeah, my mom wanted the *o-n-y* like in *ebony* or *onyx*."

"Oh, that's cute."

Tiph sits in a folding chair. A phone on either side of a pane of impossibly clean glass. The glass is so clean it's hardly visible. Not a single smudge. Tiph wonders about the allocation of resources, wonders about all the Windex it must take to keep this glass this clean. She hopes that bodes well for the treatment of her husband, but she knows better.

A guard brings in Mike. They each pick up a phone. Neither speaks for a moment.

"You okay?"

"Yeah. All good."

"All good?"

"What you want me to say? Where's Gary?"

"Are you sleeping okay? And don't gimme that 'sleep's the cousin of death' bullshit."

"I'll sleep all right. Gonna miss sleeping with you though."

"Well, what do they say, abstinence makes the heart grow fonder . . . ?"

"Tiph, where Gary at?"

"I didn't want to bring him the first time."

"You gonna bring him next time?"

Tiph shrugs.

"C'mon, Tiph, don't do it like that. Boy should see his father."

"I had a lot of conversations with my father through glass. I don't know that it helped."

"Yeah, but you don't know it didn't help neither. You turned out good."

"And yet I'm still having conversations through glass."

Mike's shoulders tense up. Tiph gets the sudden desire for Mike to be stoned. To be home and high. For his shoulders to sink. No stress, no seeds, no stems, no sticks.

"All that time I spent wishing you'd get more involved in the community, now I wish you'd been *less* woke. More toked. If you'd've just stayed home and played more video games, we wouldn't be here. Gary would have his dad. And I wouldn't have to take care of myself."

"Fuck off." Mike sits back and folds his arms across his chest.

As he leans back, she leans forward, like they're on a pendulum.

"I miss you." Tiph fights the tears.

Now Mike leans toward the glass. "Speaking on you having to take care of yourself, I maybe got a way to take care of you."

Here we go.

"I met someone in here. White dude, works in the kitchen with me. He's scrambling. Needs protection, and he doesn't want to go full-blown Aryan Nation. He's trying to do his fourteen months without getting any Nazi tattoos."

"How are *you* going to give him protection?"

"It's not me being his bodyguard, it's . . . It's more complicated."

"Okay?"

"This guy, Philip. He used to broker art. Illegal art for this other dude."

"Wait, what?"

"The guy I work with in the kitchen. His name's Philip. And Philip is an art broker. And he worked with this other dude, Chester Montgomery. Helped him buy the art he sells in his gallery in Bergamot Station. But he also helped Chester buy a shit ton of illegal art. We're talking a ton of money, right? Chester Montgomery got killed.

But his illicit multimillion-dollar art stash, according to Philip, ain't never got found."

"C'mon, Mike."

"'C'mon, Mike'?"

"Yeah, sorry if I'm twice bitten, thrice shy. But I thought we were past this shit after the Barkery. You were gonna stop this scheming shit."

From the night Tiph had met Mike eleven years ago at a backyard party in Baldwin Hills, Mike always had some scheme going. These schemes came and went. They overlapped. They varied in their levels of complexity. And in their levels of legality; they were responsible for Mike's first two felonies. These schemes prevented Mike from getting a full-time job. He was always convinced of his latest scheme; always talking about *Shark Tank*; always ripping off Shawn Carter, saying he's not a businessman but a business, man. In lieu of pursuing a career, Mike had always taken short-term (low-paying) jobs with few long-term commitments (benefits). Most of the time he couldn't bring home the Spam let alone the bacon. His latest scheme, six months earlier, involved spending a thousand dollars to go in with a group of guys starting a dog-food truck called Barkery. They planned to park it at dog parks and sell treats to dog owners. Mike didn't ask Tiph before he used a thousand bucks from their joint account. One of his partners ran off with the money before the market for a dog-food truck could be tested. Tiph had threatened to divorce him, and Mike promised never to spend more than fifty dollars on anything without asking first.

"I'm not scheming."

"You were born scheming. You were always too busy tryna make a dollar out of fifteen cents rather than tryna make a dollar out of fifteen minutes of work."

Mike rubs the stubble on his round face. "It's a real situation. Philip needs protection. I can get him protection. And in exchange, he's going to help me—*you*—find this stash of art. And then you won't gotta clean those houses anymore. We'll be on easy street."

"You never learn. Hard head makes a soft ass."

"That's cold. No ass jokes while I'm in here."

Tiph sits back and crosses her arms.

"I knew this be how you'd react. That's why I'm going to have you meet Philip."

"The guy with the art stash?"

"What? No, that's Chester. Chester's dead. Philip's the guy I work with who thinks he might know where Chester's art stash is."

"I don't need to hear the horseshit from the horse's mouth."

"This is real. I'm trying to take care of you."

"It seems like I'm going to be running around doing your errands, looking for your drawings."

"TC, this is real. Talk to Philip." Mike called her TC when he was trying to sound serious. And he was always trying to sound serious whenever he was scheming.

"When?"

"Today. In a few hours."

"I got work. *Real* work. Not treasure hunting."

Tiph shows up for work at the ironically filthy office in Del Rey five minutes early. She picks up as many hours as possible from Dee's Cleaning Services. Before Gary was born, Tiph worked as a cashier in a pizzeria on Crenshaw. The owner, Bill, was an older gentleman with diabetes and the beginning stages of congestive heart failure, so Tiph started expanding her role. She took the initiative to pass out flyers, make coupons. The shop made more money, Tiph got a raise, and Bill started calling her the head of marketing. She realized her value and was in the process of negotiating to become a partner when Bill had a heart attack and died, and the pizza shop closed. This was four weeks before Tiph gave birth. Months later, Tiph tried to reenter the workforce and find a managerial/marketing job at a restaurant or store. But on paper, she'd only been a cashier, and her one reference was dead. After six months of applications and interviews, Tiph started picking up hours at Dee's Cleaning Services.

Many of the women, all of whom are Latina, are on salary. Tiph is on a list of workers who get paid as independent contractors and fill in when one of the regular cleaning crews is missing a member.

The small-shouldered coordinator, Gloria, forces a toothy smile when Tiph walks in. "Tiphony. I was getting ready to call you. We actually aren't going to need you today."

"Girl, hold on."

"Long story but there was a scheduling snafu."

"A snafu?"

"Yeah . . ."

"Can you send me out with a different crew? I need the hours."

"We'll get you back in the mix tomorrow. Or maybe Thursday."

"No, I need it before tomorrow, as in the day after yesterday."

"Don't get angry at me."

"If I flaked"—Tiph checks her phone for the time—"four minutes before a gig, you'd fire me. You would. One fuckup. And I'd be gone. And you cancel on me last second, and there's not even an apology."

"I said I was sorry. That it was a snafu."

"I heard the snafu part." Tiph resists the urge to launch into a diatribe about how Gloria gives the Latina women on the list more hours than her. "Okay, well, please . . . I'm a single parent for the time being. My rent's going up. No money, mo' problems."

"Like I said, we'll fit you in as often as we can."

Fuck you. "Thank you."

Tiph heads for the exit. She sighs, not because of this bullshit but because she knows where she's going to go now.

A guard—the same one who led Mike in four hours ago—leads a scrawny fortysomething white inmate into the visiting area.

Philip scans the room. On the visitors' side, three Black women wait at different phones. Philip hesitates, unsure which is Tiphony.

Tiph waves, bails him out of the guessing game. They both pick up phones. Now Tiph can see he has a black eye.

"You're Mike's wife?"

"Yup. The lucky lady. Queen to King Convict. Mrs. Scheming Mike."

The comment makes Philip uncomfortable. So he moves past it. "Thanks for agreeing to hear me out."

"I already told Mike I wasn't interested in running around looking for your lost art like some kinda Indiana Jones shit."

"Well, I'm hoping you'll hear me out. This art stash is out there. And no one else is looking for it."

"You sound like Mike. Jailbirds of a feather."

"It's worth at least two million dollars."

"How do you know he had all this art?"

"I helped him get it. That's how I know. I know how much it's all worth because I was the one who took his money and gave it to the sellers. *Man with a Pipe*, Jean Metzinger. A half-burned Matisse that got stolen from Kunsthal. A bunch of others."

"That what you got busted for? Selling stolen art?"

"No. Tax evasion, and insurance fraud."

Another crooked straight white man. "Wow, triple threat, huh?"

Philip seems wounded by the jab.

Another sensitive crooked straight white man. "Why would this guy . . ." She trails off, searching her memory for his name.

"Chester Montgomery."

"Yeah, Chester Montgomery—sounds like the name for a dude who invented khakis. Or like the CEO of New Balance."

Philip doesn't get either joke.

"This Chester guy . . . why would he buy a bunch of illegal artwork? He can't tell nobody about it or hang it in his house if it's stolen, right?"

"Chester was pulling in more money than he could launder. For a long time, he had to keep the excess hidden. But he wanted to buy stuff with it. What can you buy with dirty money? Turns out, you can buy dirty art."

"Mike said this guy Chester Montgomery got killed, right?"

"Yeah."

"So don't it make sense whoever got him got the art too?"

"The police didn't have enough to arrest the guy they think did it. But supposedly it was this guy from Pennsylvania who killed Chester 'cause Chester had killed his brother. It was a tit-for-tat tap, not about art or money."

Tiph stares back, overwhelmed.

"If the guy who killed Chester did it for money, he would have taken the legal art in his home or taken the six figures in cash in the safe. But he didn't. The murder wasn't a robbery. It was just a murder."

A weeping older man two phones down distracts Tiph. She forces herself to look back at Philip. "Why are you doing this?"

"I'll take a black eye over what they're threatening next. I need help from Mike."

"C'mon, man, don't play me Boo Boo the Fool. You willing to give away all this art?"

"To live? Uh, yeah. Plus, I might not get out for a year. It may not still be there if I wait till I get out. I'd rather have ten percent of something than one hundred percent of nothing."

"Ten percent?"

"Yeah? Mike didn't mention that? I do ask you cut me in for ten percent of whatever you end up moving the art for."

"My bullshit detector is beeping bullshit. But what I can't figure is why the fuck you'd make up such a weird story. . . ."

"I'm *not* making it up."

"I could see you making it up to try to get protection."

Philip leans in toward the glass and lowers his voice. "If I'm making this up, and Mike finds out, not only will he not protect me, he'll have me killed. I'm not making this up."

Tiph chuckles about the idea of Mike having somebody killed. Although, he had almost killed that guy at the rally—that goddamn 7UP bottle being glass had pushed the charge to assault with a deadly weapon.

"You sure you wanna miss the chance to find millions of dollars?"

"You really trying to get me with FOMO, mofo?"

Philip scratches his non-black eye but doesn't respond.

"To be real honest, I'm not that intrigued," she says. "But shit, I'll think about it."

Two days of not thinking about it later, Tiphony heads out to drop Gary at his California State Preschool Program. As she opens her door to leave, Howard, who works for the property management company, takes a step back. He was taping an envelope to her door. He recovers from startled face to clown smile.

"You shutting off the water again tomorrow?" She skims the letter. "You can't do this. You already raised the rent earlier this year. You can't do it twice in a 365-day period."

"There's no such rule."

"There is. I read it online."

"That's for folks on rent control. Long as we give sixty days' notice, we're allowed to raise the rent whenever we want by however much we want. Which we're *not* doing. We're not trying to force anyone out."

"You know I can't afford this, so don't sit there and tell me you ain't trying to force me and my son out the door to Bompton. 'Cause you are."

"We're just keeping the rent at market price. Same as a gas station selling gas."

"Nah, that's apples to orange juice."

"I like apple juice and orange juice," says Gary. "How come they don't make banana juice?"

Howard smiles at Gary, then winks at Tiph. "Things have a way of working out."

"On their own? Nah, when you're Black, entropy don't solve problems, it causes 'em."

"Do you want to sit and we can talk about it?"

"No. I don't want to talk about it unless you aren't gonna raise the rent. I gotta go to work so I can try to pay the current rent price. I don't got time to try to talk about it so you feel less guilty."

"I'm sorry. This is the new rent price. Starting in sixty days. We'll prorate March."

Tiph's rent for a two-bedroom apartment has now gone from $1,230 to $1,950 in one year. She sees her new neighbors—the white hipster and his ageless Asian lady pal—returning home, perhaps from having ginger yogi tea and organic buckwheat pancakes. She holds up the piece of paper and calls out to them, "Thanks for this."

Tiph scrubs dog poop and dog puke from a Persian rug. It's hard to tell the poop from the puke. Tiph's filling in for a woman who's at her own home pooping and puking after calling in sick with a stomach bug. Tiph's happy for the work, even if the other women on this crew don't like her. They talked in Spanish the whole drive to Brentwood.

The queen of the Brentwood palace ambles into the living room, holding a yoga mat, an iced coffee, and a purse that costs more than Tiph will make in a month.

"Where's Valentina?"

"I don't know. I'm filling in. I'm Tiphony."

"Hi, Tiphony. You need to be careful in this room."

"Okay."

"I'm serious. You're two feet away from that wall *right now*."

"Ma'am, my proximity to the wall is based on the dog poo's proximity from the wall."

"Well, I need you to be careful. You're using chemicals that could destroy the $250,000 painting next to you."

Bitch, you better check your tone. "Okay. Sorry. I'll be careful."

When queen housewife walks away, Tiph sits back on her heals and takes in the painting on the wall. A piece of abstract art. One that Tiph finds concretely uninteresting. *Two hundred fifty grand . . .*

• • •

Two days later, Tiph's back at CSP-LAC, back to the smudge-free glass. Mike sits, and they pick up their respective phones in perfect unison. Like it was the hundredth time and not the second.

"Where Gary at?"

"I'll do it."

"What?"

"Get me all the info on this art shit. I'll find it."

Mike smiles. "There you go."

Chapter Five

Jody

Jody spends the majority of nights on his back, but last night he slept on his side and stomach. His ass hurts like hell after driving across the country in such a short period of time. When he wakes, his first thought is of his brother and dad, and it's like he's experiencing their deaths all over again. Who killed them? Why did someone kill them? Who/why? Who/why? When it came to his little brother, Jody used to carry around this curiosity. Across the ten years Marty was gone, it thrilled Jody to wonder where his little brother was and what he might be doing. That mystery is gone. Now, it's *who/why*.

Jody has read about LA's wild array of non-chain restaurants. But when he rises from the bed and looks out the window of his West Covina motel room, all he can see is a Hooters.

It's 6:45 a.m., what should feel like 9:45 a.m., but his binge driving and binge caffeinating makes him feel more like an astronaut returning from space than an East Coaster experiencing a three-hour throwback. He plans to infiltrate LA proper from the Inland Empire outskirts and go straight to Marty's address, but he needs to wait a couple of hours. If Marty had roommates or a landlord, dragging them out of bed at 7:00 a.m. won't be the best way to get them talking. He decides to watch more *My Dirty California* videos in a continued attempt to crack the cipher that was Marty Morrel.

There's an entry where Marty discusses his realization he was part of an early wave of gentrification in Mid-City. There's an interview with

Tony, the owner of a store called Sideshow Books. There's an essay making the case for Los Angeles as the best city for soccer in the country—with the weather, the hundreds of fields, and the immigrants from all over the world. There's a video log entry clowning Brentwood moms. Many entries document a single adventure. A trip to Pinnacles National Park. The time he surfed and skied in one day. Or just a crazy day in Los Angeles when Marty ended up on the 405 in a VW bus that couldn't go faster than thirty miles per hour headed to watch an unannounced soccer friendly between the US national team and a professional team from Norway. One entry consists of photographs of a political stunt he and a group of friends pulled on private golf courses in LA, some kind of shout-out to an episode of *Revisionist History*. There's a secret-stairwell guide with pictures and maps for twenty-five different stairwells, including the Baxter Steps, the Entrada Stairs, and the Mattachine Steps.

The entries give Jody this window into his brother's life, but that life is over, and in some ways getting to know him better only sharpens the pain.

Jody stumbles across multiple entries that mention O. Could O be a drug Marty was using? Jody hears him mention O for the first time in a simple video log entry:

"I hadn't thought about O for a while until last night. I was supposed to go to the Brewery Art Walk and meet Nicky, but I got way too high and I ended up hitching a ride from this Armenian guy who was telling me all about money counterfeiting, and I realized he was going west not east, and he tells me he's going to Malibu, to Moonshadows, and he starts talking about Mel Gibson, and so I get him to pull over and I get out and I'm on the Sunset Strip. I realize I have to piss so badly. And I'm so high and I start to think I'm seeing upside down, but then I realize the Standard's sign is upside down. And I wander into the Standard to take a piss. I walk inside, and inside the hotel lobby, there's this huge glass rectangle. A waterless fish tank. The famous and infamous Box. And there is O."

Jody searches online for O and tries googling it in conjunction with other terms like *drug* and *street drug*, but he doesn't find much. Could O refer to opioids? Jody finds a couple other O mentions on Marty's site. One entry features dozens of photographs from Lassen Volcanic National Park, and Marty wrote, *The trip was infinitely better with O.*

In a meandering, somber post, Jody finds O referenced again.

"Brick and no brick. And thinking about O and that other world, I start to smile and wonder. But it's not many-worlds, it's one, and there's no going back."

Is Marty referring to a *brick* of heroin?

Anticipation and nervousness have combined to form a kick of adrenaline. Jody's been pacing while watching videos. He can't wait any longer. He checks out of the motel, climbs in his truck, and pulls onto the 10 freeway, which at the moment resembles a giant parking lot—brake lights for days. Is there an accident? He looks at Google Maps for an alternate route. The entire city is bleeding red, from every limb and orifice, and all the connecting capillaries. Rory, who loves sticking his head out the window of a moving car, lies flat on the passenger seat. As Jody sits in traffic, Marty's words echo in his ears from a *My Dirty California* entry he watched earlier that morning:

> This is for all the LA drivers out there. All the concrete this city has is nothing short of a goddamn wonder. Concrete motherfucking jungle. I just read *Los Angeles: The Architecture of Four Ecologies* by Reyner Banham. There was a time when Los Angeles was world-renowned for our concrete freeways. "Our"? Did you hear that? When I talk shit on LA, remind me I said "our." Anyway, years ago, LA's freeway system was seen as modern. Hip. Architecturally impressive. Only in a state where we value the freeways would we call them the 10, or the 405. I-95 is a pretty goddamn helpful road. From Boston to Miami, with New York, Philly, Baltimore, DC in between. But it never earned the article of the 95. Just plain old 95 or I-95. However much respect

> LA's highways may have gotten in the seventies, somewhere between when video killed the radio star and the internet killed the porn star, LA's tangle of freeways became the laughingstock of US transportation. Los Angeles is in the process of introducing new public transpo. They're merging existing train lines, building new ones. I ride the train everywhere, def don't mistake this rant. It's a step in the right direction. But for the LA driver, all this change is meaningless. You see, at any given time in LA, there are thousands, if not tens of thousands, of people who would like to drive somewhere but they choose not to for the sole reason they don't feel like sitting in traffic. There are people who drive to work at five in the morning or leave work at nine at night to avoid traffic. So as soon as the city constructs train lines or bus lines that alleviate some of the existing traffic, that freed-up space is instantly filled by those people who weren't driving but now think there's room for them. Look, if you happen to live in Santa Monica and work downtown or vice versa, the Expo line is your escape pod from sitting in traffic. But if not, and you're still planning on driving, I don't care how many trains or buses or streetcars or Bird scooter things they implement, driving in LA is fucked for the foreseeable future. Period. All a way of saying, fuck cars.

The video had flashed back and forth between a shirtless Marty drinking a bottle of Pacifico on his transportation rant and a slideshow of photographs. Shots of the 10 freeway, the 405, the 101, the 110, the 210. Shots of exit ramps and entrance ramps. Shots of cars stuck in traffic. Fancy cars. Old cars. Economy cars. The photographs came from the vantage of a person navigating the city on foot.

Now, stuck in traffic, Jody takes in the views. Cars. Ramps. Overpasses. Dingbat apartments dot the maze of concrete. *Concrete motherfucking jungle.* Jody doesn't find any of it worthy of a photograph; Marty had a real eye.

• • •

Jody climbs out of his truck onto the neighborhood street. Google Maps had taken him west on the 10 and north on the 5 before dumping him in Mount Washington via Cypress Avenue. And now he stands outside the house that matches the return address of the last letter Marty sent him. Over the past ten years, Marty had sent Jody letters or books from ten different addresses. Marty had averaged at least one house per year.

A one-story house sits on the lot, but in the backyard there's also a separate studio apartment. No one answers Jody's knocks. He hears a rustling sound around back. He wanders down the driveway into the backyard, where a man plants marigolds in a bed of mulch.

The man looks annoyed, or maybe just startled, to see Jody. He wipes his face on his gray T-shirt. Dark stains of new sweat cover yellow stains of old sweat.

"Sorry. I knocked. I heard something back here."

"What do you want?"

"I was hoping to ask about a tenant of yours."

"Tenant? I got one tenant, and that asshole skipped out a couple weeks back and owes me a month and a half of rent."

"Marty?"

"Yeah. You know where he is? 'Cause I'm giving it another day before I put his shit on the curb. I got a mortgage. I took a chance on that kid. Gave him a place to stay, and respected his preference to do everything off book, and this is what I get."

"Marty's my brother. *Was.*"

Jody's use of the past tense brings the man's gardening to a halt. *What?* The man mouths the word as if unable to say it aloud.

"He came to Pennsylvania. And he was killed. My dad too."

"Wait, what? Who are you?"

"I'm Jody."

"Marty's . . ."

"Dead."

The man wipes the sweat off his brow with a hand that has a burn scar right below the knuckles. "Fuck. I'm sorry. I'm sorry I called him an asshole."

"It's okay. How long had he been living here?"

"Six months."

"That's it?"

"Yeah."

"What's your name?"

"I'm Travis." Travis extends the hand with the peanut-shaped scar. Jody shakes it. "I'm *really* sorry I called him an asshole."

"It's okay. You didn't know he . . . You thought he skipped out. So he was renting this unit?" Jody motions to the studio at the back of the lot.

"Yeah. I can show you?"

Jody hesitates, unsure if he can bear seeing his brother's home, but there's no version of him saying no. The cramped space includes a queen mattress on the floor, a love seat, a chest with three drawers, a stove, and a rod for hanging clothes—a sort of convex closet. One naked light bulb. A sliding wooden door closes off a tiny alcove with a shower and toilet. A tiny home, but not a hip tiny home. Just a small home. But it is a home. It was Marty's home.

A series of maps cover the walls. Nautical charts, cadastres, unfolded eight-folders, topographic maps, national park maps, state park maps, AAA maps, old historic maps. Los Angeles. Southern California. The Central Coast. The Bay Area. Humboldt County. Atop the chest of drawers sits a pile of twenty more such maps.

"He collected 'em. Old maps of California. Which is funny."

"Why?"

"Why'd he collect 'em, or why is it funny?"

"What?" Jody now confused as he scans the studio apartment.

"I don't know why he collected them. I said *funny* 'cause he didn't really have anything else. The kid had a few pairs of clothes. A pair of shoes. His computer. His phone, which he mostly left on airplane mode and mostly used to take pictures, and that was about it. But he liked these maps. I have an autistic nephew up in Washington who loves maps. I'm not saying Marty's autistic. Shit, your brother is like the opposite of autistic."

Jody explores the tiny studio apartment, examining the different maps. Jody pictures Marty lying in the bed, which makes him picture Marty lying on the carpet bleeding out. He closes his eyes to avoid crying and teeters before catching his footing.

"I can wait outside if you wanna take a minute," says Travis.

"No. It's fine." Jody opens a couple of drawers. They're empty except for a few more maps. Jody spots a cardboard beer coaster atop the chest. *Figueroa Mountain Brewing Company.*

"Like I said, he didn't really have anything. Some clothes. And them maps."

Jody goes over to the fridge. There are fifty magnetized letters on it. At first glance, all the letters are placed at random around the door. But four letters are placed together in two two-letter words. *DO RI.*

"Those letter magnets were here before Marty. The tenant I had before was always arranging them in haikus."

Jody keeps staring at the *DO RI*. The words had haunted Jody. They had become a symbol of Jody's guilt for Marty running away to California, and later a symbol of guilt for Marty's death. But maybe Marty hadn't disliked the expression. Perhaps Jody had fabricated that element of their history.

"How much did he owe you?"

"A month and a half rent."

"Which is how much?"

"Eighteen hundred."

"Eighteen hundred? Twelve hundred a month for *this*?"

"I was cutting him a deal. I could rent this space for fifteen hundred a month. Those hipsters and artists are flooding this neighborhood like it's Woodstock '69."

"Let me pay you what he owed."

"You don't have—"

"No, I want to."

Jody pulls a checkbook from his backpack. "I only ask in return you answer some questions about Marty." Jody writes a check for $1,800. "Who do I make it out to?"

"I don't feel right about this. I'll answer your questions about Marty. Truthfully, I don't know much. We didn't talk much. I mean, he could sure as hell talk, once he got going, but it was usually just about whatever. He didn't . . . I don't know what happened."

Jody is still holding the pen and checkbook.

"I feel bad, saying what I did about him, knowing he was killed. I don't want your money."

"You said he owed it to you. You said you had a mortgage."

"Yeah . . . But still."

"Well, how about this. Does the eighteen hundred dollars cover through this month?"

"What do you mean?"

"I mean, was the rent money to cover this current month?"

"Yeah. Part of it."

"Can I stay here? I'll take over his payments."

"You . . . Well, okay. I guess."

"So who do I make the check out to?"

Step one, visiting Marty's apartment, hadn't led to solving his murder, but it had taken care of step two, finding a place to stay.

Chapter Six

Pen

Pen leaves her Prius on the neighborhood street in Mount Washington and approaches a craftsman one-story house on a quarter acre lot. As she heads up the driveway, she can see a back unit that's charred black.

Pen spent the last forty-eight hours watching as many *My Dirty California* videos as possible. She tried a mobile phone number for Jody she found on the web but it went straight to voice mail, mailbox full. She found an email address online and tried sending Jody emails, but he hadn't responded. From one of Jody's videos, Pen found an address where Jody lived, which was the same place Marty last stayed. When she looked up the address, she saw it was only a mile away from the Self-Realization Fellowship International Headquarters, sometimes called the House of Hallows. Eighteen months ago, Pen looked into the former Mount Washington hotel turned temple as a possible location for Pandora's House. But after visiting the grounds and getting caught sneaking into the archives in the basement, she was given a lifetime ban.

A man answers the door. He looks in his midforties.

"Can I help you?"

"Are you Travis?"

"Yeah."

"Hi, my name's Penelope. I was hoping to talk to Jody. Is he here?"

"Jody? No. He's not here. You know where he is?"

"Me? No. I was coming here to talk to him."

"I need to know where he is."

"So he's not living here anymore?"

"No. Not after the fire."

"What fire?"

Travis points toward the partially burned back unit at the end of the driveway. "He let a friend of his stay here for a week. Some lady named Nicole. I can't get a hold of her. From my last conversation with her a couple months ago, I got a sense she's not going to be helpful. I need Jody to talk to the insurance folks or I can't get my check. Just to say it wasn't him but that his friend was here when the fire occurred."

"So he moved out?"

"Yeah. After the fire."

"Where did he go?"

"Silver Lake. Then Highland Park. Palms. I know he was downtown for a bit. I haven't been able to get in touch with him though."

"Marty lived here too?"

"Yeah."

"Do you know if Jody figured out who killed Marty?"

"No. I don't."

"How well did you know Marty?"

"I'm sorry, who are you?"

"Pen."

"And what are you . . ."

"I'm a documentary filmmaker. I was trying to figure out what happened to Marty as well. I wanted to compare notes with Jody."

"I see."

"Can I see the place?"

Travis shows Pen into the back unit. Two of the four walls are charred. Pen can see what used to be a couch. If there was a bed or mattress, it must have gotten burned. A bureau with three drawers suffered the least damage. On top, there's a pile of maps, all partially burned. Pen examines the maps. Beyond charred, many look old, like collectors' maps.

"Were these Jody's?"

"Marty's."

Pen examines the maps. It makes sense they were Marty's. And it makes sense he'd be using older maps, trying to identify anomalies that might have shown up on maps before the government started covering them up.

Pen holds up the map from the bottom of the pile. It's an old map of Lassen Volcanic National Park. Since her senior year of high school, Pen has kept a list of possible irregularities, possible gaps in the world. Lassen and its strange steaming fumaroles has long been on the list.

"Could this have been arson?"

"Arson? It was Jody's friend Nicole. An accident. She called nine-one-one herself."

Pen wants to hear from Jody if it was Nicole and if it was an accident. Or was the fire an attempt to destroy these maps?

"So how well did you know Marty?"

"Not that well."

"Did he talk about this girl Renata? About her finding Pandora's House?"

"No. I don't know what that is. Pandora's box, like the myth?"

Pen ignores the question, switches gears. "What about Renata?"

"He never mentioned her."

"Anything about a woman jumping simulations?"

"What the hell are you talking about?"

"Nothing. I need to speak with Jody. I tried a cell and an email I found online. Do you have another way I can get a hold of him?"

Travis rubs the back of his hand where he has a birthmark that's shaped like a peanut. "Lady, I don't know how else to tell you this. I'm looking for Jody. I need him to talk to the insurance company. I haven't heard from him in five weeks, all right? His phone's been off with the mailbox full. For all I know he did figure out who killed Marty and they killed him too."

"So he's missing?" Pen asks.

"Yeah, that's a word for it. Missing."

Chapter Seven

Jody

Jody walks out of his new apartment into the ninety-five-degree heat. It's hotter than Pennsylvania, but Jody's been sweating less. The heat is different here. It pulls the moisture right out of his mouth. Rory hops in his Ford truck, panting with excitement.

Jody's heading west to Santa Monica to talk to Chester Montgomery. Jody has been living in Marty's old apartment for three days, long enough to buy milk and cereal and get a sense of the neighborhood. He and Rory have walked the square mile surrounding Marty's apartment. Mostly, Jody's been digging through the *My Dirty California* videos and written entries. Working his way backward from the end. Marty's posts on Encinitas and Humboldt County are vague, but there's a specificity to the third-to-last post about going to the party in the Hollywood Hills and playing poker with that rich art dealer Chester Montgomery.

Jody has a terrible sense of direction. When he learned to drive, before Google Maps and iPhones, he constantly got lost on southeastern Pennsylvania's tangle of back roads. As he drives on the 10 freeway toward the beach, he realizes LA offers a giant compass: the ocean to the west, the mountains to the north. Now that it's been a few days, he has moments like this where a thought or interaction gives him a five-second respite from his obsessive thinking about his dead brother and father. But the lull only results in deeper heartache when the thoughts return.

• • •

Bergamot Station consists of art galleries, design firms, and cafés in a complex that doubles as a cultural center. Jody finds the CM Gallery with its door propped open. There's not much art, but maybe that's how galleries present art. Not stacked like junk in a thrift store. But spaced out.

A woman with short hair and glasses approaches. She looks like women Jody sees playing the women working in art galleries in movies.

"Hi, and how are you doing this morning?" Talks like them too.

"I'm good. How about you?"

"Excellent. Are you a collector?"

"Actually, I was hoping to talk to Chester."

"Oh, he's not here. Is it about a certain piece? I'm very familiar with our entire catalog, everything that's on display and not."

"No. I just need to talk to Chester. Could you give me his phone number?"

"I'm sorry. I can't give out his personal number. If you come back—"

Jody's ringtone echoes off the gallery walls. His childhood friend Mark has been texting him, asking where he was and why he wasn't at the funerals. Jody ignores the call; he's ignored all the texts and calls from everyone.

The gallery door opens. Jody recognizes the man from the pictures Marty posted from Chester's party. He remembers the bearlike round eyes too small for his face.

"Chester? My name's Jody."

"Hi, Jody."

"I was wondering if you could tell me anything about Marty Morrel."

Chester pauses as if searching his brain. Or pretending to search his brain. "I don't think I know a Marty Morrel."

"He was at your house a few weeks ago."

"I don't think so."

"On Saturday, May twenty-fifth, he was at your house, and you played poker until like three in the morning."

"Oh. I did have a party a few weeks back. Too many people, and I had too much Macallan. Couldn't tell you a quarter of the guests who were there."

Jody wants more information, but he's not sure what to ask.

"Why are you asking?"

"Did anything out of the ordinary happen? At the party I mean."

"No. Why are you asking me these questions?"

"He's dead. Marty is."

"Oh. I'm sorry. What happened?"

"That's what I'm trying to figure out."

As Jody navigates the string of galleries back to his truck, he runs the conversation back through his mind. From now on, he can't be introducing himself as *Jody Morrel, out to solve the tragic murder of his brother, Marty Morrel*. He doesn't have any reason to suspect Chester Montgomery killed his brother, but from here on out he'll have to be slyer.

Chapter Eight

Tiph

Outside of Philip telling her some guy killed Chester because Chester killed that guy's brother, Tiphony doesn't know much about him. Just that he had a big-ass, secret, multimillion-dollar art stash. She types *Chester Montgomery* into Google.

She clicks on a web page for the CM Gallery. She scans the website, reading about the Santa Monica location and a few pieces of the art.

"I'm Buzz Lightyear!"

Tiphony looks up to see her son, Gary, has pulled a plastic bag over his head. Tiph snatches the bag. "Don't ever do that! You hear me?"

Gary cries. The kid kind of crying where it sounds like he's going to hyperventilate.

"Go ahead and cry. Whatever makes you remember you can't do that."

Since becoming a temporary single parent, not much about parenting had actually changed except the doubling of duties. Logistically, she has time to execute all the tasks. But it leaves no time for anything else, like seeing her friends Mo and Tracy, reading the news, sleeping more than six hours, taking a long bath, having a moment of silent reflection, or maintaining basic sanity.

Gary's cries simmer to a whimper.

"Stop crying. You need to eat some fruit."

"Okay. I'll have Fruit Loops."

After she gets Gary eating carrots and apple slices, Tiph returns to the computer. She scrolls through the search results, finds a non-art-gallery mention. Chester Montgomery shows up in the Instagram of a woman who calls herself "Sierra Blaze." Tiph scrolls through the pictures. Sierra Blaze is a platinum-blond woman. Her profile picture is a selfie, a kissy face on the Santa Monica Ferris wheel. Her posts consist of her at different clubs and restaurants wearing different dresses. She may be pushing forty but she's forever shopping at Forever 21.

Tiph clicks on a few pictures where Sierra Blaze has tagged Chester Montgomery. The name isn't hyperlinked. One picture features Sierra and Chester at an Italian restaurant holding glasses of red wine. The picture's caption reads: *Me and Chest at dinner.*

Chest? Chest would be a better nickname for Sierra, since her silicon bolt-ons seem to be the through line of her Instagram account. Tiph clicks on other pictures that include Chester. Sierra and Chester at a Dodgers game. Sierra and Chester in a hot tub. Sierra and Chester hiking Runyon Canyon. Tiph clicks back to Sierra's home page. She selects Follow and clicks Message.

The supermarket is swamped for midday. An hour before, she signed in to the portal on the California Department of Corrections website and adjusted her schedule, citing she was going to Ralphs on Crenshaw at 2:00 p.m.

As Tiph walks through the supermarket, she passes by all the food she's used to ignoring. She hits three grocery stores—a Vons, a Ralphs, and a Sprouts—multiple times a week and only buys the food on sale. It's a huge time suck, but the only way she can get healthy food for her, Mike, and Gary without going broke. When she sells this art, she'll go to the store once a week. And no more skimping on parking meters and walking a mile to get to a restaurant. No more buying second-hand IKEA furniture off Craigslist. No more looking for Groupons to get her nails done. And no more signing up for Netflix and watching everything in one weekend and then canceling it. It'll be the end of worrying about making ends meet.

In the back, there's a Coffee Bean inside the supermarket. She scans the crowd of customers seeking caffeine pick-me-ups to get through their shopping escapades. She spots Sierra Blaze drinking the Coffee Bean version of a Frappuccino and sticking out like someone trying to stick out. Sticking out like someone who would change their name to Sierra Blaze. Tiph will give her half the art stash if that is her birth name. And she'll give her the other half if those are her birth tits. Tiph likes it when people call her own boobs perky. But Sierra's tits aren't perky, they're big ol' physics-defying feats. Nobody's single tit should be bigger than their whole booty, just not right.

"Sierra?"

"Yes. You Tiphony?"

"Yeah. Tiph. Thanks for meeting me."

"Yeah. Nice to meet you, girl. I was a little weirded out when you asked to meet in person."

"Oh, wow. I love your earrings," says Tiph.

"Oh, thanks!" Sierra beams with pride.

Tiph saw a couple of posts on her Instagram where she'd bragged about designing her own earrings.

"I only have a bit of time, so I hope you don't mind if I dive right in. I saw your pictures with Chester."

"Yeah. My Chest . . ." Sierra tears up.

"I'm sorry."

"What is it you want to talk to me about?"

"Well, there was a painting my mother had. She sold it a few years ago to help cover my brother's medical expenses—he had cancer. And I was looking to buy it back. And I think Chester may have owned it."

"Oh, really? Maybe at the gallery. But all that's been sold, I think. I don't know much about his art stuff."

Art stuff? She doesn't know shit about Chester's art gallery and paintings if she calls it *art stuff.* "Oh, really? That's too bad. How did you know him?"

"Chest? We . . . we were together. Sort of. He was sweet. He bought me nice things. But it became more than that. Even if it wasn't official, we loved each other." She says it like she's trying to convince Tiph. Or maybe herself. Devon, the man Tiph had been with before Mike struggled to say they were together. So had Keith who came before Devon. Tiph had given Mike an ultimatum, and he chose to make it official, to call her his girlfriend. It had been empowering and yet had also made her feel insecure.

"You saw him all the time?" Tiph asks.

"Yeah, like every day. And we talked literally a million times a day. You know you're not the first one come around asking about Chester."

"No? Who else?"

"This man. Joe . . . He came to the gym and tanning salon where I work, and I remember him because he was sunburned, which is not exactly the time to go to a tanning salon. And he had very specific questions about Chester. And I shouldn't have answered them, but Chest, he sometimes would go periods without calling me, and I was mad at him. So I answered this man's questions. And three weeks later, Chester was dead."

"Really? What did this Joe want to know?"

"All kinds of stuff. I remember he asked me multiple times about Encinitas and Eureka, wondering if Chester had gone there or talked about those places."

"Had he?"

"Not that I knew of."

"Then what happened?"

"We were talking, and he got a call from his wife and said she'd been in a car accident and he ran out. But I thought he might have been lying."

"Do you think he had something to do with Chester's death?"

"I wonder."

"When was the last time you saw Chester?"

"It was a day before he died. We had lunch at . . . I forget what it was called. But it was this Italian place right next to a Brinks. I know that 'cause he called from the Brinks and said to meet him next door for lunch."

"Brinks, the security company?"

"Yeah, he was reserving some kind of armored car."

"Really? What for?"

Sierra shrugs her shoulders in a *Who knows?* kind of way and her breasts bob chin-high. "I thought only like banks and jewelry stores used those armored trucks, but I guess people do too."

Yeah, to move their big-ass illicit art stashes. "Lemme ask you something else. Did Chester have anywhere he might hide something?"

"Chester hid everything. Shit, he hid me from his friends. But I think he just didn't want them hitting on me. But yeah, he had a whole room in his basement no one even knew was there. Trick door and all. He didn't show like anyone. But he showed it to me though." Sierra beams.

"Really?"

"Yeah. It was right by the stairwell. Door handle looked like a switchboard. Opened right up into a room."

Tiph returns to her apartment. As she heads from the carport toward the stairs, now carrying Gary, her parole officer Frank steps in her path.

"Hey there, Tiphony. Hi, Gary."

Caught off guard, Tiph tries to speak but only mutters a couple vowels.

"How was the supermarket?" Frank asks.

"Fine."

"Didn't get anything?"

Shit, fuck. She doesn't have any bags with her. A flaw in her scheme. She'll get better. "Didn't have what I wanted."

"The whole supermarket? Nothing you wanted."

"What is this? Huh? Look, I went to the supermarket. Then I picked up my son from my mother's house in Ladera Heights. Both court approved. Check the data." She holds up her foot as if the data is checked on her ankle monitor itself. "What's it, a slow day at the office?"

"Just thought I'd check in and say hi."

Go die. "Well, hi," Tiph says, pushing past him.

The morsel of comfort in seeing Philip—this white-collar white man—behind bars hasn't worn off yet. His black eye has faded. The last time she saw him, that black eye had been like a black hole and made it hard to look anywhere else. He has broad shoulders destroyed over time, probably from hunching over a computer. His callus-free fingers suggest a man who has never lifted a shovel or dumbbell. He looks like a person incapable of harming another person but who shouldn't be trusted. Calculator-is-mightier-than-the-sword kinda fella.

"I met with Sierra."

"Who's that?"

"Chester's girl."

"She one of his pro skirts?"

"Something like that."

"She tell you anything?"

"Some guy named Joe came talking to her a couple weeks before Chester got *got*. I wonder if that's the guy who you said killed Chester. She also said he had a secret room in his house. Maybe that's where the art is."

"His houses were seized after his death."

"*Houses?* You add an extra *s*? Or does Chester got an extra house?"

"He had a house in the Hollywood Hills and a house in Palm Springs."

No one in Tiph's extended family has ever owned a home, let alone two.

"She was talking about the Hollywood Hills house," says Tiph.

"The bank's selling it. There's an open house next weekend."

Tiph pictures attending a fancy open house in the hills. It would mean playing dress-up and pretending to be a multimillionaire. Luckily, she's got just the dress, and it will cover up her ankle monitor too.

"I can go, look for this secret room. But what do I do if the stash is there? I can't just walk out with a bunch of art."

"Go to the open house. Check out the room. If it's there, you can go back at night. With a crew. Maybe it's there," he says.

"Or maybe it *was* there. And this Joe guy already got it."

"If it is the same guy, his name's Jody Morrel. You should look him up."

"Why?"

"There's stuff online. I think you'll be less worried he was after some art."

There's not much on *Jody Morrel* on Google. An old LinkedIn page lists him as a middle school soccer coach/groundskeeper in Lancaster, Pennsylvania.

Below that, there's a Reddit thread titled "What happened to Jody Morrel?"

One user linked to MyDirtyCalifornia.com, suggesting an elaborate hoax. In response, another user linked to the obituary of Marty Morrel. The MyDirtyCalifornia.com page fails to open. Below the link, a user posted: *This seems like a riff on* My California, *a human interest show made by KCET that airs on California PBS stations.*

Another post: *Jody seems like an asshole who exploited his brother's death to team up with a conspiracy theorist documentary filmmaker to make some money.*

A user named PricklyPearz posted: *Can anyone confirm they've talked to Jody in the last 6 months?*

Another series of commenters debate whether Marty ever even lived in Los Angeles, pointing to articles about his death in Pennsylvania.

Other comments pertain to a Mexican teenager named Renata. Users have linked to dozens of different social media sites for different Renatas, some live in Los Angeles, some in Mexico.

The whole Reddit thread is puzzling, but Tiph keeps reading.

There are a ton of comments about a woman named Penelope. One user hyperlinks to a whole other Reddit thread about a UFO documentary called *The Flying Object*. One user calls her a *conspiracy theorist with daddy issues*. One user claims to have met Pen's father in Las Vegas in 2009. One user has linked to Penelope's Kickstarter campaign. The woman is seeking $26,000. And she has reached 3 percent of her goal. The title reads *Documentary film on the murder of Marty Morrel, the disappearance of Jody Morrel, and the existence of Pandora's House.*

The Kickstarter video features a thirtyish woman with short hair talking right into the camera:

"Hi, my name's Penelope. Some of you may know me from my first documentary film, *The Flying Object*. I'm trying to put together the necessary funding to make my second documentary. Renata is a young woman who came to California from Mexico and disappeared. She was last seen going on an organized tour of a place called Pandora's House. This man Marty Morrel started looking into her disappearance. He documented his findings but was murdered before he could find her."

The video flashes to an article from the *Philadelphia Inquirer* titled 27-YEAR-OLD MAN AND FATHER KILLED IN BRUTAL MURDER OUTSIDE LANCASTER.

"Marty's older brother, Jody Morrel, came to Los Angeles to try to find out who killed his brother. He documented some of his findings but disappeared before any arrests could be made. I believe Renata's disappearance, Marty's death, and Jody's disappearance are all tied together through this place known as Pandora's House. I believe this is a primary gap in our simulation. Finding it is crucial to proving the truth about our world and learning how to travel to other worlds. I had funding lined up to make this documentary, but I lost it. I believe there was intervention on the part of those who wish to keep Pandora's House and the simulation gap a secret. I need to raise this amount of money so I can find the house and try jumping to another simulation."

Tiph mutters, "What the fuck . . . ?"

Chapter Nine

Pen

Pen glances out her window in Topanga. The sun dips toward the horizon.

Wearing her backpack full of supplies, Pen holds up an onyx chalcedony gemstone and watches as the yellow slips behind the blue, but there's no green flash today.

When she gets back inside, Pen returns to her computer. Ever since Travis told her Jody was missing, she's been watching more of Jody's *My Dirty California* videos in an effort to track him. She found one recording where Jody said, "I think Marty may have been on some kind of a drug called O." Below the video, Jody linked to several of Marty's posts that make mention of this "O." The first link had a video journal entry that made Pen think O isn't a drug but a secret symbol Marty used. The short but somber post was from April 9:

"Today was a hard day. Maybe it was easier because it wasn't my decision. I didn't see it before, but now I see this inflection point between worlds. Two different worlds. Sliding doors. Brick and no brick. And thinking about O and that other world, I start to smile and wonder. But it's not many-worlds, it's one, and there's no going back. Someone out there would call it murder. I'm not one of those people, and yet I still feel guilty. Maybe we should have gone for it. It's too late now. Fuck. In the blink of an eye, in this world and then in no world, depending on what you believe."

Pen looked back and realized Marty posted the entry a couple weeks after he first talked about Renata and Pandora's House. Maybe this was the exact moment when Renata jumped to another world and maybe Marty regretted not going with her. Pen believes O isn't the letter *o* but rather a circle, the gap, the portal to another simulation.

The other O mentions from Jody's links further Pen's theory. In one entry, Marty describes going to Lassen Volcanic National Park "with O." Maybe Marty found out there was a breach up there, which would make sense why Pen had found a map of Lassen in Jody's burned apartment.

In another post, Marty talks about finding O in the Standard Hotel on the Sunset Strip. Could Pandora's House be hidden beneath a hotel in Hollywood? Her father had always said there was something uncanny about Hollywood. *Hollyweird*.

Later that evening, Pen drives to Sunset Boulevard to check out the Standard Hotel. Upon entering the lobby, she keeps her head low, bypasses the front desk, and heads toward the elevators. If Marty's O is in the hotel, it's got to be in the basement somewhere. She sits on a couch and pretends to text as she scans the elevators. After twenty minutes, she sees a bellhop take a personnel-only freight elevator. She waits until he returns to the lobby and then she darts inside the elevator.

She takes the freight elevator down to B2, which is below P3 and B1. She emerges from the elevator and walks down a hallway. Doors on both sides lead to storage areas. She peeks inside each one.

After forty-five minutes of searching all the storage rooms, Pen hasn't found anything more than spare couches, chairs, mattresses, and lamps. Not Pandora's House. Just another dead end.

Get back on the bike, she thinks. Her dad had taught her to ride a little red Huffy bicycle in Griffith Park when she was five. And when she fell, he told her, *When we fall, we get back on the bike*. And he later used it as an analogy each time he hit an impasse in his own search for Pandora's House.

Pen heads down the dark hallway toward the freight elevator when she sees it's already coming down to B2. She darts back into the closest storage room and ducks behind a line of stacked bedside tables. Light from a flashlight whips across the room. "Come out. We saw you on the cameras."

Pen stays low. The man turns on the light in the room where Pen's hiding. "Stand up. I see you."

As the footsteps get closer, she raises her hands in surrender.

The security guard looks like a linebacker. He sighs. "Jen already left."

Who's Jen? Pen wonders. "Sorry, I got lost," she says.

"Sure you did."

"Can I go?"

"No."

He brings Pen to a small office on the ground floor where a British man with red hair stands from behind the desk. The linebacker security guard leaves, closing the door on his way out.

"I know what you're doing here," the British man says, as he passes an unlit cigarette between fingers. "And I can help you. But I need a cut."

"You know about O?"

"What? O?"

Pen decides to stay quiet and see what he'll say next.

"Look," he says as he runs his index finger across his mustache. "Clearly you've got skills because you figured out we let them use the freight elevator to escape. I can tip you off when somebody big is leaving."

Pen stares back. *When someone's leaving? Leaving this simulation?*

"But, my cut is twenty-five percent of sale. And don't try to shortchange me. I know what *US Weekly* and *People* and all the buyers pay for pics. Do you have a card?

Pen pulls out a business card that lists her as a documentary filmmaker and hands it to the manager.

"Documentaries . . . cool. We all have a day job."

Chapter Ten

Jody

The knock comes at a good time because Jody has been burning his eyes at both ends, watching Marty's videos for three days straight. A three-day window into his brother's life. There are shorter entries on subjects like the mountain lion P-22, the corrupt town of Vernon, dead horses at Santa Anita, finding the *Six Feet Under* Fisher house on Arlington Avenue, and spending an afternoon with Christopher Dennis. And there are longer entries like the forty-five minutes of edited footage from when Marty lived homeless with no money or food or house for fourteen days as a self-proclaimed exercise in empathy. Or the thirty-minute video about borderline personality disorder—Marty had read six books on the topic when his friend Nicky confessed she'd been diagnosed with the disorder. One written entry contains an itinerary Marty made for a three-month tour of California that includes hikes, bars, restaurants, views, and museums for more than a hundred different places in the state. But whether it's a one-thousand-word ambiguously sarcastic essay on a girl's nice ass or a mosaic of surfing photographs, no post so far indicates who might've killed Marty. Jody started a spreadsheet to categorize the videos, adding columns to note the date Marty made the video, the date Jody watched the video, and any possible clues from the video.

When he hears the knock, Jody is sitting on the floor, not far from the door. Everywhere in Jody's new apartment is not far from the door. A twentysomething skater-looking fellow peers through the screen door. His flat black-rimmed cap reads 805. Rory, who for the first couple of days had paced the small apartment like a tiger in a cage, looks up from his favorite floor spot.

When the man sees Jody and Rory, he takes a step back. "Sorry. Got the wrong place."

"Wait, hold on."

But the guy continues walking away.

"Wait. C'm'here."

The guy darts down the driveway, past the main house where Travis lives and out onto the street.

Once Jody follows him, the guy takes off running. The 805 cap gets lost to wind resistance. The guy doesn't stop for it.

The man sprints down a street, Vans sneakers slapping pavement. He cuts across a lawn full of jacaranda trees, into a backyard, over a vinyl fence. Jody keeping up. Now back on a neighborhood road. Down a long public staircase. Hundreds of steep steps. They pass a couple of teens smoking pot who clear a path for the foot chase.

Jody gets close enough and leaps and tackles the guy into ivy that's overtaken the hillside next to the steep stairwell.

The two roll. And the guy slips out of Jody's grasp.

As he climbs to his feet, the guy pulls out a Smith & Wesson J-Frame pistol. Jody tackles him by the legs and takes him down again. The gun flies. Both men scramble for it. Fishing through the ivy for the upper hand.

Jody gets his fingers around the gun and aims it at the other man. Both men catching their breaths.

"Who are you?" Jody asks.

The guy appears reluctant to answer.

"Gimme your wallet. I'm not fucking around," says Jody.

The guy takes out his wallet, throws it to Jody. Jody glances at the ID. "Wyatt? How do you know Marty, Wyatt?"

"Friends. Met surfing a few months ago."

"Why were you coming to see him just now?"

"You're holding it."

"Huh?"

"The gun."

Jody aims the gun at Wyatt's center. "You were coming to kill my brother?"

"What? No. No. No. I was bringing him that gun."

"You were getting a gun for Marty? Why?"

"'Cause he was gonna pay me for it."

"Why'd he need a gun? Was he in trouble?"

"I don't know. He didn't say he was. But somebody askin' for a one-time whistle, they usually in trouble."

Jody lowers the gun to his side and ponders *one-time whistle*, translates it from white-boy SoCal surfer wannabe-gangster street lingo, assumes the gun's not registered, the serial numbers filed off. "He ask you for that, specific? A gun that couldn't be traced or whatever?"

"Yeah."

"When did he ask you to do this?"

"Few weeks ago. I came by Friday before last. I saw you, so I split, came back a couple times, but he wasn't here."

"Wait, what? Saw *me* two Fridays ago?"

"Yeah."

"I just got to town four days ago."

"Well, I saw some other dude there, then. He was fishing around."

Another guy. At Marty's place. Right around the time Marty fled town. Could this have been the killer who looked for Marty at his apartment before tracking him to Pennsylvania?

"Wait. Slow down. What did he look like? What was he doing?"

"He was just looking around. Seemed shady, so I split."

"Was he white?"

"Yeah, man, I thought you were the same dude, so any question you're going to ask me about him, you might as well look in a mirror instead."

"He looked that much like me?"

"I lost my glasses. I can't see far for shit. We're talking about me seeing him from the road. From that distance you guys might as well be twins."

"Was he tall?"

"I dunno. He was a regular-looking white dude from far away. Lean-like. Not fat. Not short."

"Was he walking funny? Like one leg was a little longer than the other?"

"What?"

"Did he have anything recognizable? Like a scar or . . ."

"A scar?"

"Anything."

"I'm sorry."

"Walk me through exactly what you saw."

"I parked. And I saw him walk from his car to—"

"His car?"

"Yeah. He walked from his car to the back unit, and I stayed back 'cause I could see it wasn't Marty. And he was fishing around, looking for a spare key and lookin' in the windows and shit, and so I left."

"What kind of car?"

"It was a black Pontiac Grand Am. Must've been a 2004 or 2005."

"How did you know the year?"

"They stopped making Grand Ams—'05 was the last year. And in 2003 they stopped using body cladding."

"You sure?"

"I used to work at my uncle's used car lot when I was a kid."

"Did Marty tell you about anything else or anyone else?"

"No, man. I just met him surfing, and we kept running into each other at the Highland Park Brewery, ya know, the Hermosillo. I didn't know the guy."

Jody realizes he still has the gun out. He shoves it in the back of his waistband.

"You're saying you hung out all these times. What did you talk about?"

"Nothing. I don't even remember."

"You're going to *have* to remember."

"We talked about all kinds of stuff. He mentioned this woman once. O."

"O's a woman?"

"What?"

"I didn't know O was a woman. You sure she's a woman?"

"Yeah, maybe *his* woman. Or *was*. Or he wanted her to be. One night we had one too many and he went off on this whole thing about how love's too complex an idea to be summed up by one word. He kept denying he loved her. But you talk long enough about *not* loving someone, and it sorta sounds like you do. Anyway, like I said, we had a few, so I don't really remember."

"What's your phone number?"

"What?!"

"Give me your number."

"Why?"

"C'mon, man, don't make me pull out the gun again."

Wyatt gives Jody a number, and Jody plugs it into his phone.

"We gonna be friends now?" Wyatt asks.

"Marty's dead. I might need your help if I get a suspect and want to know if it's the man you saw."

"Marty's . . . ?"

"Yeah."

"Fuck."

"How much was Marty buying this gun for?"

"Three hundred."

"Come grab your hat and c'mon up back to the house."

"Why?"

"'Cause I'm buying the gun from you."

Chapter Eleven

Pen

Pen parks her car at the base of the Music Box Steps, an iconic public concrete stairwell in Silver Lake. About halfway up the 133 steps, she spots a sidewalk leading to the back entrance of a set of apartments. She finds the second-floor unit labeled #3 and knocks.

Pen has been devouring and redevouring Jody's *My Dirty California* videos in an attempt to uncover his whereabouts. The best person to talk to might be this woman named Shiloh who Jody mentions across multiple entries. Pen can't tell whether she's a romantic friend or a source.

Pen knocks again. After a few moments, a woman with a ponytail and workout clothes pulls the door open.

"Shiloh?"

"No, I'm Becky."

"Oh, sorry. Does Shiloh live here?"

"Yeah. But she's not here."

"Where is she?"

"Italy."

"Italy?"

"Yeah, she works as a nanny sometimes. This family took her on their trip. Naples. Or maybe it was Rome."

"Do you know when she'll be back?"

"Three weeks."

"Did you ever meet her . . . Did you meet Jody?"

"Yeah. He broke my snow globe."

Pen perks up at the mention of *snow globe*. Sometimes people reference the idea of living in a simulation by calling it a snow globe.

"You jumped? And he broke it? Broke what? The way through? Or the whole thing?"

"Wait, what?"

"Your snow globe. Your simulation. He messed it up?"

"What? I had a snow globe. Like a snow globe." She holds her hands together like she's holding an invisible ball. "And Jody broke it."

"Did Jody talk to you about what he was doing?"

"Not really. A little."

"So you know he was trying to find who killed his brother?"

"Yeah."

"Did you know Marty?"

"A little, through Shiloh."

"Did Jody tell you anything about Marty, about figuring out who killed him and why?"

"No. Not really. Shiloh and I aren't . . . I mean we've become friendly, but we're mostly roommates."

"Is this Shiloh's number?" Pen holds out her phone.

"I don't know. Hold on." Becky disappears and comes back with her phone, cross-references the numbers. "Yeah."

"I left her a voice mail and emailed her and sent her a message on Facebook."

"I don't know if she uses Facebook anymore."

"I also sent her a tweet and an Instagram message."

"Oh wow, that's pretty thorough."

"If you talk to her, can you tell her to get back to me? I'm Pen."

"Pen?"

"Yeah, Penelope. Otherwise, I guess I'll just come back. Three weeks you said?"

Becky now appears to regret having been specific about Shiloh's return date. But she nods anyway.

"Sorry, last question. Did you ever hear Jody or Shiloh talking about a woman named Renata?"

"No. Sorry."

Chapter Twelve

Renata

¿Dónde estoy? Renata keeps circling the room, inspecting the walls and trying to understand the prison where she woke up two hours ago. She tries not to panic. Tries to breathe and think.

"Is it dawn? Or is it dusk?" Renata asks.

"That's not the sun," says Coral. "It's this level of light all the time."

Renata circles the room again. How could the room maintain this eternal golden-hour lighting?

"What's that humming?" Renata asks.

"I don't know."

Renata stops at a small hatch in one corner. She opens it. There's nothing there. Just a drawer-size space with a hatch on the other side.

"They put food in there once a day, sometimes twice. Spare clothes occasionally."

"They?"

"Whoever."

"They feed you?"

"Yeah." Coral motions to a pile of plastic ziplock bags against the far wall. "And they'll take stuff out."

Which explains why it doesn't smell awful in the room.

"Where's the door?"

"There is no door."

"How did we get inside the room if there is not a door?"

"You're asking me questions I don't have the answers to." Coral points to the far wall. "All them marks on the wall is the days I spent wondering on all the same shit you're wondering about."

"¡Eso no tiene sentido! There has to be a door. You said you were here before I? Did you see me get put here?"

"I was asleep, harder than usual. I woke up and you were here sleeping. They might have put sleeping pills in my food."

Renata thinks back to how she got here, the bus ride. She wishes she hadn't gone to see Abbott. She shouldn't have left home. Renata circles the room twice more. Looking for a door and still not finding one. "Do you talk with them?"

"I tried, the first days. Weeks. They won't open their side of the hatch unless ours is closed. If it's open, I don't get food or water or soap or a clean washcloth."

"How did you become here?"

"How did I get here? I told you. I don't know."

"Where are you from?"

"Desert Hot Springs."

"Where is that?"

"The desert. Just north of North Palm Springs."

"That is where you grew up?"

"Yeah. I had a bad breakup with my boyfriend, Peter. So I moved to LA."

"When?"

"I don't know. Maybe six months ago. I moved to LA. And I went to a party, and I blacked out. And I woke up here."

Renata keeps scouring the room.

"What are you looking for?"

"There's got to be a way we can get to another room. Back into the haunted house."

"Haunted house?"

"Yeah. Pandora's House."

Renata knocks on the wall with a closed fist. She tries hitting it. Nothing.

"You're wasting your time. It's fiberglass."

"It's not that thick. We may be able to get through it. To make a . . . how do you say it, tunnel? To another room."

"We don't have any tools. They never give us silverware or anything."

Renata pulls off the belt looped through her jeans. Holds up the buckle.

Renata and Coral take turns chipping away at the wall. The four walls are uniform. They don't pick a place based on any crack or weakness, since they can't find one. Instead, they pick a comfortable height to work.

As Renata hands over the buckle, Coral rolls up the sleeves of her long sleeve T-shirt. Extensive tattoos cover her entire arm.

"How long were you in LA before you end up here?" asks Renata.

"Two weeks maybe."

"And you were living by yourself?"

"In LA? I was sleeping in this dude's living room. Found it on Craigslist."

"You didn't know anyone in the city?" asks Renata.

"No."

"And you came alone to LA?"

"What do you mean?"

"Your boyfriend, he didn't come?"

Coral eyes the ground before answering. "Yeah, just me. Paul didn't come."

Paul. Hadn't she said Peter earlier? Yes, she had said Peter, because it had made her think of a boy named Peter she had made out with when she was fourteen. If Coral had said Paul, Renata would have thought about "Paul the wine guy" or Paul the Apostle because one of her grandmothers—the Christian one, not the one who's into Santa Muerte—was always talking about Paul from the Bible.

"Paul, this is your boyfriend?" Renata asks.

"Yeah. Ex. We broke up, and I needed a change. So I moved to LA."

Renata stares at Coral. Why would she lie? Renata contemplates calling her out now but decides against it. The two women keep alternating turns, hammering the belt buckle into the wall.

Three shifts later, what had appeared a sturdy buckle proves brittle. Renata examines the two pieces. Six or seven hours of digging, striking, scratching. They hadn't made a dent in the wall while making more than a dent in the buckle.

Coral sits on her bedding. Renata paces. With the hope of tunneling gone, she can't hold in her anger.

"You lied. You called him Peter first. Then Paul."

"No, I didn't." Coral avoids eye contact.

"Which was it?"

Coral hesitates a moment, long enough it's clear she's making a choice. "Paul."

"You're lying."

"No, I'm not."

"What else are you lie about? Do you know where we are? Are we in Pandora's House?"

"I don't know where we are."

Is Coral playing some kind of prank on her? Is this all an elaborate trick of Abbott's? Some devious part of an escape room?

"You're lying to me. Please tell me where we are."

Coral stops bothering to respond. Twenty minutes later, Coral begins snoring. Renata remains awake, observing the faint glow of twilight and listening to the never-ending insect-like buzzing. In her head, she can hear Abbott talking about Pandora's House. About the glow with no source, and the eternal echo.

That wasn't all he said. He'd also mentioned infinite levels and portals to other worlds.

Chapter Thirteen

Pen

If this girl Renata did jump simulations, Pen wonders where she might be now. Pen has watched the same video for the third time in a row, the *My Dirty California* entry where Marty describes meeting Renata and mentions Pandora's House. Pen has been up all night trying to pick the most relevant videos and journal entries from the website to show Daniel and to later use as part of her pitch to studios. Pen rereads a post of Marty's he wrote on his twenty-seventh birthday. In the post, he jokes about whether he'll make it to twenty-eight or join the "27 Club." He wrote about Jimi Hendrix, Basquiat, Kurt Cobain, Jim Morrison, Janis Joplin, and others. Pen thinks about Marty's age. Does our simulation have a flaw that causes people to die at age twenty-seven?

In another post, Marty writes about the Mandela effect, talking about Jiffy peanut butter, *Looney Toons*, and Curious George's tail. Years ago, Pen became fascinated with the Mandela effect after seeing a Reddit thread about the Berenstain Bears books, which millions of people—including Pen—remember being called *Berenstein* Bears. Most people chalk this up as a false-memory phenomenon, but in a simulated world, these could be actual errors.

Pen glances at the time on her computer. She should try to sleep at least an hour. But she gets a text from Beetle. He wants to meet. The prospect of news about her dad snaps her awake.

• • •

Pen wanders into the Coffee Commissary and spots Beetle. Without the padding of his snowboarding gear, he's skin and bones. As Pen approaches, she sees he's playing a video game on his computer. When Pen was in second grade, her dad pulled her out of school on a hot September day and they went to an arcade and played *Teenage Mutant Ninja Turtles*. They ate slices at Mulberry Street Pizzeria afterward, and her dad explained his theory that we were living in a video game. He often returned to the metaphor when talking about jumping simulations. *Don't you want to try a different game?* he'd say.

Beetle pauses his computer game when he sees Pen sit down across from him.

"Did you hear anything back?" Pen asks.

"I put the message up on the dark web."

"And?"

"I think it's been picked up. Or at least it seems like someone *tried* to pick it up. From somewhere else."

Pen sits up taller as if hit with a jolt of caffeine. "What do you mean?"

"I mean, it looks like someone was searching from outside the dark web for *your* message. Like from another place."

"My father . . ."

"I don't know. But I think someone is trying to get it. But I don't think they can access it."

"How do you know?" asks Pen.

"Because someone clicked on the message but there weren't any downloads."

"What do we do?"

"I can play around with trying to increase its accessibility through outside-the-box means."

"What do you mean?"

"I mean, I can use a program to expand its accessibility through nontraditional programming. Think a digital magnet."

"Okay. Let's do that."

"Sure. I just . . . the software doesn't exist. I'd have to customize it. It'll be a lot of work."

"How much?"

"Six grand worth of work."

Beetle averts his eyes. Like a liar might. But Pen reminds herself coders aren't always the best at eye contact.

"I can Venmo you the money today," she says.

"There's no guarantee it'll work."

"I want to do it. It's okay, I should be getting a new film deal soon."

As her agent, Daniel, watches the three videos, two of Jody's and one of Marty's, Pen keeps thinking about Beetle and her father.

"It's pretty intriguing," Daniel says. "Real hooky."

"I haven't even gotten to the intriguing ones yet." She wants to show Daniel the four entries where Marty referenced O.

"Well, the pitch should only be about twenty minutes. Tops. So why don't you finalize the exact pitch and start practicing it, and I'll schedule the meetings."

Chapter Fourteen

Tiph

Tiph is used to being in houses like this. Cleaning them, not pretending to be interested in buying them. When she gets this art money, she's going to buy a big-ass house. No more renting like a sucker. No more sweating the first of the month.

A few hours earlier Tiph had called her work and asked Gloria for a fake work slip to back her claim she was working in the Hollywood Hills that afternoon. Gloria protested it was against her morals before caving and squeezing Tiph for a hundred bucks.

The Realtor, a mousy woman named Kat, joins Tiph in Chester Montgomery's former kitchen. "Did you sign in yet?"

Tiphony writes a fake name and email. She decides to check out one of the bedrooms so it doesn't seem like she's going straight to the basement.

"Ma'am."

Tiph turns to see the Realtor glaring at her.

"We ask that only serious prospective buyers tour the house."

Tiph follows the Realtor's eyes to her feet where her multimillionaire dress has backfired by getting stuck in her ankle monitor.

Tiph motions toward the nearby couples and whispers, "'Less you want me to spill the beans on how the owner got murdered, how 'bout you let me browse in peace?"

The Realtor huffs and walks away.

The walls of the kidney-shaped basement are engraved with

concentric circles that create the impression the walls are moving. A man in a suit seems hypnotized by the walls. He and Tiph smile at each other. Once he goes upstairs, Tiph darts to the base of the stairwell. There, she finds what looks like a circuit board. She opens it and finds a latch inside. She pulls open the latch, revealing a whole secret room.

But there is no art. Just wine. At least fifty bottles of red wine. "Fuck . . ."

Tiph hears footsteps above her. She darts out and scurries toward the stairwell. But the secret door to the secret room remains open a crack. She considers turning back, but it's too late. A couple gets to the bottom of the stairs, and Tiph doesn't want to get caught snooping. She walks past them, nodding hello, leaving the secret door cracked behind her.

Tiphony makes fried egg sandwiches while Gary plays with toy dinosaurs and some fresh produce on the floor. Tiph tends to make fried egg sandwiches if she's celebrating something or wanting to take her mind off something. Ever since the open house, she's been obsessing about whether to quit this treasure hunt.

After Gary plays out an epic battle between a triceratops and a cucumber, he holds up an apple and an orange. "Mommy, if this is called an orange, why isn't this called a red?"

"I don't know. Gary, don't make a mess on the floor. Which reminds me, did you put your dirty clothes in the hamper? I told ya you gotta keep your room clean."

"LEGO Batman doesn't have to keep his room clean."

"Yeah, he does."

"How do you know?"

"I'm friends with his mom."

"What's her name?"

"Go put the dirty clothes in the hamper."

"That's a silly name," says Gary before he waddles off to his room.

Ding. A message from Sierra. *I told you he had a secret room.*

Tiphony clicks on the link on her phone. It's a clip of a local newscast. A reporter with too much makeup talking fast. "Today, at an open house for a deceased Hollywood man's home, a prospective buyer stumbled upon a secret room, which contained forty-two thousand dollars in wine."

Tiphony grinds her teeth. Wine in the hand would have been better than art in the bush. "Motherfucker."

Gary rejoins his mom in the kitchen, eyes wide in horror.

"Only adults can speak like that."

"What's wrong, Mommy?"

"Mommy missed a chance. That's all."

Doesn't rain often in LA, but when it rains it pours. Twenty minutes later, Tiph answers the door. A man about thirty on the other side. No taller than Tiph's five six, with one shoulder higher than the other, whether out of swagger or scoliosis. A greedy smile full of gold teeth.

"Help you?"

"I'm somebody who knew Mike. Dex."

"Okay . . . ?"

"Mike was in the hole. I know he went away, but that di'n't fill the hole."

"What are you talking about?"

"Talking about football picks. Basketball too. Juice over time. Your boy owes thirty-four hundred."

"Mike? I don't think so." Tiph keeps the door cracked.

"Well, he does. And I got a boss, and he got friends doing life in CSP. Could make Mike's life pretty miserable." The man smiles, letting his teeth shine.

"Even if you're telling the truth, that's on Mike. That pea's in his own pod; I ain't have shit to do with him gambling."

"Your choice. We ain't inhumane. We ain't gonna let his debt run into *your* life. But I just wanted to give you the chance to pay it. He get got in the big house, you may not want that on your conscience."

Chapter Fifteen

Jody

Now that he knows O is not a drug but a woman, maybe a girlfriend or ex-girlfriend of Marty's, Jody digs back through dozens of *My Dirty California* entries to see if he can figure out who she is.

He rewatches the video where Marty talks about being high and ending up at the Standard Hotel and seeing the "waterless fish tank." Jody reads online about "the Box." In the hotel lobby, there's a glass box where women sit, on display as some kind of weird art installation. Jody thought Marty was high on O, but now he's realizing Marty went in and saw O sitting in the glass box.

When he first clicked on it a week ago, Jody had skimmed part of an ambiguously sarcastic essay Marty had posted called "1,000-Word Dope-Ass Essay" about a woman with a nice butt. But now he realizes the entry is about O.

> Behind every great woman is a man checking out her ass.
>
> —UNKNOWN WISE MAN

This is a think piece. About the greatest piece. One that could bring peace. It's a think piece that ends with a boner joke and starts with a lesson in evolution. It's an essay about the most dope-ass ass. I'm not being cheeky, this is a serious matter. We're discussing the posterior. The backside, bottom, arse, bum, booty, buns, butt, gluteus maximus, tuchus, heinie, tush, rear, fanny. The ass. And not just any ass. But the greatest ass west of the Mississippi.

We as a species evolved from primates who boned exclusively from behind, and consequently we evolved to have an attraction to the buttocks. Note: Charles Darwin had ten kids, just couldn't stop tapping that ass. The attraction to the backside goes way back, and it's ingrained in our primal instincts. So it's not your fault you googled best ass, greatest milf ass, finest Latina ass, or badonkadonk (which is a fun word to say out loud even if you don't like larger-than-average butts).

I'm here to solve the mystery, to answer the question of the greatest butt. The first time I saw O, her ass made me envy the jeans holding it. And these had to be some custom-made jeans. It wouldn't be worth it for a company to mass-produce jeans for such a rare rump. When I met her roommate, Becky (and her roommate really is named Becky), I said to Becky, "O my God, Becky, your roommate got back."

What is it about her bum? Look, I like pancakes but not pancake butts. Hers is more like a pumpkin butt. Apple bottom. She barely even does yoga, but she's got that yoga butt. Even Adriene is like Damn, girl. We're talking gravity defying. Twice we've been in bars and she's been asked if she had a butt augmentation or a butt lift. How's she got that bubble butt? It's not junk, she's got spunk in her trunk. Two moons over my hammies. Her T&A got reordered A&T. I could stare at that hourglass for hours. Hers is an ass that makes the rockin' world go round.

Arguments over the best ass are as old as arguments over whether the earth is flat. (Even Pythagoras back in 500 BC was like, Hell yeah, 'round is better than flat.) Who has the nicest tush? No, not Beyoncé, sorry Jay. This ain't about JLaw's blue butt or JLo's insurance policy. This ain't about Kim's big asses (the one she has or the one she married). Sorry, Shakira, this isn't about who can shake it best. Kate Middleton might be next in line, but she doesn't bring up the rear. Selena's trying too hard, and Kendall just wants to break the internet. Jen Selter can ride the Instagram train, but she ain't got the best caboose. So who's got the best ass? That's O. Yup, O and her two perfect Os. She's from Maryland, and I call those cheeks the Baltimore Os. LA face with an Oakland booty, and she puts the O in Oakland. And she puts the two o's in booty too. And the two o's in too, also. And the o in also as well.

But it's not always easy being her. (Even the most beautiful painting has a crack!) Sure there are perks to her perky booty, but there are downsides to that backside. She had to delete her Instagram account because all the trolls kept telling her to turn around. When she somehow fits her phone in the back pocket of those jeans, she's always butt dialing. But that ass doesn't stop there. She butt texts, butt emails, butt Candy Crushes. Last week she butt installed an iOS update. Plus, she's gotta watch what she wears—e.g., if she wore booty shorts out in public, Garcetti would have to call a state of emergency. Getting around is hard. She can't walk without booty popping. She can't roll over in her sleep without twerking. Car accidents are twice as likely to occur when she crosses the street. Construction workers don't just whistle, they leap to their deaths. Sometimes she gets bummed when people only want to look at her bum. Her ass is so nice it's in danger of overshadowing her entire being. If she's not careful, she'll make an ass of herself.

Folks, keep your eyes peeled 'cause she's out there, fighting the good fight, converting boob guys into butt guys, making ass guys of tit guys. Even the male gays are joining the male gaze. Even the blind turn their heads. As I bring this essay to a robust end, the last thing I'll say is to be careful, gents. That Medusa ass is out there. Look right at it, and those Os will turn you to stone, ha.

The tone and subject matter stand out as different from any other MDC entry. From the thousand words, Jody writes down six. *Nice butt, roommate Becky, from Maryland.*

Jody finds another written post mentioning O, which includes dozens of photographs of hipsters and artists and hippies in Los Angeles. Apparently, O got into a fight with her manager, and her manager called O a "fippie slasher." The post talks about O's artistic endeavors. She plays in a band, she does theater, she paints, she cooks, and she got interested in acting for TV/film and was able to secure a manager. But this manager wanted O to drop her other interests to focus on acting. Marty contrasts her artistic fervor and talents against the *glut of hipsters who talk about art with other artist-wannabes and never actually do anything.* He goes on to write:

> Only in LA could a renaissance woman feel insufficient. I told her not to let them put a jack-of-all-trades-master-of-none chip on her shoulder. They always want to put you in a box. They literally put her in a box at the Standard. And fuck this manager. If he wanted to advise her to hone in on acting, he could have done it without calling her a fippie slasher. I didn't even know what those were. Fippie is faux hippie and slasher is a model/actress/singer/waitress. Cool terms, bro. Cool town. I think the comments pissed O off because she got insecure she is a fake hippie. Her parents both worked in finance, and she did reject that and move to California, and she likes walking around barefoot and shit. Our country sucks right now, so counterculture doesn't seem like a bad thing. I try to tell her all those people at the Satellite are fippies. Her band had a residency at the Satellite last year, where they played every Monday for a month or two, and since then she likes to go every Monday to check out other bands. The hipsters at this place. My god. I wish O could see how she's different from them.

Jody has no way of knowing if any of the hundred photographed hipsters are O. But he does know she goes to the Satellite every Monday night.

Jody walks down the Sunset Strip looking for the Standard Hotel. Taking it in—the neon lights, the mosaic of billboards, the honking cars, the tourists taking pictures on their phones—Jody thinks of what Marty said in one of his videos. *Hey, Los Angeles, I can see your undies.*

The sidewalk is crowded, and each passing person connects Jody to his torment. A man in a Miami Dolphins hat reminds Jody of his Sunday tradition of watching Eagles games with his dad. An Asian tourist wearing an *I ♥ LA* shirt makes Jody consider how few times he had told his dad or his brother he loved them. A family of four—two kids, a mom, and a dad—reminds him that his family of four is down to one.

Jody pulls out his phone to check the address again when he sees the upside-down sign for the Standard. Sure enough, in the hotel lobby, there's a tank. In lieu of water and fish, a woman in jeans and a tank top reading a book called *Beautiful Ruins*.

LA is a bunch of little strange places all put together as one big strange place. Jody eyes the woman. Could this be O? He approaches the front desk and asks to speak with a manager.

"What's up, mate?" asks the red-haired manager in a British accent as he pops a piece of Nicorette gum.

"What's that woman's name in the tank?"

"Why?"

"I'm looking for someone who gets paid to lay in the tank."

"Sorry, we can't give out that information."

"Does her name start with an O?"

"I can't . . . No."

"What about any of the other women? Anyone go by the name O?"

The manager runs his fingers above his lip where he's making a meager attempt to grow a mustache. "Can't tell you that. I don't even know off the top of my head."

How else could Jody narrow it down? He could tell the guy the woman he's looking for has a nice butt, but the manager already seems to think Jody is creepy.

Jody arrives at the Satellite on Monday right when the doors open at eight. He parks himself at the bar as the venue fills with black pants, mustaches, black-rimmed glasses, thrift store shirts, and yuppies all conforming to a once-nonconformist dress code. Band members and their crew set up onstage. A guy with a T-shirt that reads scriptnotes above a graphic of a typewriter sits next to Jody. Jody asks him the same question he asked the last five people who came up to the bar.

"Do you come here often?"

The guy nods, and Jody asks him the follow-up question he'd asked the others. "Do you happen to know a woman named O?"

"O?"

"Yeah."

"No. Sorry. You're looking for her? Why can't you just text her?"

"I don't have her number."

"I was half kidding. I'm a screenwriter, and cell phones are like the murderer of any problem you try to create for your characters."

Jody nods but doesn't understand what he means.

"What do you do?" the writer asks.

"I work maintenance, landscaping."

"Right on. A real job. Refreshing to hear."

A twentysomething with a long, black—perhaps dyed—beard walks past them at the bar. "Those carpenter jeans are rad." The guy's already ten feet away before Jody realizes he's talking about him.

"So you write movies?" Jody asks.

"Yeah. Well I've sold a few different things. But only one has gotten turned into a movie. It was this Nic Cage movie."

"Oh, maybe I've seen it," says Jody. *The Rock* was the first R-rated movie he'd seen in theaters as a kid. And his friends in high school had been obsessed with *Con Air*.

"No, I guarantee you haven't. See, Nic Cage is in like five movies a year no one sees. For this project, the whole budget was five million and they paid Nic three to come and work one day. They trick foreign audiences into thinking he's the main character. The movie had zero chance to be good. The whole business is pretty whack. I spend three months writing a new script, and my agent doesn't even read it. He has his assistant read it. So now I've got some girl one year out of college judging my art, and she doesn't know. She doesn't know, bro. She's just trying to get through her sixty-hour workweek and figure out a way to get a ticket to Coachella."

Jody doesn't ask any follow-up questions. A woman sat down on the other side of him, and he wants to ask if she knows an O.

She doesn't.

The first band, Massive Moth from Portland, is now mid-set after going on at nine thirty. Jody asked a couple dozen people, including both bartenders, if any of them knew an O. No one did. Three different people—two guys, one lady—have approached him and complimented his attire. After the first guy commented on his carpenter jeans, Jody thought the guy was making fun of him. But by the time he gets compliments on his Diadora sneakers and flannel shirt, he realizes by not caring about fashion and wearing the same clothes he's had for fifteen years, he's become retro hip by accident.

The crowd fills out around 11:00 p.m., when the main act goes on, this band from Australia called Cloud Control. The venue is now louder and darker, makes it harder to ask more people if they know O.

So he finds himself playing the stereotypical drunk testosterone-driven misogynistic male: wandering around looking for the woman with the nicest ass. He doesn't go out that much in Pennsylvania, but when he does, women come in all shapes and sizes. Here, in LA, and in this trendy nightlife hot spot, there seems to be less variation.

Jody feels absurd. He's walking around a music venue in Los Angeles looking for some woman who has a nice butt. Ready to give up, he heads for the door, pushing through hipsters debating the awesomeness of Beach House. And that's when his eyes fall on a particular woman who has her back to him. She's about five foot six. Dark brown hair cascades down her back. She's wearing a loose-fitting T-shirt, but her blue jeans are skintight. The tone of Marty's essay about O's butt was hard to interpret, and Jody had wondered if her butt was any different from any old (young) butt. But now that he's seeing this lady, her tail end is dumbfounding. This had to be her.

Or rather, it could be her.

Angry moths flutter in his stomach, and he has to remind himself he's approaching the woman not because of her *dope-ass* ass but because of what she might know.

As he gets closer, he sees the woman is talking to two women and a man. Jody approaches the group, positioning himself across from the woman with the tight jeans.

"Excuse me. Didn't we meet a few months ago?" Jody asks.

The woman rolls her eyes, assumes she's being hit on with a strategy as old as the retro outfits all around them. "I don't think so."

"Yeah, it was here. You were with a guy . . ."

"Oh yeah? A guy? Was he wearing a shirt? And did he have two eyes?"

"What?" Jody asks, not getting her joke. "You were here with a guy, I think his name was Marty?"

When Jody mentions *Marty*, he sees recognition in this woman's eyes.

"When was this?" she asks.

"I don't know. A few months back."

"And what happened?"

"I just remembered meeting you."

"Okay . . . ?"

"I'm . . . John." Jody extends his right hand.

The woman shakes it. "Shiloh."

Shiloh. O. Oh!

"Shiloh, that's right," says Jody, pretending to remember.

Jody introduces himself to the two women and the man next to Shiloh. A Janelle. A Tom. And another Janelle. Tom and the Janelles wander over to the bar for more fourteen-dollar drinks.

"So how did we meet?" she asks Jody.

"I think the Marty guy started talking to some friends I was with."

"I see."

Jody had this idea to pretend like they'd met before. That plan has succeeded. But now what? He could tell her who he is, but the whole idea was to see what she knows first.

"Is Marty not here tonight?"

"No, he's not. What did you say your name was?"

"John."

"John?"

"John. Saturly."

"What do you do, John?"

"I, uh . . ." *Fuck.* "I'm a screenwriter."

"A screenwriter? Have you written anything I might have seen?"

"I wrote this one movie with Nic Cage."

"Really? What's it called?"

"Uh, it was called *Con Boat*. So . . . Marty seemed like a pretty wild guy when I talked to him before."

"He *is* pretty wild. But, John, what's the plot of this Nic Cage movie *Con Boat*?"

Fuck. "Umm, well Nic Cage is on this boat transferring these prisoners, and the convicts take over the ship."

"Wow, that sounds pretty epic," she says, smiling. "So what genre do you like to write?"

Jody remembers going to Video Showplace as a kid. He remembers the VHS tapes being organized by genre. "Action/adventure."

"So what movie made you want to move to LA to become a screenwriter?"

Jody spits out the first movie that comes to him. "*Ace Ventura*."

"*Ace Ventura: Pet Detective?* You saw that movie and you were like, *That decides it, world, I'm going to move to Hollywood and work in the pictures*."

Jody stares back, takes two seconds too long to realize she's making fun of him.

"How much longer are we going to keep this going?" she asks.

"What?"

"I know you're Jody, John." She pauses a moment, waiting for him to admit it.

"Marty told me about his big brother, Jody. You share fifty percent of the same genes. No, wait, that's kid and parent. Is it? You're related. I can see it in your face. Plus, you're all *Hi, I'm John*. You're either Jody or you're a serial killer using *John* as a fake name. Marty swore you'd never come visit him. Where is he?" Shiloh's head rotates on a swivel.

Jody goes from trying to see what this woman knew about his murdered brother to realizing he has to break the news to this woman that his brother has been murdered. "You weren't together anymore?"

"Why are you asking *me* that? He didn't tell you we were— Wait, why did he have you come find me? Is he here?" Shiloh flusters. Like she's self-conscious she's the butt of a deeper joke than *Hi, I'm Marty's brother*.

"How long have you been broken up?"

"Which time?"

Jody doesn't answer. He tries to tell her Marty is dead, but the words remain in his throat, right back there with the acid creeping up his esophagus thanks to his nerves.

"Months," she says. "We haven't spoken."

"I'm sorry. I was hoping to find out something you knew. I thought that was the best way. . . ."

"What's going on?"

"He's dead. Marty's dead."

"What?" Shiloh leans in as if she hadn't heard Jody over the music.

"I'm sorry."

"This isn't funny." Shiloh looks around again. Now with a desperation. A need to see Marty pop out from behind some dancing hipsters.

"He came back home to Pennsylvania. He's dead. Shot. My dad too."

Shiloh stops looking around for Marty as the blood drains from her face.

"His phone was gone. I didn't know how to tell anyone he knew out here. I came out here to try to figure out who might have done it."

"When was this?"

"Eleven days ago."

Shiloh blinks rapidly, maybe to avoid crying, as the band plays a particularly loud song, "Dojo Rising." "I'm going to be sick."

"Are you okay?"

She darts through the crowd. Jody has trouble keeping up as she navigates the dancing drunk hipsters. Every time Shiloh bumps into someone, she keeps moving, and the person looks up to see Jody.

"What the fuck?!" asks a dude with a waxed handlebar mustache and a T-shirt that says *Cool Guy*.

"Sorry," Jody says. He loses Shiloh among bodies dancing in the dark. And he goes right back to where he was twenty minutes ago, searching a crowded bar in Silver Lake for the girl with the best ass.

His search takes him to the doorway. He pops outside. There's a line now to get in. There she is, sitting on the ground. Two dudes with band T-shirts consoling her. Kind gentlemen working overtime to prove chivalry isn't dead. Or vultures swooping in on wounded prey. Jody walks over to her. The hipsters fly off when they see Jody approaching.

He crouches next to her. "You okay?"

She looks up at him, her eyes green pebbles flooding with sorrow. "I'm sorry," she says.

"You want me to drive you home?"

"I walked. I live right . . ." She motions to her left.

"I'll walk you, then."

He walks her to the top of a concrete public stairwell.

"I'm down here," she says.

"I'm sorry. But I didn't come here to let you know. I came here to find out what you know. About Marty."

Shiloh runs her hands across her temples like someone with a migraine. "I'm exhausted. But maybe we could meet up tomorrow morning, and I'll answer whatever questions you have."

Chapter Sixteen

Pen

"And it's not just about the film, imagine what could be brought back from other simulations to this one," Pen says, trying to indulge what Daniel called *executive greed*. "Inventions. Technology. Resources. We could bring back—"

"Penelope." The oldest of three execs at Lofty Content holds both his hands in the air. "I'm sorry, but I think we'll have to stop there."

In this first pitch meeting, Penelope had ignored Daniel's advice to merely tease Pandora's House. As she grabs her messenger bag, she glances at the clock. She had been talking for an hour and forty-five minutes straight. Daniel had advised her to aim for fifteen to twenty minutes.

Daniel calls her as she drives home. "These execs and their assistants, they talk to other companies. You go around to just a handful of meetings talking about wanting to jump simulations, or try to do a two-hour pitch, you're going to be the punch line of the week at the Grill on the Alley. Look, I think you've got some real shots here with the next five pitches. But you've gotta tease the simulation part, leave it to their imaginations to fill in the gaps with the supernatural aspects. Hone in on the website, the brothers. They were ready to buy it ten minutes into the meeting. And you can't call it *The Breach*. Call it *My Dirty California*."

• • •

The next four pitches happen over the next three days. Pen holds back, which pleases Daniel. One company passes because they have a similar project. One company says they're going to discuss internally. But two companies express real interest in the room and say they're going to try to get the heads of their companies to sign off on it.

The final meeting happens on a Friday. After her eighteen-minute pitch, the meeting turns into a Q & A before devolving into a brainstorming session.

One exec suggests doing a fictionalized, scripted version. "We could team you up with a showrunner. A Damon Lindelof type. We have a good relationship with Damon."

Another executive adds, "Yeah, I think you should use it more as a seed, ya know? A jumping-off point."

They're all three talking now, *yes and*–ing one another.

"Genre bending." "Elevated thriller." "International appeal." "Four quadrant, or at least three." "Universal themes." "Solution to antihero fatigue." "Para-noir-mal." "Graphic novel adjacent." "Water cooler show." "Event series." "Actor-bait." Buzzwords fly out of their executive-bro mouths like sunflower seed shells—chewed, soggy, and empty.

They keep going for five minutes. As if Pen is no longer even in the room. Finally, one looks at Pen and says, "What are you thinking?"

"I think I'd like to be in a different simulation."

They all crack up laughing.

"This has been great," one executive says. "I'll put a call into Damon if you're open to it."

Daniel takes Pen to lunch after the last of the six meetings. While they're waiting to be seated, Daniel puts a hand on her shoulder. "It would have been nice if one of them had bought it in the room but look, you've got three places that liked it."

"So what do we do now?" Pen asks.

"We wait for them to call. And cross our fingers one makes an offer."

Chapter Seventeen

Jody

When Jody finds Shiloh outside of a diner called John O'Groats, she looks worse than she did the previous night. She's calmer, but now having processed the news, she looks more disturbed. She gives Jody a hug.

"Thanks for meeting me."

"Yeah, sorry I couldn't talk more last night." The host seats them at a booth in the corner. "So what do you want to ask me?"

"There are so many things. I mean, part of me wants to start at the beginning. But maybe it's better we start at the end."

"Okay."

"When was the last time you saw him?"

"It was maybe two months ago. We'd been off and on for a while but we broke it off for good maybe three or four months ago. I didn't see him for a bit after that. I heard through friends he had moved to Encinitas, but then I heard he was back. Anyway, the last time I saw him was random. Ran into him at Eightfold Coffee."

"What was he doing?"

"Having coffee with someone. He introduced me. It was this guy named Sal. Dunno his last name. Maybe your age or a couple years older."

"Sal, you said?" asks Jody as he jots down the name.

"Yeah, I wouldn't have even remembered Marty being with someone but there was something about their . . . I don't know . . ." Shiloh trails off.

Jody nudges her. "Please, this is helpful."

"It just seemed like I had walked in on an intense conversation."

"But you don't know what they were talking about?"

"No."

"Was Marty in some kind of trouble? I mean, it sounds like you were broken up. But did he owe people money, or was he into something?"

"Not that I know of, but again, the last couple months we haven't talked."

"What did Marty do for money?"

"You asking if he sold drugs?"

"No, why, did he?"

"No, I just . . . People think that sometimes—thought that."

"So what *did* he do?"

"All kinds of stuff. He was always taking a gig and leaving a gig. The jobs often came to him. He's like a magnet. People are drawn to him. And he'd meet people who'd pay him."

"What do you mean?"

"Like he'd meet someone who'd pay him to take them on a hike. I know that sounds ridiculous. Or he'd be playing soccer in the park and somebody would offer to pay him to train their kids once a week."

"Were any of those gigs ever . . . shady?"

"Not any shadier than paying cash, I don't think. He was entrepreneurial, like he would take photographs of businesses on spec and try to sell the photographs to those businesses, but he never stuck with anything long enough to make any real money. I always thought he should try to make money off his writing. He showed me a couple things, and they were always good, but he never tried to sell them. It was like he was self-conscious he was a narcissist by writing about his own life."

"Did he ever show you his *My Dirty California* site?"

"His what?"

"Nothing."

Marty hadn't shared the website with anyone, not even the woman he dated for over a year.

"He was a good writer, though. I met this woman who runs a writers' workshop in Iowa. And she offered to try to get him into the program. She had dropped out of college herself, and I think she was drawn to Marty's story. I filled out the application for him and told him I just needed to send a writing sample, like a thousand-word poem or essay or something. And it pissed him off, and he wrote this ridiculous essay, his way of telling me to fuck off."

"What was it about?" asks Jody.

"Nothing. It was silly, useless."

Shiloh's cheeks redden. *That's* why Marty had written the essay about her ass. When Jody had first read it, the entry had seemed out of character, purposelessly misogynistic.

Ironically, that *useless* essay had enabled Jody to figure out who O was and find her. Jody doesn't want to further embarrass her, so he doesn't say anything about spotting her in the Satellite.

He asks more questions, working backward from the end of their relationship. After a while, Shiloh asks Jody, "So you're really going to try to figure it out? What happened to him."

"Yeah."

"Do you know anything? Do you have any clues?" Shiloh chuckles when she says *clues*.

"I know, it sounds like a Hardy Boys book, but I guess *clues* are what I'm looking for." He goes on to tell her about Wyatt and the gun and the black Pontiac Grand Am.

"So you think this guy with the Grand Am, he's the one who killed Marty?"

"Yeah."

"Marty was going to buy a gun?" Shiloh asks.

Two hours after they've eaten breakfast, Jody and Shiloh order lunch, if only to temper their waiter's glares. They share stories: Jody filling in the blanks of Marty's childhood, and Shiloh giving Jody a sense of Marty's adulthood. Shiloh had known Marty for half his time in LA. They had been loose friends for a few years before the eighteen months they spent on-and-off dating.

Whether they mean to or not, the questions and stories serve as much of a function of grieving as trying to solve the mystery of who killed Marty. As references for a few different stories and questions, Jody shows Shiloh the *My Dirty California* site, but after the third video, she tells Jody she can't take it.

Jody finishes the last bite of his club sandwich. "Marty was living off the grid. He wasn't paying taxes. He hadn't finished high school. But he dated you and other women who seemed to be very much on the grid. Did he ever seem insecure?"

"When I first met him, he was in his early twenties and he had this swagger. Most of the people he'd meet, date, and hang out with had all just graduated college. Marty knew more about everything than any of them. He read so much, absorbed so much. He had this cockiness, like *fuck you* to whoever spent one hundred and fifty grand on college. But by twenty-six and twenty-seven, his peer group had started moving up. Assistants had become executives. Law students got their degrees and started getting jobs and buying condos. And Marty was still scraping by with no driver's license or high school diploma or retirement fund. Online dating didn't suit him. Marty had this cockiness and swagger when you met him in person. But on paper? He was a drifter who didn't graduate high school, didn't have a career, had lived twenty-five places in a decade, and didn't talk to any family. That's a dating profile women run from."

"Do you think he wanted a more normal life?"

"Maybe sometimes, but never for long enough to actually start living one. He was restless. He always wanted the other side of the pillow."

"And you said you were friends for a while first. When did you . . . ?"

"We'd been friends for a couple years, but we lost touch. I think

Marty lost his phone and he wasn't on social media. But then we ran into each other at the Standard Hotel and started hanging out again. And then we started dating."

"How did Marty get around in a city where you need a car? Now there's Uber and Lyft and more train lines, but he's been here ten years."

"Marty always said you can't get to know a city without walking it." Shiloh glances at her phone. "Shoot, I gotta get going. Was there anything else you wanted to ask me?"

"I wrote a couple questions down to make sure I didn't forget anything." He pulls a notebook out of his backpack. Multiple single-spaced pages of questions written in ink.

"A couple?" she asks with a smile. "Look, my friends are opening a bottle shop and taproom in NoHo, and they asked us to play their grand opening—well, they're paying us. So I gotta meet the guys. You can come, ya know, and ask more questions. Or we can meet up tomorrow."

As they drive up the 405 in the rain, Shiloh passes several cars that have their hazard lights on. "Till now, I'd been impressed with how people drive in LA," says Jody.

"We get a lot of practice driving. But not a lot of rain."

"This is how folks drive when it snows in Pennsylvania."

Jody uses the drive to North Hollywood to fire off questions from his notebook. Why did Marty move so much? Did he travel outside of California? Did he have a bank account? As Shiloh parks the car on Lankershim, Jody goes off-book and asks, "Was he happy?"

"He was searching," Shiloh says.

"For happiness?"

"For everything. Marty put in his Gladwellian ten thousand hours of searching. Twice over."

At Beeroncé, a hip hybrid between a craft beer store and a bar, Shiloh gets busy sound testing and chatting with her bandmates. Jody sips beer at the bar and chats with the guy next to him.

Shiloh plays bass and sings backup in an indie rock band called Lizards Doing Pushups. Not music Jody would listen to on his own, but he finds himself drawn to their synth-pop sound and funky eighties vibe.

Between sets, Shiloh chats with Jody. A short guy with a backward cap that reads *Radiohat* approaches Shiloh.

"Hey, Shiloh."

"Hi," she says, not hiding her edginess.

"Can we talk outside?"

"No."

"Please, I just need to talk to you for a second."

Jody turns to his new acquaintance next to him. "Who's this guy?"

"He's obsessed with the band. Well, the bassist anyway."

"Just gimme a couple minutes to talk to you outside," the guy says. He puts a hand on Shiloh's shoulder.

"Don't touch me," Shiloh says.

"I'll talk to you outside, buddy," says Jody.

Shiloh blushes.

Jody puts an arm around the guy and walks him out the back door, where the strip mall has extra parking spots.

Maybe this guy was jealous of Marty. As they walk outside, Jody contemplates threatening him, but he decides playing nice might be the best way to get him talking. Ten minutes later, Jody can't get him to shut the fuck up. It's clear he's in love with Shiloh, but it's also clear he's the kind of guy to profess his love for her to another man in a parking lot in North Hollywood, not the kind of guy who travels to Lancaster, Pennsylvania, and kills two men with a silenced pistol.

Jody watches the second set. The band had led with their stronger songs, and now they seem to be overcompensating with volume. As Jody listens, he cycles back through the questions he had asked and the answers Shiloh had given, convinced that's all the intel he'll get today. But after they're done playing, Shiloh approaches him.

"If you got someone at the DMV to help you, I bet you could get a list of all the 2004–2005 black Pontiac Grand Ams registered in the state of California."

"Yeah, but how do I—"

"When I used to live in Mar Vista, one of my neighbors worked at the DMV."

"Would she help you?"

"Yeah, she owes me. Once she found out I worked part-time as a nanny, whenever she had an emergency she'd dump her two kids on me for hours at a time. Pretty soon *emergency* became whenever she had a date. I can ask her to get me a list."

"That would be . . . Shiloh, thank you. Seriously, that would be incredible."

Chapter Eighteen

Tiph

"Where's Gary?" Mike asks.

"I couldn't bring him."

"Why not?"

"'Cause I got to talk to you about some shit. *Your* shit. Even after you're gone, you still causin' drama. The gift that keeps giving me trouble."

"What you talking about?"

"Your sheet holder came to see me."

"Sheet holder?" asks Mike, squinting through the glass in disbelief.

"Yeah. Dex. Guy said you owe thirty-five hundred. Gambling."

"I don't owe that fucker shit."

"Not what he said."

"Yeah, what else he say?"

"That if they don't get their money, some guys going to come for you in here."

Mike chuckles deep from his belly. But quickly gets serious. "You didn't pay him, did you?"

"Three thousand dollars? I don't even got McDonald's money."

"Good."

"But I'm worried about you."

"He's lying. I don't owe shit. This is what happens. These bitch-ass gangbanger wannabes come after widows and baby mamas whose fellas are doing a stint and try to get them to pay up."

"So he made it up?"

"Yeah. He's a snake."

"That spineless fucker."

"What he say at the end?" asks Mike.

"That he'd come by again. To pick up the money."

"I'll get some of my guys to take care of it. What's up with the other thing?"

"Found the secret room in Chester's house. But the art wasn't there."

"Shit."

"Yeah, but his girl, the Sierra Blaze lady, she said Chester had some armored car lined up for a couple days after he died. So I'm thinking maybe he was planning to move the art."

"Oh yeah?"

"Yeah, so maybe I can figure out the pickup and drop-off locations."

"See? You're good at this treasure shit. Like Nic Cage in that one movie."

Tiph parks her Ford Focus, dreaming about the Audi she's going to buy, across from the Brinks office on Robertson.

A tall handsome Black gentleman in a gray suit greets her. "Can I help you?"

"I hope so. I'm here to ask about armored transportation."

"We can help with that. Who do you work for?"

"Wow, don't judge a book by its book jacket. Maybe I'm here on my own. Maybe I gotta get my gold bars moved to my gold house."

"I didn't mean to offend you."

"I'm fucking with you."

The man seems surprised by her language.

"Sorry, my mother used to say I could keep a bar of soap in my mouth and it still wouldn't be clean."

"I like your mouth. Your smile I mean."

"Oh. Thanks." She tries to stop smiling, but now she can't help it.

"Yeah, that one."

She smiles more. Her hairstylist convinced her to get a curly bob because she said it brought out her smile. Tiph coughs to force herself to stop smiling.

"I'm hoping you could look up a past record for me."

"For who?"

"His name's Chester Montgomery."

"And what's your relationship to him?"

"Just a former associate."

"Associate?"

"Yes."

"Look, I'm sorry, but we can't give out private information."

"I don't think he'll mind, where he is now."

"And where's he now?"

"Six feet under."

"Oh . . . Well, that don't change the policy on our end."

"What can you give me? I don't see how it's going to come back on you if he's dead."

"How do I know he's dead?"

"*LA Times*'ll back me up. Google that shit."

He goes to his computer.

"Chester Montgomery," she repeats.

He clicks a news article about a murder in the Hollywood Hills. "Damn, he's *dead* dead. I don't mean to make a joke if he was your friend. But you said *associate*."

"Can you give me the info?"

"You let me take you to dinner, I'll give it to you."

If I wasn't married, I'd let you eat me for dinner. "Oh."

"Damn, I feel bad now. I take that back. Trying to force you into dinner. Sorry, I just like that smile. I'll look it up. No strings."

"Thank you."

"Found it. He had a reservation. Which he flaked on. Although, now I see why. My man should've moved *himself* into an armored car."

She laughs. "Can I have the details of the reservation?"

"Eagle Rock to Palm Springs."

Tiph remembers Philip saying Chester Montgomery had two houses, one in the Hollywood Hills, one in Palm Springs. "Where in Eagle Rock was the pickup?"

"The entries in our system don't have addresses. It's a safety precaution for the clients."

"You can't get the exact address?"

"No. Think about it from the client standpoint. If you were moving something valuable, would you want some sketchy customer service representative knowing where you're going and when?"

"Makes sense. Eagle Rock to Palm Springs, you said?"

"Yeah."

"And it doesn't say what's being moved?"

"No. That's normal too though. For privacy."

"Okay. Well, thank you."

"How about that dinner? Not 'cause I helped you, 'cause you like me."

"I like you, huh?"

"I think so. So what do you say?"

"I say that why-buy-the-cow expression goes the other way too."

He laughs. "You got swagger. Say whatever you want, huh? Open book . . ."

"Fuck yeah," says Tiph. Quick to drop fuck-bombs, but she's no open book. Keeps her traumas in her closet like stacked shoeboxes.

He smiles. "Well, here, take my card. You got any more questions, let me know."

DeAndre Wilson. She puts the card in her purse as she backtracks to her car. She gets hollered at from time to time from cars and side-walks, but it's not every day a nice man with a nice job asks her out on a proper date. She wonders how much the job pays. It's the kinda job she was always telling Mike he should get. But Mike was always too busy dreaming and scheming to take an honest job.

Chapter Nineteen

Renata

"I'm not lying to you," Coral says.

Renata yells back, the words echoing off the fiberglass walls of their unknown prison, "You said Peter. Then you said Paul. I know you're lying. Just tell me where we are. Por favor. Please."

"I'm not lying to you."

"Tell me. Are we in Pandora's House?"

"I don't know what that is."

"The haunted house."

"I've never heard of Pandora's House," Coral says.

"Where are we, then?"

"I *don't* know."

Renata lies down. It feels like the walls of the tiny room are closing in, feels like the walls of her brain are collapsing. Where is she? How did she get here?

She had pictured her first days in LA so many times. She'd imagined making friends with some Chicanas and finding a job in a coffee shop like Central Perk. Instead, she's locked in some prison. Trying not to cry makes it worse, so she lets the tears flow, snot coming with them.

Coral hovers over Renata. "I *am* from Desert Hot Springs. I did leave and go to LA. But I made up the part about an ex-boyfriend. I didn't have a boyfriend. Some other shit was wrong. It was fucked up. I was fucked up. And when I got to LA, I wanted to start over. And when the where-are-you-from, why-are-you-here questions rolled in every time I met someone new, I didn't wanna tell my sob story. I wanted something easier. So I said I had a bad breakup, needed a change."

"And how did you get here?"

"*That story* I didn't change. I was at a party, blacked out. And I woke up here."

"Whose party was it?"

"Some guy I met outside LACMA. The museum."

"What was his name?"

"I don't remember."

"Did you meet anyone at the party named Abbott?"

"No. I think I was talking to a Floyd. He said he was from Barbieville or Garbieville or something. He had one of those barbell nose rings. It's all so hazy."

"And no one has talked to you in here?"

"No."

"Did you try—"

"Yes, I tried. I begged. I screamed. When I would hear the food hatch open I would be right there and try to talk to them. But they won't respond. And if I have the hatch open on our side, I don't get food at all."

"But they are feeding you. So they want us to be alive. So maybe if we stop eating, they'll . . ."

"You want to hunger strike?"

Renata nods although she has never heard the term before.

Chapter Twenty

Pen

Pen's stomach growls. She missed lunch, lost track of time in LA's Central Library looking at several of the eighty-five thousand maps in their collection. She has been looking at historic maps of Palm Springs, Lassen Volcanic National Park, and Hollywood. She's considering grabbing a bite from Grand Central Market when her phone rings.

"Pen, I've got good news. We've got a bid on your project. Tower Hill Entertainment."

"Really?"

"Yeah," says Daniel. "They're paranoid about us shopping their offer. They don't want a bidding war."

"Is there a bidding war?"

"No. I don't think anyone else is interested, so I think we should take their offer."

"What's their offer?"

"They want to buy the pitch for thirty-five K. That would be for you to put together a mood trailer and a treatment. And then if they want, they'll finance the documentary."

"So I don't necessarily get to make it?"

"It's an option. They're optioning the right to finance the movie. And if they don't want to execute the option, at that point you can always go other places. Pen, this is a good thing. Where are you? I'll come meet you, and we'll celebrate."

"I'm downtown."

"I love downtown. There's a whiskey bar called Seven Grand. Right at Seventh and Grand. We can get happy."

If she stays downtown for happy hour, she'll never make it back to Topanga for the sunset.

Pen takes her first sip of a gold rush as her phone buzzes. A text from Daniel. *Can't make it. So sorry. Maybe tomorrow instead? Congrats again!*

He's always flaking like this, always hopping off their calls to take another. But she doesn't really like him that much, would just as well drink alone.

Alone proves short-lived.

"Do you come here a lot?" asks the broad-shouldered guy with a buzz cut.

Adults should have buzz cuts more often, Pen thinks.

"First time."

"What brings you here this afternoon?"

"Celebrating. I set up a new film project."

"Oh, really?" Based on his excitement and his charming face and charming body, she deems him an actor.

"Why, do you come here often?"

"First time too. I'm a consultant. Had a meeting down the street."

Not an actor. Pen doesn't dislike actors. But she finds there to be a disproportionate amount of actors in LA. She doesn't like or dislike dentists. But if everywhere she went there were dentists, and people talking about dentists, and people trying to be dentists, and magazines with dentists on the cover, and award shows for the best dentists, she might get tired of dentists.

"I thought maybe you were a dentist."

He stares back, befuddled.

Did I say actor or dentist? Pen wonders.

He introduces himself as Luke. They chat as their glasses slowly empty and the bar slowly fills. She can't tell if the whiskey is affecting her judgment, but she feels a magnetic pull to him. "Can I ask you something?"

"Ask away," he says.

"Do you believe in soul mates?"

"I thought you were gonna ask if I liked cooking or what my favorite TV show was."

"You don't have to answer."

"Yeah, I believe in true love. I don't believe everything's predestined though—free will's a little too interesting, ya know?"

"But do you believe there's one perfect person out there for everyone?"

"I don't know. Why, do you?"

"Yeah. If you believe in the simulation hypothesis, which I do, and this particular simulation was set up to have soul mates, then in theory there would be one perfect person out there for you. It's just a matter of whether or not you meet them."

"Maybe I just did," he says with a wink.

"Me too. I could feel it since we started talking. A magnetic pull."

He holds eye contact. Is he trying to discern her level of seriousness? No, he's looking for her soul. She can't help herself. She leans forward on her stool, takes the side of his face in her palm, and touches her lips to his.

Luke escorts her into his unit of the historic Biscuit Company Lofts in the arts district. Multicolor paneled dividers partition off a bedroom, but Luke leads her toward the couch in the main area. The ceiling is so high. When her eyes lower, Luke kisses her again. A pile of shirts and pants forms on the floor. She asks if he wants to go to his bed, and he answers by sliding his hand between her legs. She feels close to him, closer than she'd felt to boys and men she dated for months at a time. An electricity reminds her of doing ecstasy at Dockweiler State Beach as a teenager. They're both naked now. He's sitting back. She's over him, his face buried in her breasts. She can't let go of his buzzed scalp.

She feels closer and closer to him. But he gets up, bends her over the couch. And now she doesn't feel as close. She feels far away, but she leans into that farness, takes one of her hands off the couch, and she comes like she hasn't in a half decade.

Luke disappears into the bathroom, taking off the condom midstride. She doesn't want to rush to get redressed but she feels odd lying naked on the orange mid-century modern couch. If they were in his bed, she'd pull a sheet over herself. She puts on her underwear and T-shirt, leaving the bra on the floor, so that she can get partially re-dressed without looking in a rush to leave.

She hears Luke go from the bathroom into the bedroom. She waits, lying in a mess of her own bliss. She smells her armpit, human but not foul.

Luke emerges, now wearing different clothes. "I actually have some stuff to do."

"Oh, okay. Me too actually." Pen grabs her laptop from her messenger bag. "What's your Wi-Fi?"

He stares a moment, confused. "Uh, it's ChateauLuke and the password is *internet*."

"Oh, funny."

Luke hovers a moment before walking away. Pen pulls up a document where she jotted down several possible anomalies she found on historical maps at the library.

Now Luke comes back over. "I need you to leave."

"Is everything okay? Did something happen?"

"I just do. Need you to leave. I'm sorry."

Pen gets dressed and packs up her computer. *Does Luke not believe we are soul mates? Or maybe he knows it but he's not ready to settle down? Or maybe we weren't soul mates. Maybe I had misread the magnetic energy. Or maybe it was a chemical misfire. Or maybe this particular simulation wasn't designed with soul mates after all. Or what if a world was designed where everyone has a perfect person for them, but not in reciprocals? Like Person A is the perfect person for Person B, but Person C is the perfect person for Person A. Wouldn't that be a fucked-up simulation? Maybe that is our world, and that's why half the marriages end in divorce.*

Pen wants to stay, wants to run her hands through his hair, but Luke guides her to the door, hand on her shoulder.

"Bye. I'm sorry. Bye." He closes the door in her face.

Pen pops out onto Mateo Street, her mind and body in a tangle of satisfaction and disillusionment.

Chapter Twenty-One

Jody

Two days after their daylong adventure-filled interview, Jody and Shiloh plan to meet for lunch at Guisados on Sunset. While Jody waits for her, he watches Audis, Teslas, and BMWs cross an overpass. Underneath—in a lower class, a forgotten class—lies a tent city. Now that Jody had been in LA a couple weeks and watched hundreds of his brother's *MDC* entries, he's started to get a fuller sense of Los Angeles. To see what Marty described as *the place beyond the palms*. To see that the sunsets come with clogged freeways and smogged cityscapes. To see the nuances and cracks of the sunny place where dreams are supposed to come true.

The city of stars is more like the city of side hustles. It's not just actors; the whole city seems to be auditioning for lives just out of their reach. Everyone running the rat race, not to mention the rats; there are more rats in LA than New York. Everyone trying to get somewhere, literally and figuratively. A race to become a movie star, a race to get north on the 405 in rush hour. And in LA, rush hour lasts four hours. In theory, doctors are driving to hospitals and teachers are driving to schools, but mostly it seems like people are just trying to get in and out of the Whole Foods parking lot.

Beneath the surface of a melting pot of culture—with its undeniable glut of restaurants, museums, music venues, galleries, breweries—lies a lack of community and hometown pride. A city of transplants. So few people are from here that opponents come to play the Chargers and Rams with an away-field advantage. This doesn't include East LA and South LA where everyone worships Kobe and has an uncle with Dodgers ink. But the west side is a revolving door, and while here, people move between neighborhoods as if hopping between clubs and cliques.

There's a superficiality to Blah-Blah Land that stretches to hypocrisy. Rich liberals preaching about the environment while watering their grass that's not supposed to grow in a desert. Yuppies moving to artsy neighborhoods, meditating and doing yoga to improve not their health but their productivity. Hikers in Runyon Canyon nothing more than social climbers trying to get to the top. Media leaders claiming to want to solve the world's problems but can't even help the tens of thousands of people living on the street in their own city. A supposedly progressive town where Scientology thrives.

Beneath the neon mecca is the personality of a white paper cup. With all the glitz and glamour of Tinseltown, even the houses are constantly getting plastic surgery. Fixes and flips and makeovers and remodels. Looking at the sprawl from Mulholland, it feels like the math is visible, like the city is just a series of real estate deals. With all the new wealthy home buyers flooding in, longtime residents are forced to move farther away, drive longer commutes. Housing shortages. Eviction crisis. Tent cities like the one in this underpass. So many people are getting pushed out of LA that now one out of five people living in Oregon was born in California.

But hey, 329 days of sunshine a year.

After *hello*, Shiloh says, "My old neighbor said she'd get the list, so we'll see."

"That's great. Thank you."

"What else can I do?" Shiloh asks.

"Well, I guess I want to talk to more of Marty's friends."

"Might be hard. I didn't have their numbers or even know their last names. Marty wasn't into social media. And you don't have his phone?"

"No."

"I have Nicole's number."

"Who's Nicole?"

"Friend of Marty's. I'm not close with her. She's one experiment away from being an addict. And she's . . ." Shiloh struggles to find the right word. "She's a borrower."

"A borrower?"

"Yeah, always asking to borrow something."

Shiloh introduces Jody to Nicole over text. Nicole calls Jody crying after hearing the news. Jody asks if they could get together and talk about Marty. Nicole feels like they need to tell more of Marty's friends.

"No one knows, no one even knows," she says again and again, sobbing.

Later in the day, Nicole texts back that she's going to get a bunch of Marty's friends together. A send-off party. Jody's not interested in the *party* aspect but getting a bunch of Marty's friends together in one place at one time would be great. A makeshift focus group think-tank thing.

Nicole changes the venue multiple times. A restaurant, then a bar, then a hotel bar. Later, she texts Jody an address for a loft in Bunker Hill. She says it's a filming location that also rents out the space for parties. She texts that the password to get into the party is *Marty*.

In the lobby, a security guard steps in front of Jody. "Going to floor eight," Jody says, then adds, "Marty."

Jody can't believe how many people are there. Over a hundred. Maybe two hundred. A DJ in a seersucker suit spins nostalgia. People are dancing and drinking. Lots of tattoos, ironic and less ironic. Jody scans the scores of people; Marty touched so many lives. Jody feels a swell of endorphins in his gut and forehead. The deceased living on through the lives they touched. . . . It's about as close to immortality as an atheist can imagine.

He scans the crowd for Shiloh. Doesn't see her. He texts Nicole, *Are you here?* At a card-table bar, he orders a Golden Road lager. A woman comes over to order a drink.

"How do you know Marty?" Jody asks.

"Who's Marty?"

While he waits for Shiloh and Nicole to get there, he asks seven more people if they knew Marty. No one knows what he's talking about. One guy in a bowler hat says, "*Marty-party*, that's the password I was given."

By the time Shiloh shows up, Jody is convinced not a single person here knew Marty. Shiloh joins Jody, collecting stares as she walks across the loft in her yellow dress.

"Do you recognize anyone here?" Jody asks.

"I think I see a few friends of Nicole's that I met once or twice. But I don't know if they were friends with Marty."

"Which one is Nicole?"

"I don't see her." Shiloh scans the crowd for a moment. "Let me text her." Shiloh fires off a text message.

"Do you go to places like this a lot?" Jody asks.

"I don't know. I feel like I *end up* at places like this a lot. Ya know? A night starts off with wine or getting together with friends and inevitably ends at a place like this with everyone having trouble hearing each other. Every once in a while, you go out, and you have the right amount to drink, and you're with the right group of people, and the right music is playing, and everyone dances and has this great time. But that seems to be the exception that proves— Oh, here, she texted me back. Yeah, she's not coming. She says she can meet you tomorrow. Anytime you want."

Jody struggles to hear her over the beat blasting from the speakers. He had thought the party might be a good way to connect with different friends of Marty's and collect intel. But now the whole evening is about as useful to Jody as the pounding music in his ears. The song's beat sounds like gunshots, and Jody flashes back to firing the shotgun at the fleeing murderer in his backyard. It leads to a chain of flashes. His brother bleeding out. His dad dead, bleeding out. Giving his brother chest compressions. Now the growing crowd and the echoing music feel like they're closing in on him.

"Are you okay?" Shiloh yells to him over the music.

"What? Yeah . . ."

"Come with me."

Jody—and a few turning male heads—follow Shiloh across the room, over to the hallway where the elevator is. But she goes into the stairwell.

The rooftop offers a panoramic view of Los Angeles. A sea of lights in every direction. Flickering pixels below a hazy marine layer. Headlights moving through the fixed glow of buildings, streetlights, traffic lights, billboards, and houses. A giant neon portrait, ever shifting.

"Thanks, air feels good." Jody looks out at the sprawling city of lights. Beautiful but intimidating. So many buildings, roads, and cars. So many people. So many people who could have killed Marty.

"In one of his videos, Marty said LA's a city confused about where the suburbs start."

"That sounds like him," Shiloh says.

"Do you like living here?"

"There are definitely times where I'm stuck in traffic and wondering why I'm here, and I realize I could take my rent money and more than cover a mortgage somewhere else. Have a little house. With a little garden. And one of those tire swings. It is cool though. LA. Have you been to the La Brea Tar Pits yet?"

"No. What are they?"

"Big pits of tar. There's a museum there. All these animals died and were preserved. I guess there's this natural asphalt that comes up from the ground. But water would collect on the top level of dirt and leaves. Thirsty animals would try to drink the water and get stuck in the tar and slowly die."

"Oh."

"Sometimes I feel like LA is just a big tar pit."

"And you feel like one of the animals stuck in it dying?"

"Sometimes. And sometimes, I love this place."

Jody's eyes go from the city's yellow lights to Shiloh's yellow dress. She smiles at him. The impulse to kiss her causes a pit to form in his stomach. That would be fucked up.

He stares into the starless charcoal sky, then looks back down at the endless lights on the ground. A capsized version of small-town Pennsylvania. Headlights zip across the upside-down sky like shooting stars. Jody looks down to see Shiloh holding his hand. He leans in and she meets his lips.

Nicole turns up at Jody's house ninety minutes after she said she'd be there. She had sent texts updating her level of lateness four times before she stopped altogether. When Jody opens the door, he sees a thirty-year-old woman with sleeve tattoos and blue streaks in her hair.

And a periwinkle upright spinner suitcase.

"Hey. Sorry I'm late."

"No worries. I'm Jody. Come on in."

Nicole enters Jody's tiny studio unit. Her suitcase fills a quarter of the floor space.

"You don't mind if I crash here for a bit do you?"

Jody does mind. He struggles to sleep in general, so he's not keen on adding a roommate, especially someone he doesn't know. As much as he wants to tell her he can't have her stay here, he also needs information from her. And she knows that. And in a way she seems to be holding this over Jody. *I'll give you what you want to know about your brother, but I need a pillow for a few nights.* Or maybe she hasn't made that calculation.

She's a borrower, Shiloh had said.

"For how long?"

"I'm not sure."

Even Rory, sniffing Nicole's bag, seems to grasp his space just shrank.

"Okay. I guess it's fine. It's not that big, so . . ."

"I'll be fine. Just need a couch."

Small talk leads to Nicole telling a twenty-minute story about her stepbrother getting arrested after getting in a fistfight at the wharf in San Francisco. As she rambles on, Jody wonders what would have happened if he had visited Marty in California years ago. It leads him into a spiral of other what-ifs. What if Marty hadn't moved to California? What if Jody had spent more time with Marty when he was a teenager? What if their mother hadn't died? What if his dad had been harder on Marty when he got more rebellious? What if Jody had chased down the killer rather than going back in the house to call 911 and check on Marty?

Jody's relieved when Nicole pauses and asks, "So what do you want to know about Marty?"

"Anything. Everything."

"This is crazy. I just saw him in Encinitas."

"What was he doing there?"

"I don't know. It wasn't out of the norm for him to go spend a few weeks somewhere. That guy, rest in peace, he conquered this state." She laughs.

Jody wonders about the connotations of *conquered*, but Nicole keeps going. "But when I got there, he was stressed, which is weird 'cause Marty wasn't normally stressed. I mean analytical, opinionated as hell, sure. But there was a palpable dread. The weird part is all he did was surf all day and pick up a few shifts washing dishes at this breakfast burrito place called Mozy Cafe. It's like he was in Encinitas on the most zen chill laid-back weeks ever, but his attitude was the opposite. And it kinda felt like he didn't want me there."

Had she had shown up uninvited when she visited Marty? Today, she'd shown up and wedged herself into Jody's apartment, asking to stay for an unspecified amount of time. Not surprising Marty wouldn't have wanted her popping in and staying with him in San Diego.

But maybe Marty's supposed anxiety was more than being annoyed with Nicole. Maybe whatever got Marty killed had to do with his trip to San Diego.

"Do you think Marty could have seen something that got him killed?"

"Sure. What though, I dunno. Dude lived on his tippy-toes, always trying to see a little more."

"Did Marty ever mention a guy named Sal?"

"No, why?"

"Shiloh said the last time she saw him, he was with some serious-looking guy named Sal."

"I dunno a Sal."

"What about women? Shiloh told me a lot about Marty, but he might not have discussed other women with her."

"I know he was sleeping with this Japanese chick for a while. Marty had this simpler side to him where he wanted to meet new people. But then he'd go through periods of self-inflicted abstinence. And he was the one who forced me to go to the Women's March downtown. He was always analyzing his encounters. Like one time, I guess some girl asked to use handcuffs, and Marty did it, but then he spent like four hours talking to me about whether or not the girl had been getting off on the idea of being raped, and where that fantasy might have come from, and whether he was at all complicit."

Marty had his own moral code he struggled to arbitrate.

"Just shit like that," Nicole adds. "Everybody used to call him a free spirit. But if you knew him, really knew him, he was a free spirit trapped in a cage."

Jody stares at her arm and thinks about how people with tattoos tend to be friends with people who have tattoos.

Nicole has been in the shower for a half hour when Jody hears a knock. Shiloh, holding a yellow envelope.

"Hey," she says.

Jody's about to invite her in when Shiloh's eyes go past him to Nicole, who emerges from the shower, towel—Jody's one towel—around her hair.

She waves, says, "'Sup, Shiloh," and goes to her suitcase.

Jody wants to explain, anxious for Shiloh not to misinterpret the nature of his guest, but Shiloh appears amused. Jody steps outside and closes the door.

"I thought she was coming over to answer a few questions," Jody says.

"And she moved in? That's how she rolls." Shiloh holds up the yellow envelope. "My former neighbor dropped this off. She didn't want an electronic trail. So it's a hard copy."

Is that the whole reason Shiloh brought it over in person? Jody takes the envelope. "Thank you. Did you . . . did you look at it?"

"Yeah. One hundred and eighteen people. Every registered black 2004–2005 Pontiac Grand Am in LA County. "

Jody opens the envelope and pulls out a printed spreadsheet that lists 118 different people, including addresses. "This is a lot of people. But *this* is helpful. Really, Shiloh, I can't thank you enough."

"Of course."

"I gotta go. But . . ."

"What?"

"Nothing."

She pecks Jody on the mouth and walks back to her car.

Chapter Twenty-Two

Renata

The first day is harder than the second day. But on the third day, the true suffering sets in. Whether it was when her father got laid off from the cement plant or when they got evicted and had to live in a shed behind her grandparents' house for two weeks, Renata had never gone twenty-four hours without eating. Now she'd gone more than forty-eight.

Each time the food came, Renata and Coral left the food in the hatch. These meals were replaced with fresh meals that Renata and Coral left in the hatch. Now the cycle has continued for three days.

"It's not working," says Coral. "They don't care."

"Or maybe we just have to wait them better."

"I can't do it."

"You can. We've come all this way. If we eat now, it's all wasted."

Coral stops arguing. She lies there, moaning. An hour later, Coral says, "I'm sorry, Renata."

Renata beats her there, scrambling over to the hatch. She takes the food dish and dumps it right into a large ziplock bag that has their waste in it. She shoves the bag into the hatch so their captors will see the rejection.

"Fuck you," Coral says, tears streaming down her face. She goes back to her makeshift bed.

The next half day stretches on, the seconds counted in pangs of hunger. A headache comes and goes. Intermittent nausea. Sleeping avoids suffering, so Renata tries to keep her eyes closed and remain as still as possible. Dozing, she dreams she's back in Tijuana at her sanctuary. Amid the rampant crime, widespread poverty, the feral chickens and stray dogs, there's a bunker-like community center in Camino Verde run off private and government grants. What used to be a waste-filled arroyo that divided two gang territories became a public seam of soccer fields, classrooms, dance spaces, and a digital library called Casa de las Ideas. Renata hung out there on weekends and most days of her summer breaks.

Renata wakes to the sound of the hatch closing. Their next meal has arrived. Renata is too weak to move. Coral crawls over toward the food. Renata wants to get up and stop her. But she feels too queasy to move. It feels like her stomach is digesting her liver and heart and lungs.

She watches as Coral shoves chicken and rice into her mouth. Like a tiger hunkered over captured prey. When Coral finishes, she crawls back and lies down.

There's no point to continuing the hunger strike now. All Renata wants to do is eat. But surely Coral ate all the food. Maybe there are crumbs left. It hurts to move. She gets the strength to crawl over. Half the food—chicken, rice, and broccoli—remains. Her half. Renata eats it, licks the plate when she's done.

She crawls over to where Coral is sleeping and lays next to her. Coral wakes up as Renata spoons her.

"Lo siento," Renata says.

Chapter Twenty-Three

Tiph

While she waits for them to arrive, Tiph pays seven different bills online. When she finds this multimillion-dollar art stash, she'll enroll in autopay. No more living out of fear of overdraft fees.

The doorbell rings. On the other side stand two men. One tall and wiry, moves like an inflatable-tube man. The other built like a fridge, wears a backpack that looks small compared to his frame. Mike had told her two men were coming, Philly D and L-Chubbs. She eyes the fridge-shaped fella, who has kind eyes and a neatly trimmed beard.

"You must be L-Chubbs."

But the tall wiry guy nods: *That's me.*

"And you're Philly D?" she asks the other guy.

"Yeah. Deon." He sets down the backpack.

L-Chubbs smiles at Tiph and crosses his long arms behind his back. *Hmm, he has kind eyes too.*

Staring at the two big men, Tiph feels the loss of control, and she starts to doubt her decision to have Mike take care of this situation rather than the police. "Well, this guy Dex should be here in an hour or so."

"Okay, cool," says L-Chubbs. The two men move past Tiph.

"Hold on, shoes off."

They pause in the entryway to take off their shoes. Once inside, L-Chubbs sits in the recliner. Philly D stretches.

"Wait—what's the plan here?" asks Tiph.

"What do you mean?" asks Philly D.

"When Dex gets here."

"Yeah, we're going to make sure he doesn't bother you anymore," says L-Chubbs.

"Right. But you're going to take him somewhere, right?"

Philly D glances around the apartment. "We can do it here. Or in a bedroom."

"Wait, you're going to do it *here*?!"

"You thought we were gonna take him out for hoagies?" Philly D motions to the apartment. "He's coming here. So *here* is the easiest place. Otherwise we gotta tie his ass up and transport him, risk making a scene in the courtyard or on the street."

"I did not understand this was the plan. My son is in the other room."

"Little man won't bother us," says L-Chubbs. "It'll be cool. Nothing's gonna happen."

"Now that's not true," says Tiph. "Something's going to happen. Can't teach an omelet a lesson without breaking some eggs."

"It ain't gon' come back on you's what we're saying," says Philly Deon.

"We've done this kinda thing before," adds L-Chubbs.

Sweat forms across her lower back and behind her knees. Should she back out? But Dex is coming back tonight at 7:00 p.m. If she tells Philly and L-Chubbs to leave, she'll still have Dex knocking in forty-five minutes. And she doesn't have $3,400 for him. She wants this problem gone. She doesn't want to have to wonder when the next time Dex is going to show up.

"Are we cool?" asks L-Chubbs.

"I guess."

"Cool," says Philly.

"I'm going to go check on Gary. You guys good? You want something to drink?"

"I'll take a beer," says L-Chubbs.

She hadn't meant alcohol. But okay. "How about you, Deon?"

"Do you have green tea?"

"Uh, no. I have black tea."

"That's okay, I don't fuck with black tea. Water's fine," says Philly D, still standing in the middle of the room.

"You can sit on the couch if you want," says Tiph.

"Nah," says Philly. "Sitting's the new smoking."

An hour and a half later, the doorbell rings. L-Chubbs puts down beer number four and stands. Philly was already standing. Philly goes to his backpack and pulls out a semiautomatic gun. Tiph had figured what was in the bag. But it's still jarring to see it. She opens the door. Dex on the other side.

"You got my money?" asks Dex.

"Yeah. Come in."

Once inside, Dex sees L-Chubbs and Philly waiting for him. Philly aims the gun right at him. Dex raises his hands in the air.

"Shoes off, motherfucker," says Philly Deon, which gives Tiph a newfound confidence this is going to go okay.

"I'll be in the back," says Tiph. She disappears into her bedroom, where Gary plays with LEGO bricks on the floor. She locks the door.

"What are you building?"

"A bike," says Gary. "Maybe by tomorrow, it'll be big enough to ride."

"You're building a bike to ride?"

"Yeah. Dad kept saying he was going to get me one and teach me how to ride it."

Tiph and Mike had a big fight six months ago when Mike wanted to buy Gary a bicycle from Target. *He's got to learn the essentials*, Mike had said. *Groceries are essential*, Tiph had snapped back. Now Tiph wishes she'd let him.

Tiph hears the sound of muffled voices out in the living room. To fend off the anxiety, she tries to picture a vacation in Cabo once she gets this art.

Twenty minutes later, Tiph can hear yelling. "Stay in here," Tiph tells her son.

Tiph steps out of the bedroom. Dex has a bloody lip and bloody nose and a bloody cheek—a bloody face. L-Chubbs hovers over top of Dex, tossing a grenade in his hand like it's a baseball.

Tiph pulls L-Chubbs into the second bedroom.

"What's up?" he asks.

"What's up? I'm on house arrest. If I so much as steal an apple or go outside when I ain't supposed to, I'm going to actual prison."

"Right?"

"Right, so I can't be having you detonate a grenade in my apartment is what I'm saying, not to mention I'm not tryna get blown up."

"This shit ain't real."

"Oh."

"So we cool?"

"The gun's real?"

"Yeah."

"So yeah, that could still send me to prison. I appreciate what you guys are doing. Just promise me you won't fire the gun or get the police brought."

"No problem."

Tiph goes back into the bedroom with Gary. She helps him construct a yellow and blue and red house with the hodgepodge of LEGO bricks. A few minutes later, there's a knock on the door.

"Stay here, baby." Tiph goes out into the living room, where all three men are standing in their socks. Dex continues to bleed from multiple wounds on his face. He's panting like a child with asthma.

"Man's got something to say to you," Philly says.

"I'm sorry," says Dex.

"And?" asks Philly.

"And I won't bother you anymore."

"Okay," says Tiph.

"Now get the fuck out of here," says L-Chubbs.

Dex dashes out.

"Thank you," says Tiph, ready for them to leave too.

"I use your bathroom before we go?" asks L-Chubbs.

Later that night, Tiph takes a long shower, trying to wash the images of Dex bleeding out of her mind. Trying to wash the guilt away. To get her attention elsewhere, she focuses her thoughts on the art stash. She finds herself wondering yet again about Jody. Maybe the best way to find him would be to talk to this Penelope woman, the crazy lady who'd made the Kickstarter video for that documentary film about Jody and his brother and simulations.

Chapter Twenty-Four

Pen

Olivia, the peppy junior exec overseeing her film project, invites Pen to lunch at Akasha to get to know each other. Olivia shows up thirty minutes late, but the lunch is otherwise pleasant. After they eat, Olivia slips her corporate card onto the mini clipboard holding the bill.

"Thanks for lunch," says Pen.

"Of course. Hey, I meant to ask you. One of my friends works at Lofty Content, and she said you pitched there too but had this whole spin involving simulations? I sometimes wonder if we're living in a simulation."

"Yes! And my lame agent kept talking me out of mentioning that part. Some people just can't handle the idea there is no spoon." Pen goes on to tell Olivia about her theory of what Pandora's House is and the connection to Marty and Jody. They have to give up the table, so they grab a coffee down the street at Cognoscenti.

Midafternoon, Pen hops on the 10 to the Pacific Coast Highway to Topanga, invigorated by an exec being open to the documentary's ultimate direction.

The next morning, Daniel's assistant emails Pen to come to Century City at 2:00 p.m.

Daniel's assistant leads Pen though the agency's maze of hallways. But they go past Daniel's office.

As they turn the corner and approach the glass conference room,

Pen sees fifteen people inside. She recognizes them all. An old roommate she lived with in Del Rey. Her former agent who left and became a manager after she was sexually harassed. A cousin named Felix who she hadn't spoken with in two years. A documentary filmmaker friend named Chelsea.

Why are all these people from her life gathered here? Can't be a surprise party, her birthday is in May. Perhaps Daniel's assistant got her birthday wrong.

The folks who were sitting stand, and the folks who were standing sit.

"Hello, Penny," Daniel says.

Pen hasn't gone by the name Penny since she was six. Her mom used to call her dad Johnny, but when she left, he was devastated and he started going by John. In solidarity with her dad, she started going by Pen.

"What is this?" Pen asks.

"Thank you for coming in," Daniel says. "We wanted to talk to you as a group."

"Okay . . ." Pen says, looking around.

"The studio called. They're backing out of the offer."

"Why?"

"The lunch you had with Olivia."

"She asked me to go to lunch. It went fine."

"Well, as a result of that lunch, the company became concerned about your mental health and about the scope of the project, and they pulled the offer. But this isn't just about that project or that film or that deal or that money. It's about you. We're concerned about you, and I wanted to get your friends and family together and share our concerns with you as a cohesive group of people. Who care about you."

"Who think I'm crazy . . ." says Pen as she shakes her head.

"We don't think you're crazy," says Daniel. 'We think you have a tendency to find connective tissue where it doesn't exist. And we think you need a little more balance in your life."

"Balance is for people who don't know what their purpose is," says Pen. "I'm confused. What happened to the film project? What did Olivia say?"

"She told the other execs about your conversation at lunch," says Daniel.

"Olivia's the one who brought up believing we're in a simulation."

"Well, she baited you," says Daniel.

"That makes no sense. She said she was all into Buddhism. The Eastern traditions all suggest the world around us is not *the real world*. They believe it's a world created by our minds. And that's just Eastern religions. You want to talk déjà vu, angels, NDEs, OBEs, resurrection, some god creating the world in six days, afterlife, synchronicity—pick your unknown, and simulation hypothesis can explain it."

Daniel turns to his assistant. "Didn't you say a physics professor from UCLA was coming?"

Daniel hadn't brought this group of people together. His assistant had.

A bald man with a gray beard and two earrings raises his hand. Professor Laskey. When he taught her sophomore year—Pen's last year before she dropped out of film school—the two became such close friends that he asked her to call him Henry.

"Great," says Daniel. "I can respond too, but maybe you can talk her through the science of it all?"

"Well, I don't agree with Pen. We've had many debates about this. To liken it to Schrödinger's cat, we don't disagree on whether the cat is alive or dead, we disagree about whether it's possible for the cat to move to another box."

Pen points an angry finger. "You're choosing a simple analogy that defines a single *sealed* box."

Laskey smiles. Daniel waits for him to respond. Daniel assumes because Laskey disagrees with Pen, Laskey agrees with Daniel.

But Laskey turns to Daniel. "Look, she already knows how much I disagree there are breaches or wormholes connecting different simulations. But to be clear, I'm fairly certain we *are* living in a simulation. It's a matter of probabilities. Not to mention the fact that fractal geometry appears in nature; there's clearly computation. And I'm not on an island in my field. Stephen Hawking has said we have a fifty percent chance of being in a simulated reality. Neil deGrasse Tyson thinks it's *very likely*."

Daniel turns to his assistant and gives her a death glare. He looks ready to throw his iPhone at her, and she looks scared he might do it.

"And I find it amusing the simulation hypothesis remains unhip outside the scientific community, and yet it's become popular to believe someday we'll be able to download our consciousness into a computer and extend our lives indefinitely. If you accept the latter, then you accept we are just digital information, which should make the leap to simulation theory rather easy. I mean . . . accepting consciousness as digital is the challenge, the rest is just pixels. Think about how compression could be used to show a black night sky, and—"

"Sir," Daniel repeats until Laskey stops talking. "Thanks for joining us, but maybe we're going to go with a closer-knit family-style discussion here. I'll have them validate your parking."

Henry Laskey grumbles under his breath. As he trudges out, he looks to Pen, and she shrugs.

Pen's friend Ben, a twentysomething with clear-framed glasses, raises his hand. "I also believe in the simulation hypothesis. Should I go or stay?"

Daniel groans and motions to the door. Ben mouths *I'm sorry* to Pen on his way out.

"Before we go any further, I would like to make sure everyone in the room is here because they're concerned Pen is not taking care of herself emotionally."

A thirty-year-old guy who goes by the nickname Feather, who

Pen hasn't seen in eighteen months, stands. "I was confused what this was. I got the call from the agency . . . I thought it was about my writing. I've been looking for representation." Feather holds up a bound screenplay. "Who should I give this to?"

Daniel sighs. Feather turns to the assistant who looks like she's going to cry.

"I'll leave it here on the table. It has my contact info on the front." He heads to the door but stops. "It's science fiction. I just wanted to make sure the tone isn't lost. I know we've been having a lot of scientific conversations just now, and I didn't want you to think . . . It's a story's what I'm saying. But it is *hard* sci-fi so I could see it being tonally confusing in light of the ambiguities we've been discussing just now."

Feather stops, but starts again. "Great role for a Chris. Chris Pine. Or Chris Evans. Or Chris Hemsworth. Or Chris Pratt. Chris Abbott."

"Please get out." Daniel points to the door.

Feather speed-walks out of the conference room.

"Maybe this was a mistake." When he says *mistake*, Daniel again glares at his assistant.

"I have to go. I have a five-year-old at home." Chelsea, the documentary filmmaker, stands. They met on the festival circuit a couple of years ago. "But I do want to say something first. Pen, I care about you. I don't agree with many things you say. I'm not here to try to talk you into seeing through my lens. But I often worry you're not taking care of yourself."

Pen uses her sleeve to wipe her eyes. Chelsea gives Pen a hug and walks out the door.

"Everything she said, I agree with," says Daniel. "First and foremost, that's all that matters to us. But our relationship is one of agent and client, and my job is to help you get jobs. And I am here telling you I can't help you if you're going to keep going down this road."

Fuck it, Pen thinks as she drives home to Topanga. It would have been easier to have a company front the overhead, but oh well. She thinks through a possible crowdfunding campaign as she drives down Sunset toward the PCH.

She's clutching the wheel when laughter bubbles up and becomes uncontrollable. An intervention. Like there's something wrong with her.

Chapter Twenty-Five

Tiph

"Dad said I should pick my own clothes, and I want to wear them over top like this."

After Tiph makes Gary put his underwear *under* his wears, Tiph drops him off at preschool. Once home, Tiph finds a website for Penelope Rhodes, documentary filmmaker. The website includes a link to a short film about UFOs. The contact tab lists Penelope's agent, Daniel Hudson at Beacon Talent Agency.

"Daniel Hudson's office."

"Yeah, can I talk to Daniel?"

"May I ask who is calling?"

"Tiph."

"Does Daniel know you?"

"No."

"What's this in regards to?"

"Penelope Rhodes."

"Hold on," the assistant says.

"This is Daniel."

"Hi. This is Tiph. I'm trying to get a hold of Penelope."

"She's in the hospital."

"What happened?"

"She's in a locked psych unit. Metropolitan in Norwalk."

"Oh. Since when? What happened?"

Call ended.

• • •

The trace of cleaning products burns Tiph's nostrils. The security in Metropolitan State Hospital seems stricter than the security at the prison where her husband is doing fourteen months. Mike has an estranged aunt in this hospital. In terms of her home confinement, Tiph was able to get the visit approved under the label of "tending to family obligations." But she's not here to visit Mike's aunt.

An administrative assistant walks her to a hallway where there are twenty-four separate tiny meeting rooms. Tiph sits in the small room with white walls. There are two white chairs, no windows, and no decorations. It looks like a normal room covered in snow. Ten minutes later, a nurse brings in a white woman in sweatpants and a sweatshirt.

"Hi, Penelope," Tiph says.

"Who are you?"

Her skin is pale, nearly the same color as the room's white walls. The woman's eyes are wide, her eyebrows thrust toward her hairline. As she stares Tiph down, Tiph struggles to maintain eye contact.

"I'm Tiphony."

"Okay?"

"Okay, so I was hoping you could answer some questions for me."

"Like what?"

"I need to know where Jody is."

"Jody?"

"I know you two were working together to figure out what happened to Jody's brother, Marty. I watched your Kickstarter video."

"Okay."

"Okay, so can you help me find Jody?"

"Why do you need to find Jody?"

"I need his help finding something."

"The other side?"

"What other side?"

"Nothing. What do you need his help finding?"

"Chester Montgomery has something of mine. And I think Jody can help me find it."

"I see."

"Do you know Chester Montgomery?"

Pen stares back. Doesn't answer.

"Do you know where Jody is?" Tiph asks.

"Yes."

"Where?"

"I need something from you first."

"How about Berenstein Bears," says Tiph as she flips through a stack of books on Gary's bedside table. After Tiph gets Gary to fall asleep, she climbs into bed. Just as she drifts off, she hears a rustling at her window. She flips on the lights, but now she can't see outside well. She sees movement, a figure running from the window. She turns the light off. A black Honda Civic with yellow rims pulls away from the curb. Tiph double-checks the front door is locked. Who was in the Civic? Would Dex risk coming back to shake her down for a few grand even after he'd had his ass properly kicked by Mike's guys?

Tiph posts up outside an office building on Rose Avenue to talk to a man named Beetle. Pen had given her his real name, and Tiph found a LinkedIn profile that led her here to Venice. A couple of hours pass. People watching. Dog watching—Tiph decides she's going to buy one of those Akita dogs when she gets the art. Finally, a young man in a beanie emerges who matches the LinkedIn photo.

"You Beetle?"

"No."

Fuck off. "You sure as hell look like a Beetle."

"What do you want?"

"Penelope sent me."

"She paid me fair and square. I didn't do anything wrong."

"You talk like somebody who done something wrong. Look, I'm not her bounty hunter. Came to ask if there were any messages from her father."

"No."

"I gotta go back to that locked psych unit. Gimme a little more than *no*."

"Locked psych unit?"

"Yeah. She tried to play the real version of *the floor is lava*."

"What? Is she okay?"

"Seems like she's where she's supposed to be. What can you tell me about her father?"

"Look, she paid me to put up a message on the dark web."

"Dark web, what's that? Internet for Black folks?"

Beetle looks uncomfortable.

"I'm kidding. Why would she have you do that?"

"'Cause she thinks her father's in a different simulation."

"As opposed to . . ."

"This simulation. Her stance, not mine."

"This is making as much sense as seahorses."

"Me trying to tell you how Pen thinks will only result in deeper confusion. Look, I work *here* now." He motions to the office building. "But I used to do odd jobs. Coding."

"Hacking."

"We got introduced through a friend, and she paid me money to put up a message to her father on the dark web. I did that. And I *shockingly* never got a reply."

Tiph heads out of her apartment, off to see "Mike's sick aunt." She spots the Honda Civic with yellow rims again. This time parked across the street.

Tiph debates getting Mike to call Philly Deon and L-Chubbs. But if last time didn't spook Dex, what would they do this go? Kill the guy?

Tiph decides to call the local LAPD precinct in Inglewood. Once she realizes it's going to take a while, she gets in her car and heads to Norwalk, finishing answering the LAPD's questions as she drives.

Tiph has to wait a full hour before Pen gets brought into the visitation room. Halfway through the wait, an orderly in scrubs brings Tiph a cup of coffee and asks how she knows Pen. Tiph wards off the question with a casual *just friends.*

Pen has a fresh wound under her right eye.

"What happened to your face?" When Pen doesn't offer an answer, Tiph proceeds. "Well, I went and found Beetle. He works for a tech start-up in Venice now."

"Silicon Beach."

"Yup."

"Silicon is just sand."

"What?" Tiph asks.

"'Silicon Is Just Sand'—you want to know what's really going on with tech in Venice and Santa Monica, you should read it. And they don't even get to the part about why Google wanted that building so bad."

"Okay. Um, look, Beetle said he never got a message back from your father."

Pen rubs her cheeks with the pads of her fingers, then puts her head on the table.

"Sorry it's not the news you wanted," adds Tiph. "Where is Jody?"

Pen doesn't answer. She appears lost in thought, and Tiph is both curious and afraid to know what's going on between this lady's ears.

"I bit the bullet, did what you asked. Now please tell me where Jody is."

"It's Jody who bit the bullet. He's dead." Pen stands, motioning to the orderly in the hallway that she wants to return to her room. "Sorry it's not the news you wanted."

Chapter Twenty-Six

Jody

At first, the DMV list of 118 people who owned 2004–2005 black Pontiac Grand Ams is so overwhelming, Jody isn't sure it's the best use of his time. He looks into the first person on the list, and it seems like Steven Shoemaker, a thirty-seven-year-old man in Pasadena, could very well be the man he saw in Lancaster who killed his brother and father. He finds a few pictures online, and the guy looks similar enough to Jody that Wyatt's bad eyes could have mistaken one for the other. Great, so the killer could be Steven Shoemaker or it could be any of the other 117 names on the list.

But the second name is a seventy-nine-year-old Korean woman who lives in Mid-City, and Jody realizes he'll be able to eliminate many car owners by age, race, and gender. The fifty-year-old, four-hundred-pound man never could have jumped the fence in his backyard in Pennsylvania. The twenty-six-year-old Black woman from Compton would be pretty hard for Wyatt, even with his poor eyesight, to mistake for Jody.

Jody eliminates dozens of names. Some come easy. A name leads to a Facebook account. But others prove harder to link with social media profiles, like a man named William Johnson, who's forty-two years old and lives in Azusa. No shortage of Bill Johnsons in LA. Though tedious, the task gives Jody something tangible to do rather than just thinking about his brother and father.

• • •

Jody's shoulders, neck, and back ache from hunching over his computer for the bulk of the last twenty-four hours. He took breaks to eat a couple of meals, walk Rory, and sleep for three hours. He might've slept longer if Nicole hadn't been snoring on the couch. He's reduced the list from 118 to thirty-six. But he's starting to see double, and his head throbs, and he wonders if he risks crossing off a person who doesn't warrant being eliminated.

Shiloh's text comes at the perfect time. *What ya doin?*

He texts back, *Working on this list.*

Did you eat?

Not yet.

They meet at an Italian restaurant she likes in Eagle Rock called Casa Bianca.

"Wow," she says after Jody updates her on his progress.

"But it's also flawed."

"What do you mean?"

"The car could have been stolen. Wyatt could have seen the wrong color car. Or maybe I cross some seventy-year-old man off the list and it was his son who was using his car. Or maybe the guy doesn't live in Los Angeles County."

"Oh. Right," Shiloh says.

"But I still think it's the best way to proceed."

While they wait for the check, Shiloh reaches across the table and finds Jody's fingers. "What are you doing tomorrow?"

"More of the same."

The next day, Jody wakes at dawn and gets to work on the list. Nicole arrives home at 8:30 a.m. after not coming home the night before. She makes three melodramatic phone calls from the couch. Seeking white noise over Nicole's noise, Jody walks to a coffee shop. He could use the caffeine anyway. The hipster refuge is full of screenwriters slapping the keys of their MacBook Pros, but Jody manages to find a table in the back.

Even when a person matches the age, race, gender, and size, Jody's able to eliminate people from the list in other ways. Jeff Richards, a thirty-three-year-old former marine, would know how to handle a gun, but his public Instagram account shows him on his honeymoon in Maui the week Marty and Joseph Sr. were killed.

At 4:00 p.m., Jody has narrowed the list to four men who he thinks might be the killer. He stretches, drained from staring at the computer screen for two straight days but also energized by narrowing 118 names to four. One of these four people may have killed his brother and father. He glances at his phone. Shoot, he hadn't responded to a text from Shiloh six hours ago or a text from her two hours ago. He calls her.

"Where are you?"

"I'm at home," she says.

"Come meet me. I'm at Civil Coffee."

Shiloh finds Jody at a table in the back twenty-five minutes later. She's wearing a salmon-colored sundress.

Jody stands, smiling. "I got it to four people."

"Wow. How did you do that?"

He updates her on the strategies he employed.

Her face falls. "You sounded so happy on the phone. I didn't realize it was about the list."

Jody realizes she'd rushed to get ready. Her hair. The outfit. The touch of makeup.

"That's awesome. I can't believe you got it down to four."

They walk outside together. On the sidewalk, they dodge a young man riding a Bird scooter and a woman texting while walking.

"So what's next?" she asks.

"I need to see who has one leg that's longer. And *that's* the guy."

When Jody reaches for her hand, Shiloh steps off the busy sidewalk into a bus stop shelter.

"Jody. I think we should stop this."

"Stop what?"

"I think you're in *this* because I provide some connection to Marty. A connection to your dead brother."

"Is that what I am to *you*?"

"No. Maybe. No, I don't think so."

"If that's what it is to you, then we should stop."

"I think it would be natural," she says. "I mean you lost your brother and you come out here and you meet me, and I have this window into who he was."

"I don't want something with you *because* of Marty. That makes it kinda weird. I like you despite that aspect. I like you," he repeats.

She kisses him. But less tender this time. She pulls him closer, pressing their bodies together. "Did you walk here?" she asks. "Yeah," he says. "I'll drive you. Do you want to come to my place?" she asks. He nods. "Yeah." Not sure of the implication. But pretty sure.

They ride in silence until Shiloh points out the red-tailed hawks in the Verdugo Hills and the Goodyear Blimp over Griffith Park. The garage holds four sets of tandem spots. After she turns off the car, Shiloh leans over and kisses him. She takes his hand and guides him, cutting from the garage across a patch of grass to the concrete steps that lead to her second-floor apartment. They move in unison up the steps, the rhythm between them building, certain to transcend into another rhythm as soon as they get inside.

Inside, they're met with the sound of laughter. Becky has seven friends over. They're drinking margaritas, getting ready to barbecue.

Becky introduces Shiloh and Jody to her seven friends and encourages them to hang out.

Shiloh glances at her room as if debating bringing Jody inside and closing the door. "We were going to head out."

Shiloh and Jody trudge back toward the garage. The anticipation and buildup and desire dissipated.

"I guess we could go eat," Shiloh says.

"Sure."

Instead, Shiloh climbs across the armrest and cup holders into

Jody's lap, straddling him, kissing him. She pulls off his shirt. Undoes his belt.

His hands go from her ribs to her thighs, up her dress.

And they fuck in the parked car in the garage like teenagers. It's been a couple of weeks since he's masturbated, a couple of months since he had sex. Jody finds an escape he hasn't felt in what feels like forever, and he wants it to last all day. But she quivers and comes without warning, and it pushes him over the edge and he comes too.

Chapter Twenty-Seven

Renata

Renata and Coral had never set out to teach each other English and Spanish, but it happened. Their exchange of ideas isn't limited to language. They discuss food. Yoga. Religions. They alternate telling each other about books they've read and stories they've heard. Renata tells Coral about her recurring dream where she's flying in a red hot-air balloon, and Coral tells Renata about her childhood obsession with the Disney princesses. They argue about whether "The One with the Jellyfish" is the best episode of *Friends*. When one slips into despair, the other tries to cheer her up. When they're cold, they cuddle. They exercise together, doing push-ups, sit-ups, and yoga to stay healthy but also to prepare for some future possible escape attempt. They eat their meals together. They don't have a choice but to become best friends. Even their periods sync up.

But like lovers, siblings, roommates, or best friends, their relationship ebbs and flows. One—and it could be either—turns to fatalistic thoughts as a defense mechanism at a time when the other is trying to hold on to hope. Coral tends to sleep nine hours while Renata grows restless after six. Sometimes Coral masturbates in the middle of the night. The first time, Renata thought Coral was having a bad dream as her breathing picked up. Renata pretends to be asleep rather than push the issue. Coral picks strange times to sing. She likes singing rap songs and banging one hand on the wall to create a beat, her favorite being Tupac's "California Love."

Whenever Coral infuriates her, Renata reminds herself how much worse it would be stuck in this prison alone.

When they hear the hatch open, Coral and Renata scramble over for their daily meal. Next to their two sandwiches and two apples, there are six green twelve-ounce bottles.

As they eat their sandwiches they stare at the six bottles.

"You think it's beer?" asks Coral.

"Why there are no labels?"

"I dunno."

"It doesn't matter anyway," says Renata. "Can't open them. Maybe it's just a cruel joke."

Coral goes over to the hatch, where the food comes in. She lines up the bottle cap's rim on the latch that opens the hatch, and she smashes her fist down on the top of the bottle.

The cap flies right off. Coral smells the liquid. "It's beer." She's about to take a pull from the bottle.

"Don't drink it!"

"Why?"

"We don't know what's in it."

"Would they go to the trouble of feeding us every day just to try to kill us with some poisoned beer?"

Renata tries to think of a retort, but Coral dips her head back and lifts the bottom of the bottle. She swallows. Burps. "I don't even like beer that much, but this is the best goddamn beer I've ever had."

"When was your first time?" Coral asks.

"Drinking?" asks Renata.

Coral shakes her head.

"Oh," says Renata, realizing Coral's buzzed. "It was when I was sixteen. This guy who lived down the street named Tomas."

"How was it?"

"Fine," says Renata. It had been fine once it happened. But when they first tried, Tomas had come into the condom when he was rolling it down. He took out his humiliation on her, yelling at her. She had cried. He felt bad. Two hours later they tried again, and it went fine.

Coral nods, clearly wants Renata to reciprocate.

"How about you?" asks Renata.

"I was fifteen too!" Coral says, even though Renata had said she was sixteen. "It was my brother's friend Skip. He was nineteen. I worshipped him. He made me promise afterward I wouldn't tell my brother. My brother would have killed him. He looked out for me." Coral wipes her eyes. "He died of an overdose. Fentanyl. After that, there wasn't anyone looking out for me. He created a shield around me, and I didn't even know it was there until it was gone, until *he* was gone. Things got bad, and they got worse. That's why I had to leave."

Renata gives Coral a hug, which turns to gentle swaying, and Coral starts laughing and slow dancing with Renata. Coral drinks more of her beer and smiles, her meltdown already behind her.

Coral has often tried to get Renata to sing along with her, and Renata always refuses. But today, after two and a half beers, when Coral sings Tupac's "California Love" and uses her hand on the wall to create the beat, Renata sings along with her.

Coral tries to dance like Renata, holding her hands up high and shaking her ass, impersonating her in jest, but she drops the last bottle of beer.

"Coral!" says Renata, giggling.

"Whoops."

Renata and Coral pick up the pieces of glass. Renata holds up the biggest piece's most jagged edge. "Hey. Coral."

They alternate shifts. Renata uses her right hand to scrape. When that hand gets tired, she switches to her left. When her left hand gets tired, she hands off the shard of glass to Coral.

During one of Coral's shifts, Renata lies on her back to rest, tired from the work, tired from the beer. She's half-asleep when Coral shrieks. The blood spills out of her wrist at a pace that makes Renata wonder if Coral had done it on purpose. Like she had discovered another way to get out of this room. Renata scrambles over to Coral to try to help her. Coral, seeing the blood, panics, yelling and waving her arm. Renata grabs her. She tries to hold the wrist with her hand, but blood pours out.

Coral cries and continues to flail, to panic, making it harder for Renata to hold the wound.

A gas starts to fill the room. Coughing, Renata uses one hand to cover her mouth from the gas and keeps the other hand on Coral's bleeding wrist. Coral seems to welcome the gas, sucking in air as she continues to panic. Coral nods off, unconscious. Renata thinks it's because of how much blood she's lost, but she feels herself slipping away. She breathes into her shirt, trying not to take in gas. She loses grip on Coral's arm and slumps over. Before her heavy eyelids close, she gets a glimpse of otherworldly figures entering the room.

Chapter Twenty-Eight

Jody

Six minutes before El Condor closes, Jody grabs takeout and heads to Shiloh's house. He's been sleeping at her place since they *slept* together. But even though he crashed there the last four nights, they've barely seen each other. Jody has been trying to find the man with the leg discrepancy from his list of four. It took him two and a half days of staking out his garage, but once Jody got a visual of Edgar Rodriguez, a mechanic who lives in Burbank, the brown skin, potbelly, and lack of a noticeable leg-length discrepancy told Jody it wasn't him. Trent Hufton was hard to find. Like Jody, he wasn't staying at his own apartment but was staying with a lady friend. But once Jody tracked Trent down, it was easy to knock him off the list. Trent went for a jog on the street, allowing Jody to see his running form and confirm he didn't have a leg-length discrepancy of two-plus inches. With two more names off the list, he's now down to two.

Jody finds a street spot right next to the happy foot/sad foot sign that's walking distance from Shiloh's apartment. As he parallel parks, a single-word text comes in from his unwelcome guest Nicole.

Sorry.

Jody types back a question mark. He waits for a response while Rory barks at a passing poodle. Nicole doesn't respond. Jody abandons the gem of a parking spot and drives to his apartment in Mount Washington.

Two fire engines are parked on the street. The flames have been extinguished but smoke still rises from the burned back unit. The flashing lights of police cars and fire engines take Jody back to seeing the wheeled gurneys lit up with the flashing lights of the emergency vehicles. He feels like he's going to faint, so he sits down on the ground. After taking a moment to collect himself, Jody finds a livid Travis talking to two firefighters. In a tantrum, Travis tells Jody someone named Nicole called 911 about the fire but didn't stick around once the firefighters arrived. Jody apologizes. He calls Nicole three times, leaves two voice mails.

Now two hours later than he said he'd be, Jody pecks Shiloh hello. Shit. He left the food in the car. It reminds him of the night when he left the propane tank in the car and had to circle back to get it. And for the hundredth time, he wonders if it would have changed how the events went down. Would he too have been shot and killed if he'd walked in thirty seconds earlier? Or would he have apprehended the killer?

As they eat at Shiloh's kitchen table, she invites Jody to stay at her place. He feels bad accepting, but he's already been crashing with her the last few nights. Shiloh picks up a taquito but sets it down. "Are we ever going to go on a date? Like a normal date. Like normal people do?"

"I'd like that," Jody says.

"You and Marty both. It's funny."

"What?"

"Just that neither of you would take me on a normal date. But for wildly different reasons."

"I'm sorry," Jody says. He wants to go on dates with her. He wants to go on walks with her. Hikes with her. Wants to go camping with her. He wants to travel to Asia with her. Europe. He wants to watch movies with her. He wants to be the person she wants.

They eat the rest of the meal in silence. After dinner, Jody has to walk Rory and asks if she wants to join. She declines, seems irritated. Jody knows she'll ask him not to stay in her room tonight. He'll sleep on the couch and find a new apartment. He didn't even have the time or mental capacity to take her out on a normal date. It's too soon for them to live together.

Jody cleans up and takes out the trash. When he comes back up, Shiloh is in her room. Becky's door is closed. Jody plans to sleep on the couch. He won't make Shiloh ask him. He just needs to take a quick shower first. As he's drying off, the door swings open. Jody throws the towel around his waist, unsure whether it's Shiloh or Becky. It's Shiloh. Presumably to tell him to sleep on the couch or to find a new place to stay. She moves to Jody. Like she's moving to hit him, and he staggers back and knocks a snow globe off a shelf next to the sink. She comes right into his body, kisses him for a fraction of a second before she drops to her knees, pulling his towel down as she goes to the ground. She rises to her feet and her gym shorts are somehow at her ankles and she sits on the sink's edge and pulls Jody between her legs, pulls Jody into her. Over her shoulder, the mirror grants a view of the greatest ass west of the Mississippi.

Later, Jody climbs into bed, and Shiloh curls up to him. Another mystery he may never solve, the mystery of women.

Chapter Twenty-Nine

Pen

"Thinking about O and that other world." Pen reads Marty's words aloud from her own transcript. Pen had decided to edit together a video to include in her Kickstarter campaign for her documentary film *The Breach*. She's been going back through *My Dirty California* videos to find clips to include. Her agent, Daniel, and the film execs had trouble tracking her leap from Marty and Jody to Pandora's House and the simulation gap. She tries to find the best clips to make the relationship clear between Marty's death and the breach. She's debating using this whole entry that Marty made back on April 9, where he mentions *thinking about O and that other world*. In a notebook, she had transcribed the whole video journal entry. She stares at the O, imagining it's a gap, imagines slipping inside it and jumping to another place, imagines finding her father, imagines him saying, *I knew you'd find me, Pen.*

Chapter Thirty

Jody

For the second day in a row, Jody follows Ross Lemon from Ross's house in El Segundo to an office in Larchmont Village. Jody's down to two names on the DMV list. While staking out the office in Larchmont and hoping to get a better look at Ross, Jody kills time by looking at Marty's *My Dirty California* project on his phone.

He hones in on a particular post. He had watched it before, but at the time he thought maybe O was a drug.

"Today was a hard day. Maybe it was easier because it wasn't my decision. I didn't see it before, but now I see this inflection point between worlds. Two different worlds. Sliding doors. Brick and no brick. And thinking about O and that other world, I start to smile and wonder. But it's not many-worlds, it's one, and there's no going back. Someone out there would call it murder. I'm not one of those people, and yet I still feel guilty. Maybe we should have gone for it. It's too late now. Fuck. In the blink of an eye, in this world and then in no world, depending on what you believe."

Jody watches the entry again and again. It stands out against every other video and essay and blog post. Marty looks distorted, unsettled. He fidgets and avoids eye contact with the camera. His voice sounds insecure, shaken, fatalistic. Jody keeps thinking about the words *someone out there would call it murder.*

He watches the entry four more times while he pets Rory, waiting outside the building where Ross Lemon works. He follows

Ross home to El Segundo and still manages not to get a good look at the guy.

By the time he gets back to Shiloh's in Silver Lake, it's 9:00 p.m. He'd spent four and a half hours driving and another ten hours sitting in his car looking at a house, then an office building, and then a house again.

After they eat eggs and toast for dinner, Jody asks, "Will you watch something for me? One of Marty's videos."

"I told you they made me feel weird."

"I know. I'm sorry, Shi. I won't make you unless I have a specific question." It was the first time he called her *Shi*. The back of her first name was taken by Marty, so Jody went with the front.

As Shiloh watches the video, Marty watches Shiloh. Her face tightens.

"I told you I didn't wanna watch these."

When it's over, Jody asks, "Is there something you're not telling me? About Marty being involved with some crime or something?"

Shiloh keeps scrunching up her face; she's holding in the tears. And she can't do it anymore. The dam breaks, and the tears flow.

Jody waits for an explanation. Rory nestles up to Shiloh's leg.

"I got an abortion."

It all clicks. The mood, the tone, the euphemisms for life and death. Murder. Regrets. Guilt. Spiritual undertones, afterlife or lack of one.

"I'm sorry," Jody says.

He's so focused on the entry not aiding his investigation that a couple of minutes pass before he thinks about the abortion. If she hadn't, would they have stayed together? Would Marty have avoided whatever trouble he found himself in? Would Marty still be alive? Would his father still be alive, on his way to becoming a grandfather? Maybe Jody would be an uncle. Uncle Jody.

"I care about you, Jody. What's it going to do to you if you figure out what happened to Marty and you find out he got himself into some mess? That he's not just some innocent victim but that he did *something*?" Shiloh continues crying. Jody's not sure how to answer.

Shiloh stops crying even faster than she started. "I'm going for a run," she says.

Jody knows whatever they have going can't last. She'll break it off. Maybe not when she gets back from her run. And maybe not tomorrow. But it will happen.

Chapter Thirty-One

Tiph

Tiph's phone rings, the caller ID reads *California State Prison*. She slides right to answer the call, wondering if it will be Mike or Philip.

It's Philip.

"Just checking in," he says. "Mike told me about the Brinks armored car reservation."

"Yeah, Eagle Rock to Palm Springs. Makes me think the art stash might be in Eagle Rock."

"I agree. He had been doing a remodel on his Palm Springs house. Makes sense he would take the art there when he was done."

"Okay, so what did Chester have in Eagle Rock? An office or storage unit or something?"

"I don't know."

Tiph thought Philip was calling with information. "You have no idea?"

"No."

"C'mon, man. I'm out here killing birds with stones and leaving none of 'em unturned."

The doorbell rings. A Latina LAPD officer on the other side of the peephole.

"I gotta go." Tiph hangs up the phone.

"Ti-phony?" asks the cop. She's got a soft body but hard eyes.

"Yeah, Tiphony."

"You called about the car with the yellow rims."

"Yes."

"My partner and I spoke with the individual."

"Was it that Dex guy?"

"No. It was a woman. I don't believe it had anything to do with you. She was looking for a man she was involved with named Mike."

"Wait, what? Mike? That's my husband. Who was this?"

"I'm sorry, ma'am, report said you lived alone," says the officer as she shuffles her feet.

"Who said they were *involved* with my husband?"

"Ma'am, I don't want to get involved."

"Too late. You involved. Who was this lady?"

"Alexandra."

Tiph's whole body tightens up—her throat, her fists, her shoulders. "And she said what now?"

"She said Mike wouldn't call her or text her back, and she was waiting for him to get home to confront him," the cop says.

"Well, she gon' have to wait a year."

Tiph makes Gary go to bed early and then drinks glasses of wine. Wine tends to make her mellow, but there's no mellowing to be had tonight. The buzz turns melancholy to rage, like adding water to an oil fire. She'd never once suspected Mike of cheating. But maybe she shouldn't be surprised *Scheming Mike* had a sidepiece. Her girlfriends Tracy and Monique had always warned her Mike was the type who couldn't keep his dick in his pocket. They saw all his semi-duplicitous moneymaking plans as indicators of an adulterer. Tiph had always defended Mike to her friends, saying he was loyal as a dog.

Mike is a dog. The metaphor hasn't changed. Just the implication.

Tiph wakes up hungover. She spends the whole morning hating Mike. After lunch, she fishes out a business card from her purse.

"Hello?"

"DeAndre?"

"Yeah."

"It's Tiphony."

"Who?"

"I came into your work a few weeks ago. You gave me your card."

"Girl with the heartbreaking smile."

"Your offer for dinner still stand?"

"Most def does."

"Are you free?"

"Yeah. When's good? This weekend?"

"How about tonight?"

"Tonight, no I got . . ." He pauses, starts over. "I can move it. Yeah I can be free. You like Italian? There's this place in Culver City. Novacento."

Tiph was so nervous about calling him she forgot about her current travel limitations. "How about I make you dinner at my place?"

Tiph has her mom pick up Gary for the night, telling her she has a stomach bug. Tiph wears her long blue sundress from Sabrak. The dress drags and picks up dirt so she rarely wears it. But it's one of the few outfits she has that will cover up her monitor.

DeAndre talks and talks, whether out of confidence or insecurity, bouncing without transitions between hip-hop, nineties nostalgia, politics, and his family.

"Few years from now, everybody's gonna be ghostridin' the whip."

"What?" asks Tiph, realizing her mind was wandering.

"Self-driving cars."

"Oh."

They move to the couch after eating chicken tacos.

"Hold on." She gets up and hits the light. Hoping he won't see the monitor in the dark. When she gets back on the couch, he pulls her dress over her head, lays her on the cushions.

"Oh," he says, his mouth lingering in an o-shaped look of shock.

"Shit."

"You on house arrest?"

"I was hoping you wouldn't see that." Flustered, she reaches for her dress to put it back on.

"Nah, it's cool. It's hot. How long you been stuck in this place? Huh? Called me up to come take care of your needs?"

She smiles as he pulls her on top of him. Mike's betrayal had motivated her to fish out DeAndre's card from her purse. Even if it began that way, it isn't about revenge or spite now. Just raw attraction. There's clunkiness in the newness of it all. But there's passion in the newness of it all too.

As they get dressed after, DeAndre gazes at her for a moment.

"What?" she asks.

"I was going to ask you about that day in Brinks. Why you were asking about that Chester Montgomery guy."

"Oh." The question takes her out of the post-sex bliss. It takes her right back to the treasure hunt she'd quit. Right back to Mike. And his schemes. And her marriage. And her bills. It takes her right back to everything she wanted to escape by having DeAndre come over. "It was something I was looking into, but it didn't work out."

"Okay?" DeAndre appears offended by her vagueness. The salesman with the swagger who had artfully navigated every crevice of her body now seems delicate. Tiph doesn't have space for his emotional neediness. And she knows how to get rid of him.

"I gotta go pick up my son," she says.

"You got a kid?"

"Yeah," Tiph says unapologetically. "I do."

Chapter Thirty-Two

Jody

After multiple days of following Ross Lemon from his house to his sales job and back again, Jody comes up with a new strategy. He pretends to be a potential customer and sits in for a thirty-minute tutorial on a coworking office space. Ross does the presentation standing, which gives Jody a half hour to analyze the man's posture. His legs are even. Ross Lemon is not the killer. Jody has now ruled out 117 of the 118 people on the DMV list.

Jody waits in his truck parked across the street from the house of Derrick Fletcher. Derrick is the last remaining possible suspect on his DMV hit list. He's a thirty-nine-year-old man who worked for a private security firm in Yemen for a few years and later worked as a researcher for a law firm in Los Angeles. As much as anyone else, his profile matches that of a contract killer. Jody watches the man's house in Little Ethiopia for several hours. Anxiety keeps him from falling asleep, anxiety over what he'll do if Derrick doesn't have a leg-length discrepancy. Will he return to names he crossed off the list? Will he expand the list to cars registered outside LA County?

He's drifting off again when the door opens across the street. Out walks a man wearing carpenter jeans and a T-shirt two sizes too big. He's the exact shape of the man Jody'd seen in Lancaster.

But as he steps off the porch toward the street, he takes long, even steps. Stable core, even hips. No leg-length discrepancy. This wasn't the man Jody chased out of his house back in Pennsylvania.

Jody's mind fidgets. Should he second-guess his gut instinct that the killer had a leg-length discrepancy? Should he question Wyatt's memory of the car? Or his theory the same man who had been searching Marty's apartment in LA was the same man who came to Pennsylvania and killed him? Should he not have assumed the driver of the car was the owner of the car?

He turns his eyes back to the street, where the man climbs inside a blue van. On the side, it reads *S&L Heating and Air-Conditioning*. He isn't Derrick Fletcher. He's a heating and air-conditioning guy at Derrick Fletcher's house. Jody watches as the blue-collar red herring van pulls away. The black 2004 Pontiac Grand Am remains in the driveway.

When Jody returns his gaze to the house, another man has stepped out onto the front porch. The actual Derrick Fletcher. He walks out into his front yard.

Jody doesn't have to be close to him to see it.

Without a doubt, this man has a significant leg-length discrepancy. The right leg longer than the left. His head leans to the right. Pelvic tilt. Excessive foot pronation on the right. When he walks, his arm swing is greater on the left. Jody's knuckles crack from clutching the steering wheel. His heart thumps, the validation sends this blast of adrenaline—nearing euphoria—through his blood. But there's also an anger bubbling in his veins. This man, not twenty-five yards away from him, killed his brother and father.

And Jody's not the only one to know it. Rory leaps out the open passenger side window and runs straight for Derrick, who's walking across the yard toward his Pontiac.

Jody can only hope now Derrick doesn't recognize his mutt from their encounter on the other side of the country six weeks ago. Jody slumps low in the driver's seat as Rory runs across the neighborhood street.

Jody hadn't yet worked out what he'd do once he found the man who he thought had killed Marty and his father. A leg-length discrepancy and a witness account from a near-blind weapons dealer wasn't going to get the cops interested let alone a warrant. Jody had thought about ways he might interrogate a suspect. Break into their house. Follow them, learn their schedule. He had the advantage in finding Derrick without Derrick knowing anyone was onto him. But the minute Derrick knows, Jody's edge will disappear.

Staying low in his seat, pulse hammering, Jody watches Rory run to Derrick, barking. Derrick raises his hands. "Whoa! Whoa, boy!"

He won't recognize the dog, Jody tells himself. Yes, Derrick had seen Rory back in Pennsylvania, but it was in a moment of chaos in the dark of night. And Rory isn't a particularly recognizable dog.

Rory bites and barks and circles and howls and snarls. Derrick uses his foot to step on Rory's neck and pin the dog, exposing Rory's collar. Derrick takes Rory's collar in one hand. And now he must be seeing the name on the tag, Jody Morrel.

Derrick looks up from the dog, his face white, his eyes wide. He scans the street, his callous gape honing in on Jody's gray Ford truck.

Chapter Thirty-Three

Renata

Renata wakes, eyelids heavy and brain foggy. She feels woozy most days, stuck in this prison or whatever it is. But today, she feels sluggish and disconnected. The gas that had knocked her out had put her into a deeper kind of sleep. Across the room, Coral lies on her side. Is she dead?

Renata speed-crawls over to her.

Coral is breathing. Her wrist is bandaged with layer upon layer of white athletic tape.

Renata crawls back over to her bedding. She rests a while before a metal object catches her eye. She crawls over to the center of the room and picks it up. It's a metal foot. Like a charm or a large key chain, about one-eighth the size of a human adult foot. Engraved on the bottom is *DAVEY*. She assumes it must have fallen out of a pocket when the two men came in to patch up Coral's wound.

As Renata fiddles with the foot, the pinky toe moves. And now she knows what it is.

Coral sleeps for a couple more hours. Renata stares at the greenish fiberglass walls and thinks, a plan forming in her head.

When Coral wakes, she clutches her bandaged wrist and looks at Renata. "How did you do this?"

"I didn't. They came in."

"You saw them?"

"Yes, when I was part awake. Before I passed out too. I think they were wearing masks."

"Masks?"

"To breathe." Renata points toward the hatch where their food comes each day. "The hatch is in the middle of the door. If you look close, you can see the cracks."

"So there is a door . . ."

How could they have gotten inside if not through a door? And yet both had ended up in the room through such bizarre circumstances that being stuck in a room with no door still might not have been the hardest part to accept.

Coral can't stop rubbing the bandaged wrist with her other hand.

"Do you feel okay?" Renata asks.

"So-so. Maybe the hunger strike would have worked," Coral says, holding up her wrist. "I just mean, they saved me, so maybe they would have done something if we had refused to eat."

"Maybe, maybe not. I have a new plan. For how we can escape."

"How?"

"Like you said, they saved you. This means they saw you were bleeding. Which means there must be a camera in here. I think I found it." Renata points to the upper corner, left of the wall where the hatch and door are. "So if there is a fire, we could let smoke fill the room. And they will see it on the camera. And when they come in to put out the fire, we leave out the door."

"You think they'd let us run out?"

"Once the room fills with smoke and they can't see, we crawl over to the hatch, hide off to the side. Then they come in to put out the fire, and we slip right out the door."

"It would take a lot of smoke to fill the room."

"We have our clothes. The two blankets. The pillows."

"Do you think that will be enough?"

"I don't know."

"It's a good idea. Too bad we have no way to start a fire."

Renata holds up the metal silver-colored Davey-inscribed foot. "It must have fallen out of one of their pockets when they came in."

"What is it?"

Renata uses her body to shield the camera from seeing the foot. She holds it toes pointed up. She pulls the pinky toe out from the ring toe, and a flame pops up from the top of the big toe.

Chapter Thirty-Four

Pen

Pen looks up from the 1933 map of Hollywood to see a man in a tracksuit divert his eyes. Is he following her? She's been in the LA Central Library all morning. Her mind cycles through who might be tailing her. She walks out of the room, glances back. The guy in the tracksuit stays.

Riding the escalator, Pen gets an alert on her phone, another pledge to her Kickstarter campaign. She logs into her account and sees a user named BrianTilTheEndofTime has made a $20 commitment. There's also a new comment from the same user. *Just pledged twenty bones to see this crazy lady's wack movie.* After a full week, Pen's Kickstarter campaign has gotten $190 in commitments. How could there be so few? Is the government blocking pledges? She thinks again of the man in the tracksuit.

Another alert goes off on her phone. But it's not a new Kickstarter pledge. It's a reminder from her calendar app: Shiloh gets home from Italy today.

A woman answers the door with a red towel around her wet hair. She's wearing the tiniest shorts and a big T-shirt that reads *Lizards Doing Pushups*.

"Hi, are you Shiloh?"

"Yeah."

"My name's Penelope. I'm a friend of Jody's."

"You *are*?"

Pen senses Shiloh sizing her up. Is it out of jealousy?

"Yeah. I came by a few weeks ago. And your roommate said you were on a trip."

"I got back late last night."

"How was it?" Pen wants to make conversation before milking Shiloh for intel.

"I didn't get to see much. Mostly babysat in hotel rooms while the kids' parents drank wine. Not a bad way to pay rent though."

"Cool," Pen says. *Maybe that's enough small talk.* "I was hoping you could tell me where Jody is."

"You said you're a friend of his?"

Pen senses Shiloh's skepticism and tries to think of a lie that will put her at ease. "He hired me as a researcher, to help figure out what happened to Marty. I'm a documentary filmmaker. But he's not answering his phone. And I'm worried something happened to him. I was curious when was the last time you talked to him?"

"It was a few weeks before I went to Italy."

"Did anything significant happen?"

"He wanted to know if Salvatore Jenkins was the Sal I met through Marty. He showed me a picture, and I said it was him."

"And what happened?"

"That was all that happened."

"Do you know where Jody's staying?"

Shiloh stares at Pen, hesitates.

Pen adds, "I know he had to move out of his place in Mount Washington after the fire."

Shiloh lets down her guard. "Yeah. I think he's still renting a room in Palms. This little yellow house across the street from the Cheviot Hills Shopping Center. Maybe on Shelby. Or Castle Heights."

Pen finds the house Shiloh described, nothing more than a stucco shanty. A forty-year-old man with a beard answers the door.

"Hi," he says.

Something about him reminds Pen of her father. She struggles to speak.

"Can I help you?" His mannerisms, his beard, his brown eyes.

"Sorry, uh, I was looking for Jody. Does he live here?"

"He used to. You a friend of his?"

Pen can't look at him without flashing to memories of her father. Buying her an ice cream sandwich at Diddy Riese and telling her it's always ice cream weather in LA and warning her their world might not make it through Y2K. Playing with his beard when he was working a problem out in his head. Explaining to her at Mel's diner why her mother had moved to Missouri. Taking her to this bridge with Gothic turrets in Franklin Hills. Asking a stranger to take a picture of them in front of the Great Heron Gates at the LA River. Leaving her with a babysitter and telling her he'd be back in a few hours the night he disappeared.

"Sort of. Friend of a friend."

He invites her inside. After some small talk, Pen asks, "Do you know where he is?"

"No. But wherever that is, he was going for three months."

"What do you mean?"

"Well, he moved out, but he asked me if he could leave some stuff here. A plastic bin. He said he was going on a trip for three months. I didn't mind throwing it in the linen closet." He motions down the hallway when he says *linen closet*. "Anything else?" He had seemed generous with his time to invite her inside, but now he seems anxious for her to leave.

"No, guess not. Well, thank you. Actually do you mind if I use the bathroom first?"

"No, right there on the right."

Pen dips into the bathroom and turns on the fan. She unravels fifty-some squares of toilet paper, throws them in the toilet, and flushes. It all goes down. She doubles the amount of toilet paper. And when it runs out, she throws in five tissues for good measure. She flushes the toilet. This time it jams. Pen emerges from the bathroom. "This is so embarrassing. I think the toilet's clogged."

"Oh," he says, equally embarrassed. He jogs into the bathroom, where water runs over the toilet bowl's edge.

Pen scoots down the hall, finds the linen closet, and opens the pantry-style doors. She spots a blue polypropylene tub. Inside: clothes, books, and a computer. She grabs the computer. She wishes she had a bag with her. She shoves the laptop up the back of her T-shirt. She keeps her hands on her hips to hold the T-shirt in place. He'll be able to see the computer's shape if he sees her back. She returns to the kitchen as he emerges from the bathroom.

"Sorry about that," she says. She keeps pivoting to face him.

"That's okay," he says, irritated.

"Thanks again for the info on Jody."

She keeps her hands on her hips and walks backward to the front door.

On Jody's computer, Pen finds the folder with all of Jody's *My Dirty California* video files. Jody hadn't uploaded twenty of the more recent videos to the *My Dirty California* site. The videos seem to be therapeutic exercises for Jody as opposed to specific updates on his investigation. But four stick out to her as helpful.

In one, Jody says the man who shot his brother and father is now dead. He appears distraught, like he's confessing to a murder. Easy to fathom why he didn't upload this video. Jody never names the person who killed Marty. *Who was it?* In this same video, Jody mentions losing Rory. *So Jody found out who killed his brother and then killed him? And lost his dog in the process?*

In another video, Jody complains about not being able to figure out who Roller is. Pen can imagine why a person with a nickname that simple and common might be hard to identify. In this video, Jody, maybe drunk, goes from venting about Roller to venting about his own videos.

"I'm never going to solve this thing. All I'm doing is making videos, just a list of videos. It's no different from the list of possible careers I made. Or the list of houses for sale. Didn't pursue any of the careers or buy any of the houses. Just lists. And now I've got another one."

In a video weeks later, in the midst of a thirty-minute sob-fest into the camera, Jody complains about overlooking Chester Montgomery. Pen remembers Marty's *My Dirty California* video about going to Chester Montgomery's house in the Hollywood Hills. And she also vaguely remembers Jody's post about looking into Chester and writing him off.

In the last video saved on his computer, Jody goes on long rants broken up by strange, sometimes unintelligible tangents, but at one point he mentions Marty having worked with a dirty cop. He says multiple times in a row, "Shiloh was right. Marty got himself in trouble."

Chapter Thirty-Five

Jody

Once Derrick Fletcher spots Jody sitting in his Ford truck, Jody doesn't have a second to waste. He throws open the door of his truck, jumps out, and sprints straight at Derrick. Pulling out Wyatt's pistol as he runs. Derrick might have made it inside the house, but when he takes his foot off Rory to run, Rory bites his ankle. Derrick's able to kick his leg free, but it delays him long enough that Jody reaches him before Derrick reaches the front steps.

"Stop," Jody threatens, gun aimed at the man's head. Derrick raises his hands.

Rory runs around the front yard in circles, barking, growling, then barking again.

"Get in your car," Jody says.

Derrick hesitates.

"Go. Walk."

Derrick walks, hands still in the air, toward his Pontiac Grand Am parked in the driveway. Jody follows behind him. Rory keeps running in circles in the yard, barking.

"Rory! Come on!"

If he keeps barking this loud, people will come out.

"Rory, let's go."

But Rory keeps barking. Jody's exposed, holding the gun on a man in broad daylight. He'll have to come back for his dog.

"Get in your car."

When Derrick hesitates, Jody presses the gun into his back. Derrick climbs in the driver's seat, and Jody climbs in right behind him.

"Drive."

"Where are we going?" asks Derrick, putting on his seat belt.

"Turn right out of the driveway. I'll tell you where to go. Just drive. Straight here. Left at the stop sign."

Jody remembers an out-of-business Ross store where he'd posted up on an empty rooftop parking lot on one of his DMV-list stakeouts. A good place to interrogate Derrick.

Jody was planning to wait until he gets there. But he can't. "You know who I am?"

"No."

"You remember me. You remember seeing me the night you killed my brother. And my dad."

"I don't know what you're talking about."

"Fuck you. Turn right here."

Derrick turns. Up ahead, at the next red light, there's an LAPD patrol car waiting in the middle lane. Jody's and Derrick's eyes meet in the rearview mirror.

"Don't do anything funny. I will kill you. You killed my family. I'll do it."

Derrick stays in the far-right lane and pulls up next to the cop. Jody makes sure to keep the gun out of view. Derrick glances over at the cop but then looks straight ahead.

The light turns green.

"Turn right." Jody doesn't want to go right, but he wants to get away from this cop. Derrick complies, right on Orange Grove. "I want to know why."

"I don't know what to tell you."

"You don't even know why, do you? It was a contract? That what you are, a contractor?"

Derrick doesn't answer.

A contract killer? A hit man? Jody repositions his weight and tightens his grip on the gun. Derrick may try to lunge for it.

"Left at the light."

Derrick turns left. Now on La Brea.

"Stay in the right lane. You're going to tell me who hired you, then."

Derrick doesn't answer. Jody reaches his hand along the center console and shoves the gun into Derrick's ribs.

"Who hired you?"

"Roller."

"Roller?"

"See you haven't gotten very far yet."

"Fuck you. Who's Roller?"

Derrick looks at Jody in the rearview mirror again. Jody takes his eyes off the road and retains full eye contact with Derrick. Waiting for him to answer. There's a glimmer in Derrick's eyes. Jody doesn't understand why until he looks back to the road as Derrick plows into the car in front of them going thirty miles per hour. The car in front, a Chevy Blazer, was at a complete stop at a red light.

Derrick's deployed air bag—and seat belt—catch him. Jody goes flying through the gap between the two front seats, over the cup holders. The forward momentum sends him all the way up onto the dashboard and into the windshield but not through it. The glass spiderwebs but holds. Jody bounces off the windshield and rolls back headfirst onto the floor beneath the passenger seat.

Throughout the turmoil, Jody tries to protect his head and hang on to the gun.

Once Derrick realizes Jody didn't die or drop the gun, he opens the door to flee.

Jody scrambles to get upright and go after Derrick. He's right side up in time to witness Derrick get out of the car and get struck by a silent monster—a Tesla Model 3 in the center lane. The light had turned green, and the Tesla must have been coming down the center lane, no cars in front of it, approaching a green light.

Jody, still trying to get his bearings, remains in the car, looking in every direction. He spots Derrick, twenty-five yards away in the middle of the intersection. All in one piece—flesh, bones, head, limbs. But the piece is lifeless.

It's not hard for Jody to pretend he has to throw up.

Various firefighters and police huddle in groups. Jody is in the middle of giving his statement to a cop when he feigns—half feigns—the need to vomit. He darts over to a jade plant in a front yard, and as he bends over, he pulls out the gun and shoves it under the plant. His story will have a better time sticking if he's not holding Wyatt's *one-time whistle*.

He walks back over to Officer Spencer, the fortysomething LAPD cop who's been taking his statement.

"You okay, Jody? Maybe you got a concussion. We better get you to the hospital."

"I'll be okay. Thought I was gonna puke, sorry. I'm fine though, really." He hadn't told them he'd hit the windshield. He hadn't told them he'd been in the back seat or that he wasn't wearing a seat belt.

"Okay, well if you change your mind, I'll have one of the guys give you a ride. If you're worried about the money, there's an urgent care a mile from here."

Jody shakes his head.

"All right, well, let's finish up so you can get outta here. So how did you know Mr. Fletcher?"

"I actually didn't. He was doing some work on his house and wanted to hire some workers . . . ehhh, for ehhh, well, for cash."

"It's okay. I don't have to write that down. I can say you were associates or colleagues. So you didn't know him well?"

Jody starts to get paranoid about appearing in the accident report. About Derrick's employer coming to kill Jody. But what can he do?

"Jody?"

"Sorry, I didn't really know him. No. It was my first day helping him. We were going to the hardware store."

"And he hit the car in front of you."

"Yeah. And he was getting out to make sure they were okay. And he stepped right in front of the Tesla."

"Okay. Well, I've got your info. Here, take my card if something comes up. Or you want someone to show ya around, I know you said you just got here."

He hands Jody his card. Is the cop hitting on him? Jody pretends like he doesn't pick up on it and shoves the card in his back pocket.

Jody takes an Uber back to Derrick's house to get his truck. And to get Rory. He's worried a neighbor might have seen him pull the gun and there might be more cops around, but the street is quiet as a morgue when he exits the Nissan Uber.

Rory doesn't come bounding over to him. Jody finds his truck empty; Rory hadn't hopped back in the window. He tells himself what he told himself when he left Rory there. Somebody will find him and call the number on his collar and Jody will go pick up his dog. Nobody would steal an ugly mutt like Rory. That's when the setting sun catches a piece of metal in Derrick's yard. Jody jogs over to the shiny object, hoping it's a coin or a piece of scrap metal. But he knows what it is. He picks up Rory's collar. Jody's name and phone number engraved on it. It must have come off in the skirmish with Derrick. Which means it's not as easy as somebody finding Rory and calling the number on the tag.

Jody knocks on doors, walks the whole block. He calls every shelter and animal control place within two square miles. He goes full Ace Ventura, Pet Detective. But no hits.

At 10:00 p.m., it sets in that Jody might not get his dog back. That Derrick, the hit man who had taken his brother and father, has now in a way taken his dog too.

Jody alternates hours of sleeping and lying awake. In the morning, he lies still in bed, trying not to wake Shiloh. His shoulder throbs too much to move anyway. He had come in late the night before, after stopping to pick up the gun he stashed, and he'd been too drained to tell Shiloh about Rory. And he wasn't sure he should tell her about Derrick. She knew something was off and asked what happened, but he played coy, took a shower, and got in bed. Now, he stares at the ceiling, one word echoing in his brain. One big little word. *Why*. The *who* was handled, but it's the *why* that matters.

When she wakes, Shiloh glances at him, sees he's awake, and disappears into the kitchen.

As they eat breakfast, Shiloh eats slower than normal. For an elegant woman, she tends to eat like a fourteen-year-old boy. But today, she chews slowly. When she's done, she says, "I need to talk to you."

"Okay."

"Did you know I had a brother?"

"No."

"He died. When he was sixteen. I was fourteen."

"I'm sorry." So they'd both lost a brother, thinks Jody. He ponders what it would have been like to lose Marty at different ages.

"Sixteen years old. A kid."

Based on the age, Jody guesses car accident or drug overdose. "What happened?"

"Car accident."

"I'm sorry."

"It was a long time ago. But not a day goes by I don't slip back into that place of thinking on it, obsessing over it, missing him. That event, it changed my whole family dynamic. I was depressed for years, had to see a shrink, got put on pills, had to work my way off them. My parents got divorced; I dunno, maybe they would have anyway. But I'm saying this tragic event seemed to shape my whole life. On top of the grief you're going through, you're trying to figure out what happened to Marty. And if I can help, I want to. Still. If there's anything, any time of day, call me. But mixing that with *this*, whatever we're starting, I can't do it. I feel myself slipping back into that previous fourteen-year-old version of myself."

"I get it."

"I don't want you to feel like I'm bailing on you when you need me."

"I don't think that." He'd anticipated this and had anticipated sadness and rejection. But instead he feels relief. Falling for Shiloh had become complicated by the guilt over not being able to be the right kind of man for her. Jody has enough guilt.

Chapter Thirty-Six

Tiph

Tiph scrolls through Netflix, trying to pick a show to watch. She's done with the wild-goose art chase, the mapless treasure hunt. Thinking about the art stash makes her think of Mike, and that makes her think of Mike's betrayal. Plus she doesn't have any leads. She lets it all go. The dream of finding the art. And the dream of a new life: Jimmy Choo heels, American Express card, espresso maker, hot tub, Nobu sushi, rain shower.

Her days slide into a pattern. When she's not looking after Gary or picking up the occasional shift cleaning houses, she lies around and watches whatever the algorithms suggest. She assumed DeAndre wouldn't call now that he knows she has a son. But he does call. A couple of times. Followed by texts. Tiph doesn't respond.

On her fourth night in a row streaming mediocre programs, she gets another text from DeAndre. *Yo.*

Tiph stares at the text. She can't put him off any longer, him being Mike.

Tiph picks up the phone.

"What the fuck?"

She stares back at Mike through the glass, greeting his nervy tone with an icy glare.

"Why you been ducking me? Where's Gary?"

"I didn't bring him."

"Why not?"

Again, Tiph stares him down through the glass.

"You can keep on with that cold shoulder. Shit, being in here, cold shoulders ain't exactly what I fear."

"I know about your sidepiece."

"What?"

"She came by looking for you, saying you wouldn't return her texts or calls."

"This a joke?"

Go ahead and lie through your busted-ass teeth. "Go ahead and lie through that gap in your teeth."

"How you think I got something on the side up in here?"

"Must've been from before. She stopped hearing from you 'cause your dumb ass in prison, so she came to our house."

"I don't know if you're trying to trap me into saying somebody or saying something. I can't tell you who it is or worry about who it might could be 'cause there ain't nobody. After that last time we made it official and you got pregnant, I ain't been with nobody."

He stares, the Scheming Mike poker face trying to bluff her.

"Alexandra," Tiph says as if laying down an unbeatable hand.

"Alexandra? Are you serious? That's the bitch I told you I had to get a restraining order against like three years ago. Xanny."

Tiph hadn't forgotten about the crazy girl Mike met when he got into a scheme selling studio space to musicians. She hadn't forgotten how funny turned to troubling when Mike said she had started stalking him. And she hadn't forgotten about Mike getting the restraining order. But she managed to forget—or maybe she never knew—Xanny was short for Alexandra.

"Why the fuck would I cheat on you with that crazy bitch? She ain't even hotter than you. I wouldn't cheat on you, and I haven't, but if I was gonna, she'd have to be fly as hell." Mike laughs. "Tiph, I'm kidding. What's wrong?"

"Nothing."

"Tiph? What? Is there something else?"

Tiph had never strayed in her marriage. She hates it when cheaters claim it's a selfish act to tell your significant other you cheated because it's your way of relieving your own guilt. Tiph always thought that was bullshit, a way for assholes to justify tacking deceit onto adultery.

But Mike is already trying to get through hell-in-a-cell, and she's not about to make his life any harder by telling him how she had sex with the dude from Brinks after she made him tacos, Mike's favorite food.

Chapter Thirty-Seven

Jody

Jody sublets a bedroom in a three-bed/two-bath apartment in Highland Park. Since Nicole burned down his last rental, he'd been crashing with Shiloh, which he shouldn't have done. It was too much, too fast.

Every day he spends an hour or two looking for Rory, calling shelters, putting up posters. He tries and fails to find out who Roller might be. He watches and rewatches various *My Dirty California* entries. He makes near-daily videos himself, reporting his findings. Because he's not finding any fresh leads, the videos end up as sessions for brainstorming new possible avenues or reviewing old intel. OCPD lists of lists.

He attends Derrick Fletcher's funeral. A hodgepodge of folks show up. A couple of friends. A neighbor. No one seems to have known him. An estranged brother flies in from Alaska to handle the arrangements, but two minutes into their discussion, Jody realizes he knows more about Derrick than his brother does.

Jody drinks beer in the evenings, trying to dull the pains and anxieties. Nausea follows in the morning, also serving to dull the pains and anxieties. But he ends up hating himself for being less productive as he pedals through the endless loop of investigation. Look for Rory. Watch *My Dirty California* videos. Dig through the infinite wasteland of the World Wide Web for information on Derrick, Roller, and Marty.

In the midst of all these searches, multiple times a day, Jody tries to convince himself he got the guy who killed his brother and father.

That it's over. But he can't ever go more than a fleeting moment without confronting the reality *somebody* hired Derrick. Derrick was an extension of the gun. Not the one who had decided Marty would die.

His two-week sublet at the dingbat in Highland Park runs out, and he finds a new place to crash in Palms, another sublet, this one a room in a yellow house. From the east side to the west side, his home base different but his routine the same. His grit and determination keep him on a cycle yielding zero results, and Jody wonders again if he shouldn't have left his antianxiety medication back in Pennsylvania.

Chapter Thirty-Eight

Renata

Renata and Coral eat sandwiches and apples. Sometimes the food comes with napkins, sometimes it doesn't. Today it does. They've been storing whatever paper and cardboard products come with their meals, adding them to their stash of flammable items. Two weeks ago, they used their blankets to clean up a fake digestive disaster and spent the night pretending to shiver. The next night, it got cold enough they didn't have to pretend to shiver. After their third night of consecutive shivering, they were gifted two more blankets.

Coral stops chewing. "I just thought of something."

"What?"

"What if they're not here?"

"What do you mean?"

"I mean what if we start the fire, and they're not watching. The whole plan is contingent on them rushing in here to put out the fire, which is contingent on them seeing the fire in the first place."

Renata hadn't thought of this. She'd been too proud of the idea, hadn't tested every aspect.

"I mean, they're not just sitting there watching us twenty-four hours a day. How could they be, right? So if they don't put out the fire, what, we burn to death?"

"I think it'll go out on its own." Renata thinks back to bonfires her neighbors had on fall nights. She remembers being given the chore of *feeding the fire*, remembers finding sticks, adding kindling in a race against the fire dying out.

"But you're talking about a level of smoke where they can't see us. Won't that be enough smoke to kill us?"

"I don't know."

"Well, fuck, dude."

Disappointed with her flawed plan, Renata looks away. And her eyes fall on her half-eaten sandwich. "We do it right when the food comes. If they're giving us food, then we at least know they're right here. So maybe they're more likely to be seeing the video."

Coral nods her approval. "Cool."

With that problem solved, Renata relaxes. Until the dread creeps back in . . .

Chapter Thirty-Nine

Jody

A full beard covers his neglected face. It's now been five weeks since Jody indirectly killed the hit man Derrick Fletcher. It's been five weeks since Shiloh broke it off with him. It's been five weeks since he lost Rory.

He keeps rewatching Marty's *My Dirty California* videos, telling himself he's looking for more clues, but a part of him watches to spend time with his brother. He continues to make lists of possible leads, checking them off as he rules them out. He makes lists of further questions to ask Nicole. He makes lists of places Marty lived. He makes lists of details he remembers Marty saying in Pennsylvania before he was killed. He makes lists of possible reasons why someone would kill Marty. He makes lists of people mentioned in Marty's *My Dirty California* videos. Jody keeps creating tasks, convincing himself the case is active, because it's the moments between leads—the moments when he accepts he has no leads—that feel the hardest to endure. Drinking and the nausea drinking causes make it easier to endure. Those and walking. Jody takes long walks. They started as specific walks in specific neighborhoods, chosen out of their proximity to where he lost his dog or where Marty lived. He tells himself he walks to keep the investigation going, but he walks because standing still hurts his stomach.

Today, he explores a neighborhood in Atwater Village, where Marty lived a few years ago—at least long enough to send him a letter and a copy of Joan Didion's *Play It as It Lays*.

He turns a corner, passes a tattoo parlor, craft beer store, bike shop, yoga studio—subcultures competing for attention. He sees a dog park where the road ends in a T. He's gotten into the habit of checking dog parks. He walks to the chain-link fence. Happy dog owners look on as happy dogs run, play, and shit. But no Rory.

Jody heads back toward his truck, planning to drive back to Palms and go to Boardwalk 11, a karaoke bar with happy hour beers on draft. Jody circumvents a food truck selling dog treats. When he gets around it, he sees a taped-off, freshly built memorial. A bench with an inscription for slain LAPD detective Salvatore Jenkins. Jody's about to move past it when his gaze falls on the date: June 25, 2019, exactly a week before Marty and his father were killed. He stares at the bench. The date. Then the name. When he asked Shiloh about the last time she saw Marty, she said it was a few weeks after the last time they broke up, and she ran into him and he was with a guy named Sal.

Could this Salvatore Jenkins be the Sal who was talking with Marty? Was Marty working with the LAPD and the guy he was working with got killed and that made him flee town?

Jody hadn't realized how much anger he'd been carrying toward Marty. Beyond the obvious anger he had toward Derrick and whoever hired him, it was Marty who had brought the trouble back to Pennsylvania. It was Marty who had gotten their father murdered. But maybe Marty was working with the police. Trying to help someone or get important intel. The bench in front of Jody suggests LAPD detective Salvatore Jenkins was a hero. Maybe Marty was a hero too.

When Jody gets to the restaurant called Public School, he spots Shiloh sitting on the patio. He stops when he sees she's sitting across from a thirty-year-old yuppy-looking fellow with combed hair and a shirt that suggests *I have money and I used some of it to buy this shirt.* A glass of white wine in front of her. A dark, frothy beer in front of him. They're both leaning in, expressing polite intrigue but not holding hands. A first date, maybe second. Jody stops, realizing he should wait outside and text her and let her come out.

Jody is pacing next to a rat king of locked bicycles when Shiloh emerges from the bar slash restaurant.

"Are you okay?" she asks.

"Yeah. Sorry I'm interrupting." He regrets the wording. He can tell she can tell he saw her date.

"It's okay. What is it?"

Jody pulls his phone out. He flashes her a picture he found of Salvatore Jenkins. "Is this the guy you saw Marty with the last time you saw him? The Sal guy."

"Yeah."

Jody had been 99 percent sure she'd say yes, but he still needed to confirm it.

"Why? Who is he?"

"He's a cop. *Was*. He was killed. A week before Marty. I think Marty was working with the cops. Maybe it wasn't just a scam or drugs or something. Maybe he was trying to help the cops." He's not trying to convince her as much as he's trying to convince himself.

"Yeah, maybe, Jody, but . . ."

"What?"

"I'm just worried about you. If Marty was doing something with a cop and it got the cop killed and him killed . . . I want you to be careful."

"I will. I'll let you get back to your . . . I'll let you go." Jody can see from her face she wouldn't go back and have a nice date. That this event now had dominated her evening.

"Couldn't you have just texted me the picture?" asks Shiloh.

He had told himself he wanted to show her in person so he could judge her face, her level of confidence, but he had just wanted to see her again. "Yeah, I'm sorry. I should've. I'm sorry."

She sighs, shakes her head in anger. Trying to be an asshole. But she just doesn't know how. Her eyes tear up. "Bye, Jody." She walks back into the restaurant.

• • •

Jody picks a spot in Miracle Mile for his lunch with Officer Neal Spencer so he can get there early and look around for Rory. He parks ninety minutes before he's meeting Officer Spencer. From Derrick's house, the last place he saw Rory, he works his way outward in circles. Flashing a picture he has on his phone, he asks anyone out walking their dog if they've seen Rory. Dog people are the best helpers to find a missing dog. But they all say no, and they all suggest the same animal shelters Jody had already checked. He gave all the shelters copies of a picture of Rory and put his number on the back.

Jody returns to his truck. Driving toward Wilshire Boulevard, where the restaurant is, he realizes he might as well park here in the neighborhood rather than try to find a spot at the restaurant. He parks, walks toward Wilshire, past pastel bungalows. He's walking alongside a high brown fence when a dog barks at him. Granted, barks are hard to differentiate, but the bark sounded familiar. He could feel the bark in his right hand, the one he broke in high school, the one that hurts when it's about to rain. Prepared to climb up and see a yellow lab or a Dalmatian, he hoists himself enough to see over the fence. In the backyard, there's a mini paved basketball court, painted Laker yellow and purple.

And an ugly brown mutt. Rory.

Jody lands hard on his heels. Rory bounds over to Jody, licking him. Jody falls to the ground, hugging his dog.

"Hey! What are you doing?!"

Rory wasn't the only one in the backyard. There's a man wearing a suit who's talking to a woman. The woman holds a sweaty glass of lemonade. There are kids toys strewn about the backyard.

"This is my dog." Jody's prepared to give a deeper explanation, but the man and woman stare in awe as Jody leads Rory out of the backyard, now using the gate. He pulls the new shiny collar and tag off Rory and drops them in the yard before he takes Rory to his truck. Jody feels a buzz in his chest ranging on euphoria. First he got the clue that Marty was linked with an LAPD detective. Now he's found his dog.

But the jubilation is short-lived; he can't shake the feeling bad news is coming soon.

"I'm glad you called." Neal Spencer, the LAPD officer who'd given Jody his card, smiles at him across the table. They were planning to eat at a diner, but now that Jody had Rory, he picked the sandwich spot next door because it has outdoor seating where Jody tied up Rory and can keep an eye on him. He wasn't about to leave Rory in the truck twenty minutes after finding him.

"I wasn't sure if you would," Neal says.

Jody was making conversation before he got into asking for a favor. But now he'd misled the guy.

"I was wondering if you knew anything about this cop Salvatore Jenkins."

"Heard a lot about him. Why?"

"Asking for a friend."

"I see." Neal looks disappointed, realizing Jody didn't ask him to go to a meal socially.

"I saw the memorial."

"A lot of people were pissed about that."

"Pissed about him getting killed?"

"Well, initially, yeah. Anytime a cop gets killed, that shit reverberates around the department. But rumors came out about him."

"About Sal? What kind of rumors?"

"Apparently, he was trying to get into evidence off-hours."

"To take something?"

"Yeah. There was an IA investigation but then he got killed, so they decided to drop it. Cop gets killed, normal for there to be a memorial, but because a lot of people think he was dirty, there was pushback. I know civilians out there hate dirty cops. You know who else hates dirty cops? Clean cops."

"What was he trying to get from evidence?" Jody asks.

"People say coke."

"How do they know?"

"So three days before Sal dies, there's this wild shootout in Frogtown. I mean people opening fire on a neighborhood street. Stray bullets entering homes. This happened right outside a known Latin Kings hot spot. The shootout turned into a vehicle chase. Which the cops end up joining. The chase ended with an Acura going into the LA River. The driver gets away. Now look, all this is rumor, pure speculative puzzle-piece assembly. But a lot of cops think Sal wanted to sell some coke. He tried to go through evidence. That failed. So he robs these Latin Kings. They retaliate and kill him three days later."

"I think I follow you. But how does Sal get blamed for the drug heist in Frogtown?"

"Oh, yeah, I left out a key piece. Sal was a narco detective and he had a CI in Frogtown. In the Kings. So through his informant, he would have known where a stash house was. The logic dots connect, but not in a way that made sense for IA to follow through with a huge investigation. Sal's dead, and with no other evidence, they let the case rest with his body. But if you drop the investigation, then you look bad to not give a memorial. His family laid on the pressure thick. So they do the memorial, and a bunch of cops end up annoyed."

"So the guy in the Acura robbed the drug dealers presumably? Whose car was it?"

"Owner of the Acura called in his whip stolen the next morning."

"So he's lying?"

"Maybe. But not out of the normal for a heister to use a bent car."

"Who was the Acura registered to?"

"The guy's name?"

"Yeah."

"I don't know it off the top of my head."

"Could you find out for me?"

"Remind me, you're looking into this for a friend, you said?"

Jody's going to have to give Neal more. He tries to come up with a reason, but he can't stop thinking about Marty. For this brief moment in time, he had believed Marty was working with the LAPD, that he was killed trying to help the police. But maybe he had been part of some drug heist.

"Jody?"

"Yeah, sorry."

"I'm confused here, man. I meet you at that car accident. And you say you'd just gotten to LA. And now you're asking me about this slain cop. What gives?"

"Sorry. I haven't been fully honest with you." Jody wonders if he should come clean about everything but decides against it. "My friend is trying to do one of them true-crime podcasts on murdered cops. She started looking into Salvatore."

"You can't quote me on this stuff. All that was rumors."

When Jody gets to his truck, he searches news articles about the shoot-out in Frogtown. He finds an *LA Times* article that mentions several Latin King gang members were arrested for possession of illegal firearms. It also mentions the owner of the Acura that was called in stolen. Tyler Gotchel. Poking around online, he finds a Tyler Gotchel who works as a bartender at Figueroa Mountain Brewing Company up in Santa Barbara County. Jody isn't positive this is the same Tyler Gotchel. But then he remembers the beer coaster he found in Marty's studio apartment.

Chapter Forty

Pen

Pen's computer drops to 5 percent battery life. Over the last four hours, she's done a battery's worth of Google searches. Between her conversation with Shiloh and watching the videos on Jody's computer, Pen has three leads to pursue, all people. Roller. Chester Montgomery. And Salvatore Jenkins. She can't figure out who Roller is. But she scrapes up real info on the other two names.

Salvatore Jenkins was a decorated detective and, even outside of the LAPD, seemed active in the community. No article paints Sal as anything less than a heroic detective who gave his life to protect his community, but Pen wonders if he's the *dirty cop* Jody mentioned. In reading his obituary, Pen notes that before Sal worked in Narcotics, he worked in Missing Persons. The detective who had worked her father's case twenty years ago, then a young man, Miguel Sanchez, still works in MPU.

Chester Montgomery owns an art gallery in Santa Monica and two homes, one in the Hollywood Hills, where Marty detailed going to a party, and one in Palm Springs. Because her father became fascinated with Palm Springs before he disappeared, Pen has long suspected Palm Springs as the location of Pandora's House. She's looked into several locations over the years. One of them is Korakia Pensione, a historic resort built in 1924 supposedly haunted by the Lady in Red. Another one is the Hope house, built for Bob and Dolores Hope, designed by architect John Lautner. The mushroom-looking house is famous for its undulating triangular roof and central light shaft. During its initial phase of construction, several eerie events occurred. A fire destroyed the house in 1973, and later the chief interior designer died. Over the years, Pen had researched dozens of homes in Palm Springs. She'd talked to residents and even snuck into several houses, but she'd never found any evidence of a breach. Could Chester's home in Palm Springs be Pandora's House?

At 11:30 a.m., Pen enters the DTLA LAPD precinct on First Street. The Missing Persons Unit is located on the third floor. An administrative member, an older woman who's seen it all, raises her eyebrows toward her gray hairline.

"I'm here to see Miguel Sanchez."

"Your name?"

"Penelope Rhodes."

"Hold on." She picks up the phone and dials a number. "Hey, I've got a Penelope Rhodes here to see MS." She holds up a *one moment* sign to Pen. "Yeah. Okay. Thanks." She hangs up the phone. "It's his day off."

Beyond the woman, down a hall and through a room with glass walls, Pen swears she sees Miguel dip into a personnel-only elevator.

"Are you sure?" Pen asks.

"He'll be in tomorrow," the admin says.

In the reclined seat of her Prius, Pen stakes out Chester's desert vacation home. She plans to return to the MPU tomorrow, but she figured she might as well use the open window today to drive to Palm Springs. Construction workers go in and out. Are they doing construction? Or is the remodel a guise? Maybe these aren't construction workers but people exploring the portal under the house.

One of the workers grabs a sandwich from his car and sees Pen sitting in her Prius. Her heart rate hastens as the man returns to the house, twice turning back to look at Pen. She considers abandoning the stakeout, but her curiosity overrides her fear.

At five thirty, the workers pack up and leave. The glass walls make it easy to peek inside. She can't see anything out of the ordinary. Except a pricey alarm system. Which means she can't have a look inside. When she turns around to go back to the front of the house, she sees an animal hopping. And it's not a rabbit. It has a pouch. Pen stares as the Eastern Grey Kangaroo hops across the yard.

Pen heads back to her Prius with a dopamine kick, knowing the kangaroo is a sign there's a breach here. The kangaroo traversed from a different simulation. How else would a kangaroo get to Palm Springs from Australia?

Chapter Forty-One

Tiph

Now that the confusion over Alexandra/Xanny has been cleared up, and now that her revulsion with Mike over his conjured affair has turned to disgust with herself for her actual affair, Tiph finds herself thinking about the lost art stash again. She knows it's not over. The lady isn't even fat yet, let alone singing.

She still hadn't gotten the chance to go to Palm Springs to see the house where Chester was presumably going to move the art. And the timing is working out. By the end of today, she's finished her home confinement sentence. She plans to drive over at four to get the monitor taken off at five. To kill the time, she handwrites a list of all the information she has on the art. At the bottom, she writes *Penelope says Jody Morrel Dead.* She wonders who killed him. And reminds herself this isn't a game. She's not trying to be the cat curiosity killed.

Chapter Forty-Two

Jody

The Figueroa Mountain brewery in Buellton doubles as a brewery facility and taproom. Jody scans the bar. Two lady bartenders and an old Latino bartender. Tyler must not be working tonight. Jody turns to leave when he spots a stairwell that leads to a brew deck. He heads up the stairs where there's another bar. And a white male bartender looking after a half dozen customers. Tyler.

Tyler hands him a beer list. Jody nods a hello.

"'Sup, bro. Let me know if you want to taste anything." Tyler has a scar on his throat that makes it look like somebody tried to take a bite out of his Adam's apple.

Jody scans the list, wants to try them all. If he has a beer at this hour, he'll feel like shit tomorrow. "I'll have the Danish Red Lager."

Tyler pours him a pint. "Are you Tyler?" Jody asks.

"Yeah."

"Did you know Marty Morrel?"

Tyler shakes his head, tries to feign confusion, but he also checks the doorway, and gives Jody a more thorough look-over.

"I'm his brother."

Tyler's confusion wanes, but his seriousness does not.

"My name's Jody."

"Need to check your ID. For the beer."

Jody takes out his wallet and hands his ID to Tyler. Tyler checks his name, hands it back. "I'm sorry about Marty."

"Most people out here haven't heard about it."

"I saw it on the news."

"It didn't make national news."

"All news can be read anywhere, man."

Jody wants to ask how he knew to look for it. But he waits to see what Tyler will say next. Tyler seems happy to take an order from two women who have strolled up to the bar. Jody sips his red lager and waits impatiently. Twenty minutes go by before Tyler circles back to Jody.

"So, look, I'm working. You obviously came here for answers. And I can respect that. The unknown ain't nobody's friend. But I'm working, can't be discussing this shit with you here."

"When do you get off?"

"I'll meet you tomorrow morning. Grass Mountain Trailhead. It's right off Fig Mountain Road. Easy to miss it, hard for Google to."

"Okay. What time?"

Jody wakes up at 6:00 a.m. hurting from his one pint of red lager. He has an hour before he's supposed to meet Tyler at Grass Mountain. The name Grass Mountain makes him think of marijuana, and that makes him think about the name Roller, but he knows he's forcing a constellation of unconnected stars. What he doesn't know is what Tyler plans to do. Did he blow him off last night so he could get Jody out into the wilderness where Jody might fall down a ravine?

"It's this way," Tyler says as he walks from his car past Jody, not stopping and not making eye contact.

Jody alternates between walking side by side with Tyler and walking behind him depending on the trail's width. Once they get a couple hundred yards into the hike, Jody lets Rory off leash. They hike at a steady clip for twenty minutes without Tyler uttering a word. Jody wonders if Tyler *has* brought him out here to kill him or hurt him or threaten him. But at the next switchback, Tyler says, "So, look, I thought about not showing up. I thought about feeding you any ten of the fake-ass stories

I cooked up lying in bed smoking weed last night. But I figure I owe Marty to speak the truth. But if you go to the authorities—ya know, cops or whoever—on any of this? I'll deny it: your word against mine. And that would be snitching. I don't bring harm to nobody who didn't have it coming. You snitching, you got it coming."

"Fair's fair."

"I'll also say, not sure you wanna go down this road. Might be better to roll over, head back East. Forget it all."

"Not an option."

"I respect that." Tyler now talks in a quieter voice even though they're alone. "So, look, Marty came to me about wanting to rip off some drug dealers. How Marty knew I was the kind of a guy you come to when you're in a situation like that is a story for another day. Don't ask me. So Marty tells me he's in league with this LAPD narco."

"Sal."

Tyler stops walking, flustered that Jody knows the name. "Yeah. Salvatore Jenkins. So he says Sal was supposed to get this coke from evidence and Marty had this buyer lined up, this rich dude who lived in the Hollywood Hills, Chester Montgomery."

Chester Montgomery—the art dealer Jody went to see when he first got to LA. The guy who had the party and poker game Marty described.

"But the evidence hookup fell through. So the plan was off, I guess. But Marty had this buyer lined up, and through one of his CIs, Sal got intel on a drug-stash house in Elysian Valley, Frogtown or whatever. Minimum security, Sal told Marty."

Jody thinks back through Marty's post about playing poker with Chester until 3:00 a.m. Marty was at this party, meets this guy who's in need of cocaine. Marty goes through his cop friend Sal, who says he can get it, but that falls through, so Sal tips off Marty on another way he can score the cocaine.

"So, look, Marty and me, we hit it. Middle of the night, came in, hoods up, guns out. Sal was right about it being a stash, but he was wrong about the amount. It was supposed to be one hundred grand of blow, a lone sleepy, stoned, street kid on watch. We got to the spot. It's a garage. A mechanic, but off-hours. We go in, and there wasn't even a lookout, so we're thinking it's easier than cake. We go under a fence and break inside. There was more like seven figures of coke and four gangbangers. I don't even think we fired back. They chased us. Emptying rounds. We got in my Acura. They chased us. They hit a tire, we flipped, rolled down the embankment. They were coming to finish us off. Now usually the LA River's just a stream of polluted water in concrete but it had rained for two days. So we just got out of the car, let the current take us. Climbed through a drainage ditch five hundred yards downriver. Marty and me feel like we escaped. It was crazy. Kinda event that'll make two guys thick as thieves, real *rethink your life* typa shit. I was worried 'cause I knew the Acura could be traced to me. Wasn't as worried about Marty 'cause I didn't think anything could come back to him.

"I hadn't heard from him in a couple days. Wouldn't text me back. I tried calling. Phone was off. I had an eerie feeling already. Then I read about this LAPD narco detective getting shot. Eerie turned to *scared as fuck*. I hit Marty up again. Still nothing. A week later, I put his name into the computer, how I came to read about him and your dad."

"Nobody came for you?"

"Not so far. But you can imagine why I near shit myself when you come into FMB asking about Marty. At this point, I figure if someone was coming for me, they'd've already came. So look, I'm sorry for my role in it, but if clarity's what you're looking for, where I'm sitting, Marty got killed by the drug dealers we tried to rip off. That confidential informant probably *informed* the other way, ya know? Big-time operation almost gets robbed, planned by a hippie drifter and a dirty cop? Ego and rep on the line, so they send a message."

They still have to hike two hours back to the cars. Jody tries to think of more questions to ask Tyler. But he can't stop picturing Marty trying to steal drugs from a gang. It doesn't track. Marty robbing drug dealers? But as he passes the currently dry Maple Creek, he thinks about what Shiloh had said about Marty. About how in his early twenties he had this swagger, but in his last couple of years, his peer group had surpassed him, become more successful, wealthier. Maybe those feelings of inadequacy were enough to explain why Marty broke bad at twenty-seven and organized a cocaine heist. From *do ri* to *get mine*.

His temporary reprieve from harboring feelings of anger toward Marty and guilt toward not being a better brother is now gone. His stomach tightens, adds to the nausea from drinking.

Chapter Forty-Three

Renata

For several weeks now, Renata and Coral have been exercising on a daily basis and hoarding whatever they get that might burn. They pretend to go through toilet paper faster and hide layers under their pillows.

But the increases in their flammable items are marginal. At a certain point, they're delaying. Having three or four more squares of toilet paper won't make the difference.

One morning, Renata crawls over to Coral, nudges her. "I think we should try it. Today."

"Okay," says Coral.

They spend the next six hours preparing. Every blanket, spare T-shirt, sweatshirt, napkin, and piece of cardboard now sits in the place they want it.

But they still have to wait for the day's meal to come.

They wait for two hours that feel like two hundred. When they hear the hatch open for the day's meal, neither reacts. Now that the moment arrives, both are too petrified to move.

Coral stands first. She does an attention-grabbing yoga pose. Meanwhile, Renata, while lying on her side and facing away from the camera, pulls out the lighter and lights the paper under her blanket on fire. She goes to the hatch and gets their lunches.

Coral screams. The fire spreads across both bed areas, the blankets and pillows erupting in flames. Renata drops the lunches on the floor. She grabs a bottle of water. She makes it look like she's trying to put out the fire but she aims for the top of the flames. This causes the flames to smoke more. As the flames grow higher, Coral and Renata drop to the ground. They don't have to pretend to cough. The room has filled with smoke. The heat rises and it has nowhere to go.

"Let's go," says Renata. She and Coral crawl across the smoky room and find the hatch against the far wall. Renata waits on the left side of the door, Coral on the right.

Smoke cycles through the room in a three-dimensional counter-clockwise circuit. The flames wither. The blankets, pillows, and paper products have all burned to ash. But they continue to smoke.

Renata and Coral try to stay low to the ground and breathe into their T-shirts. Still the door remains locked.

"Coral?" Renata says, worried she might've passed out.

"Yeah," says Coral.

Another minute passes, and their epic plan seems like it will end in a smoky double suicide when the door flies open. Below the cloud of smoke, two pairs of feet rush past. Coral goes first, crawling right out the door the two men came in. Renata follows right behind her. Crawling out. But something grabs her foot. She sees large fingers clutching her ankle. She tries to break free, but she can't breathe because of the smoke. The man flips her onto her back. She's not even trying to escape now. Just trying to breathe. Panic offset by joy; Coral escaped. The hands drag her closer to the masked man. A foot smashes the masked face. Again. Now her foot is free. Smaller hands pull Renata to her feet and out the door into a tiny chamber, a room one-tenth the size of the room where they'd been trapped. This chamber has already started filling with smoke. Renata and Coral push through a door.

Outside. The sky not much brighter than their cell. But they also see grass and trees. They run. Everything looks strange, their depth perception hampered from being in that room so long. And their atrophied legs feel like pozole. But they run across the yard. Through trees.

A hill. They're falling. Rolling. Scrambling. Pine needles, leaves, and dirt become rock and sand.

They stand. A beach with black sand. A brilliant sunset. The coast in both directions rugged and untamed. The air wet and cold. This cannot be Los Angeles.

Chapter Forty-Four

Pen

Pen returns to Los Angeles from Palm Springs, and the next day she returns to the DTLA LAPD MPU and asks the same seen-it-all-before admin to see Miguel.

Miguel Sanchez stands from his desk when Pen steps into his office. She'd seen him several times in the years since her father disappeared. Miguel had seemed ageless the first ten of those twenty years, but his age shows now. His undyed gray hair points to a man comfortable with his age.

"Hi, Pen," Miguel says, extending his hand.

She shakes it. "I saw you run out yesterday."

"Well, it *was* my day off. Came in to take care of one quick thing. And to be frank, when you come see me every so often, it's not a simple conversation."

"Fair enough," says Pen.

"So what's up?"

"I've been hired to work as a grip on a new documentary film about a narcotics detective, Salvatore Jenkins."

"Sal Jenks?"

"Yeah. I saw he used to work in MPU."

"Yeah. Really sad what happened. We weren't friends, but we . . . he was a good shield."

"The filmmakers seem to think he was a dirty cop. But I'm wondering if there's another side to the story? I don't want to be part of a film if they're bashing the wrong guy, especially a guy who's not alive to defend himself."

"Sal wasn't a straight cop who turned crooked as much as an overzealous cop already walking the line. As soon as I heard he was getting linked to a cocaine heist, I knew there must be more to the story."

"What cocaine heist?"

"In the weeks after Sal got murdered, a bunch of stuff came out about him. There was a whole IA investigation that eventually got dropped about him supposedly trying to take drugs from evidence. And some other stuff."

"What stuff?"

"The short of it is one of the gangs Sal was investigating for dealing cocaine was robbed. But the whole thing was botched, big shootout and car chase. This happened a few days before Sal gets killed. It turns out Sal had a CI in the gang, so speculation grew that Sal used intel from the CI to set up this cocaine heist."

"You said there was more to the story," says Pen.

"Yeah. So back when he worked MPU, Sal was keen on linking this rich art gallery owner to a couple of missing girls."

"Chester Montgomery?"

"Yeah," says Miguel, surprised she knows the name. "Sal never could get evidence on Chester. Our commander asked him to let it go, but Sal wouldn't. He shit the bed on other cases 'cause he was so focused on these missing girls. Eventually, he got pushed out. They weren't going to take his badge, especially when he was just a few years short of his pension. But they said he had to go. Lateral move. *Pick a department*. So he picks Narco. Why do you think?"

Pen shrugs, doesn't know, but leans her body weight forward onto her elbows, wants to know.

"This art dealer Chester Montgomery's been on the LAPD's radar since the nineties. Guy was a massive marijuana kingpin. So I'm thinking Sal goes to Narco prolly hoping he can bust the guy on something drug related and use those warrants to get something on those missing girls."

"And you think Sal stealing the cocaine has something to do with this marijuana kingpin art gallery Chester guy?"

"Maybe it was Chester Montgomery, maybe something else. But if Sal was involved, it wasn't to score X amount of money in cocaine. Wasn't in his blood. He was a true detective."

Pen ponders Chester Montgomery as a former marijuana kingpin. "Could he have gone by the nickname Roller? Chester, I mean."

"Maybe."

"And the stuff in the evidence room?" Pen asks.

"This is all conjecture, but a lot of folks think he was having trouble getting Chester on anything, so maybe he was working with a CI to set him up, ya know, sell him coke or whatever. He needs the coke to do it."

Pen chimes in, finishes off the theory. "He tries to get it from evidence. When he can't, he sets up this heist."

"Yup."

Miguel walks Pen out to the lobby. "It's good to see you, Pen. I was pleasantly surprised you weren't here to talk about your dad and simulations."

Pen is tempted to tell him she believes Chester Montgomery has found a gap. To tell him that Sal too had discovered the breach, and that's probably why he got killed. She's tempted to share her theory that if Chester was linked to other missing persons, he might have been experimenting with sending people to other simulations. But instead, she smiles. "Thanks for your help, Miguel."

Pen lies in bed, thinking about Renata. Is she still in another simulation now? Is it the same simulation where her father went?

Her mind shifts to Jody. The guy left LA thinking his brother got killed over a cocaine deal. When he gets back to LA, she'll find him and tell him the truth, how his younger brother was trying to help the police. Jody's old roommate had said he'd be gone three months. Where did he go for three months without his computer?

As she drifts off, an image of an itinerary forms amid more dreamlike shapes. She rushes to her computer and pulls up the *My Dirty California* website. Where was Marty's post about a tour of the state? Wasn't it a three-month itinerary? She scrolls down the master list of links and finds it. *Three-Month Tour of California.*

The next day, Pen drives her Prius southeast three hours to Anza-Borrego. Looking over Marty's itinerary, assuming Jody left right after he recorded his last video, he should have gotten to the desert yesterday or the day before. When she gets to Anza-Borrego Desert State Park, she drives to several trailheads listed on Marty's itinerary, looking for Jody's truck. She stops at Carlee's, a restaurant and bar in the middle of Borrego Springs, a town in the middle of the state park. She doesn't see Jody's truck but eats a great cheeseburger. After lunch, she drives past Ocotillo Wells to a long canyon running between Fish Creek Mountain and Vallecito Mountain. She drives along the sandy wash and finds the trailhead for the Wind Caves Trail. A half dozen parked cars, among them a gray Ford truck with a Pennsylvania license plate.

Chapter Forty-Five

Jody

Jody looks out at the Carrizo Badlands from the wind caves, a stone-igloo-like sand formation carved out by eons of breeze. At the beginning, he had doubted he'd need three months to see California, but now he feels like he could spend three months exploring Anza-Borrego alone. But after tomorrow, he'll stick to Marty's itinerary and move on to Julian and Alpine. He has a week left on his epic three-month California journey.

When he started the trip, he had to drag himself. After leaving LA, he camped in Topanga, then Leo Carrillo State Park. He ate fried oysters at Neptune's Net in Malibu and walked Carbon Beach, the billionaires' beachfront backyards. And in Ventura, he camped at Hobson, watched beginner surfers catch the big rollers at Mondos against the backdrop of the Channel Islands, ate pizza in a bag from Tony's, tried the fish tacos at Spencer Makenzie's, and drank beer at Topa Topa surrounded by Ventucky 805 Bros. But over that first week, all he seemed to think about was Marty. Marty stealing cocaine from a street gang. And getting himself killed for it. And getting their father killed for it.

He was considering bailing after Ventura, but something changed in Ojai. Maybe it was going to Bart's outdoor bookstore or seeing the pink moment at Meditation Mount, but Jody figured he'd at least make it up the coast. Carpinteria came next. Jody hit the Island Brew Company, Busy Bee diner. North and saw a Phoebe Bridgers concert at the Santa

Barbara Bowl. Found another Topa Topa in the Funk Zone. Giraffe with the crooked neck. Tri-tip sandwich at the Cold Spring Tavern on the way to Figueroa Mountain. Lizard's Mouth.

Neverland Ranch. Santa Ynez Valley. No need to hike Grass Mountain again. Los Olivos to Solvang to Los Alamos to Buellton. Sideways. After Pea Soup Andersen's, he went to Jalama, camped two nights, sampled the on-site store's famous Jalama Burger, and hiked to a remote beach called Tarantulas. Up the coast to a beach with three shark-attack fatalities in as many years. He drove by the Flower Fields in Lompoc. Hiked the Pismo Preserve.

By the time he got to San Luis Obispo, Jody began releasing the anger he was carrying. Ate great meals at Novo, Flour House. Walked a state-famous Thursday night farmers market. He bought a couple of gems in Phoenix Books. Added a piece to Bubblegum Alley. He camped two nights and stayed two in the Lamplighter Inn. He saw a minor league baseball game and drank at Central Coast Brewing. Over the four days, he went on six different hikes. San Luis Obispo brought out something akin to spiritual in Jody.

On his way to Morro Bay, he hiked the West Cuesta Ridge trail, great views of the coast—and if timed right—the Amtrak Surfliner train snaking its way through the hills. In Morro Bay he saw "the Rock" and ate rockfish at the Galley.

It was Big Sur where Jody turned a corner, where a lingering reluctance yielded to an openness. He camped six nights. Hiked. Saw the Bixby Bridge and the Instagrammers snapping photos. He ate a shrimp BLT at Nepenthe and caught a secret outdoor concert at the Henry Miller Library featuring a band called the Americans. He reread Jack Kerouac books Marty had sent him seven years ago.

He left Big Sur fueled with a hunger to see, eat, learn, absorb, and grow. With a hunger to *live*. Over a ten-year period in California, Marty had experienced the lifetimes of two or three men. Over those same ten years, what had Jody done? Hid behind an easy job, antianxiety medication, and beer? Made lists of things he'd do later in life? Jody had committed to doing this three-month tour of California, and yet he hadn't committed to the *living* part of it.

Jody went into Monterey with a new attitude. He went to Cannery Row and the aquarium. Combated his introverted tendencies, conversed with more strangers. He went to Capitola and Steamer Lane. He visited Santa Cruz and the boardwalk, the Ocean City of the West Coast. Asked a woman named Sharon he met at a fish stand to go for a walk, watch the sunset. San Gregorio, lost in time. San Jose. Saw a 160-room house, stairs to nowhere. He went to Half Moon Bay. Promised himself he'd try surfing, but maybe not at Mavericks. Next Oakland. San Francisco. A nonprofit worker mistook him for homeless and offered him a bed in a shelter. After making sure he wouldn't put anyone out, he stayed the night, bought everyone dinner, and asked to hear their stories, to hear about their heartbreaks and triumphs, their addictions and afflictions. He stayed an extra day in the Bay Area and went to the Outside Lands music festival and drank with some Chinese foreign exchange students and danced to some band called Tanlines and almost talked himself into trying Molly. Charles M. Schulz Museum in Santa Rosa. Saw a mountain lion in Ukiah, thought about P-22. Mendocino County was on fire, skipped ahead to make up the extra day he'd spent in Frisco.

He visited Garberville, saw the drifters drifting on his way to Shelter Cove. He did a three-day twenty-five-mile hike called the Lost Coast, where he had to bring a tide chart.

From Shelter Cove, Jody spent a week in the Redwoods, *been to Hollywood been to Redwood*. Avenue of the Giants. Ewoks. Shrine Drive Thru Tree. Eureka—Lost Coast Brewery, Booklegger, and Sea Grill oysters. On to Huell's northwest corner. Waved hello to Oregon. East along the line to State of Jefferson. Lava Beds. Huell's northeast corner. Lassen. Sacramento, reread some Joan Didion and watched *Lady Bird*, so many good films he hadn't seen. Truckee, Donner.

Three days in Tahoe. Aces and threes. Gambling and counterculture Kirkwood. Bailed a stranger out of jail.

On to the gold rush towns of Columbia, Sonora, and Jamestown, where he had a sarsaparilla milkshake, went to a railroad museum, and did a hike at Coyote Creek that led to a cave where he saw bats and thought about Batman. He went to the Steinbeck museum in Salinas and saw California condors at Pinnacles. Hiked with a widow and her three young kids. Was reminded he wants kids someday.

In Paso Robles, he tracked down Marty's favorite painter, Jordan Hockett. Jordo cried when he learned about Marty's death and tried to give Jody an acrylic painting, a beach-town landscape with conflicting patterns and divergent color combinations. In Atascadero, Jody went to the Tent City brewery and did the Three Bridges Oak Preserve trail. Tamale Festival. In Templeton, he drank beer next to a man who kept boasting he was a fifth-generation Californian and kept insisting Jody try a pancake shot, which apparently is whiskey, butterscotch schnapps, and orange juice, with a strip of bacon laid atop.

Jody stopped by the Pozo Saloon, drank two too many beers and entered the acceptance stage of grief, walked into the woods on the other end of sober, cried for hours. Two nights in the Carrizo Plain—he'll have to come back in a superbloom. Penny Bar in McKittrick, eavesdropped as oilmen argued about America. In Taft, beer and Thai food at the Black Gold Brewing Company owned by a brewer who'd traveled to Thailand and came back married to a chef.

Five days in Kings Canyon and Sequoia. What up, General Grant. Hairy tarantulas. He went to Madera—*where the palm tree meets the pine*—before heading to Yosemite. Climbed rocks. Heard tales of Alex Honnold. On to Mono Lake and Bodie—the preserved ghost town made him ponder the future.

Mammoth Mountain out of ski season. Schat's bread in Bishop. Two days in the Ancient Bristlecone Pine Forest, couldn't find the oldest tree in the world either. Imagined trees with opposable thumbs. Stopped at Manzanar. Japanese internment camps—will we learn from our history? Hiked Mount Whitney and carried out his poop. The start of the Kern River. *I might drown in still water, but I'll never swim Kern River again.*

Alabama Hills Cafe in Lone Pine, pancakes never tasted so good, and nice to leave the poop behind.

Four days in Death Valley. Burned his Crocs sliding down 150-foot sand dunes. Coyotes lounging like lazy house cats.

From there, Jody spent three days in the Mojave National Preserve. Lava tubes, more sand dunes. *Motherfucking Tatooine.* Stopped in Nipton, *nearly Pottown, USA.* Rottweilers. A hike out to a mine in Wrightwood. Huck Finn Jubilee in Victorville, reread some Twain.

Jody spent three days in Arrowhead and Big Bear, made sure to do the Pinnacles hike and check out the Alpine Slide. Met an actress who'd fled the biz fifteen years ago. Couldn't find Marty's quaking aspen grove—lost to wildfires. Four days in Joshua Tree, camped off the Boy Scout trail and found the unlisted hike to Eagle Cliff Mine. Helped a poet tripping on acid find her friends. Crossroads Cafe on the way out, best decaf coffee he ever had. On to Idyllwild, hiked Suicide Rock.

Palm Springs, Palm Desert, Salvation Mountain. Before arriving to Anza-Borrego, he'd spent two days at the strange Salton Sea—dead fish for miles. And then he came to Anza-Borrego, where he's been the last few days and managed to see a roadrunner and a coyote.

As Jody hikes the mile and a half back, he keeps his eyes peeled for bighorn sheep and debates returning to Carlee's for another burger. Calling for Rory to catch up, Jody approaches his truck. The tailgate is down, and there's a woman sitting on it.

"Jody?"

"Yeah."

"My name's Pen."

Chapter Forty-Six

Renata

Renata and Coral look from the sunset on the horizon to the rocky coast to the hillside where they half scrambled, half fell.

"We gotta go," says Coral, trying to catch her breath. They're both out of shape, having been stuck in a room for months.

Left or right? Each direction of the coast looks rocky, black, and ominous. North—assuming the magnificent medley of colors on the horizon is a sunset and not a sunrise—looks more navigable, so Renata points right. They jog up the beach. The stretch of sand goes for about seventy-five yards before it bends around a rock outcropping. Coral pulls Renata behind a giant tree trunk that washed ashore. Renata's eyes follow Coral's finger. Her rods and cones are disjointed from months in that box, but she can make out what Coral sees: two men coming down onto the beach from the hillside.

"They don't know which way we came," says Coral.

But the two men head toward them.

"Our footprints," says Renata.

They run around the bend to another stretch of beach. Bowling ball–size rocks cover this beach. The whole shore is a series of unstable rocks. It makes it impossible to go fast.

"They're gonna catch us," Coral says.

"They won't be able to go fast either."

Renata moves faster by finding the larger, flatter rocks. Coral starts to fall behind. "Don't try to step between the rocks. You're making it harder. Find the big ones and push off those."

While she waits for Coral to catch up, Renata looks ahead. They've made it a third of the way across the one-hundred-yard stretch of rocks before the next bend in the coast.

Coral gets the hang of walking across the rocks. By taking an extra half second between steps and finding the best rocks, she's going much faster. She's only five yards behind Renata now.

"There you go," says Renata. Right after she says it, beyond Coral, Renata sees the two men come around the bend. "Coral, c'mon!"

Renata and Coral move down the beach, rock to rock. The two men behind them. Like a race in slow motion.

When they're about halfway across the rocky beach, Renata looks back. The two men are a third of the way across the beach, only twenty or so yards behind them. They won't make it at this pace. Renata scans the cliffside. Could they move inland from the beach? It's all steep, jagged black rock. They could try going into the ocean, but Renata isn't a strong swimmer, and the surf looks violent.

Coral must sense the men gaining on them because she starts to sob. As Renata takes step after step, her mind cycles through what will happen when they catch up. Should Renata and Coral try to fight back? Renata imagines trying to pick up a rock and defend herself.

Renata hears a squeal of pain. She fears it's Coral, but she sees one of the men has fallen. He holds his ankle, wailing in pain. The other man goes to his side. Renata and Coral keep moving. Now is their chance to put space between them.

"C'mon!" Renata says.

Coral falls in line behind her, tracing her steps. Renata seeks out the larger, more stable rocks, leaping from stone to stone. Coral behind her, copying every move.

Renata glances back. The man who fell now limps. His counterpart leaves him behind. Renata spots a stretch of open sand to her right. It's only ten yards long, but Renata takes the detour. Now able to sprint across the tiny pebbles and sand. Coral follows the move. But the line of sand ends, and it's back to slow rock-stepping. They're ten yards from a huge outcropping and the next bend in the coast.

At the outcropping, waves slam into the rocks. They have to time it, try to run through knee-high water between waves. Renata makes it, but Coral gets hit by the next wave and flung into the rocks. Renata pulls Coral to her feet, looking back and seeing the uninjured man approaching, making his way across the stones.

Renata and Coral turn the corner, now on another beach, and this one looks different from the previous two. No rocks, just brown sand. Lighter than the original beach's black sand. The cliffs are as high, steep, and unwelcoming. The beach itself is much narrower. Two yards of sand separate the water from the cliffs. Renata and Coral run down the beach, cold whitewater hitting their feet. They suck in air and push through the pain. Renata glances back.

"He's not there," she says between gasps of air.

Coral hunches over, breathing hard, desperate to stop.

"We should still keep moving." Renata speed-walks down the beach, letting her breathing slow to a manageable tempo. Coral trudging along behind her.

Above the horizon, pinks and oranges have given way to reds and purples. The beach seems to get narrower with each wave. The tide advances.

They keep looking back, but the man never comes around the outcropping from the stone beach. Maybe he went back for the other guy, the one with the sprained ankle. Or maybe he can't swim and didn't want to risk running through the water the way they had.

Five minutes later, they get to a dead end where huge waves slam into the rocky cliffs. Maybe at a lower tide it would be passable but not now.

"What do we do?" asks Coral.

Renata scans the cliffs. She can see the rock's color, the range of how high the tide can rise. At its highest point, they'd be submerged right now.

That's why the man didn't follow them around the outcropping. At high tide, this beach isn't a beach at all. For several minutes, Renata scans the rocks, trying to find a way over.

"We have to go back," Renata says.

"Back?"

"We'll drown. This will all be under water."

They head back across the narrow beach. The sky now in a golden hour, matching the light of their prison cell.

"What if they're waiting for us?" asks Coral.

Renata fears they will be. But what other choice do they have? Stay here and drown? "We'll get there and look around and see if they're there."

This satisfies Coral. But when they get back to the rock outcropping, they hardly recognize it. Instead of whitewater coming up the slanted beach and flowing into the rocks—like the water that had hit Coral—now waves crash every few seconds right overtop the rock outcropping.

Renata watches the waves coming in, tries to see if there's a long enough gap. She pictures wading out, making her way around the outcropping, and getting thrown into the jagged rocks.

Renata wonders if they can go over the outcropping as opposed to around it. But the rocks are high, wet, and slippery. She finds the section that looks most accessible to climb. She tries to reach up and find a hold for her fingers, but they slip right off. Coral gives her a boost, but again Renata slips and falls into the water.

The sky has turned charcoal. Renata and Coral jog down the beach. As waves come up, the water runs knee-high. They scan the cliff, trying to find a nook or some accessible high ground. But the cliff is steep. A monotonous black edge. They keep going, hoping they'll find a cave or place where they can climb up and wait out the high tide. At a couple spots, they try to scramble up, but each time they slide back down into the water.

The water ranges from knee to waist height now. The sky, the water, the cliff—they're all the same color of black, dark shadows closing in on them from all sides.

They find a part of the bluff that has a slope, and they scramble up. They have to hold on to the rocks above them to keep from falling into the water below. Waves slam into them again, again, each time threatening to loosen their grips enough for Neptune's magnet to pull them back into the sea.

Coral cries for fifteen minutes straight as they hold on. Renata tries to think of a plan. But there is no plan. All she can do is hold on and hope the tide maxes out soon. The stars have come out. The light reveals the colors of the cliffside, shows the ranges of tide. At its highest tide, the area they're clinging to will be under water. If this is one of those tides, they'll drown. She can't have made it this far on her journey from Mexico to die here tonight. But the pessimistic side of her asks why not. *Santa Muerte will find you.*

"Renata!" Coral screams over the sound of water hitting rock.

"Yeah?"

"I can't hold on."

"You can hold on. Just hold on. You can do it."

"I can't. I'm not strong enough. I can swim. I'm a good swimmer."

"What?"

"I'm going to swim. I'll swim out past the waves. And I'll swim back around the rock. And I'll get help."

"Coral, stay here!"

"I can't. I'll come back for you. I'll bring a boat. A raft, something. I'll get help."

"Coral, stay here. You can do this. You can hang on."

"I'm going."

"Coral, por favor, no. Please . . ."

A wave comes up and strikes their lower halves, water splashing up to the area of cliffside where their hands grasp whatever rock they can hold. As the water goes back down, Coral lets herself go, and the water pulls her out to sea.

"Coral!" Renata screams.

Renata watches as Coral tries to stay above water as the tide sucks her right into the path of a crashing wave. Coral attempts to duck-dive the wave at the last second. She goes under, and Renata doesn't see her again. Renata searches the waves for her, head on a swivel, trying to spot Coral in the starlight. But another wave comes, and Renata has to press herself against the rock to avoid being swept out to sea. She nearly slips but holds on. Now she looks back, tries to find the spot where Coral went, but she only sees the angry ocean throwing waves against the rocks. She hangs on as the tide continues to rise.

Chapter Forty-Seven

Jody

Jody stares at Pen. Who is she? And how did she find him out here in his three-month off-the-grid tour of California?

"Who are you?"

The woman bends and scratches Rory behind the ears before answering. "Pen. Look, this will sound strange, but I've been looking for you 'cause I was looking into Marty's death too. I guess I've been behind you on the trail."

"You knew Marty?"

"No."

"How did you find me here?"

"Marty's three-month-trip. Based on when you left, I knew you'd be coming through Anza-Borrego. Jody, I know you thought you had figured it out. And you did figure out some of it, but Marty wasn't stealing the drugs to make money."

"What are you talking about?"

"The cop who died, Salvatore Jenkins? Him and Marty? I think they were looking into Chester Montgomery because they thought he had something to do with this Mexican girl's disappearance. Renata. So they were trying to bust him on drug charges so they could use that to look into Chester more."

"What? How did you, how do you . . ."

"I know a guy in Missing Persons. Sal went to Narcotics from the Missing Persons Unit. I guess Chester had been associated with some missing women a couple of years earlier, and Sal was never able to take him down."

"Holy shit." Little brother Marty. He *was* working with the police. *Do ri*. And that's what Marty was trying to tell him as he died. He wasn't saying *de nada*. He was saying *Renata*. Jody wishes he'd discovered this sooner, wishes he hadn't spent the last three months bumming around. So Chester had Marty killed, not the gang he and Tyler had robbed. Which explains why Tyler wasn't targeted even though his Acura would have made him easier to identify than Marty.

Marty told Jody about *My Dirty California* because he was in danger. Maybe Marty told him because he knew if something happened to him, that his detective work was hidden in the *My Dirty California* entries.

"Pen, you said?" he asks.

"Yeah."

"I don't know how to thank you. Wait, why are you looking into this though?"

"I'm a filmmaker. Documentaries."

"Oh," Jody says, assuming she's interested in making a documentary about Marty and his website and his death. He's not sure how he feels about that prospect, but he is sure this woman has helped him. "So what was your plan next?"

"We go back to LA, and we look into Chester."

We sounds good to him. He's a mediocre wannabe gumshoe running on grit alone, and this lady seems like she knows what the hell she's doing. Jody motions toward her car. "This your Prius?"

"Yeah."

"All right, let's do it. I'll follow you."

"Okay."

The rush of endorphins lingers; Jody feels like he's floating. "Thank you, again. I can't tell you how much this means to me."

"You're welcome. I wish I could say I was doing it out of the kindness of my heart, but this is all about Pandora's House for me."

"The haunted house thing the Renata woman told Marty she was going to?"

"Yeah. There's more you don't know, Jody. Do you have a good grasp of the simulation hypothesis?"

For the next twenty minutes, as the desert sun cooks them, Pen tells Jody about Pandora's House, jumping simulations, her father, her theory Chester has access to one of the breaches, the government cover-up.

A few moments ago, Jody had felt like this great detective had just joined his team. Like he could be Scottie Pippen and let this lady go all Michael Jordan on the investigation. And now he wasn't sure if she was partially insane or fully insane.

"We can talk more about it when we get to LA. We better get driving," she says.

Jody follows her out of the desert in his truck, never once second-guessing the first theory she'd presented, the theory Marty had been working with the cops to try to take down Chester Montgomery and figure out what happened to a missing young woman.

Chapter Forty-Eight

Jody

Pen lets Jody crash with her in her bungalow in Topanga the night they get back from the desert. The house—with its Faraday cage, books on astrophysics and quantum mechanics, UFO periodicals, and various unrecognizable electronic tools—doesn't grant Jody any more confidence Pen is stable. Jody sets his bag down as Pen comes in with his computer.

"Here's your computer. Sorry I took it."

"How did you . . . . Never mind." Jody spots a shelf with fifty empty beer bottles on display. "Fan of craft beer?"

"Oh. No. That's my earthquake detector."

Jody doesn't ask a follow-up question, assumes she has a different interpretation of earthquakes than seismologists.

Before they go to sleep, they brainstorm ways they can look into Chester Montgomery. Pen finds a woman online named Sierra Blaze who has posted tons of pictures with Chester. They see Sierra Blaze works at a tanning salon and gym in North Hollywood called Summer Shape. "I'll go see her in the morning," Pen says.

"Okay, I got something else I need to do," Jody says. He wants to ask Shiloh if Marty ever said anything about Chester Montgomery. But he also feels an obligation to tell Shiloh what Marty was doing that got him killed.

Jody takes the Music Box Steps two at a time toward Shiloh's apartment.

Shiloh wipes the sleep out of her eyes. She's wearing a red pajama onesie. Her hair is ruffled. Maybe she's not alone? Although, she probably wouldn't be wearing these pajamas if she wasn't alone.

Looking at her in these ridiculous pj's for some reason causes him to picture her married. But in this fabricated glimpse of a hypothetical future, she's not married to Jody, just the silhouette of the future Mr. Right. Even in his own vision, he can't manage to wedge himself in there as her husband.

"Did I wake you?"

"No," she lies. "How are you? Are you okay?"

"Yeah."

Jody hears footsteps in the apartment. Maybe there is a man here with her? After another moment, Becky, her roommate, walks by holding a steaming cup of coffee. Shiloh steps outside and closes the door.

"Sorry. I got this for some pajama party a few years ago, but it's comfortable."

"It's . . ." He wants to say it's cute but it's not. He wants to tell her it's because it's not hot that it *is* hot. "I wanted to come tell you Marty was working with the cops. I know you've doubted his motivations or suspected he might have gotten himself into something illegal. And that was fair. But he was trying to find this woman, this Mexican girl named Renata."

"Oh. Oh my God."

"It's given me some peace of mind. I thought it might . . . you too."

"I never doubted Marty was good."

"I know."

"He was good."

"I also wanted to ask if Marty ever mentioned a guy named Chester Montgomery?"

"I don't think so."

"He has an art gallery, big house in the Hollywood Hills."

"Doesn't ring a bell."

"Okay, thanks."

"How have you been?" she asks.

"Okay." They meet eyes, divert eyes.

"Is that all you wanted to tell me?"

That's all he wanted to tell her, but now that she's standing in front of him, he wants to be here for a different reason. He wants to be a different person who can go inside and hang out. Be a person who can hug her. He wants to be the one who could peel off her weird onesie pajamas. To be the one to fuck her slow, fast, then slow again. To lounge with her all morning and read the news and complain about the media and scroll through Netflix and debate the meaning of paradox of choice. To grow into a relationship as comfortable as an old pair of jeans and bicker about shit like who's going to do the dishes.

But that's not Jody. He hadn't come here as that person, and he can't magically become that person. They'd had a conversation about Marty's life and death. And that's all Jody is. A man trying to figure that shit out.

"Yeah, I just wanted to let you know."

"Oh. Okay. Thank you. I should . . ." Tears form in the corners of her eyes as she trails off. "I have to run a couple of errands." The last time Jody saw her, she'd tried to hide her tears behind anger. This time, it's errands. Unable to bear seeing her cry, Jody averts his eyes and mutters a goodbye.

After leaving Silver Lake, Jody finds a new sublet on Craigslist, a bedroom in a two-bed/two-bath apartment in Chinatown with a view of the dragons on Broadway. After Jody hands him a check, Ralph says he hopes they can have nightly barbecues out on the balcony. The guy wants a friend not a roommate.

"Sorry, man, I'm trying to figure out why my brother got killed."

"Oh."

When Jody gets back to his car, he has a text message from Pen. *Meet me at this costume shop on Melrose.* There's a link. Jody clicks it. What wild idea does Pen have now?

Chapter Forty-Nine

Pen

Pen browses costumes. Earlier that morning, she went to the gym and tanning salon where Sierra Blaze works. After Pen mentioned having a film at Sundance a year ago, Sierra invited Pen to come to a dress-as-your-favorite-movie-character party at Chester's house that night.

The costume-store owner asks Pen if she needs help. A conversation about the party leads to a conversation about Pandora's House, which leads to a conversation about a book the costume-store owner reveres. By the time Pen drives to Chevalier's Books in Larchmont Village, buys the book, and returns to the costume shop, Jody is waiting for her outside the store.

"Sorry, I had to buy this," Pen says, holding up the black dictionary-size book for him to see.

Chapter Fifty

Jody

Jody feels ridiculous dressed as Batman, but he had to pick a costume that would cover part of his face. He and Princess Leia approach the front door. The party spills onto balconies. They can see guests—most dressed in costumes—in different windows and in the backyard.

When they enter, a woman dressed in a yellow jumpsuit, the Bride from Kill Bill, runs over to them. She squeals as she hugs Pen. This must be Sierra. Her breasts are so big it would be impossible to do kung fu.

"Chester, c'm'here."

Jack Sparrow joins Sierra.

"Chest, this is Pen."

"Nice to meet you," Chester says, not in character.

All eyes go to Batman. Jody extends a hand. "Joe."

"A Star Wars, DC Universe crossover event, huh?" Chester says. It takes Jody a moment to get the joke.

"Pen's a filmmaker," Sierra says.

"That right?" Chester says, before he looks back at Jody. "Have we met before?"

"No, I don't think so."

"All these people coming to my house in masks, it's hard to even know who's here," Chester says.

Jody resists the unspoken pressure to lift his mask.

"Chester, look at this Scarface asshole!" a voice calls out from farther inside.

"Duty calls," Chester says. "Nice to meet you both. Have fun."

After Chester walks off, Jody turns to Pen. "I'll let you two chat. I'm going to use the bathroom." They had decided on the half-mile walk from the car that they should split up to cover more ground.

Jody explores the house, popping in and out of rooms, taking a lap around the backyard. His brain keeps misfiring, thinking Marty is going to be beneath one of the costumes. He tries to strike up conversations whenever possible, curious who might know Chester, but most people seem to be friends of friends. The whole party—the whole city—seems to be comprised of artists, wannabe artists, and people trying to make money off artists. In Pennsylvania, conversations start with the weather. Maybe because of the *seventies and sunny* monotony, but here conversations start with "What do you do?" After forty-five minutes of chitchat with Cruella de Vil, Katniss Everdeen, Doc Brown, Quailman, Zack Morris, and a woman who says she's dressed as Sloane Peterson, Jody makes his way upstairs. The doors along the hallway are all closed. Bedroom. Bedroom. Bathroom. The fourth door opens to Chester's office. Jody slips inside. An antique wooden desk takes up a quarter of the office. Jody searches the drawers. But none hold anything interesting. The door pops open. Jody darts away from the desk as Edward Scissorhands and Harley Quinn—a goth super couple—barge inside.

"Thought this was the bathroom," Jody says. He squeezes past them.

Harley Quinn giggles. "Wanna join us, Bruce?"

Jody thinks she's insinuating something sexual until he sees Edward holds more than scissors. A baggie of white powder dangles from his fingers.

"I'm good," Jody says, slipping out the door.

Downstairs, in the kitchen, a man in a suit is digging through a cooler of craft beers. "You want one? I can't find what I'm looking for."

"What are you looking for?" asks Jody.

"Anything that's not an IPA."

Jody laughs. "Californians and their IPAs."

"I give up," the man says.

"Are you Gordon Gekko?"

"Oh, no. Just came straight from work."

Jody laughs. "How do you know Chester?"

"Oh, actually, I broker art for him."

"Oh, that's cool."

"How about you? How do you know Chester?"

"Came here with a friend. Princess Leia. She's around here somewhere."

"Her?" The man points to the next room where Pen is talking to two people dressed as Minions. Pen stretches her arms to the sides as if to measure the wall with her wingspan.

Chapter Fifty-One

Pen

"The family realizes the house is a half inch shorter on the outside than the inside, which is impossible right?" Pen shortens her wing-spread arms by a half inch to show the difference.

"That's . . . crazy. I think we're going to go mingle." The Minions wave goodbye and scamper off.

Pen walks down the stairs into the finished-off basement, where a dozen heroes and villains drink and chat. The peanut shape is better suited for a swimming pool than a basement. Pen scans the crowd for Sierra, but the walls catch her eyes. Engraved concentric circles create an optical illusion the wall is moving. Pen gets lost in the circles. They're all centered at one particular point. The larger circles form a pattern encompassing the smallest circle.

Maybe this is the breach, the gap, the hole, the O.

Chapter Fifty-Two

Jody

Jody wanders through the house. Philip was the first person who seemed like he might be involved in Chester's business dealings, but the art broker had excused himself after a five-minute conversation, saying he had to get home.

In the foyer, Jody spots Sierra Blaze whisper yelling at Chester. She storms out, her attempt to slam the door thwarted by the pneumatic door closer. Chester appears relieved she's gone and heads back into the kitchen, approaches a group of four people. Jody snakes his way through the room and positions himself with his back to the group. This puts him next to a woman standing by herself who's dressed as Dorothy. She holds a stuffed dog.

"How's it going?" he asks.

Jody makes small talk with Dorothy. Once he asks the follow-up question of how the acting is going, she goes on a diatribe, which works out well for Jody to nod along as he eavesdrops on Chester's conversation. A man with a European accent keeps asking Chester about an Asian woman, and Chester keeps laughing.

A short woman with a deep voice saunters into the kitchen. She approaches Dick Tracy. "Some lady downstairs just tried to pull this art off the wall."

Dick Tracy says something Jody can't hear, and the woman responds, "Yeah, she was like trying to climb into the wall or something. It was insane."

Jody steps away from Dorothy, who's still bumping gums, now about headshots. "Excuse me."

"Oh, sure."

Jody pushes past her and darts downstairs. A crowd of people surround a man and woman yelling at Pen. The man, who's dressed as Shaggy from *Scooby-Doo*, holds Pen's wrist.

"Go get Chester. I'll hold her here," the man says to the short-haired woman dressed as Harry Potter.

Jody jogs over to the skirmish. "Let her go," he says, putting an arm around Pen's shoulders.

"No, listen, guy. She just pulled that sculpture—"

"I don't care. Let go of her."

The guy won't release Pen. More voices call up the stairs.

"Go get Chester!" "Has anyone seen Chester?"

No more time to mediate this dispute. Jody hits the guy with a right hook. Right in his left cheek. Shaggy goes down hard, Scooby Snacks flying. Jody grabs Pen and pulls her toward the stairwell.

Up the stairs, where they spill out into the kitchen.

"There she is!"

"That's the lady!"

Jody and Pen dart out of the house, but now they're on a deck overlooking the backyard. No way down. They head back for the door when they see a couple of guests leading Chester through the kitchen.

Jody and Pen run to the edge. A twenty-foot fall. But the pool water will break it.

He and Pen climb up on the deck railing.

Folks in the yard around the pool assume it's a party stunt. As Jody and Pen climb out, other guests jump in, copying the movies that copied *It's a Wonderful Life*. The chaos proves helpful. Up on the deck, a few people point and yell. "Grab them!" But most people are paying attention to a guy in a Jabba the Hutt costume who jumped in—perhaps chasing Leia—and now has trouble swimming because of the bulky costume.

Jody and Pen run out of the backyard. It's one long hill. The Hollywood Hills. Their costumes provide extra protection as running regresses to sliding. The hill levels out, enough to stand and jog. They go across a flat yard. Crawl under some toyon shrubs. They pop out into another backyard. With another party. That they might have blended into. If only they weren't dressed as Batman and Princess Leia. Wealthy Angelenos holding martinis stare at them as they sprint across the yard. There, they get to a road.

Chapter Fifty-Three

Pen

When she gets back from Chester Montgomery's costume party to her bungalow in Topanga, Pen climbs in bed. After a few minutes of staring at the copper-colored dots on the ceiling, she turns on the light and opens the book she bought earlier that day. It's not a story, but a story within a story. The fonts are different for different narrators. The words are black except one word that's blue every time it's written. She looks up the footnotes. Some seem real. Others don't. She realizes it's not a book but a maze. Realizes it's not a maze but a puzzle. With each turn of the page, the layout changes. Hours later, she turns the physical book in circles as the sentences go inward one by one.

Chapter Fifty-Four

Renata

Each wave comes up higher. Thoughts of drowning terrify Renata, but the gradual change in tide makes it torture.

Chapter Fifty-Five

Jody

"Thanks for meeting up with me," says Jody. He struggles to find the words. He'd gone over it in his mind earlier as he drove to the chicken joint in Beachwood Canyon, but now that he's here, the message seems dismantled in his brain.

Before he can say more, Pen chimes in. "I wanted to talk to you too. You know how I showed you that book the costume-store owner is obsessed with?"

"Yeah."

"I stayed up all night reading it. I think it's all related."

"What do you mean?"

"So the book is about this guy who works at a tattoo parlor and he gets a new apartment and he finds this manuscript from this previous resident Zamponà. And the manuscript is about this documentary film called the *Navidson Record*. And the *Navidson Record* is about this family whose house starts to change. Like they realize one wall is a half inch bigger on the interior than the exterior and—"

Jody becomes worried she's going to try to tell him the entire plot. "And you think the house in the book is this Pandora's House you've been looking for?"

"No, that's crazy. The book is fiction."

"Oh, okay, good," Jody says.

"I think the house in the book is based on the real Pandora's

House. Like maybe the author had seen the real Pandora's House, and it inspired this fictional story he came up with."

"I don't follow."

"It might sound strange, but I think the author might have known my dad. The author lives in LA. The main character, this guy Johnny Truant, is a grungy tattoo artist who lived in Hollywood in the nineties. My dad lived right off Sunset on Wilcox and got a bunch of tattoos and all he listened to was Mudhoney and Soundgarden and Alice in Chains. And my dad's name is John, but he used to go by Johnny. I think this character is based on my dad. Or like a hyperbolized version of my dad."

"Pen, I think you're—"

"Guess what year the book came out?"

"I don't know."

"The year 2000. The year my dad disappeared."

"Pen—"

"Every single time the word *house* appears in the book it's in blue."

Jody stares back, unsure if he's supposed to understand the relevance.

"There are all kinds of rumors about Pandora's House. I'm not saying they're all true. But many involve a blue light. That can't be a coincidence."

"So what is it you're thinking to do?"

"I'm going to get in touch with the author. He lives in LA. I want to see if he did know my dad. See if he knows where Pandora's House is."

"Look, I can't tell you how much I appreciate everything you've done. If it wasn't for you, I wouldn't have known Marty was trying to help the police. But I don't want to focus as much on the Pandora's House aspect. So maybe we can just keep each other in the loop."

"Sure, fine."

Jody can't read if she's wounded. It's as if she's calloused from a lifetime of nonbelievers.

Chapter Fifty-Six

Pen

Pen reads the book cover to cover twice, including the footnotes and the footnotes' footnotes. The story has nothing to do with simulations, but it makes her think about simulation jumping in a different way. She wonders if other worlds out there might be labyrinths. Is her dad trapped? Is that why he hasn't come back?

She tries knocking on the author's door, but he doesn't answer. She sends him an email asking to get coffee. When he doesn't respond, she sends another email, asking if he knew her father and again requesting to meet. He emails back and tells her the book is fiction, he doesn't know her father, and he would like her to respect his privacy. Pen's not sure whether to believe him.

Even if her suspicions about the book are true, she knows she has to focus on *My Dirty California*. The ergodic nature of the book reminded her of how much could be hidden below the surface of Marty's entries. Marty had known he was in danger, and he left *My Dirty California* behind in case something happened to him. He had mentioned Chester Montgomery in an entry—maybe that was one of many bread crumbs.

Pen rewatches the *My Dirty California* video where Marty mentions Chester Montgomery. Each of the three times Marty mentions his name, he rubs his left eyebrow. Is it a signal?

Pen goes back through other videos Marty made and notes the words Marty said when he touched his left eyebrow. *Zócola. One-eyed Gypsy. Arbor. Naomi Hirahara. El Pino. Kook. Lassen. Harrison Wills. Cobalt FC. Diddy Riese.*

Rodney King. Soccer Kids USA. Mount Baldy. Hobson. Ryder Bach. Atwater Carl. Barney's Beanery. Jeff Bridges's prosthetic head. Dead whale. Hans Jordi. Hollyhock. Imperial Beach. Golden Road. Potato tacos. Garth Ancier. P-22. CicLAvia. Andrew McMahon. Lizard's Mouth. Lotus flowers.

After a day and a half of watching videos, the list of words stretches onto a second page. Pen decides to put a pin in her plan to track every time Marty touched his left eyebrow and instead hone back in on certain entries. She returns to an entry of Marty's she's watched more than any other.

"Two different worlds. Sliding doors. Brick and no brick. And thinking about O and that other world, I start to smile and wonder. But it's not many-worlds, it's one, and there's no going back."

Pen still believes this entry connects to when Marty must have found a breach. Did Marty leave clues in the post? She watches it three more times. She transcribes it. Reads it backward.

She goes to the next entry listed on the MDC website. It's a video post where Marty describes going for a hike in Horsethief Canyon outside Alpine. He had tried to identify species of wildflowers on the hike, and he listed them at the end of the video. Pen rewatches the video, and this time she writes down the list in a notebook.

Live-forever
Alkali mallow
Sticky phacelia
Scarlet bugler
Elegant clarkia
Narrowleaf milkweed

Live-forever? Was Marty talking about jumping simulations? As a path to digital immortality? She's about to watch the next video when she looks at the first letter of each of the six flowers. Going down the page, it spells LASSEN.

Marty had the map of Lassen Volcanic National Park. And he had an entry about going there. She finds the exact post, which was from a mere four months before he died. She looks through the pictures and sees where Marty wrote *The trip was infinitely better with O.* And Marty had touched his eyebrow when talking about Lassen in one of the videos.

Jody answers on the first ring. "Hey."

"Jody, I think I found something on the *My Dirty California* site."

"What?"

She walks him through her findings.

"Pen, O isn't a gap or a breach or a hole. O is Shiloh," Jody says, sounding impatient. "Marty went to Lassen with Shiloh. And that other post, the one you're talking about, Shiloh had an abortion. That's why Marty was talking about different worlds. He was imagining a world where she hadn't gotten an abortion."

They're not mutually exclusive, Pen thinks. "Maybe Marty was using the nickname for his girlfriend to describe the breach so it wouldn't be obvious. As a way to hide it."

Jody doesn't respond, and Pen thinks the call might have been dropped.

"You there?"

"Yeah."

"What about him spelling out *Lassen* with the flowers?"

"I dunno. There are hundreds of videos. You're going to find something."

"It's not a coincidence, Jody."

"So what are you saying?"

"The breach is in Lassen. Maybe that's where Renata went through. And Marty found out. And they killed him."

Again, Jody doesn't respond.

"You there?"

"Yeah. I'm not sure what to say."

Pen climbs the Music Box Steps, then the steps to the second-floor apartment.

Shiloh opens the door after the second knock. "Hi, Pen," she says.

"Can I come in?"

"Jody isn't here."

"I came to talk to you."

Shiloh ushers her inside.

"You went to Lassen with Marty?"

"The national park? Yeah. A while back."

"Why did Marty want to go there?"

"Why did he want to go to Lassen? I remember him saying it was one of the few places in California he hadn't been yet."

"Why did he want you to go with him?"

"We were broken up. But kinda back together on that trip."

"It makes sense you'd get involved with the two of them."

"What do you mean?"

"I mean they're brothers. If you believe in soul mates, you could have a misfire pretty easily with siblings."

"I'm confused."

"Just saying, if someone's your soul mate in a simulated world, their brother might cause confusion, like a false positive."

"I'm not saying I agree with you. But in your scenario, which brother is my soul mate?"

"It's not my scenario, Shiloh. Let me ask you this. Did Marty say anything about Renata or Chester Montgomery on this trip?"

"No."

"Was he looking for something there?"

"Marty was always looking for something."

Pen stares at Shiloh. Does she know more about Lassen? What is she hiding?

"Hold on one sec." Shiloh heads into the bathroom but scoops up her phone from the counter on her way.

Pen inches closer to the bathroom door where she can hear Shiloh whispering on the phone. Pen dips out the door and heads back to her car, taking the Music Box Steps two at a time.

Chapter Fifty-Seven

Jody

Jody watches Chester's house in the Hollywood Hills from his truck parked on the street. After diverging paths from Pen, he wasn't sure how to proceed other than stake out Chester's house.

Yesterday, he followed Chester to a liquor store. An Uber Eats driver brought Chester lunch. And a Postmates driver brought him dinner. Hungry himself, Jody had ordered from Grubhub and had it delivered to his parked truck. Today, Chester hasn't left the house. A gardener working next door eyes Jody each time he returns to his landscaping truck. Jody is contemplating moving farther down the street when his phone vibrates. *Shiloh.*

"Hey."

"Hey."

"I can't hear you."

"I can't talk louder," she says. "Pen's here. She's asking weird questions. I think you should come over."

"I'm coming."

Jody turns on his truck, pulls a U-turn to head to Silver Lake. Right as his phone buzzes. A text from Shiloh: *Never mind she left.*

Jody fights the urge to go see Shiloh and claim he hadn't seen the text. He goes back to watching Chester's house, tries to get his mind off Shiloh by thinking about other ways to look into Chester. At the movie-character costume party, Sierra Blaze stormed out after an argument with Chester. Maybe if they'd broken up, she'd talk to Jody.

But he worries if he approaches Sierra asking questions, she may warn Chester.

An hour later, a car pulls up to Chester's house. This one a Honda Accord. A twentysomething fellow—maybe over the bunny hill to thirty—makes his way down the driveway with a bag. Looks like a thermal bag. Does this Chester dude ever cook or eat out?

Ten minutes later, the Honda Accord is still parked there. Maybe not an Uber Eats/Postmates fellow after all.

A red bumper sticker catches his eye. *Mozy Cafe.*

Mozy? Wasn't that the name Marty's friend Nicole had said? She said when Marty was in Encinitas, all he did was surf and pick up a few hours washing dishes at a café. Was it Mozy? Jody grabs his phone. He types *Mozy Cafe* and Google finishes it for him, suggesting *Mozy Cafe Encinitas*.

Jody snaps a picture, making sure he can see the license plate.

Five minutes later, the surfer-looking dude walks back to his car. Jody has a better angle to see what the guy is carrying. It's a gym bag. And now it's full of *something*.

Chapter Fifty-Eight

Pen

Multiple times on the hike, Pen gets the sense someone's following her. Is it the ranger? She's about halfway out to the hydrothermal area.

Yesterday, it took Pen nine hours to drive to Lassen Volcanic National Park. The park was closed by the time she got there. Today, hers was one of the first cars in line to enter the park. At the ranger station, she read Lassen is part of the Ring of Fire, a zone of mountain-building volcanoes that surround the Pacific Ocean. Pen wondered if the true Ring of Fire is a series of breaches in our simulation, a big O of smaller o's. She asked the park ranger about Bumpass Hell and the hydrothermal area, and whether anyone had entered the lava pools. "Luckily, no one has died in a long time. We try to educate people about the dangers of falling in," said the ranger. When she left the station, she looked back and realized he had followed her outside and watched her walk to the trailhead.

It takes Pen an hour to hike the 3.1 miles out to Bumpass Hell. The hike offers views of jagged peaks and clear alpine lakes. She knows she's gotten there when she sees smoking sulfur rising off a cyan pool. The bubbling liquid looks like boiling Gatorade. It hisses. She doesn't want to do anything rash, so she reviews the steps that led her there. She found a map of Lassen in Marty's old apartment. Marty found something in Lassen he knew was dangerous to discuss so he coded a message into his video. Marty was killed after his trip to Lassen.

She stares at the boiling hydrothermal O-shaped pool. The sun comes out from between clouds and hits the boiling green lava, creating a sort of flash. A green flash.

She knows what she has to do, her father's words ringing in her ears. *The question for you, pumpkin, is when we find the gap, will you have the guts to jump in?* She pictures herself reunited with her father in another world, and she steps forward to leap into the breach.

Chapter Fifty-Nine

Tiph

The bare skin on her ankle, free of the bracelet, feels smooth, clean, good. Tiph drives east on the 10 freeway. She's always wanted to go on a spa trip to Palm Springs and never let herself believe it was possible. When she finds this art, she'll come back and do it right. Weekend trip with her girlfriends: spa, salon, brunch, the works.

Google Maps takes her to Chester's giant desert house. She rings the doorbell, not expecting anyone to answer, knowing Chester died with no will and no family to inherit his estate. She checks under the doormat for a spare key. No go. She's about to head around back when a gruff voice says, "Hello there."

A man walks his Pomeranian down the adjacent driveway.

Shit, fuck, balls. "Hi," Tiph says back. Had he seen her lift the doormat?

"Hope you weren't looking for Chester."

"I am. We were friends in LA, sort of fell out of touch, but he had invited me to stop by his Palm Springs house anytime. I'm a bit of an architecture buff."

"Oh dear. Chester's dead, ma'am. I'm sorry to be the one to tell you."

"Oh no. Cancer?"

"No. He, well he . . . They think he was murdered."

"Jesus Christ."

"I can show you the house. I'm sure he'd love for you to see it. If you believe in heaven or wherever, he'd be looking down, still wanting to show off his houses and his art."

"You don't mind?"

"No, he had me watering his plants and feeding his shark whenever he was in LA. I've kept doing it. I guess the house is going to the city. Or the state rather. He didn't have any family."

The neighbor, who introduces himself as Raymond, gives Tiph a tour. A labyrinth of rooms, hallways, nooks, closets, balconies, and stairwells. Plus a tank with a baby wobbegong shark.

"In his LA house, he had this secret room where he kept his wine."

"If he had something like that here, I still haven't found it. If anyone would know it would be Jean-Marc."

"Who?"

"You ever meet Chester's friend Jean-Marc? A carpenter. Or woodworker. I'm not sure what to call him. But he made most of the pieces in this house. Lives right down the road."

Tiph looks out the window at the sun, low on the horizon. A jaguar skulks across the desert-scape backyard. Raymond follows her eyes.

"Oh," he says. "My wife said she thought she saw a jaguar. Chester had all these exotic animals. Animal control came to pick them up after he died, but a bunch of them got away."

Tiph watches as the jaguar sits in the dirt and licks itself.

Forty minutes later, Tiph knocks on Jean-Marc's door. The Frenchman answers the door in a pink bathrobe. "I always say Palm Springs needs more Black women."

Tiph chuckles.

"Just tell me you aren't selling me anything, especially not Jesus."

"Christ, no," laughs Tiph. "I was a friend of Chester's back in LA. We fell out of touch, and I just found out he passed."

"Oh, yes, it's been very sad. I just tried to make risotto. Want to help me judge how bad I botched it?"

Tiph drives back to LA from Palm Springs with a belly full of risotto and a new lead. Jean-Marc babbled about Chester, art, wine, and parties.

Tiph couldn't tell for sure whether he knew about the stash of illegal art, but based on the way Jean-Marc spoke about the purity of art and art collection and museums, Tiph suspects Chester wouldn't have shown him an *illegal* art stash.

Jean-Marc mentioned a nineteenth-century Wooton desk Chester had him restore. Chester had put the desk in the second-floor office of his Hollywood Hills mansion. Jean-Marc said it's up for auction along with the rest of the furniture from the LA house.

According to Jean-Marc, Chester had him build a secret compartment in the back of the Wooton.

"What did he put in the compartment?" she had asked him.

"I'm not sure I wanna know," Jean-Marc had said, laughing, before adding, "He was a good man." He seemed to add this last part less out of honesty and more out of respect for the dead.

As she drives back to LA in the dark, Tiph yawns. Growing wary of growing weary, she listens to old Ice Cube songs and imagines what could be in the secret compartment.

Chapter Sixty

Jody

Jody follows the Honda Accord from Chester's house to DTLA and onto the 5 freeway, headed south, Rory's fur blowing in the wind. By the time he gets to Long Beach, Jody assumes they're going to Encinitas. In between views of the crashing blue Pacific, the drive offers glimpses of the San Onofre Nuclear Power Plant and Camp Pendleton. Before long, Jody's taking exit 44 for La Costa Avenue, which dumps him right in Leucadia, a beach community on the northern end of Encinitas. In Marty's second-to-last *My Dirty California* entry, he'd alluded to being *disappointed with his trip to Encinitas.* And there's Nicole's description of Marty seeming stressed out in Encinitas. Had Marty linked Chester to Encinitas and come down here to investigate further?

The surfer leaves his Honda parallel parked along Highway 101 and steps inside a noisy bar with live music called Le Papagayo. Jody parks in a dirt median between two surf vans. And watches. Twenty- and thirtysomething guys in board shorts, tank tops, and flip-flops—clones of his mark—spill out of the bar every few minutes. An hour later the surfer he followed to San Diego emerges with two such clones. The trio walks to the back of the Honda. After a moment, the original guy hands the two guys brown paper bags. Jody assumes he's just broken up the cash he got from Chester three ways. Or maybe drugs they're all going to sell? The three guys give each other fist bumps and semi-sarcastic *hang loose* signs before dispersing.

Jody follows the Accord four blocks to a carport on W. Glaucus

Street. Jody watches the surfer walk up to his apartment. Jody checks the time. Ten forty-five. After he waits another half hour, he assumes the guy's in for the night. He'll pick this up tomorrow. He grabs dirt-cheap but tasty tacos from a place hidden inside a gas station called Cancun Mexican and Seafood. He checks into the Rodeway for a mere $59 a night. He'd read Leucadia was as expensive as hell, and yet the dinner and room seem closer in price to Lancaster than LA.

The next morning, Jody gets to the surfer's apartment at 7:15 a.m. He sits in his truck on the hill outside the apartment units for two hours. Unlike in LA, in Leucadia his Ford pickup blends right in. The hillside street is full of trucks, SUVs, and surf vans. By nine thirty, he's thinking how this fellow likes to sleep in. Just as the guy walks right by Jody's truck with his surfboard, wetsuit stripped down to his waist, returning to his apartment. The two guys from last night are with him. They'd left before Jody had even gotten there.

They emerge from the apartment at 4:00 p.m. with their boards. Jody follows on foot from a cautious distance up the hill to Neptune Avenue, which runs along the bluff. The occasional house has glass walls or large windows that offer a view from the street straight through to the Pacific. The guys arrive at a stairwell that leads to Grandview Beach. Jody hangs back as they head down the stairs and disappear into the water. They return to the apartment on Glaucus at six thirty. The other two guys leave at ten. Jody heads back to the Rodeway at eleven.

The next day plays out the same. The guys surf in the morning and late afternoon, and that's it. If he's going to try to meet them, it'll have to be in the water.

Jody can't believe how much the surfboards cost as he browses the Encinitas surf shop. Most are over a thousand.

A teenager with sun-bleached hair and a T-shirt that reads *Surfing's the source* approaches Jody. "What you looking to ride?"

"Never been before. Maybe I should rent one?"

"If it's your first time you probably wanna go longboard, maybe a foamie."

"All right. How much do they cost?"

"Here, man, take this Wavestorm with the single pink fin. It's like twenty-five bucks a day. Just gimme fifty and you can bring it back whenever you're done with it."

"Okay. Do I need to fill out a form or anything?"

"If you want."

Jody chooses a beach called D Street. Even though they're closer, he wants to avoid Beacon's and Grandview this first time.

The sun, the bare feet, the beach town—it takes him back to the East Coast. To his childhood. A week or weekend in Bethany or Rehoboth or Ocean City. The shore. Sun-kissed shoulders. Pelicans flying low over the water. Maryland blue crabs. But in all these nostalgic flashes, whether he's a younger kid or an older kid, he has a little brother. With Marty dead, with his father dead, all those memories inflame the ache in his gut. He wants to go back to the shore. To be thirteen and Marty six. To go crabbing on the dock. Yes, to teach Marty how to bodysurf, but from there, he longs for life to take a different route with different outcomes. Outcomes where his father and brother are still alive, and they could go to the shore together today and reminisce past beach trips and form new family memories.

Jody paddles out into the surf. The water is frigid. That's why everyone is wearing a wetsuit even though it's seventy-five degrees outside. Jody grew up going to the beach a week or two per year. He boogieboarded as a young kid before turning to bodysurfing as a teenager. Paddling out on the foam surfboard isn't out of his comfort zone. He turns and paddles back toward shore with a wave, and he catches it. All that is second nature with bodysurfing. But once the wave picks up the surfboard, Jody tries to stand and falls onto the face of the crashing wave.

He tries again and again. But can't seem to stand. He remembers learning to ski the one time he went. It was Blue Mountain in the

Poconos, and Jody was seven, and by lunch he was skiing. Is surfing that much harder than skiing? Or is it that much harder to learn a sport as an adult? He watches surfers to the north and south of him and tries to replicate the *popping up* motion, but he can't seem to get it. After about twenty tries, he sees a huge set coming in. He lets the first pass and goes for the second wave. Same result: he paddles, the wave catches him, he tries to stand, and he falls. Except this time, as the wave crashes, it picks up the board and slams it onto his legs. His ankle is bleeding. Though plastic, that single fin is capable of inflicting real damage.

When he gets back to the parking lot of the Rodeway, most of the spots are taken and he has to park at the edge of the lot, along the highway. A long line to get into a seafood restaurant called Fish 101 stretches into the motel parking lot. As Jody takes the Wavestorm out of his truck, he catches looks of condescension from the surfer types in line. An SUV drives by and Jody hears "Kook!" right before a smoothie hits him in the chest. Everyone in line at Fish 101 laughs. Jody doesn't know what a *kook* is, but based on the strawberry banana beverage thrown along with it, it must not be a compliment.

Staying at the Rodeway is not the way to garner respect from the locals. The next day, Jody moves into a weekly rental two blocks over on Avocado Street. The ad on Craigslist called it the Avocottages. There are four one-bedroom cottages on one lot. The landlord, a woman in her early fifties named Karen, is happy for Jody to stay as long as he wants as long as he pays two weeks out. The unit includes a fenced-in backyard perfect for Rory.

After buying a cheap wetsuit, he takes his board back to D Street. The rideable waves are less abundant today. He has to stay out twice as long to get the same number of attempts. The experience resembles the previous day's but on one particular wave, Jody goes from lying down to a one-knee proposal-style stance, and he manages to stand and ride the wave for a half second before he loses his balance and wipes out. Even though it was a mere half second of surfing, the activity's appeal ceases to be a mystery.

• • •

The next morning, Jody wakes up at six. He stretches for the first time in a few years. That half wave he caught yesterday has given him confidence he's ready to go surfing at Beacon's and Grandview. He waits four houses down from the apartment on Glaucus. At six forty-five, his mark emerges, walks up the hill toward Neptune, and turns right toward Grandview Beach. Jody watches the three friends rendezvous at the stairwell.

Jody waits for them to paddle out before he heads down to the sand. He straps the leash to his left ankle. D Street, where he'd gone the last two times, is a beach break similar to the beaches where he grew up swimming. But this is different. Wall after wall of whitewater comes at Jody. He can see the surfers fifty yards out. But he can't seem to get there. He paddles ten yards, and the whitewater sends him back ten yards. His back, shoulders, and arms burn from paddling. A surfer on a short board passes by him, but when Jody gets thrown back, the other surfer duck-dives with his board and goes under the wave. Jody tries to replicate the maneuver on the next wall of whitewater but his big foam board is too buoyant, and he gets a face full of water as he's thrown back ten yards. Jody keeps paddling. Sheer will gets him out past the whitewater to the takeoff zone where thirty other surfers sit on their boards. Jody climbs up, straddles his board, and tips over. He climbs on again and manages to balance. It takes five minutes for his heart rate to even out.

After thirty minutes of hovering nearby the three guys, Jody picks up their names. Zack is the guy he followed from Chester's house. Geoff is the stocky, short one with the striking facial features. And Ken is tall and quiet with a shaved head. Aside from their names, Jody doesn't learn much. They mostly talk about prior waves, future waves, beer, whiskey, and some girl named Tonya who Geoff aspires to fuck. They all catch waves, often two at once with one going left and the other right, but they always paddle back to the same spot, which makes it easy for Jody to eavesdrop without having to follow them around.

A set of four waves goes through. All three guys catch one. A teenager nearby mutters, "What's this guy waiting for, the perfect wave?" If Jody's going to keep eavesdropping, he's got to go for a wave or two. The next time a wave comes through, Jody paddles. Unlike the beach break, here, despite being bigger, the waves roll rather than break. Which makes them easier to catch. Jody paddles and he feels the wave grab him, an exhilarating moment, and he's about to try to stand when a body and board smash into him from the right. Jody hits the water and goes under. He can no longer feel the leash around his ankle. It must have come off in the collision.

Jody resurfaces. The guy who hit him, already back on his board, waves his arms. "What the fuck are you doing?"

Jody had been so focused on the wave, he hadn't looked left or right. The surfer was already riding the wave and Jody had dropped in on him.

Jody treads water, searching for his board, but it's nowhere to be found. "Sorry, man."

"Fuck you, kook." Maybe his being called a *kook* before had more to do with his foam surfboard than staying at the Rodeway.

Jody thinks the incident is over, but the guy's rage intensifies.

"Drop in on me with your Costco board." The guy swings down and punches Jody, connecting with his nose. The punch sends him underwater. He comes back up, eyes watering and nose stinging. Jody tries to throw up his forearms to protect his face, but he can't do that and tread water. Twice, Jody goes underwater to avoid punches. But that gets him more out of breath. Jody feels like this is a test he's failing. He sees the three guys on their surfboards a mere fifteen yards away. If this were in the parking lot, Jody would scrap it out, and, win or lose, at least he wouldn't lose all street cred. He takes another shot to the face, this one to the jaw. He can't fight; he'd drown. So it's flight. The agro-psycho surfer is between him and the beach. Jody swims the opposite way. Out into the deep blue. Headed for China.

Chapter Sixty-One

Renata

The larger waves bring water all the way up to Renata's back. She uses all the strength in her arms and fingers to hold on as each wave wants to drag her back into the sea. She stopped looking for Coral an hour ago. The moon now adds to the starlight, throwing a spotlight on the cliff.

In another thirty minutes, the water will come over her shoulders, and she won't be able to hang on. What will she do? Should she swim out the way Coral had tried? She fears going into the path of the crashing waves. But by staying closer to the cliffs, she'll risk getting tossed over and over again into the jagged rocks.

Neither option is viable. She's not a good enough swimmer to make it past the breakers. And to what end? Swim parallel to shore fifty yards in the dark? Even if she were to make it that far, it will be hard to see the shore from the water. How will she even know when she's swum far enough that she can make it in again? A wrong guess could send her body surfing face-first into a wall of rock.

She accepts her fate. She accepts she gave it everything she had. She thinks about her mother and father, memories as a child. Gabriel. Going to the park. Escondidas. Thinking on the past readies her for inevitable death. She can't bear to think about the future, about the possible life she had chased coming north. The thought of the future causes fast and uneven breaths, causes her to dread the moment of death. But when she focuses on the past, she finds comfort in joining things past.

Twenty minutes later, the water hasn't gotten any higher than her upper back. Though her shoulders have been splashed, they still haven't been submerged. Maybe the tide has maxed out.

She shoves that previous fatalistic acceptance far back in her consciousness. She clings to the rocky cliffside with every last bit of strength she has, knowing even if the tide starts dropping, she may have to stay like this for a couple of hours.

Chapter Sixty-Two

Jody

Jody sucks air into his lungs as he drags himself from water to sand. He had swum offshore from the agro surfer about forty yards. After the first twenty, he looked back and saw the guy paddling after him. He kept going. Headed west for the horizon. After forty yards, he saw the surfer had given up. From there, Jody had swum south, steering clear of the cluster of surfers by half a football field as he swam to shore.

Catching his breath, Jody scans the water. He can't tell who's who from this far away. The surfers all just bobbing stick figures. He spots his board washed ashore. The pink fin is gone, he assumes snapped off by the surfers.

Jody trudges back to the Avocottage. This was not how he had wanted to get in with the trio of surfers. He'll have to find another way other than undercover friendship to figure out their connection to Chester. And he'll have to be more careful now that the three guys saw him get his ass whooped. They'll recognize him if they see him again.

The next morning, Jody finds Mozy Cafe, the breakfast burrito spot where Nicole said Marty had picked up hours washing dishes. Jody orders a Great breakfast burrito—there are seven different kinds. Despite liking eggs and Mexican food, Jody has gone thirty-four years without eating a breakfast burrito. He sits outside on a patio where hanging plants create a Costa Rican rain forest–like atmosphere and eats his breakfast burrito, which is pretty *great*. He's strategizing how he'll ask about Marty when the blond girl who took his order sits at the table next to his, taking the twenty-first-century version of a smoke break.

"This was good," Jody says.

"I know, right?" she says, before going back to her phone.

"What's your favorite kind?"

"I dunno. They're all pretty good. Except the one with plantains. I'm not down with plantains."

"Me neither," says Jody even though he has no disdain for plantains. She keeps texting. "Hey, you ever work with a guy named Marty here?"

"No. But I just started like three weeks ago. Why?" She shoves her phone into the back pocket of her jean shorts.

"My friend used to work here."

"You can ask Janet." She motions toward the kitchen. "But she just started too. Kind of a high turnover rate, I guess. You live here?"

"Visiting."

"Yeah? Whatya been doing?"

"Tried surfing."

"Caught the bug already? Contagious around here."

"Yeah. Everyone seems nice. I was surfing with these guys, Zack and Geoff and Ken."

"Oh yeah, they're dope. Especially Kem, dude can shred."

Jody realizes it's Kem and not Ken. "You know them well?"

"Just from chillin'. I see them at Swami's from time to time—that's my spot. But yeah, they're chill."

"What do they do for work? I feel like since I got here, everyone's just hanging out."

"Not all of us," she says with a smile. "I dunno. They go on these trips too, and I'm like, how can you afford to do that and not work? I think Geoff is rich. His dad owns a chain of restaurants in Orange County."

"What kind of trips?"

"Mexico, like twice a month."

"Really? Huh. That's cool. They go surfing down there?"

"I dunno."

Jody thinks about twice-monthly surf trips to Mexico. Could they be bringing something back? Like cocaine?

"Shit, I gotta go back in before I get scolded by the man from down under." She says *man from down under* in a mock Australian accent.

Over the next three days, Jody tries to replicate the ease of asking the cashier about Zack, Geoff, and Kem. He buys a new fin for his board. He surfs in the mornings and afternoons. He goes to restaurants, bars, and coffee shops, striking up conversations. But most folks don't know the guys, and the few who have met them don't know too much about them—or at least they don't offer any details. Jody goes back to Mozy for breakfast burritos three different times. The one with plantains—the Tropical burrito—tastes better than great. There seems to be a different attractive beachy girl behind the counter every day. None know Marty and none have worked there longer than a few months. Jody approaches the manager. The Aussie denies having employed Marty and gets nasty fast. Jody wonders if Marty worked for cash under the table.

Filling the rest of his days, Jody tries to follow Zack, Geoff, and Kem, although he has to proceed with caution now. On the third such night, the guys have been barhopping, and Jody loses them. By the time he spots them, they're headed right for him on the sidewalk. With nowhere else to go, Jody ducks into Pandora's Pizza. It's as much a bar as a pizza joint. Fifteen beers on tap and a bunch of buzzed white surfer types sampling them. All under a sign that reads NO SHIRT, NO SHOES, NO PROBLEM. Jody finds himself thinking about Pen and her quest to find Pandora's House. He turns and sees Zack, Geoff, and Kem coming through the glass door. In an effort to avoid being seen, he'd hid in their next destination.

Jody darts from the entryway past the bar and into the men's bathroom.

Just as Jody closes the door, it opens. Kem. Jody steps up to a urinal. He fake pisses, trying to face away from Kem, who's at the adjacent urinal. Kem joins him at the sink.

"Yo. You're . . ."

Jody looks at him in the mirror, unsure what he's going to say.

"You were on a Wavestorm when that guy Worm attacked you."

Jody contemplates playing dumb as Kem keeps going.

"That guy is such a psycho. That was gnarly how you swam out to sea. Yo, bro, you gotta come with me. Lemme buy you a beer. My guys are gonna laugh their asses off."

Jody follows Kem to a booth where Zack and Geoff are planted across from each other.

"Yo," says Kem. "Look who I found."

"Oh shit," says Zack.

"Heeey. That guy," adds Geoff.

Jody tries to smile, still not sure about the tone of their amusement.

"That was fucked up," says Zack. "I mean I was right there, you did drop in on him, but that dude is a fucking psycho. He just started wailing on you."

"I didn't know what I was doing. First time on a board and suddenly this nutjob is punching me. I thought I was gonna drown."

"We thought maybe you *did* drown," says Kem.

"What you want?" asks Zack. "This one's on me."

Since the surfers had done nothing as the guy attacked him, Jody thought they were all one singular force. But the guy who attacked him was an outlier. And the others were ambivalent. And felt guilty for not coming to the aid of a man being attacked. Hence the insistence on buying him a beer.

"I'll have a Scrimshaw."

Jody drinks with the trio the rest of the evening. When they ask, Jody says he's on a trip, taking a break from life in Pennsylvania. He worried they'd connect him to Marty, but he's not sure they knew Marty. Plus, with his PA tags, he doesn't want to get caught in a lie.

He asks questions when he can, but they're all met with broad responses. What do you guys do for work?

"Ya know, make just enough to stay out of a nine-to-five."

Jody can't push too hard, knows he has to play the long game.

The next morning, he paddles out and joins the guys at Grandview. The agro dude is there, but his hollow eyes don't even seem to recognize Jody. Jody makes sure to check left and right whenever he goes for a wave. He tries a dozen waves, falling on each one. Kem tells Jody he has to stop going up to his knee first.

"You don't gotta stop at one and a half to get from one to two, bro. The old guys out here gotta do that 'cause they can't get it up. You're young and vibrant, man. You gotta just pop."

Even though Jody hasn't caught a wave yet, he's still tried to stand up a hundred times now across a week, and the muscle memory is ingrained.

On the third day of surfing with the guys, Jody sees a big wave forming. "This is you," says Kem.

Jody paddles hard. The wave picks him up. Its crest is high, and Jody rides down the wave on his belly. He tries to pop up, but he still puts his left knee down first. Even so, the wave stays smooth and forgives the superfluous step, allows him the moment to go from belly to knee to standing. And now Jody is riding the wave. Headed across the face on his board. He can hear whoops and hollers behind him.

"Yeah, old man!"

Jody rides the wave forty-five yards before it tapers. He paddles back out, trying and failing to wipe the grin off his face.

After surfing that morning, the guys invite him up to Geoff's aunt's house. She lives right on Neptune in a house on the bluff. And Auntie Rachel is nowhere to be found. In the backyard, there are two dozen teenagers and twentysomethings. A few folks in their thirties. Surfers and burnouts. Empty bottles and cans strewn about among leashes, fins, and boards. Blunts and vape pens and bongs. In the pool, two thirteen-year-old boys playing beer pong against two thirty-year-old men on a floating table. Old Jack Johnson songs on poolside speakers. Jody brought a six-pack of Mother Earth Cali Creamin', and he sets it on a table. He spots Zack, Geoff, and Kem.

"Old man . . . ," says Zack with a big smile.

"Thanks for inviting me. This place is . . ." Jody motions to the house, the view.

The other guys smile, but Geoff seems annoyed.

They sip beer for hours. Jody accepts a blunt as it's passed around. He hadn't smoked in years. Like riding a bike. His stomach settles in a way it hasn't in forever. He forgets what he's doing here, but then he thinks about Marty being stoned in some of the videos. He'd never smoked weed with his brother and he never would. The seven years between them had been a chasm as children, but the older they got, the less that gap would have mattered. Jody saddens thinking about them as peers, the age gap between them shrinking relative to their ages.

Four hours later, Zack approaches Jody. "Yo, we're gonna bounce, but we're hitting Beacon's tomorrow, dawn patrol, if you wanna get wet again."

This wasn't a party. This was a Tuesday. And Wednesday doesn't look much different. He surfs—*gets wet*—with them at Beacon's in the morning, and they invite him to the Neptune "beach palace" again in the afternoon. About 50 percent of the people are the same as the day before. The activities haven't changed. Beer. Weed. Lounging. Stoner/surfer music. In trying to infiltrate the Encinitas surf scene, Jody had felt like an impostor, but most people who can afford to live here are impostors. It's no different from Venice Beach or Brooklyn. The authentic culture made it hip, which brought wealthy people, which drove up the price and made it hard for the original *authentic* folks to stay.

He's sitting with Kem, and Kem's talking about surfing in Mexico when a teenage girl in an impossibly small bikini comes over. "Who's the newb?"

"Hey, I'm Joe."

"Tonya."

Jody recognizes the name. The girl Geoff talked about in the ocean. She looks about eighteen. Maybe nineteen or twenty. She sits with Jody and Kem. Chitchat. A quick shot at the president. Weed. Waves. Water temperature. She complains about her older sister for a few minutes. "You guys want another?" she asks.

Jody nods, *sure*.

"I'm going to go to the bathroom," says Kem.

When Tonya returns, she hands Jody a beer and plops down next to him. Her laugh devolves into a giggle, and she edges closer to Jody on the chaise lounge. Maybe it's the weed or the beer or her tiny polka-dot bathing suit, but Jody pictures what it would be like to kiss her, to untie the swimsuit. Or maybe it's her carefree mock-zen attitude that's making Jody want to hit pause on his all-consuming investigative quest and give in to his most primal of instincts. Or maybe it's the unique ability of the beach to foster fantasy. Whatever the cause, Jody gives into thinking what it would be like to have sex with her, picturing the foreplay, putting her nipples in his mouth, switching positions, trying to make her come. But the thought experiment is fleeting. It all leads him to think about Shiloh, and he wonders where she is, how she is. And that leads him back to Marty and his father and Chester Montgomery and the whole reason he's in San Diego.

Tonya slouches more, shifting weight to her elbow and forearm. Her medium-size breasts, barely retained by the tiny bikini top, roll across her chest as she adjusts her posture. Jody's eyes move to her bikini bottoms. And he goes right back to imagining having sex with her, to letting her straddle him like a surfboard. This time, it's the *do ri* Jody Morrel moral code that wakes him out of dreamland. Whatever the circumstances, he could never go through with sleeping with her.

Tonya wanders away to answer her ringing phone as Zack sits next to Jody. "She digs you. I can tell."

"Yeah?"

"Geoff's always being territorial about these girls he's not even dating. Don't let him stop you. She's hot."

A man in a sun hat comes over asking how the waves have been in Mexico. Jody pretends to text as he listens. They talk about Mexico for thirty minutes, but it's all about barrels and offshore winds and tides and reefs and twin tailfins, and nothing they say explains what's behind Zack's cryptic surf trips. While he's eavesdropping, Jody unconsciously pounds his fresh beer.

An hour later, Jody gets up to take a piss, the one-two punch of pot and booze causing a stumble. When he comes out of the bathroom, Tonya stands at the kitchen island trying—and failing—to open a bottle of champagne.

"Help me?"

Jody pops the champagne. "What are you celebrating?"

"I dunno," she says with a goofy smile.

Ten minutes later, she takes his hand and leads him into one of the many bedrooms. Turns out he could go through with it after all.

Afterward they're lying in bed, drinking more champagne. Tonya keeps giggling and trying to replicate Jody's southeastern Pennsylvania accent. *Wooter-ice.* Jody tries and fails to say the word *home* without adding an extra half syllable and then changes the subject.

"What's up with these Mexican surf trips?"

"I dunno," Tonya says. "I tried to go one time. Ya know, ask if I could go, and they shut it down. Those guys'll buy you a brew, lend you a board, invite you to their sick crib by the beach. But I guess those surf trips are sacred or something."

"Yeah," says Jody. "And I could kinda get that if it was once a year. But they go twice a month?"

"Yeah, it's weird. We should start our own trip!"

"How well do you know them?"

"So-so. Geoff's always texting me. I like Kem, he's rad. I thought Zack was a dick when I first met him, but I found out his dad had died like the week before. I dunno, they're all cool, I guess."

When Jody returns to the pool thirty minutes later, Zack smiles at him. Geoff shoots Jody a glare before killing the rest of his beer.

The partying takes a brief respite as the pack of drunks walk down to Beacon's to check the conditions. It's windy, blown-out, and someone suggests going to O'Hurley's.

Jody nurses his first beer, recognizing he's gotta slow down.

"Who's got the next round?" asks Kem.

"How about Joe?" says Geoff. "Maybe the leech could get this one for once."

Jody's not surprised at the remark after what happened with Tonya earlier, but he's surprised when Zack laughs.

Geoff stares down Jody, taunting him. "What do you say, old man? Maybe it's your turn to buy a drink. Or maybe it's all for you? The waves? The party? The beer?"

"I can get the next round," Jody says.

"Fuck it, I'm going home." Zack sounds drunk and angry. He slips out of the bar.

Kem avoids eye contact.

"It's not just me," says Geoff. "Zack thinks you're a leech too. Where'd you even come from? You weren't here, and then you were."

"It's been a long day. I'll see you guys." Jody heads for the bar's exit.

When Jody gets back to the Avocottage, he can't sleep. The booze has him exhausted, but he's wrestling with what he's doing. He's been here almost three weeks now. All to get in with these guys who are never going to invite him to Mexico. He's not even sure it's still cool to hang out with them. His mind races through other options. Maybe he should have risked talking to Sierra, Chester Montgomery's girlfriend, instead.

Jody wakes up feeling terrible. He throws up three times in an hour. He debates whether he should go see if the guys are out surfing. Instead, by 10:00 a.m. he's on the 5 freeway headed north to LA.

He finds Sierra Blaze at the gym and tanning salon where she works in NoHo. Jody recognizes her bleached hair and fake breasts from the costume party.

"Hey, are you Sierra?"

"Yeah."

"I'm Joe. We met a while back, and you told me to come into the salon."

"Oh. Cool." Sierra stares at his face. Maybe trying to remember him? Or maybe just looking at his sunburn?

"Yeah, you were with some guy named Chester. It was at a Dodgers game."

"Oh, okay. Cool."

"Is Chester your husband?"

"No. We, uhhh, we're kind of on a break. He'll call though. We always find our way back to each other."

Jody tilts his head, offering a sympathetic nod. "What does Chester do?"

"He's kinda retired. Still owns this art gallery."

"Oh, cool. I think when I met him, he was talking about business trips. Like in Encinitas? Or maybe it was Eureka?"

"Business trips? He travels but not really on business. Maybe to pick up art."

"He never mentioned Encinitas or Eureka? Are you sure?"

Sierra shakes her head no. Now eyeing Jody with more skepticism. "When was this you met me and Chester?"

Jody can sense he's pushed as far as he can push, and it doesn't seem like she knows anything anyway. Wanting to get out of the conversation, he pulls his phone out of his pants and pretends he has an incoming call. "Hello? Babe, are you okay? What? Oh, my God. I'll be right there." He turns to Sierra as he darts out. "My wife got in a car accident. I gotta go."

Jody spends the next day in Los Angeles. He's split between thinking he should go back to Leucadia or stay in LA and pursue other leads here.

But most of his leads have dried up. He thinks about Marty's investigation and about the post he made about going to Chester Montgomery's party. Was it a clue he'd left behind because he knew he was in danger? Are there more clues? When Marty told Jody about the *My Dirty California* website when they were hiking in Pennsylvania, was he telling him because he wanted Jody to be able to get to know him better? Or was he telling Jody about the website in case something happened to him?

Jody's been going through Marty's *My Dirty California* posts for twenty-seven hours—minus four hours of sleep—when his phone buzzes. A text from Zack. *Yo. I'm picking you up.* He hadn't heard from the guys since two nights ago, when Geoff had called him a leech and Zack had walked out of the bar. Jody texts back, *Cool, gimme 90 minutes.*

Thirty-six hours ago, when he'd driven up to LA from Encinitas, it took him three and a half hours. But now, middle of the day with no traffic, Jody pushes eighty the whole way, going south as if downhill, and he's there in eighty-five minutes. He's just parked and walked inside the Avocottage when a horn blasts. Zack in his Honda Accord.

"Get in."

Jody climbs in the car. With no idea if his cover's blown. Maybe Zack's driving him out to the desert to kill him.

Zack drives a couple of minutes before he says anything. "Sorry about the other night. When Geoff goes dark, it makes me wanna go somewhere else."

"No worries," Jody says as Zack pulls into a parking lot for Coffee Coffee.

"Enough of the bullshit," Zack says.

Jody's sure he's about to call him out for trying to infiltrate their group of friends when Zack breaks a smile.

"We gotta snag you a real board."

Coffee Coffee neighbors a surf shop called Surfy Surfy.

Jody surfs with the guys the next three days. He bought a used board the sales clerk said the previous owner had nicknamed the Death Cloud.

Jody's not sure why. It's an eight-foot fiberglass Walden. It's harder to use than the foamie but he gets less eye rolls hauling it around. Geoff pretends like nothing was ever wrong.

On the second day, Zack, Geoff, and Kem bring Jody to a paddle-out for a Black teenager named Jarmon Wade who was shot by the police up in LA earlier in the week. More than five hundred surfers gather on the beach, but because the water gets rough in the afternoon, the surfers stay on shore and use their boards to spell out a giant *UNITY* in the sand.

On the third day, Jody and Zack eat lunch at Haggo's while Geoff and Kem stay out to catch more waves.

Halfway through cauliflower tacos, Zack asks, "What are you really doing out here, man?"

"Truth is, my dad passed away a couple months ago. I tried to stick it out, ya know, just go on, but . . ." Jody trails off.

"That's a bummer." Zack tightens his fists to hold back tears. "Sometimes you ride the wave, sometimes the wave rides you."

The maneuver works. Zack asks Jody to hang out more and more. Surfing in the mornings and evenings. Lunch. Beers at Geoff's aunt's house one of the days—where Tonya latches on to him again, this time in an outdoor shower stall.

One evening, Jody and Zack stay out surfing late. Kem's leash broke, and he and Geoff had paddled in for the day. The waves turned to shit an hour ago, but Jody and Zack sit on their boards watching the evening sky, a kaleidoscope of blues, oranges, reds, and purples. Looking at the colors, Jody senses this is the moment.

"Yo? Can I ask you something?"

"Sure," says Zack.

"I got a sister back East. I quit my job after my dad passed. But she's . . . well, she's got some health issues, and I need to send her money. I'm just wondering, whatever you guys are doing, I want to help."

"I don't know what you're talking about."

"I just need to make some money's all," says Jody.

Zack catches the next wave and rides it all the way to shore.

Jody doesn't hear from Zack the next day. He checks Grandview and Beacon's in the morning but doesn't see them. He's a month into this Encinitas operation. He brainstorms his options. He could come clean with Zack, tell him about Marty. He could pull Wyatt's gun on them and interrogate them. No option seems advisable. If they'd never bring him to Mexico, what could he do? Follow them in a boat? Slip a tracking device into their bag like some James Bond shit? No amount of considering his options helps Jody narrow in on a good one.

Two days later, Zack knocks on his door at 6:30 a.m. to go surfing. And on the walk up Avocado Street to Beacon's, he asks Jody if he wants to go on a surfing trip to Mexico and make a little cash on the side.

Chapter Sixty-Three

Pen

The nurse hands Pen a pill and a six-ounce paper cup of water. "Down the hatch," she says.

The first time the nurse handed her a pill two weeks ago, Pen tried to use sleight of hand to palm the pill. The nurse caught her and forced her to swallow it. The next day, Pen tried spitting the pill back into the cup, but the nurse caught her again.

"Go ahead," she had said. "And you're gonna try to cheek them tomorrow. Guess what, we'll start crushing them up into a powder, and if that don't take, we'll use a needle. I recommend you just take the pills."

After the Lassen park ranger tackled her, Pen was tased and arrested. She was transferred to Metropolitan State Hospital in Norwalk.

Pen takes the pill from the nurse. "Thank you," she says. She puts the pill in her mouth and uses her tongue to shove the pill into a gap where she's missing a molar. She makes sure not to swallow so hard it pulls the pill out.

"Let me see," says the nurse.

Pen opens wide and moves her tongue in a circle.

"Good."

She had slept the whole first day of her involuntary psychiatric hold. On the second day, she met with her treatment team—a psychiatrist, a psychologist, a social worker, and a rehabilitation therapist. The psychiatrist prescribed her clozapine, an antipsychotic drug. The 5150 seventy-two-hour hold was extended to a 5250 fourteen-day hold. The team met with her every day that first week, where they completed various clinical evaluations and assessments. They informed Pen these meetings would now be held once per week. It reminds her of signing with agents, a manager, and an attorney after her documentary went to Sundance. She kept having these team meetings where each meeting's sole purpose seemed to be planning the next meeting.

After the nurse leaves, Pen takes the pill out from between her molars and tosses it in the toilet. She lies down, tries to wrap her mind around the cover-up. If Lassen is a breach in the world, the national park rangers could be helping to keep people out. And when someone does figure out the truth, what do they do? They throw them in a locked psych ward. And force them to take medications. Her new *team* has told her the goal for all patients is to prepare them for discharge. But all the patients Pen has met in group therapy and in the cafeteria and in the garden have been here for months or years.

Chapter Sixty-Four

Tiph

It smells like perfume and lemon-scented air fresheners in the auction house. Tiph watches as folks—mostly old white folks—bid on furniture, antiques, expensive cookware, and even some sports memorabilia. Tiph finds herself daydreaming about which items she'd want in the house the art stash will buy.

A man sits next to her, which causes Tiph to pull her purse closer. The purse that holds two thousand dollars in cash she got from pawning an antique gold pocket watch that she borrowed two days ago from a house she was cleaning. The owners are away for a month. Tiph plans to resell the desk and use the money to buy back the pocket watch and replace it before they know it's gone.

The fourteenth piece to be auctioned off is Chester's desk. "It's a nineteenth-century Wooton desk that was restored two years ago." Projected photographs showcase the desk from various angles. "We'll start the bidding at five hundred dollars. Anyone? Five hundred dollars for the Wooton desk?"

Tiph raises her paddle.

"We've got five hundred. Anyone else?"

Tiph glances around the room. Most folks are on their phones, came here for a different item.

"Anyone else? Six hundred for the desk? Last call."

Tiph smiles. Based on her research, she'll be able to resell the desk for a couple grand. She might be able to get the contents of the secret compartment and then resell the desk for a profit too. Make Scheming Mike proud.

An old Italian man in a fedora raises his paddle.

Damn it.

"Okay, we've got six hundred for the desk. How about seven hundred?"

Tiph raises her paddle.

"Lady offers seven. Do I hear eight hundred? Fedora at eight. Do I hear nine hundred? Lady offers nine. Do I hear a thousand? We're at a thousand. Do I hear eleven—"

"Eleven hundred," says Tiph.

"Okay, that's eleven hundred. Twelve anyone?"

Fedora hesitates a long moment before raising his paddle. Tiph relaxes. If he hesitates at twelve, he won't go to two grand.

"Twelve from the man with the hat. Anyone want thirteen hundred?"

Tiph raises her paddle confidently—no reason to give the Italian man any idea she's close to her ceiling.

"Thirteen says the lady. Do I hear fourteen?"

The door opens, and an old Asian woman wheels into the room, pulling her chair up to the fourth row.

"Fourteen hundred? Last call for fourteen."

The man in the fedora raises his paddle, lower than last time, as if hoping the auctioneer doesn't even see it.

"That's fourteen hundred from our friend in the fedora."

"Fifteen hundred," says Tiph.

"The lady takes fifteen hundred. Anyone for sixteen?"

All eyes fall on the man in the fedora.

"Do I hear sixteen?" The auctioneer looks right at the old Italian man, but he shakes his head. "Okay, last call for the Wooton. Sixteen hundred from the woman with a hat of her own."

Tiph looks over to see the woman in the wheelchair has her paddle raised.

"Do I hear seventeen hundred?"

Tiph, flustered at the newcomer's bid, raises her paddle.

"That's seventeen hundred from our original bidder. Do I hear eighteen hundred?"

The woman in the wheelchair raises her paddle.

"How about nineteen hundred?"

Tiph raises her paddle.

"Do I hear two thousand?"

The woman in the wheelchair throws up her paddle.

"Do I hear twenty-one hundred?"

Two thousand was Tiph's ceiling. She has maybe another seventy-five dollars in her purse. She could scrape together twenty-five from her car. "Twenty-one hundred," Tiph says.

The woman in the wheelchair doesn't wait for the auctioneer. She holds her paddle high to the sky.

"Is that two thousand, two hundred, ma'am?" the auctioneer asks.

The woman in the wheelchair nods.

"Do I hear twenty-three hundred?"

This would be three hundred over her ceiling. Maybe she could run to a pay advance place. But she doesn't have a paycheck with her. What jewelry does she have on her to pawn? Maybe she could get a couple hundred dollars.

"Last call for twenty-three hundred," says the auctioneer.

Tiph hasn't finished the math yet, but she thrusts her paddle up.

"That's twenty-three, how about twenty-four hundred?"

The Asian woman in the wheelchair holds her paddle high. Had she even put it down from her last bid? "Twenty-four hundred. Do I hear twenty-five?"

Tiph doesn't have five hundred dollars to make up the difference. She might have failed to scrape together the twenty-three.

The auctioneer looks to Tiph. "Two thousand five hundred for the Wooton desk, last call."

• • •

Crestfallen, Tiph trudges toward the exit of the auction house. She's about to leave the lobby when an employee carries an antique lamp out of a room past a security guard. The inventory room. Tiph doesn't need to own the desk. She only needs to access the desk. If the secret compartment is the size the carpenter had described, its contents should fit in her purse.

Tiph approaches the guard. "How you doing?"

"Fine." He doesn't look fine; he looks annoyed.

"I was hoping to look at one of the pieces."

"No can do."

"I'll just be a second."

"Same answer."

"I'm not going to steal anything, just steal a glance. I promise you."

"I promise you, all I get paid eight dollars an hour to do is make sure people do not go in the room."

Did he bring up his salary to suggest he makes his decisions based on economics? Tiph reaches in her purse and pulls out two twenties. But he won't take them.

"C'mon. I'll be in and out. Fast as this analogy."

"Nope."

"I'll give you a hundred."

"See that camera over there?"

Tiph follows his finger to a security camera on the far side of the lobby.

"C'mon, ace, let's call an ace an ace, they're not checking that footage unless there's an incident. There won't be an incident. I just need to *see* something for two minutes."

"Lady, you can talk to me all day. I get paid to sit here whether you ask me a hundred times or whether you leave and I go back to staring at the wall."

Fuck you, fat man. "Fuck you, fat man." She walks away wishing she hadn't brought his weight into it.

Tiph goes outside. She has a voice mail from Dee's Cleaning

Services canceling her next gig. By losing this gig, she's not only losing the $35, she's losing the chance to return the antique gold pocket watch once she buys it back from the pawnshop. She calls Gloria, the coordinator, back.

"You get my message?" Gloria asks.

"Yeah, I can't lose that gig."

"I'm sorry."

"Nah, girl, hold on, sorry's not sharp enough to cut it. You done me like this too many times. I gotta plan my schedule. I got a son. You take me off this gig tomorrow, I'm out. And I'm calling Rayya and telling her about this shit too."

There's a long pause. "Fine, it's yours," says Gloria before hanging up, not bothering to say goodbye.

While on the phone, Tiph had stress-paced around the side of the building along a walking path that dead-ends. When she returns to the courtyard outside the auction house, Tiph sees the huge security guard taking shade under an evergreen ash tree. Yelling into the phone and pacing. Is another guard at his post?

She reenters the auction house lobby. The security guard's chair is empty. Without any hesitation, she slips into the inventory room.

She thought there might be a few dozen pieces in the room, but there are hundreds, maybe thousands. She searches the rows of furniture.

She spots the desk right as she hears the door opening. She opens an antique steamer trunk and climbs in. Pulling the lid over top herself.

She waits what feels like five minutes. She opens the lid to climb out but sees two men on the other side of the room waiting to pick up a couch. She lowers the lid, now keeps it open a tiny crack. She listens as they carry the couch, knocking into other pieces, before leaving the room.

The carpenter in Palm Springs had told her about the secret compartment, but it still takes Tiph five minutes to find the latch. She pops out the false back. Fuck. Is the compartment empty? She reaches her hand farther and her fingers find a key. She pulls it out, the metal cooling her palm. She looks at the key on the black and red key chain. A number on the key chain reads 302.

Two employees walk inside to grab another piece. Tiph shoves the key in her pocket. The two guys see her. She does her best to look like she hadn't snuck back here. They either buy it or don't care. As the two employees head for the far side of the room, Tiph heads for the exit.

The security guard is back at his post. He steps in front of her. "What I tell you? Now you're going to have to come with me."

For a moment, Tiph can't find any words, her brain too busy screaming at her that she's on probation, that she can't let this happen. "Oh, fuck no. Don't be throwing stones from your glass house. You do that and you'll have to tell your boss instead of sitting in your chair, you were outside talking on the phone with your girl."

She heads for the exit, still not sure whether he'll try to stop her. She doesn't hear any heavy footsteps following. Once out the double doors, she runs for her car.

Chapter Sixty-Five

Jody

Jody paces in the Avocottage, waiting for Zack to pick him up. When Jody had asked what he should bring, Zack had said, "Just clothes for two days, one night. And your stick." His landlord Karen was happy to watch Rory for a couple of days.

Jody hears a car horn and heads outside. He straps his board on top of Zack's Honda. They meet Geoff and Kem at the harbor parking lot in Oceanside.

"The Death Cloud has arrived," Kem says with a smile.

Geoff nods a hello, as nice as he's been to Jody. They lead Jody through a forest of masts to a beautiful—albeit old—fifty-foot sailboat named *Kelly*.

"I'm stoked you're here. You know how to sail?" Zack asks.

"Don't even know which side is starboard," Jody says.

"C'mon, you'll learn," says Zack as the four of them pile on the boat.

It takes them eight hours to sail down to Campo López, which is about halfway between Tijuana and Ensenada on the Baja Peninsula. Zack seems to enjoy teaching Jody how to sail, showing him the intricacies of this particular boat. Jody learns that Geoff is going on a trip to Fiji with his dad for a few months, and the guys need someone to take his place while he's gone. It's dusk by the time they get to Campo López, dropping anchor about seventy-five yards offshore. From the boat, in what's left of the day's light, Jody can make out a beach, the bluff, some rocky terrain, and farther back, dirt roads and two-dozen one-story homes on a hillside.

They go to bed at 9:00 p.m., planning to surf at dawn. Jody hadn't asked any questions. Not out of a lack of curiosity but an attempt to hide his intentions. He lays his head down as Zack says, "Yo."

Jody watches as Zack pulls the wall, where an extra layer of fiberglass has been added, painted, and sealed. The concealed compartment is the size of a walk-in closet.

The guys seem to be staring at Jody as if to gauge his reaction.

"What are we taking back with us?" Jody asks.

"What's a who," says Zack. "Just helping some folks who want a better life."

"We figured it was safe to assume you're not a build-the-wall kinda guy," says Kem.

"No, 'course not," says Jody. This was the scheme. But was this it? Would Marty have gone to such lengths to try to take down a few surfers who were getting paid to help undocumented Mexican immigrants cross the border?

Twenty minutes later, Jody can hear the three surfers breathing as he lies awake wondering how tomorrow will go.

At dawn, they load their boards up on the dinghy and head to shore. The waves are pounding, an unusual early-morning onshore wind making them close out fast. Jody paddles out but doesn't try to catch any waves. Kem catches a few—he can surf anything it seems. Geoff and Zack each try for a couple and wipe out. Geoff curses under his breath, ego bruised. After an hour-long break, they head out for more waves at 10:00 a.m. The conditions have grown steadily worse since they first got out there. Jody still doesn't go for a wave, instead retains the sole goal of trying to survive.

They're on a lunch break, nestled under the shade of a palm tree, when they hear the sound of an automobile. A police Jeep drives over rocks and sand.

A twenty-five-year-old Mexican police officer gets out of the Jeep.

None of the three surfers seem rattled. They put down their food and beer and stand to greet the officer.

The police officer pulls out his gun when he gets closer. All of them raise their hands, now rattled.

"What are you doing here?" the cop asks.

"Equipo Aguilar," says Zack.

The officer pauses. "¿En dónde has oído eso?" He laughs. "Where did you hear that?" he asks.

"We're on a surfing trip," says Zack.

"Say the expression again," says Kem.

"Equipo Aguilar," says Zack.

"Put your wallets in a pile here," says the Mexican cop.

"They're on the boat." Zack points out to the sailboat anchored past the breakers.

The cop shoves the gun against Zack's temple. "I will wait here. Go get all the cash and wallets from the boat. And the phones." Keeping the gun to Zack's temple, he motions to Geoff. "You. You go."

Geoff drags the dinghy into the surf and heads toward the sailboat.

Now the cop turns to Kem. "Put all the boards in the Jeep. Except *that* one." He points out Jody's longboard.

Geoff gets back with the wallets and phones from the sailboat. The surfboards—minus the Death Cloud—have been loaded in the Jeep. They all hear the sound of another automobile. This one a pickup truck. Also Mexican police. An older officer, more like fifty, walks over toward the group.

Zack speaks up. "Equipo Aguilar. Equipo Aguilar."

This grabs the older cop's attention. He looks at the younger cop. The younger cop laughs and shakes his head. "Lo escucharon en alguna parte."

The older cop motions for the younger cop to step away with him. They walk back to their cars.

Jody, Zack, Kem, and Geoff wait. Their bare feet burning in the hot sand. Kem says, "They think we heard it from somewhere."

Two minutes later, the older cop returns. "We are sorry for confusion. Please enjoy stay of yours."

The surfers step back into the shade.

"Jesus Christ."

"What the fuck was that?"

"Dude, that was heavy."

"I almost shit myself."

"Bro, that was almost fucked, bro."

They watch as the cops unload the three surfboards. The older cop gets in his truck and drives off. But the Jeep stays. The younger cop walks back toward the surfers. Before, the younger cop appeared amused as he robbed them, but now he looks ready to exercise a vendetta.

"What do we do?" asks Kem.

No one has an answer.

The younger cop steps into the shade of the palm tree, joining them. He reaches toward his hip, and it seems like he'll pull his Glock again when he reaches into his back pocket and pulls out a wad of cash. He hands it to Zack.

"I'm sorry for the . . . mix-up. Confusion. I was wrong. Please, I ask that you keep that incident for us."

"No problem, man," Zack says.

The fear on this alpha male cop's face signals that Chester must be in league with an intimidating party. A cartel.

The cop hands back their wallets and phones in a plastic grocery bag.

"Give him the money back," Geoff whispers.

Zack tries to hand him back the wad of cash. But the young cop won't take it. Instead, he turns and walks back toward the Jeep.

None of them feel like surfing. But after sitting in the shade for a couple of hours, an offshore wind picks up, causing the waves to hold up and form clean barrels. The near-perfect conditions are enough to abate their nerves. All four paddle out. Kem gets the first barrel, dropping down a wave, going right before he disappears into a tunnel of water and emerges ten yards on the other side. Geoff and Zack each get a great left soon after.

The waves crest and crash faster than at Beacon's and Grandview, and Jody can't get up in time. He manages to catch one, going from belly to knee to standing in record time, but he rides down the wave instead of across it. He stays on, but as he reaches the base of the wave, the sheet of water slams down on him from above. The chaos—being pushed and pulled in multiple directions—reminds him of the car accident with Derrick. He surfaces in time for another wave to smash down on him. While underwater, he opens his eyes and sees the coral and rocks, all the hazards that could've busted his head open. He surfaces, finds his board, and paddles out of the crash zone.

Kem laughs. "You're a wildcat."

"Careful in there, old man," Zack says.

Jody stays out in the water but doesn't paddle for any more waves.

Zack checks his watch and motions for the shore. "We should head in."

Jody isn't sure what he expected to see. But it wasn't a man in a straw hat walking toward them followed by thirteen women and children. As they get closer, Jody can see the man in the straw hat is no farmer. It isn't the guns on both hips that suggest he works for a Mexican drug cartel as much as it is his cold, vacant eyes.

The surfers stand to greet the man. A recognition in the nods exchanged. They must have dealt with this man before. Jody looks past the group. Rocky terrain and tide pools filled with combinations of rainwater and seawater. The police Jeep and pickup had made it all the way to the beach, but whatever vehicle had brought these thirteen individuals must have only made it so far. Jody wonders how far they walked.

The women and children—with tentative smiles—look nervous but excited about the new adventure that awaits them. The man in the straw hat leaves the thirteen Mexicans with the surfers and trudges back the way he came.

It takes two trips in the dinghy to get them all out to the sailboat. There's a teen girl with hot pink fingernails. A pretty twentysomething woman with a gap between her two front teeth. An eight- or nine-year-old boy clutching something in his hands, maybe a harmonica. A young girl with a Barcelona shirt reminds Jody of a girl who played on the middle school boys' soccer team last year.

While Jody helps Zack get the anchor up, Kem addresses the women and children. "El compartimiento es pequeño. En el viaje, pueden estar en el casco del barco. Pero si se acerca la Guardia Costera o la migra, tendrán que meterse rápidamente en el compartimiento."

Kem and Geoff have the women and children climb down into the hull to test the smuggling compartment. They all fit. And they could fit another full-grown adult or two children.

A boy with a buzz cut cries, and Jody senses he's seasick even though they haven't left yet. He gives the boy a Dramamine.

Once they're sailing back north, Zack walks over to Jody and reties the jib sheet. "This is the easy side of the border."

Jody doesn't have to fake an uneasy smile.

Looking out at the water, Jody thinks about the thirteen migrants. All women and children. No men, no one older than the age of thirty. These women and children are under the impression they are being smuggled into the United States for a better life. But they aren't. They are being trafficked. Jody thinks through a plan. Once he knows where they are, he'll call the police. They'll come. The ring will be busted. *This* is what Marty was trying to stop. The human trafficking ring he was trying to bust. And Jody might be doing it in a matter of hours.

The excitement and nerves give him diarrhea. A smell that lights up the boat's tiny bathroom. A smell that permeates the whole hull. A smell that gets blamed on the Mexican women and children.

They're maybe a mile away from the coast of San Diego now, and Jody realizes how many unknowns there are. He plans to call the police, but at what stage? Where are they taking the women and children? Are they taking them to some warehouse or maybe a home? He doubts they're going to return to the busy harbor in Oceanside, so where will they get ashore? He wants to make a decision about when he'll call the police, but he doesn't have the necessary information. He has to wait.

As the dread builds, so does his nausea. He hears Zack say, "Oh shit." A Coast Guard boat bears down on them from the north. Geoff darts below deck.

Jody feels a rush of ease, his blood cooling. The Coast Guard is bailing him out. *Semper Paratus—Always Ready.* Once they arrive, he can alert them to the situation. The Coast Guard will board the ship, find the compartment, and it will be the same result as Jody trying to get the police.

He hears the clatter and rush of bodies below deck as Geoff gets the women and children into the smuggling compartment. He hears the compartment door sliding shut. Geoff appears above deck as the Coast Guard boat pulls up next to them.

"How's it going, gentlemen?" asks a white man in his fifties, nose forever reddened by exposure to the sun. A stout woman in her twenties stands next to him. Both wear US Coast Guard gear.

"Good," Zack says.

Jody steps forward not wanting to risk waiting any longer before he sells out his three surfer friends and alerts the Coast Guard to the human beings being trafficked below deck. He doesn't know what Zack, Geoff, and Kem will do. What can they do? They're on board a sailboat with no weapons—as far as Jody knows. They can't outrun the Coast Guard's motorboat with their sailboat. All they'll be able to do is stare down Jody with icy glares at his betrayal while they await their fates.

The words are on the tip of Jody's tongue when his mind skips ahead to the events that will follow. He miscalculated. The surfers may wait to ask for lawyers or maybe they'll talk, but either way, the three think they're part of an illegal immigration ring. Jody doubts the same three guys who brought him to a BLM paddle-out would knowingly take part in a human trafficking ring. And even if Zack knows the operation is about more than getting these women and children over the border, he won't volunteer that information. The victims themselves don't even know they're victims, so their story will match the surfers'. Jody doesn't know what the penalty is for aiding illegal immigration, but it's more lenient than the penalty for taking part in a human trafficking ring. However far up the chain this arrest goes, whether it stops with the surfers or they can get other middlemen, everyone will claim it was a border-crossing scheme. The penalties won't be great enough to scare anyone into giving up Chester Montgomery. Chester will walk. His human trafficking ring can continue. Even if right now the Coast Guard can get Zack, Geoff, and Kem to give up the details of the meet-up and they manage to arrest someone else, *that* person will just claim to be the last in a line of people helping undocumented immigrants get to the United States. In an operation this complex—one with smuggling compartments and a Mexican drug cartel—there would be plans in place. There may already be a lawyer on retainer. This was an operation that killed his brother and an LAPD detective. It was an operation willing to kill to protect itself. Those on the rungs of the ladder between these surfers and Chester Montgomery won't talk to the police. They'll take their few years in prison like any midlevel criminal in any successful criminal operation. By tipping off the Coast Guard, all he'll do is get these surfers arrested and alert Chester Montgomery that he, Jody, is onto him.

Jody had stepped forward, planning to make his great reveal. All eyes remain on him. To fill in the blanks, now he asks, "How are you guys doing?"

"Good," the man says. "What are you all up to?"

"Just a day surfing trip," Zack says.

"We're going to need to come on board," says the woman, killing the motor.

"No problem," Zack says.

The woman stays on the Coast Guard boat. "How were the waves?" the man asks.

"Pretty epic," says Kem.

"Show me down?"

Zack nods for Geoff to show the man down into the hull. Jody stays up top. He stares out at the ocean. A few moments ago, he was getting ready to show these two the women and children in the smuggling compartment. Now he's praying to a god he doesn't believe in that they won't find it. The Coast Guard woman is looking at him, reading his unease. Jody takes a cue from Kem and tries to emote surfer nonchalance.

Two minutes pass, and Jody fears the officer found the compartment. He hears footsteps. Geoff and the Coast Guard officer appear on deck, mid-conversation about flounder.

"All right, gentlemen, be safe." He steps back over to the motorboat, and they zoom off.

Zack turns to Jody. "That's happened three times. But it's still nerve-racking."

"Should we get going?" asks Kem.

"We got an hour. I kinda want to watch this gnarly sunset," says Zack.

As the four guys watch the sunset from the rocking sailboat, Jody steals glances at the coast. Is that a harbor about twenty miles north? Could that be Oceanside? Or is it the main harbor in downtown San Diego? He scans the coast for airplanes. If he can find San Diego International Airport, that should give him a good indicator of where they are. The marine layer makes it hard to see the skyline.

"What ya looking at, dude?" Geoff asks.

"Oh. Uh, was trying to see if I could spot the track at Del Mar," Jody says, pointing.

"You can't see it from the water," says Kem.

None of them have offered any details about what the plan is. "Where are we going in?" Jody asks.

"You'll see," Zack says. The other three guys all return their gazes to the setting sun, sharing stories of seeing the green flash.

After it gets dark, they sail the ship toward the shore. A cove below a cliff. It looks like it could be near Carlsbad, Solana Beach, or any other ritzy, remote residential Southern California beach community. It looks like the last place where they would bring thirteen undocumented immigrants from Mexico. But maybe that's the point.

As they get two hundred yards away from the shore, they cut the lights, pull in two of the sails. Sailing stealth mode.

About thirty yards outside the breakers, they lower the last sail and drop the anchor.

"Is it there?" asks Kem.

"Yeah, I see it," says Geoff.

"Be patient," says Zack impatiently.

Jody can make out the silhouette of a box truck at the edge of a lower section of the bluffs. He can't be sure from this distance in the dark, but it looks like a switchback trail goes up from the sand to the top of this lowest section of bluff.

So from here, will they take the women and children somewhere in a truck?

Headlights flash twice. This must be the signal the coast is clear because Zack, Geoff, and Kem spring into action. Before Zack and Geoff disappear below, Zack says to Jody, "Help Kem with the dinghy."

Jody swallows, the taste of rust lingers in his throat. If someone is in the truck flashing the headlights, maybe they're taking all thirteen women and children. Does that mean Jody, Zack, Geoff, and Kem are sailing back to Oceanside? Then how will Jody track the women and children to the next step of the human trafficking ring?

By the time Jody and Kem get the dinghy in the water and strap the ladder to the sailboat's edge, Geoff has the first group of women and children waiting. One by one, they go down the ladder into the dinghy where Kem helps them down. Seven in total now, plus Kem. Jody is supposed to wait here with Geoff and the other half of the migrants.

Jody watches the dinghy head for the shore. Zack and Kem time it to ride the momentum of a wave. A wave big enough to take them toward shore but small enough to avoid capsizing the dinghy.

From the sailboat, Jody can see the shape of a man open the back of the box truck. For the third time today, Jody enters a state of panic. He had envisioned the surfers themselves taking the Mexicans somewhere, which would have allowed him to take down more of the human trafficking ring when he went to the authorities. Instead, they're being picked up by a man in a truck. And from Jody's perspective, all the way out here, it's the mere silhouette of a man and a truck.

After the dinghy lands ashore, Zack and Kem lead the Mexican women and children up the switchback path where the truck awaits them. The seven of them walk up a ramp and disappear into the truck. Zack and Kem jog back down the path to repeat the process for the other half of the women and children.

Jody had wanted to do more than save these thirteen individuals. He'd wanted to break the whole ring, to save past victims and future victims. But now these thirteen individuals are going to get sold into who knows what.

He races through his options. He could still call the police now, although he'd have to either do it without Geoff hearing him, or he could try to overpower Geoff and push him overboard. But even if he calls the police, he's not sure they'd get there in time to get the truck.

"What time you think we'll get back?" Jody asks.

Geoff stares at him. "You're asking a lot of questions, bro."

Jody has to get ashore. That way he can at least get a better view of the truck and the driver.

Zack and Kem pull up the dinghy to the starboard side. The other six women and children emerge from below deck, led by Geoff. Kem helps each of them to the ladder, where Zack waits in the dinghy below. Once all six of them are in the dinghy, Jody clutches Kem's arm.

"Yo, you mind if I go? I got seasick sitting here in the waves." It's not hard for Jody to fake the nausea.

"Sure, bro."

Kem steps aside. Geoff looks on, arms crossed at his chest.

Zack looks confused why Jody joins him rather than Kem. "Gotta get my feet on solid ground for a minute. Feel sick."

Zack smiles. "Yeah, anchored can be worse than sailing on high seas."

Zack picks a medium-size wave, and they ride it ashore. The youngest boy smiles as they take the wave toward the sand.

"Is that fun?" Zack asks.

The boy doesn't speak English but seems to understand the sentiment and raises his arms like a kid on a roller coaster.

Jody helps Zack pull the dinghy up to dry sand. Zack leads the second group of women and children up the sandy switchback, Jody in the rear.

When they get to the top, Jody gets a better look at the white or cream-colored box truck. One by one, the women and children climb the ramp. The vehicle is parked parallel to the water about ten feet back from the bluff's edge where Jody stands just behind Zack. The youngest boy has a hard time making it up the ramp, and Jody moves to help. This will be his chance to see the license plate, but Zack grabs his arm. "Stay here. He hasn't seen you before, and he's kinda intense. Better to stay over here." Zack motions to the driver, who at this moment is on the other side of the truck.

Zack helps the boy up the ramp. Jody keeps scanning the truck for any possible detail. He looks through the window to get a view of the driver. But it just looks like a white dude with a ball cap low over his face. Maybe sideburns. Zack goes over and talks to the driver. Jody takes out his phone. He makes sure to turn off the flash before he snaps pictures of the side of the truck. Zack closes the back of the truck as the driver climbs back in the front. Jody snaps one more picture, this one includes the driver at the wheel, and shoves the phone in his pocket before Zack sees.

"Let's roll," Zack says as he moves to the switchback.

As the driver turns the ignition, Jody hesitates, hoping he'll get a view of the plate. But the driver backs up instead of pulling forward, all to do a K-turn, and now a sand dune blocks Jody's view. He gets one more glimpse of the truck, but now it's forty yards away, and he can't make out the plate.

As they sail north to the harbor in Oceanside, Jody remains on the verge of vomiting, continues passing it off as seasickness. He can't stop picturing the women and children disappearing into the back of that truck. To be trafficked.

On the drive back to Encinitas, Jody's nausea builds. "I thought it was seasickness, but I think I swallowed too much water surfing."

"You all right?" Zack asks.

Jody gets that distinctive bilious feeling in the center of his body, knows vomiting is imminent. "Pull over. Pull over."

Jody climbs out. He throws up in the grass. When he walks back to Zack's car, he sees Geoff and Kem have climbed out of Geoff's SUV to talk to Zack. Geoff holds Jody's wallet. Kem, standing next to Geoff, holds Jody's opened backpack.

"Joseph Morrel?" Geoff asks, reading Jody's ID. "Thought you were Joe Bell."

"What the fuck?" asks Zack.

"Just wanted a new start is all," Jody says. At first, he's paranoid they'll connect the name to Marty, but he doesn't think they know anything about Marty.

"That's shady, man," says Kem.

Geoff takes the bag from Kem and throws it in the grass. "Find your own way back." Jody looks to Zack, hoping he'll intervene, but Zack avoids eye contact.

Jody watches their cars disappear. If they knew he'd befriended them to figure out their Mexico operation, they'd've never let him go like this.

He throws up again while he waits for a Lyft.

• • •

Unable to sleep, Jody paces his beach cottage. Twice he picks up the phone to call the police and changes his mind. The image of the truck driving away haunts him, but a call to the police will only result in the police questioning Zack, and Zack or some attorney alerting Chester. He needs to deal with a cop or FBI agent he can trust so the authorities can go after Chester without tipping him off.

Early the next morning, he looks out the window of the Avocottage and sees Karen watering her snapdragons. Jody asks if she knows any San Diego cops that she trusts.

Kenny, a SDPD homicide detective, orders a vegetable scramble and a coffee at A Little Moore Cafe. Jody sips on a decaf coffee, not up for a meal.

"Karen said you needed help."

"I need to know I can trust you."

"This about that Worm guy?"

Jody had previously told Karen the story about the surfer attacking him, and she must have passed the story along to Kenny.

"No. It's nothing like that. It . . . it goes deep. Sprawl to it."

"What are you talking about?"

Jody lays it out for him. He tries to summarize it as much as possible, but by the time he's done, the scramble has come and so has the check.

Kenny asks a series of follow-up questions, and Jody answers them. Jody's had to do so much lying and pretending over the last few weeks. It feels good to spit the truth.

Kenny remains quiet for a long minute. "I know one guy in the FBI. He's in financial crimes. But I think if I get this info to him, he can get it to the right folks in human trafficking."

"And there's no reason why the LAPD has to know, right? I'm saying, they can't tip off Chester or whoever by asking around the LAPD. 'Cause then that truck full of women and kids . . . I don't know. If he feels the heat coming, I imagine he'd have to get rid of them."

Chapter Sixty-Six

Renata

The water has gone from Renata's shoulders to her knees. Enough so she's able to loosen her grip on the cliffside one hand at a time. Her muscles so fatigued it feels like a thousand needles are poking her.

Now that she knows she'll survive, her mind shifts to Coral. She keeps picturing the moment Coral let go, when the water sucked her out to sea. Had the wave slammed her into rocks below the surface?

Another hour later, the tide has dropped more, and the incoming waves bring water no higher than shin level. Renata lets go of the rocks, her fingers bleeding from hanging on for hours. It's still dark, still the middle of the night. Renata stays close to the cliff's edge and heads south, working herself back the way they came. She gets to the rock outcropping they originally went around the previous evening. Between waves, she steps into waist-high water and peers around the outcropping. She can't see anything other than starlight cast on tens of thousands of stones, whitewater ebbing and flowing. No sign of the two men who had chased them.

Renata clocks the rhythm of the waves, watching several cycles. Right as the water goes down, she darts through the knee-high water and around the outcropping before the next wave of water hits the rocks. She's back to the stone beach now. She had hoped to see Coral alive on the other side, had feared seeing her dead body washed up on the rocks. She sees neither. Just ocean, sand, rocks. An epic, rugged, wild coastline that can't possibly be LA.

Renata stares out at the ocean, wondering if Coral's body is floating out there. Her mind goes to sharks, and she starts trudging back across the stones.

Chapter Sixty-Seven

Jody

Jody moves out of the Avocottage and checks into the Leucadia Beach Inn. It feels good, like he's taken the case as far as he can and passed it off to the FBI.

But without some investigative task to occupy his mind, he can't stop replaying memories of his father and brother. He doesn't want to risk running into Zack, Geoff, or Kem, but Jody craves the escape of riding waves. So he surfs at Swami's every morning at dawn, the water his one solace.

After two days, Kenny texts him and says he talked to his guy at the FBI, and it went well, and he should know more soon. For the next three days, Jody falls into a routine. He wakes up and surfs at Swami's, eats lunch, goes to a bar called the Regal Seagull where he spaces out three pints over as many hours before grabbing a chicken burrito and returning to his hotel room.

The next day, he catches a big left, and shoots across, exploring the plane with a zigzagging pattern, the longest wave he's caught. He's in the middle of drinking an amber ale and talking to a good-natured bartender named Pat when he gets a ping on his phone. He had set up a Google alert for several names, including his brother, Penelope, and Chester Montgomery. Jody clicks on the *LA Times* article. Chester Montgomery is dead, found drowned in his pool in the Hollywood Hills.

Kenny doesn't want to talk on the phone. He texts Jody to meet him at Moonlight beach by the volleyball courts.

"Did you see?" he asks Jody.

"Yeah, read it on the news. Found dead in his pool."

"Guys at the precinct were talking about it. A couple of 'em have cop friends in LA. Apparently, it was made to look like he cracked his head open diving in, but it won't hold. Coroner's office was confident he got the skull fracture before he entered the water."

"He was murdered."

"Might not come out in the press for a couple weeks, but yeah."

"How did they . . . someone . . ."

"Look, it could have been a coincidence. Chester was wrapped up with seedy folks. We knew that. There does exist the chance this had nothing to do with you."

"It's too—"

"I know. I doubt it's a coincidence. I went to my guy in the FBI, and he kept it internal. No one outside the bureau would have heard something about Chester, not this fast. So if whoever's higher on the mountain than Chester has a mole, it must be in the FBI, not the LAPD."

"What do we do now?" Jody asks.

"Jody, I don't know what to tell you. I got two kids. I'm going to take them to my wife's mom's in Minneapolis. Go off the grid for a bit." Kenny looks spooked. He's pacing and talking fast. "You should think about getting out of town too."

"I can't do that. I n—"

"I know. I know you're not going to stop. But there's nothing else I can do for you. I'm sorry."

Chapter Sixty-Eight

Tiph

Tiph pulls her car into the seventh storage center she's been to this morning. She assumes the key she found in the desk's secret compartment is for a storage unit. The armored car Chester had reserved was supposed to go from Eagle Rock to Palm Springs. Last night, Tiph made a list of all nine storage centers in Eagle Rock.

The first two didn't even have three floors, so she didn't think she'd find unit 302 there. She found herself thinking, *First is the worse, second is the best, third is the one with the treasure chest*, and the third one did have a unit 302, but the key didn't match. She had trouble getting into the fourth place, the swankiest so far with the highest level of security. The fifth one was closed, set to be torn down to make way for condos. The sixth one had a unit 302, but the key didn't work. Now she's on lucky number seven, the largest of the storage facilities. She waits in her car until a man and his son approach the lobby from the parking lot. He uses a key to enter the lobby and holds the door for Tiph. She thanks him and heads for the elevator.

Tiph walks the maze of hallways on the third floor. She's in the 340s. She turns left. 380s. Now she's in the 360s. 363 is next to 365 and across from 362 but the hallway with the 360s does not lead to the hall with the 370s or the 350s. Ten minutes of wandering later, she spots the storage unit labeled 305. Across from it and one to the left, there it is. Unit 302.

Tiph inserts the key into the lock and turns it. It pops open. She pulls up the garage-style door. To reveal a spacious storage unit. A spacious, *empty* storage unit. Tiph steps inside. She turns in a slow circle. This was it. This had to have been it. But the art is gone. An empty storage unit at the end of the rainbow.

Tiph sits on the dirty, dusty concrete floor. She lays her head back and closes her eyes.

After a few moments, she rises to go home. To get back to her life. And leave this whole treasure hunt behind. When she stands, she spots a camera in the upper corner of the storage unit. She reaches up and pulls it down. It's a 720 HD battery-operated motion sensor camera.

When she gets home, she uploads the footage off the s-card.

Two weeks.

She was two weeks too late. She watches the footage from two weeks ago. Where a storage unit full of art—most of it wrapped up—goes from full to empty. A man makes nine trips into the storage unit. The art—her art, the art *she* was supposed to have—disappearing with each of the nine trips. The man loads paintings and sculptures onto a cart and returns twenty minutes later. The camera is cheap, and the footage makes it hard to get a good look at the man. A white dude with sideburns. Late twenties to early forties.

Tiph watches the footage twice. It's validating she followed the right clues and made it to the end. But it's also tragic she was too late. The second time she watches the footage, her mind circles back to every step of her hunt, wondering if she could have gone faster.

She pictures the look that will come over Mike's face. He'll hide his frustration. He'll lie and say everything will be okay. Maybe she shouldn't tell him. Maybe the hope of finding the art is helping him do his time.

Chapter Sixty-Nine

Pen

"Where did SARS come from?" Pen asks.

"The epidemic in 2002?" her psychologist, Dr. Murphy, asks.

"Yeah."

"I believe it originated in Foshan. China."

After a set of assessments and hearings and a bullshit determined *Post Certification of Dangerousness*, Pen's fourteen-day hold had been extended to a further hold for up to 180 days at the discretion of the facility manager.

"That's what we're told," says Pen. "But there are so many inconsistencies. SARS came from another world, another simulation."

"Penelope, our sessions continue to be dominated by your trying to convince me of something. I'm not here to agree with you or disagree with you. I think it would be helpful for you to take some time before our next appointment and make a list of all the data points you find yourself repeating."

Pen has notebooks full of such lists. Just not with her in the hospital. Over the next week, she writes it all down again. In her next session with Dr. Murphy, she gives her the list. Eighteen single-spaced pages, front and back.

"I thought we could discuss this today, but if you want me to read it, we'll have to wait until next session," says Dr. Murphy.

• • •

The following week, Pen sits for her session with Dr. Murphy. "Did you read it?"

"Yes."

"What did you think?"

"I told you. I'm not here to convince you of anything. And I'm not here to be convinced by you."

"Then why'd you have me write everything down?"

"I wanted you to see if it would make you feel differently to have it all down on paper. Sometimes, it's helpful to write something down, so we don't have to feel the need to keep repeating it in our heads out of some fear we'll forget it."

"Okay."

"Did writing it down change your opinion about any of it?"

"The cover-up."

"What do you mean?"

"When I wrote it all down, I lumped everyone in on the cover-up. LAPD. FBI. This hospital. The park rangers in Lassen. I do think *some* people might be covering up the existence of a breach. But I admit, I don't know who exactly."

Dr. Murphy suppresses a smile. Her expression reminds Pen of the look her dad gave her as a kid when she showed him a short movie she'd made on his Canon PV-1 camcorder.

That night, lying awake, Pen lets doubt creep into her mind, doubt that there's some kind of comprehensive government cover-up.

But the next day she's in the visiting room staring at a Black woman she's never seen before who's asking where Jody Morrel is. She's a Fed. Or she's working with the Feds. To protect Jody, Pen lies and tells her he's dead. And she reminds herself she can't trust Dr. Murphy. As soon as Pen let her guard down, they'd sent a visitor in to try to get intel from her.

Pen needs to get in touch with Jody to warn him. They're coming for him too.

Chapter Seventy

Renata

Renata wanders down the beach for several hours. She's so weak she's not sure she can trust what she's seeing. Each bend in the coast brings a different beach with different colored sand or rocks. Even the ocean seems to shift from a greener blue to a midnight blue to a cooler blue. She pictures going around the corner to a city or town, but each turn brings more coastline, rugged and remote. The trees and marine fog don't make her think of California. She'd been to playas de Tijuana and Rosarito four or five times each as a kid. And the impression she had of Los Angeles and San Diego was that the beaches were similar, with colder water, and more houses. Wandering down the beach, she doesn't even feel like she's in America. Her throat burns. She was thirsty before she and Coral had run. Now she hasn't had any water in a day and a half.

Chapter Seventy-One

Tiph

Tiph chooses not to tell Mike about the art, but he keeps asking for updates. His *hope machine* pumping out optimism like usual.

This is our time, TC, he keeps saying.

When Tiph climbs in her car in the visitors' parking garage, she lets out an angry scream and throws her phone against the dashboard. It hits the windshield then bounces under her seat. She reaches down to pick it up. Fishing around for it, her fingers grasp a piece of paper. It's a flyer that says *Balcony Advertising—make easy money today!* It was an idea Mike came up with to link businesses that were looking for cheap advertising opportunities with people who had balconies, windows, and rooftops that overlooked busy streets like Slauson. The scheme started making money, but within two weeks, the landlords of his customers shut it down.

Tiph stares at the flyer, and she cries. Ever since she found that empty storage unit, she herself has felt empty. It wasn't about the treasure. It wasn't about the fortune not favoring her boldness. It wasn't about her greed. It was about Mike. Mike was the treasure. Their relationship was the treasure. She spent so much time complaining to him about his schemes, but it didn't mean she didn't want them to be successful. She wants to believe in Mike's schemes. Were his schemes even that bad? He wasn't off selling drugs or cheating on her. His schemes were attempts to support her. She had hated on him for scheming even while in prison, but underneath, it was romantic. He was risking his life to try to take care of her. And she was rooting for him. She wanted it to be legit. Not a scheme. But a quest, a journey. Not hers. Not Mike's. But theirs.

Tiph stops crying. She starts the car, and she leaves the parking lot with a new plan. Just because someone got the art before her, doesn't mean she can't still get it.

The next day, after dropping Gary off at preschool, Tiph goes back to the storage facility in Eagle Rock. She approaches the attendant in the lobby, a slim, skim milk vampire-looking dude. "Excuse me, I was hoping you could help me. A few weeks ago, my boyfriend, well ex-boyfriend, came and took all my shit from my storage unit. He's denying he took it but if I can spot his car here on the day it went missing, then I can prove it was him. I saw you had cameras at the garage entrances. I was wondering how long you keep the footage."

"We keep it for a month. And then it gets deleted."

"This was maybe three weeks ago that I think he took it."

"Okay. And what's the name on the account?"

Fuck. To start crying, she thinks about Mike in prison. Scheming Mike. In prison, working an elaborate scheme to take care of her.

As Tiph sobs, the attendant grows more and more uncomfortable. "Okay, okay, calm down, let me get the footage."

She knows the exact time Mr. Sideburns entered Chester's storage unit, and she knows what time he left after getting the last batch of art. Based on those two times, she should have a pretty good sense of when to look for the car or truck arriving and leaving.

"The good news is we still have the footage from the afternoon you're talking about. The bad news is we have two entrances to the parking area, and only one of the cameras was working that day."

"Can I look through it?"

"Quickly, sure."

A few other customers come in. While the attendant helps them, Tiph saves the footage to a thumb drive. When the attendant comes back over, Tiph says she couldn't find his car. "Thanks anyway."

Once she gets home, Tiph uploads the footage. There are nineteen vehicles that could have been the guy with the sideburns, and the angle doesn't show the drivers, just the cars. The problem is the guy could have driven in but waited ten minutes before walking up to the unit. And when he came down with the last batch, he could have left right away or he could have spent an hour loading up the last batch and making sure the art was secure in the back before he drove away. She also doesn't know whether he used this entrance/exit. His vehicle might not even be one of the nineteen.

Gary decides it's his birthday even though it's not. After getting him to settle down and putting him to bed, Tiph paces around her Inglewood apartment. She has grainy footage of a guy with sideburns plus the license plates of nineteen different vehicles, one of which *might* be his. If he knew about the art, he had to know Chester. Maybe she can cross-reference people who knew Chester with the grainy footage of Mr. Sideburns. She tries to identify people who are in any way associated with Chester. The few she finds aren't a match.

She finds herself going back to the Reddit page that focused on Jody and his brother, Marty, and that crazy filmmaker lady Penelope. She sees there's been a flurry of new activity. A user claiming to be Jody Morrel has posted a request to help ID the man he thinks killed his brother. There's a picture that features the side of a box truck and the profile of the driver. The picture was taken at night, and it's difficult to see the driver, but it is clear he has bushy sideburns. Tiph pulls up the footage from the motion sensor camera she found in the empty storage unit. She pauses the grainy footage on a shot of the man taking the art. She puts the still shot against the picture from Reddit. It's the same guy.

Now Tiph goes back to the nineteen vehicles she marked. This box truck in the picture on Reddit is white without any logos or branding. She rewatches the footage. Of the nineteen vehicles, seven were sedans or SUVs, and twelve were box trucks. However, ten box trucks are branded with U-Haul or other names. And one is a *blue* box truck. There's only one unmarked light-colored box truck. It left the parking lot sixteen minutes after the last piece of art was taken from the storage unit. Tiph pauses the footage and zooms in on the back of the truck, copying the license plate number.

Chapter Seventy-Two

Jody

The side of a regular-looking box truck. And the profile of a regular-looking white dude with sideburns. That is all Jody has. He stares at the photo for hours. He transfers it to his computer and zooms in and out. He tries looking at the wheels. The man's face. He does hundreds of reverse image searches but the photograph isn't clear enough for Google to match it. He tries to figure out the make and model of the truck. Since Marty's entry on Encinitas ended up being relevant, Jody wonders about the subsequent entry about Eureka and Humboldt County. But there's not anything to go off other than Marty saying he was *curious* about that area. There's no real way for Jody to do internet searches for men and trucks in Northern California, but it doesn't stop him from trying. Hours turn into days, and days turn into days wasted.

During the daytime, he obsesses over ways of identifying the man with the sideburns. He contemplates going to Zack and the surfers and demanding answers. But he suspects they only know so much. Plus, if he asks them questions, and they tip off the man with the sideburns, the trafficking ring will hide their tracks or maybe even dispose of the women and children.

At night, he can't stop picturing the women and children on the boat. The excitement in their eyes, thinking about a new life ahead of them in the United States of America. He balked on telling the Coast Guard about the compartment because he was worried about not cracking more of the human trafficking ring, but as a result, those thirteen women and children are being trafficked, and he's no closer to stopping the ring. Better to have saved thirteen women and children than save no one. The guilt and regret eat away at him, excess acid filling his stomach in a constant gnawing churn.

He rarely leaves his room at the Leucadia Beach Inn. If a mole in the FBI led to Chester being killed, the same higher-ups may be coming after him as well. That real fear exists, but it's overshadowed by the guilt.

Jody is trying yet another reverse image search when his phone rings. Unknown number. He worries it's the party that killed Chester trying to track him down. But when he listens to the voice mail, it's from a patient in Metropolitan State Hospital asking him to visit. The voice mail is from Pen.

Chapter Seventy-Three

Renata

Renata spots a stream of water running down the hill, where it hits the sand and runs right into the ocean. She climbs down a cluster of rocks to the stream. She cups her hands, dips them in the water. It's icy cold, appears clear in her hands. She sucks the water down. Her dry throat tingles with relief. She cups her hands, goes back for more.

"STOP!" She looks up to see a man three feet above her. Holding sticks in a threatening way.

Renata crosses the stream. Leapfrogging from rock to rock. Up the bank. She steps on a loose rock and slips, lands on her back. She tries to get up to run, but the man hovers over her. The sticks appear to be hiking poles, and the man's holding his hands palms up.

"Are you okay? Sorry I scared you. You're not supposed to drink the water unfiltered."

Renata looks from the man to her bleeding elbow back to the man. Can she trust him?

"How did you get here?" the man asks.

"Where are we?"

"About halfway between Big Flat and Shipman Creek. Where's your pack?" When she doesn't answer, he moves to a broader question. "Are you doing the Lost Coast hike?"

"Hike?

"Yeah. The Lost Coast."

"You're lost?" she asks.

"No, it's called the Lost Coast."

"Where is that?"

"Are you okay, miss?"

"Please, just tell me where we are."

"We're on the Lost Coast."

"California?"

"Yeah."

"Near Los Angeles?"

"No. We're like a ten-hour drive from LA. Are you from LA?"

"No. Uhh, yes."

"Why don't you follow me? We'll get you some water and food."

Renata follows the man a few hundred yards along a path that goes through the woods and up over a bluff, then down to another beach and into the woods, where there's a campsite. Four tents, eight people. They all look shocked to see Renata.

"Hold on one second," the man says. He and the others congregate. Renata stands by herself outside the huddle.

Renata's tummy turns with paranoia. She darts away down the path.

"Wait!" she hears behind her.

She breaks into a run. They don't seem to be following, but she keeps jogging. Until her lungs burn. She walks for an hour. She hears a few birds chirping, and she looks up. An old building sits on the bluff. A stone staircase leads up to it. Her legs ache as Renata walks up the stairs. A sign reads INN OF THE LOST COAST. Inside the lobby, there's a huge map. Analyzing the map, she grasps she's on the Lost Coast, a fifty-mile stretch of beach in Northern California. According to this map, there's only one road that goes out. Shelter Cove Road.

"Can I help you, ma'am?"

A clerk approaches.

"No, that's okay. Thank you." She walks outside as a Toyota Camry pulls up to the loading zone. A couple in their sixties climb out, their back seat full of luggage. The driver leaves the keys in the car as they head inside. Renata hops in the car. She turns it on. It's been a long time since she's driven. Brake pedal on the left, gas pedal on the right.

She follows the signs for Shelter Cove Road. She's been driving up a winding stretch for five minutes when she passes a man standing on the side of the road. He peers in her window as Renata passes, and Renata can see his septum ring. In the rearview mirror, she sees the man limp to a gray sedan as he pulls out his phone. The guy who sprained his ankle. A place with only one way out had made it easy to keep watch. She drives as fast as she can, but the road follows one S curve after another, and Renata hasn't driven much in her life. The sedan remains fifty feet behind her. Renata gets to a narrow section of the road, and as the road banks right, a navy blue Chevy Blazer pulls out from a driveway and blocks the road. Renata has to slam on the brakes. She tries to turn around, but the sedan pins her in. She gets out of the car and runs. A man with sideburns jumps out of the Blazer as the limping man gets out of the gray sedan. She runs for the woods, but the man with the sideburns tackles her. Renata screams as loud as she can, but the two men throw her in the trunk of the sedan and slam it shut.

Chapter Seventy-Four

Jody

"I was worried about you," says Pen.

"Why?" Jody asks. He feels uneasy in the Metro State Hospital visitation room, like it's a police interrogation room or something.

"I was worried the Feds might have found you."

"What are you talking about?"

"A Fed came to see me about you."

"What? Who?"

"A Black woman. Asking all kinds of questions about you."

Jody thinks about Chester's cracked skull. Thinks about the FBI looking into him as a possible suspect. Or maybe a corrupt FBI agent looking into him to kill him.

"Don't worry. I told her you were dead."

"Thanks."

"I think the Feds are behind the Reddit thread too."

"What Reddit thread?"

"There's a whole Reddit thread on *you*."

"What do you mean, on me?"

"About you and where you are. There's comments about me. My Kickstarter. Marty's *My Dirty California* site."

Jody wonders what cocktail of medications they've given her. "I'm glad you called. I wanted to tell you I looked into Chester. There's a whole ring. A human trafficking ring. They're bringing in women from Mexico. And children. I just wanted you to know. Renata was a victim of human trafficking. Not of jumping simulations or whatever."

Pen stares back at Jody but doesn't say anything.

"I will forever owe you, Pen. I had quit, and you came and found me. And pointed me in the right direction. I'm grateful."

He reaches across the table and puts his palm out. She sets her hand atop his. Her eyes well up with tears.

They sit like that for a long moment.

"The human trafficking makes sense."

Jody nods. He had worried she might not be willing to see it this way.

"If there's a corporation or a government, or some individual who's found the breach. They could be using humans as test subjects. To cross over. Maybe it's dangerous or difficult to control where you're jumping."

"Pen . . ."

"It does make sense."

"That's not what's happening."

"How can you see so much of it and not see the rest? Many people wouldn't believe in a human trafficking ring. They'd think Marty got killed by a crackhead looking for crack. But you see it. And yet you get so close to the truth and then get tentative."

"Pen, I don't know what to do. You helped me. I wish I could help you."

She takes his hand this time. "You *can* help me. Get me out of here, Jody."

"I can't."

"Please."

"How? There's nothing I can do. I'm sorry." Is there anything he can do? "They took you on an involuntary hold. If you're telling them about simulations and . . . And if you refuse to take the medicine. They'll never let you out. Are you taking the meds?"

Pen nods, but Jody suspects she's lying. "They'll give you a blood test to see if you're taking them. You should start taking them. If you want to get out, you've got to stop with the theories. And if you can't stop with the theories, at least stop talking about them."

When Jody gets back to his hotel room from visiting Pen, he pulls up his laptop. He googles *Reddit Jody Morrel*. Pen wasn't lying. There's a whole thread. It covers him and Marty, and much of it branches off into discussion about Pen and her Kickstarter. The thread consists of fifty people commenting back and forth. It doesn't appear to have broken out in a viral way.

He reads the entire thread. He had hoped maybe he'd get details on Chester or Roller or the human trafficking ring, but he doesn't. But how were they able to piece so much together? There are posts about Jody, his background, his childhood. A few people had uncovered pictures of Jody he didn't even know existed. There are pictures of Marty at different ages, plucked from social media sites. And there's a ton of info on Pen, her father, her films.

After three hours Jody has had enough. His growling stomach rousts him out of the chair. But a new idea sits him right back down. Maybe these internet sleuths can help. Maybe, sitting here in his armchair, he can activate an army of armchair detectives.

Jody has exhausted every strategy he could think to employ to figure out who owned the truck and who the man with the sideburns was. But maybe others could help. Jody creates a Reddit account. He calls himself Jody_Morrel; JodyMorrel is taken. He replies to the original Reddit thread:

This is Jody Morrel. I am still trying to figure out the parties involved in my brother's murder. As part of my search, I came upon this man in this truck, but I was unable to get his license plate. The picture was taken near Solana Beach in San Diego County. I'm not sure where the man lives, but I suspect it's either San Diego, Los Angeles, or Humboldt County. If you can figure out the identity of this man, please direct message me.

To go along with his message, Jody pastes the grainy nighttime picture of the truck and the profile of the man with sideburns. He contemplates the risks of uploading the message, says *Fuck it*, and presses Enter.

An hour later, the Reddit thread activity picks up. Several users seem interested in helping, but a consensus builds that Jody_Morrel is not the real Jody Morrel. Jody walks to a coffee shop called Pannikin and buys an *LA Times*. He takes a selfie of himself holding the paper and posts the picture to Reddit.

Jody grabs fish tacos and a Duck Foot blonde ale from Fish 101. When he comes back, he sees there's a flurry of new responses. Various folks sharing strategies for how they can identify the man. A woman with the username Bahdee Dansan posts a link for a private Facebook group where folks can share tips without them being seen by the public. If anyone wants to join, they can send her a request, and she'll invite them.

Jody's request to join the private group gets denied.

As hours pass, Jody starts to doubt the Redditors will produce a name. He may be back to square one. He revisits old lists and makes new lists.

But six days later, Jody receives a direct message from Bahdee Dansan. According to her, the man in the truck is named Davey Richards, from Eureka, California. He's thirty-three years old. The message includes a link to a Facebook wedding picture where people have been tagged. There are seven people in the picture, and one—the one tagged as Davey Richards—is the guy with the sideburns from the truck.

Jody paces in his hotel room. *Holy shit*. These internet sleuths did it.

Chapter Seventy-Five

Pen

Maybe because she took Jody's advice and stopped talking about simulations and began taking her meds, or maybe because of budget cuts, Pen gets out today on a conditional release. She called her filmmaker friend Chelsea, who promised to be there at two o'clock. But now it's two thirty, and Chelsea is nowhere to be found. Pen had tried calling the bike-shop owners where she used to rent the bungalow, but they said it was no longer available. What are her other options? She could take an Uber to a hotel. But she could only afford a couple of nights. She fumbles through her phone. Who would put her up for a night? She looks up from the contact list on her phone to see Chelsea walking into the lobby. Her five-year-old son walks right behind her.

"Is that her?" a nurse asks.

"Yeah, that's her," says Pen.

"I'm so sorry," Chelsea says, embracing her in a gentle hug as if Pen's a fragile antique. "Carter bit one of the kids at school."

"She bit me first," Carter says.

"They made me pick him up," says Chelsea. "But we're here, the welcome-home party one stronger."

"Thank you so much," says Pen.

As Chelsea drives Pen on the stretch of the 110 that cuts through the heart of downtown, Carter asks Pen questions. "Mommy said you were sick for a while?"

"Yup," says Pen.

"Did you have a runny nose?"

"Sort of," says Pen. She looks out the window at the snowcapped mountains to the east.

Chelsea pulls into the driveway in Sherman Oaks. "Carter, run inside and say hello to your daddy." After the boy climbs out of the back seat and darts inside, Chelsea turns to Pen. "We converted the garage to a little creative office space. You can stay here. As long as you want."

"Just a couple days, thank you so much."

"No, Pen, I'm serious. As long as you want. But there are a few rules. You have to go to your appointments." As part of her conditional release, the hospital assigned Pen a psychologist for mandatory twice-weekly outpatient sessions.

"Okay," says Pen.

"And I don't want to hear any more about the simulation stuff. I used to think it was interesting, even if I never believed it, but you crossed the line. When I heard you . . . what you tried to do . . . Look, Pen, I have a kid here. My friends think I'm crazy for letting you stay. So it's a zero-tolerance situation. You want to live here, be friends, watch movies, whatever, let's do it. I can get you hours teaching kids documentary filmmaking with me. But you gotta follow those couple rules. So what do you think?"

Pen wipes the tears from her eyes. Even through the fog of her meds, she sees what a kind gesture this is. "It sounds good. Thank you, Chelsea."

Chapter Seventy-Six

Jody

Jody drives the ten hours from LA to Eureka. He had done the drive in the first leg of his three-month tour of California. In that one, he'd stopped fifty-some places. Now it's a straight shot. Right to the bungalow Davey Richards owns in Eureka. Jody parks across the street. There's a Chevy Blazer in the driveway, but after three hours with no movement or light through the windows, Jody starts to doubt he's home. But thirty minutes later, a woman with a pizza rings the doorbell. A man opens the door and takes the food. It's Davey Richards, the guy from the box truck in Solana Beach, the guy with the sideburns. Jody watches the house until 2:00 a.m., but no one comes, and no one leaves. He drives to a cul-de-sac several blocks away and sleeps for a few hours, returning to Davey's street at 6:30 a.m. Jody watches the house all day. Davey comes to the door for an Amazon delivery and an Instacart delivery.

That night, when it seems like Davey won't be going out, Jody drives a few blocks away where he finds a stretch of bars and restaurants. He enters a dive called Clancy's and orders a chicken cobb salad and an Anchor Steam. He asks the bartender if he knows a Davey Richards, but the guy is standoffish, either knows Davey and didn't want to admit it or doesn't like the idea of Jody coming in asking questions.

Jody asks for the check, and he's about to leave when he hears a drunk forty-year-old man with a mustache and a Warriors T-shirt say, "I think he met her at one of Roller's parties a few years back." The guys at the end of the bar are all drunk. Jody nurses his beer, and keeps listening, but the guys now only talk about Colin Kaepernick and the Splash Brothers. The other guys leave. Now Jody approaches the man with the mustache. "Hey, I hear you say *Roller's party*?"

The man with the mustache turns and eyes Jody a moment before nodding.

"I keep hearing about his legendary parties."

"Oh yeah, they were the bomb. I mean he doesn't really have 'em anymore, but a few years back, wasn't a better time to be had. We used to call them the Energizer parties, 'cause they just kept going. He'd get kegs, start up around dinnertime, and those things would flow until 5:00 a.m. sometimes."

The bartender comes over, glaring at Jody. Jody ignores him and says to his new friend, "Let me get you a drink. What are you having?"

Mustache looks at the draft handles. "Lemme getta Great White."

"Make it two," Jody says to the bartender.

"Thanks, I'm Kyle."

"Hey, Kyle. Joe."

The bartender brings over two pints of Belgian-style witbier. Jody buys Kyle three more over the next hour. The guy goes from merry to slurring.

"So who is this Roller guy?" Jody asks.

"Why do you want to know?"

"I told you already," Jody says, lying. "You need to slow down drinking!"

Kyle laughs. "Roller? He's a weed guy. *The* weed guy. Guy pulls so much pussy too. I've been to his house like three or four times, always with a friend of a friend. That place is like a castle. And he always has ten girls living with him."

"Really?"

"Yeah, man. He's a boss."

"Who are the girls?"

"I don't know. He gives them a place to stay."

"In exchange for what?"

"I don't know, for being hot?" Kyle laughs, and Jody forces a laugh. "No, it wasn't like that. The girls had a place to stay if they were between spots or new to town. I think he just liked having'm around. Party or whatever. I'm sure he fucked some of them sometimes. I heard he liked to watch'm have sex with other people too. Just one big party."

"Sounds like some kind of rap star who doesn't rap."

"Yeah, well his music is his weed biz. And my man had hits. Biz has gone sideways since it got legalized."

"Is he still in the game?"

"Yeah. Actually, I don't know."

"What's his real name?"

"Rob Stoller."

Rob Stoller. Roller. Jody suppresses a smile. Finally has a real name for the nickname the hit man mentioned just before he died.

"And where's this crazy house of his?"

Kyle is about to answer when the bartender comes over. "I think it's about time you left, friend."

Jody drops forty bucks on the bar and walks out.

That night, Jody checks into a Knights Inn. He finds everything he can online about Rob Stoller aka Roller. Little exists, but he does find him mentioned as a consultant in a business plan for a start-up called GroTown. He finds his address online and uses Google Earth to check out the property. A massive plot, fifty acres, right off Walnut Drive on the east end of town. The property backs up all the way to Ryan Creek.

The next day, Jody heads over to the property. He parks a quarter mile away at a community park trailhead. He brings a backpack containing among other items duct tape and zip ties. He finds Roller's property, a dirt driveway off Walnut. A huge metal gate with a keypad blocks the entrance. Jody debates hopping the fence. For now, he decides to wait across the street in a clump of western hemlock trees that sit in the shadows of several old coast redwoods.

Chapter Seventy-Seven

Pen

Pen goes to dinner with Chelsea, Chelsea's husband, Caleb, and Caleb's work friend Anit, whose chiseled face looks like it has its own gym membership. The four had gone out to dinner the week before. Though it wasn't a blind date, it felt arranged. Pen had fun, and according to Chelsea, Anit did too.

Pen's life has been different since she got her conditional release from the hospital. She's been enjoying teaching documentary filmmaking as an after-school enrichment program at Crossroads School in Santa Monica. Chelsea leads the classes with Pen helping out. For Pen, a fog has lifted. She comes to terms with her mistake at Lassen. She still thinks there's a good chance it's a portal to another simulation *but* she recognizes there's some chance, however small, it's not. In which case she would've died. When she accepted this, it opened up a Pandora's box—pun intended—of other doubts. Doubts that feed and grow and linger. For two decades, she'd sensed other people's fear for her. But she hadn't felt the fear for herself. Like she had some outer shell that wicked away doubts and fears. But when she stopped trusting her instincts, she started to feel the fear, to experience doubt. It's been helpful to discuss this with her new therapist, Dr. Green.

After dinner, Chelsea and Caleb apologize that they're tired and want to head home. Anit asks if Pen wants to extend the evening and go for a drink.

Anit orders a whiskey, and Pen gets a cranberry juice. She doesn't like mixing alcohol with her medication.

After two hours of banter, Pen asks Anit, "What has Caleb told you about me?"

"I know you were in the hospital, if that's what you mean. I know you received a lifetime ban from the Magic Castle for breaking into their cellar."

Pen laughs, and Anit smiles.

"I think you're interesting. I like that you don't accept things are the way we're told they are. You question things. They say kids ask like three hundred questions a day. Society would be a better place if adults asked more questions." Anit smiles in a way that accentuates his jawline.

Pen smiles. "I should get home, but I'd like to do this again."

"Me too."

The next morning, Pen wakes up to an email from a woman named Fay. She says she found Pen's email from a Kickstarter campaign. She claims she has been in Pandora's House, and she wants to talk to Pen.

Pen sits up in bed, feeling light-headed. For weeks now, she'd been pushing simulation-jumping-related thoughts out of her mind. And now they all flood back.

Pen and Fay find each other and sit at a table in the patio section of Intelligentsia Coffee. Fay asks Pen questions about her film project.

Pen answers them before asking, "You said in your email you think you were in Pandora's House?"

"Yeah. I was with my boyfriend at the time. This was maybe six months ago. We were doing a lotta drugs. I'm clean now. But at the time, we were . . . every night. He took me to this party his friend called a Narnia party. The house was bizarre. Just this little blue house in Glassell Park. But then we went down this stairwell, and it was like a giant mansion. But underground. There were other people there partying, but they were different; I dunno how to explain it. Like they were from another place. And my boyfriend wanted me to fuck this other woman. And I didn't want to. And he was pressuring me. So I ran. And I got lost. There were so many rooms and hallways. And then I found this one room and there was this hole. I don't know how to describe it. It was in the air in the middle of the room, but it was like a gap. And I stuck my hands in it, but I felt myself going away and I got freaked out, and I pulled out my hands. And then I ran. Got lost for an hour. Finally got outside. And I kept running. And I saw a police car, and the cop drove me home."

"Did you go back?" Pen asks.

"I've been too scared. The whole thing freaked me out. I stopped using. And I've been going to meetings. I talked about what I saw, and at first people were supportive, but they wanted to dismiss it as a bad trip, but I know what I saw. The group leader asked me not to bring it up anymore, said I was freaking people out. But I needed to talk to someone, to understand. So I started researching all kinds of stuff, haunted houses, and iceberg houses, and I came across your Kickstarter."

"Where was this house?"

"It was a blurry night to begin with, definitely a blur when I ran. I might have run a mile or two. But I remember getting to Division Street and then Cypress, that's how I knew the house was in Glassell Park."

"What else do you remember about the house?"

"There were these stone lion heads on the front porch. Two of them. And a big California black walnut tree in the front yard. I know that's what it was 'cause I used to read in this grove of them, Walnut Canyon."

"Are you sure you can't remember seeing anything else?"

"Mushrooms."

"You took mushrooms?"

"No, we did other drugs, but not mushrooms. I *saw* mushrooms though. I can't remember where, but there were mushrooms."

Pen has long been fascinated with mushrooms. Some scientists think mushrooms came from another planet. Their spores are made of sporopollenin, which is the hardest natural material in nature, which makes mushrooms ideal for space travel. Genetically, mushrooms are closer to humans than plants. They're weird, and Pen has always wondered if they came to our simulation from another.

The next day, Pen meets up with Fay, and they drive through Glassell Park, keeping their eyes peeled for Californian black walnut trees, stone lions, and blue houses.

Later in the day, Pen gets a text from Chelsea. *Where are you?* Pen lost track of time. She and Fay have been searching for six hours, and she missed the class she was supposed to teach with Chelsea.

Chapter Seventy-Eight

Renata

The car goes up steep, windy roads, and Renata gets carsick rolling around in the trunk. She vomits. Being trapped in the trunk with her vomit makes her vomit twice more even once the grade levels out. The car comes to a stop. The trunk pops open. One man holds her down while the other puts a blindfold on her and then ties her hands behind her back. Carrying her, they struggle to walk in unison. Eventually they drop her and one man throws Renata over his shoulder.

She can hear the echo of footsteps now. Is she being taken into a tunnel? She hears the creak of a door. Her hands are cut free and she's tossed to the ground. She removes the rag tied around her eyes. She's in a cell, a six-by-six-by-six metal cube. A shipping container or industrial freezer. She goes to the source of light, a tiny slit. She can't see much. A narrow corridor.

She hears a knock to her right. She puts her ear to the wall. There must be a box adjacent to hers. Another knock. She knocks back.

More knocking. Over and over. Why is the person banging like this? Are the knocks in a particular rhythm? She listens, catches the beat. It's the Tupac song "California Love."

Coral's song.

Coral is alive.

Renata bangs on the wall in celebration.

A sense of joy washes over Renata that Coral hadn't drowned. But part of Renata had wanted to believe Coral had escaped and run and stolen a car and driven to Ohio. Where is Ohio? It's a state, Renata is pretty sure. And she had hoped Coral was now in Ohio. Living. And dating. And eating ice cream. And complaining about her job. And getting head. And giving head. And watching *Friends* reruns. But she's not. She's right in the cell next to Renata.

Chapter Seventy-Nine

Pen

Pen walks along Kinney Street in Glassell Park, headed back toward her car. She wanted to cover another stretch of houses, but it's less effective searching in the dark. Plus, she needs to find a good parking spot where she'll feel safe overnight.

Five weeks ago, Chelsea asked Pen to move out of her house. Pen had missed several documentary film enrichment classes in a row. She stopped taking her medicine. When she was home, she talked to Chelsea and her husband, Caleb, about Fay and the breach. But she was rarely home because she spent most of her time looking for Pandora's House in Glassell Park and Cypress Park. She got home one day, and Chelsea gave her an ultimatum: get back on the meds, come back to work, and stop looking for the house or move out. Pen moved in with Fay. The pair continued their daily search in Glassell Park. But one Wednesday Fay said she had to visit a friend, and Pen didn't see her for two days. Pen thought maybe she had found the house and jumped simulations, but she also worried Fay might have overdosed. Pen came back to Fay's house after a day of searching and found Fay in bed, alive albeit in a bad way. High, sleepy. Fay told Pen she blamed her relapse on searching for the house, on the dread of finding it. She regretted coming to Pen, she wanted to forget the whole mess. She needed Pen to move out. Pen resumed looking for the house on her own. She's been sleeping in her car for three weeks.

Chapter Eighty

Renata

Renata has been in her industrial freezer–size lightless box for three days when two men blindfold her and take her outside. She's placed on a tarp. She can feel the breeze and hear birds. She'd give up the ability to see if she could be free.

"Usually we'd try being nice and asking before we resort to this, but I'm in a rush."

Renata hears another man, this one breathing heavier. As he approaches, she hears a swooshing sound. Some kind of liquid in a bottle or tub being shaken. Liquid splashes on her skin. It feels thicker than water, like syrup. The smell hits her nose.

Gasoline.

She hears a clicking sound. She's not sure what it is until she can feel the heat, the flame of a lighter. Inches from her face. She wonders if it's the foot. And she wonders if they'll burn her alive.

"If you lie to us, even once, I'll drop this lighter. Okay?"

"Okay," Renata says.

"Do you know Sal?"

"Who?"

"Salvatore Jenkins."

"No."

"Don't lie to us. Did you get busted for drugs? And a narcotics cop named Sal tried to get you to go undercover to bust me?"

"No. I don't know what you're talking about."

"Do you know who Chester Montgomery is?"

"No," says Renata.

"How about a man from Pennsylvania named Jody Morrel?"

"No," says Renata.

"C'mon, do you know Jody?"

"No."

"What about Marty?"

Marty? The man she met playing soccer who'd asked her to breakfast? How could they know this man? Or know that Renata had met him?

"No," says Renata.

She didn't know why, but she felt in her gut if she said she knew Marty, they'd kill her. Or they'd want to know more information about Marty she wouldn't have. And they'd torture her. Or kill her.

"You paused. Are you lying?"

"I'm not lying."

Renata feels the flame close to her face again.

"Please, I'm not lying. I paused only because I knew a Marita back in Mexico."

There's a long pause. Renata thinks she can hear the two men whispering. The leader says, "Well, it's time for your trip to begin."

Renata gets taken back to her box. She's been in so many cells and holes, like different coffins she's been testing out. A man comes by and gives her a fresh bottle of water and a sandwich and dumps out her waste bucket. The next day, a couple of men retrieve her, putting duct tape over her mouth and a hood over her face. They load her in the trunk of a car. There's another person in there. Renata can't see or talk. But the other person finds her hand and holds it, and Renata knows it's Coral. Renata squeezes the other hand. And for a moment, the terror dissipates, and all that exists in the whole world is her bond with Coral.

After an hour-long car ride, Renata gets pulled from the trunk.

"Walk."

She still can't see, but a man's firm grip guides her. She crosses a long yard. She can feel the dirt and grass beneath her feet. They go down a hill. She can hear the sounds of a forest around her as the hike continues. A bird keeps calling out. *Fee-Bee. Fee-Bee.* And it makes Renata think of Phoebe Buffay. After a series of switchbacks, they go into a canyon, or maybe it's a basement. It's darker and colder but still breezy.

One of the men pulls the hood from her head and rips off the duct tape. They're in a cave or a mine. In front of Renata and Coral is a cage. It's pretty dark, but she can see two dozen women and children. The two men shove Renata and Coral inside.

Renata and Coral hug. Together again. Imprisoned together again.

Chapter Eighty-One

Tiph

L-Chubbs and Philly Deon don't show up together. L-Chubbs arrives first, driving a rented U-Haul. Tiph walks outside as L-Chubbs climbs out of the truck. He's wearing a designer T-shirt that reads *Current*, a relic from one of Mike's failed schemes.

"U-Haul? You serious?" Tiph asks.

"Yeah. What's wrong?"

"Nothing. You said you'd take care of the box truck. I thought you meant you had access to one. I didn't know you were going to rent a U-Haul."

"Truck's a truck, no?"

She had pictured a subtler vehicle. But in its own way, a U-Haul truck is subtle. People don't tend to pull heists with a U-Haul. "Where's Philly?"

"Said he had to stop at the store."

Tiph checks the time on her phone. They have a long drive ahead. Using the license plate on the truck, she found the identity of the man with the sideburns, Davey Richards. After that, she went to see Mike, and he encouraged her to take Philly D and L-Chubbs. They agreed to do the job for 10 percent of the take, 5 percent each. Even after they shell out 10 percent to Philip and 10 percent to Philly and Chubbs, that still leaves 80 percent for her and Mike.

Think of it as paying taxes, Mike had said.

"Where's Little Man?" asks L-Chubbs.

"At my mom's." Her mother made a fuss over watching him

because she wanted to make Tiph feel bad, but Tiph knows she was excited to have her grandson for a two-day sleepover.

Philly Deon pulls up in his old Lexus sedan. He pops the trunk and pulls out a brand-new round point shovel. Tiph and L-Chubbs both bag up.

"What?" asks Philly D.

"It's not treasure in the ground. We ain't gotta dig it up, you Hulk-shaped dumbass," says L-Chubbs, still laughing.

"You don't know that."

Tiph tells them Davey has two houses, one in this isolated neighborhood on the Lost Coast called Shelter Cove plus a bungalow in Eureka. "We'll go to Shelter Cove first."

It takes eleven hours to drive to Shelter Cove. For at least a whole hour of this, Philly Deon and L-Chubbs argue over the superior coast. L-Chubbs's *West Coast is the best coast* stance can't be beat because no matter how many valid points Deon makes, L-Chubbs keeps asking, "Then why you here?" The argument only subsides when Deon says he has to do his daily meditation.

They pull up in the U-Haul to Davey's house in Shelter Cove. The whole neighborhood appears empty. There are dozens of houses. But not a soul in sight. "We don't even need the FedEx shirts," says Tiph. They knock on the front door. No one answers.

They walk around to a side door. Philly Deon peeks through a hopper window adjacent to the door. "I don't see an alarm system."

"We can't fit through that window," says L-Chubbs.

Deon smashes the window with his shovel. He puts the shovel all the way through the window, stretches his arm, and uses the shovel to slide the dead bolt off the door from inside. "Yeah, shovel's not so funny now, is it?"

The three of them search the house. In one room, they find six old arcade games including *Street Fighter II*. "Oh shit. 'Bout to go Guile on your ass," says L-Chubbs to Philly Deon.

In the living room, sitting on the coffee table there's a cardboard box. Inside, there are several hundred condoms.

"Damn," says Philly Deon. "I never seen so many rubbers."

"Yeah, man, how's this video game nerd getting so much play?" L-Chubbs says, laughing.

"Maybe why he's got a bunch of *unused* condoms," says Tiph.

They search every closet and drawer but find no sign of the art.

There's a second structure on the lot, a box-shaped building at the back of the property. It's locked. Philly Deon picks the lock with a torsion wrench. They step into a little entryway room. Tiph pulls a chain hanging from a naked bulb. Now they see a hatch that looks like a garbage chute. A two-foot gap before a hatch on the other side.

Above the hatch, L-Chubbs finds a door handle. The room has twilight-level lighting that seems to be coming through the fiberglass walls. The room is empty. It would be a good place to store art, but there is no art. One wall has a bunch of scratch marks, maybe a hundred. Someone counting something. There's a pile of ashes in the center of the room.

"What's that noise?" Philly D asks.

They all listen. A humming noise coming from the other side of the fiberglass wall. They walk back out into the laundry-room-size entryway. From here, a door leads to a neighboring room that shares a fiberglass wall with the large empty room.

Dozens of humming UV lights, a complex watering system, and a solar power converter fill the room. On one side, there are ten marijuana plants. But the space is set up to handle ten times that many. L-Chubbs walks over to the plants.

"Yo, we gotta go," says Tiph.

"Look at this Mary Juan . . . ," L-Chubbs says. On their drive, L-Chubbs had told Tiph how he got kicked out of the US Army on his second day after he got caught smoking marijuana.

"A lil' herb is a crucial part of self-care." Philly Deon stares at the converter. "Using solar too. Going green to get the green."

"They do that so they can't be tracked," says L-Chubbs. "DEA works with the department of power to see who's using extra juice. To find the grow houses."

"Shit, really? I thought—"

Tiph interrupts Deon. "The art's not here. Davey's not here. So we gotta drive to Eureka. FedEx doesn't come late at night, so we gotta get there at a reasonable hour." The two men can't take their eyes off the marijuana plants.

"Two handfuls," she compromises.

Chapter Eighty-Two

Pen

Pen walks a stretch of Maricopa Drive she'd walked a dozen times in the last month. The houses are meager, but the plots of land stretch far back into the hillside, which makes them great candidates for iceberg houses.

The last three days have been a grind. Her car got impounded, and she's been sleeping beyond a thicket of California mugwort next to the 101 freeway. Her athlete's foot got exacerbated by a lack of clean socks. She lost her bucket hat, and her face got sunburned. Her stomach has been rocky after going to a soup kitchen and eating a sandwich with questionable lunch meat. Pen has started to wish she hadn't left Chelsea's. She had a place to stay. She was working, doing a job that made her happy. And she wasn't alone; she had a real friend in Chelsea. Plus, she liked Anit and was excited to see where that relationship might go. But she gave all that up, all to chase another clue that had led her to another dead end.

Pen scans front yards for California black walnut trees. She looks at porches for stone cats. She surveys hillsides for blue houses. Up the street, she sees a teal-colored house. She remembers it. It doesn't have the tree in the yard or the lions. As she passes by, she spots a stump partially hidden from view by a pair of barrel cacti. She walks into the yard around the cacti to get a better look at the stump. The top has a light tan color and there's sawdust in the grass. It could be a California black walnut. Her eyes jump to the front porch, looking for the stone lions.

As she gets closer, she scans the thick ivy growing on either side of the porch. Something gray behind the green. She parts the ivy, exposing a stone lion. She goes to the other side of the porch and fumbles with the ivy, finds the second stone lion. A bluish house with two lions and a California black walnut tree.

Pandora's House.

Chapter Eighty-Three

Tiph

It's around 5:00 p.m., and the Eureka neighborhood street is busy. Folks walking dogs. Kids playing football and riding bikes. Porch chairs rocking.

Tiph leans over to Philly Deon. "Stay out here. Call us if anything happens or someone's coming in."

"Okay."

Tiph and L-Chubbs walk to the front door. L-Chubbs carries an empty cardboard box. Both wear FedEx uniforms.

"You ready?" Tiph asks.

"Hell yeah."

Tiph knocks. They wait. Tiph knocks again. They wait for thirty seconds, no answer.

"All right, let's go in."

"Wait," says L-Chubbs. "I swear I hear something in there."

Tiph knocks a third time. And rings the doorbell. They wait forty-five seconds, but no one comes to the door. L-Chubbs pulls out a torsion wrench to pick the lock.

"Hold on," says Tiph. She pulls up the welcome mat, spots a spare key.

They search the house. They sift through mail on the kitchen counter. They search Davey's bedroom. L-Chubbs checks the spare bedroom while Tiph looks in the dining room area. They meet back in the kitchen. Where they see there's one more door. They hear a yell of excitement from inside followed by a loud grunt. Someone is home, fighting or fucking.

They inch forward. L-Chubbs holds up his gun, and Tiph throws open the door.

Davey Richards swings a sword toward them. L-Chubbs nearly fires. But Tiph waves him off before he squeezes the trigger. They watch as Davey swings a sword-shaped device in midair. He has virtual-reality goggles covering his face. L-Chubbs and Tiph look at each other and laugh. L-Chubbs picks up a baseball bat. Dodging the video-game wand, L-Chubbs cracks Davey across the face with the bat. Davey lands hard. He tugs off the cracked virtual-reality goggles, looks up at L-Chubbs and Tiph standing over him.

"We got some questions for you, Lancelot," says Tiph.

"About the treasure," adds L-Chubbs.

"My wallet's in the kitchen."

"We're here for the truckload," says Tiph.

"Truckload?" he asks.

"Hell, you want to go to hell in a hand basket quick, keep playing dumb, dumbass," says Tiph.

L-Chubbs holds the bat in one hand, his gun in the other. "Look, motherfucker. It's time to sing. I can hit you with the bat. Or . . ." He sets down the bat to free up a hand. He pulls out the grenade. "I can shove this up your ass, pull the pin on my way out the door."

"They're gone."

"Who's gone?" asks Tiph.

"The truckload."

"Well, who's got the art now, then?" asks Tiph.

"The art?"

"Yeah, the motherfucking art," says Tiph.

"C'mon, man. I'm just a driver."

"Cool. So you can stick to your skill set, driver, and drive us to where the art is then," says Tiph.

"He's not home."

"*Who's* not home?" Tiph asks.

Now Davey looks like he doesn't want to talk anymore.

L-Chubbs tosses the grenade a couple of inches in the air. Catches it. Repeats. "Lady asked you a question."

"We're not fucking around 'round here," says Tiph.

"Roller."

"Roller?" asks Tiph.

"Yeah, Roller. But he's not home."

"Great, even better," says Tiph with a smile. "Then he won't be there to stop us from taking it."

L-Chubbs uses zip ties to bind Davey's feet and hands.

"All right, let's go," L-Chubbs says.

"Hold on," says Tiph. "We can't just walk out there with him all tied up. It's like the Roaring Twenties out there, man. People drinking lemonade on their porches and shit."

"You got a duffel bag?" L-Chubbs asks Davey.

"C'mon, man," Davey protests.

Tiph struggles to carry the *feet* end of the bag. She and L-Chubbs fail to walk in unison as they head to the truck. Tiph loses her grip, and they drop the bag. Davey grunts in pain. Philly Deon jogs over from the truck and takes Tiph's half. They put the bag in the back of the truck.

L-Chubbs pulls over two blocks later on a remote cul-de-sac. They need to get Davey up front so he can tell them where to go.

It's a tight squeeze across the front bench seat of the truck. Philly Deon driving. Tiph and a bound Davey in the middle. L-Chubbs on the other side.

It's dusk when they pull up to the driveway on the outskirts of Eureka. There's an iron gate with a keypad.

"Those are some big-ass trees across the street," says L-Chubbs. "Endor-looking things."

"What's the passcode to get in this jawn?" asks Deon.

"You keep saying *jawn*, he's gonna know your ass from Philly."

"You dumbass," says Tiph.

L-Chubbs makes a *whoops* face. "Whatever, we'll kill him after. Just playing, Davey Boy. You get us this art, you can be playing your medieval virtual-reality Nintendo shit in no time."

"What's the code?" asks Tiph.

"Four twenty, four."

"Four hundred twenty-four?" asks Deon.

"Four, two, zero, four."

The automatic gate opens outward.

"He'll hunt you down," Davey warns.

"Hunt down *who*?" asks Tiph. "All you got is one asshole from Philly, and there's a lot of assholes in Philly."

"Don't be giving us a reason not to leave you alive," says L-Chubbs.

Deon drives the box truck onto the property. The winding dirt road and overgrown estate don't scream wealth, but as they go around the bend and out of the trees, they see a massive three-story Victorian house with stained glass windows, turrets, ornate gables, and a steeply pitched roof. In LA, it would be a fifty-million-dollar property. In Eureka, maybe 10 percent of that.

There are seven cars in the driveway. A red Mustang, a Jaguar, two SUVs, an old Porsche, a retrofitted VW van, and a Sprinter van. "You said he wasn't here," Tiph complains.

"He isn't. Just likes cars."

Deon clips the zip tie around Davey's ankles so they don't have to carry him. His arms remain bound behind his back.

"You got a key?" Tiph asks.

"No."

L-Chubbs tests the knob, smiles. *Unlocked*. He and Deon pull out their guns. Tiph swings the door open. They step into the foyer. A grandfather clock chimes, and L-Chubbs nearly pops a cap in it.

L-Chubbs laughs but sees Tiph looking up. A blond woman with scraggly hair and a white T-shirt with no bra looks down from the banister above.

"Shit," L-Chubbs says.

The woman runs. Deon goes up the stairs after her. Tiph follows. L-Chubbs stays with Davey in the foyer.

Tiph runs up the stairs, falling behind Deon with every step. She follows Deon to the end of the hall, where a door slammed. It's locked. Deon lowers his shoulder. Wood splinters, and the momentum carries Deon right through the door into the bedroom. Not one but two blond scraggly-haired twenty-year-old women.

"Drop the phone," Deon says, waving the gun at the two girls. She drops the phone.

Tiph runs over and grabs it.

"They call the cops?" Deon asks.

"No. Cell. Eureka area code. Only lasted eighteen seconds." Tiph looks at the girls, already forgetting which one had the phone in her hand. Their identical looks of horror making them look like identical twins. "Who'd you call?"

"Floyd."

"Who the fuck is Floyd?"

"He works here."

"He answer?"

"No."

"Check her texts."

Tiph looks through her text messages. One text to a *Rolla* that says 911.

The two white drifter-looking ladies are now bound with zip ties on their hands and feet. Duct tape stifles their whimpers. Deon puts the two women in a closet, using more zip ties to bind them to a water pipe.

"Where to?" says L-Chubbs.

"This way," says Davey. They follow him down a hallway.

"You pull our leg, I'll shoot your leg," says L-Chubbs.

Davey leads them to the end of a corridor. For a moment, it looks like Davey is killing time. But then he says, "Pick up that painting."

L-Chubbs lifts the painting off the wall. Behind it lies a small door handle.

Deon turns the handle and pushes open the door.

Tiph goes in first. The room is full of art: paintings and a few sculptures. About forty pieces in all. They're not on display so much as being stored. Much of it is still wrapped up like when Tiph saw the art in the storage-unit surveillance footage. Tiph smiles at Mike's scheme come true.

Deon and L-Chubbs step forward to see the art.

"Is this—"

Before Deon can finish talking he gets kicked in his ass, pushing him out of the doorway and into the room. Davey uses his bound hands to grasp the door and close it as he steps out of the room.

Deon reaches to open the door, but there's not even a handle on this side.

"Fuck."

Deon tries to lower his shoulder and run through the door. But it holds.

L-Chubbs pulls out his gun and aims it at the door.

"Hold on!" says Tiph. Her and Deon step back to avoid a ricocheting bullet to the face.

L-Chubbs fires a round of bullets into the door. No-go though.

Tiph scans the room. No windows. No other doors. No crawlable air vents. She looks back to see L-Chubbs holding the grenade.

"You said it was fake," says Tiph.

"I lied."

L-Chubbs looks at the door, as if thinking about where to place the grenade.

"Hold on," says Deon. "You're going to blow up the art. Maybe us too."

"What good's the art if Davey kills us or calls the police or whatever the fuck he's doing right now," says L-Chubbs.

"Between a rock and a hard place, I think I pick the rock," says Tiph as she points to the grenade. Her eyes go past L-Chubbs to a filing cabinet against one wall. "Here!" Together, they bring over the filing cabinet and put it a couple feet from the door.

"Is that going to protect the art? Is it going to protect us?" asks Deon.

Tiph and Deon move to the far side of the room. Here, they're a good thirty yards from the door. They drop to the ground and cover their heads.

L-Chubbs pulls the pin and tosses the grenade between the door and the filing cabinet. He sprints, dives on the ground. Joining Tiph and Deon on the far side. For a long moment, nothing happens—maybe it is a fake? Or a dud.

But the grenade explodes. Metal from the filing cabinet flies everywhere. Smoke clears, and the door is gone. They run through the smoke and ash, back down a hall where they find Davey using a kitchen knife to cut the zip ties that bind his hands. He manages to get his hands free as the trio storms into the kitchen. Deon grabs him and body slams him. Davey's nose breaks on the kitchen floor.

"Damn, man, that was some Ultimate Warrior shit," says L-Chubbs.

Tiph grabs a fire extinguisher from the kitchen and heads back to the art room while Deon and Chubbs put fresh zip ties on Davey.

Chapter Eighty-Four

Jody

Hidden in the clump of western hemlocks, Jody has been watching Roller's property the whole day. No one has come or gone. Jody walked up and down the road. He explored the adjacent property and found a way to get onto the grounds without going through the gate. He's contemplating sneaking in to have a look around. By dusk, he still hasn't made a decision yet. A box truck passes Jody on the road and heads toward Roller's property. It stops at the gate. The driver must have entered a code or called the house because the gate opens. Jody watches the truck enter the property. This could be a truck bringing humans. Or picking up humans to transport elsewhere.

Jody contemplates his next move. Should he sneak onto the property on foot? Or wait here? The property is expansive. If he sneaks in on foot and is deep on the grounds when the truck leaves, he won't be able to get back to his own vehicle in time to follow it.

He decides to wait here, but not with any confidence. Acid swirls in his belly like suds in a washing machine.

Two hours later the same truck approaches the gates to leave. Jody had once let a truck full of women and children go. He isn't going to do it again. He stays low and tiptoe-sprints across the tree line.

As the truck gets to the end of the driveway, it has to stop for the gate to open. As the gate swings open, Jody runs and sticks his gun right in the open window of the driver's side. A lanky Black guy at the wheel. In the passenger seat, a Black woman.

"Put on the brake." Jody waves the gun at the driver's temple. "Do it."

The driver puts on the parking brake.

"What's in the truck?" Jody asks.

"Nothin'," the man says.

"Fuck you. Keep your hands in the air. Okay, now, sir, you first, slowly get out. Ma'am, stay there with your hands on the dashboard."

The man complies, gets out. He's tall and wiry. His shirt reads Current.

"Keep your hands in the air."

Jody pulls a Glock from the man's waistband.

"What's in the truck?" Jody repeats.

"Nothin'," the man repeats.

"Walk to the other side." Jody needs to get him on the same side as the woman. "Good. Now get down on the ground. On your stomach."

The man complies. Jody aims the gun at the woman in the passenger seat. "Get out. Slowly."

The woman gets out, keeps her hands in the air.

"Do I gotta search you for a gun?"

"I don't got a gun."

"Show me your waist."

She raises her shirt an inch. Twirls. No way she has a gun on her. "What's in the back, ma'am?"

"Nothing."

"You stay on the ground," Jody threatens the man. "Lady, I need you to come open the back of this truck for me."

"All right."

Jody keeps his head on a swivel between the woman and the man.

The woman lifts the roll-up door.

Jody first glimpses a tied-up man, and for a brief moment, he's sure the whole truck is full of bound, trafficked human beings. But as the door goes up, he sees the tied-up man is being held up—held hostage—by a Ninja Turtle–shaped man holding an automatic weapon pointed right at Jody. "Drop the little pistol, white boy."

Jody raises his gun at the man. He doesn't have a shot because of the bound hostage. Plus his gun is outmatched. Not to mention the high ground this man has.

"Drop the pistol!"

Jody drops his gun. He stares at the truck. It's filled with wrapped objects, maybe paintings, not people.

The guy with the automatic weapon lets the bound hostage fall to the metal floor of the box truck. He leaps down, comes right at Jody and hits him with the butt of his gun. Right in Jody's jaw. Jody lands on his back. Pain shoots through his limbs. Looks up to see a boot hit him in the face. It's the other Black man who ran over to help. Jody tries to cover his face and curl up into a protective ball as the two guys show no sign of relenting.

"Stop. Wait."

The two men stop. But continue towering over Jody. The woman joins them, looking down at him.

"Thought I recognized you. You Jody?"

Jody wonders if being Jody is good or bad. The situation can't get worse. "Yeah."

The woman turns to the other two men. "He all right. He's not after us or the stuff."

She offers a hand and pulls Jody to his feet. Jody has no idea who this woman is and how she knows him.

As Jody stands, everything from his feet to his face hurts, but he doesn't think anything's broken. He wipes blood from his lip onto his sleeve.

"Bring him over," the woman says. The guy with the automatic weapon nods to his counterpart. The tall wiry guy goes over to the truck and pulls out the bound man. He lifts him, brings him over, dumps him on the ground between the four of them.

Now the moonlight casts a glow on the bound man's face. Davey Richards.

The woman points to Davey. "We were gonna dump his ass, tied up, in Big Sur. To give us enough time to get south. But maybe you want'm?"

"Uh, yeah," Jody manages to say.

"Okay," she says. "We're out. Good luck."

The woman and the two men climb back in the U-Haul truck.

The U-Haul truck drives off into the night. Leaving Jody with Davey Richards, who's wrapped up at his feet like a gift. Jody rips off the duct tape from his mouth.

"Is Roller here?" Jody asks, aiming his pistol at Davey's nose.

"No."

"You remember me?"

"No."

"I was in Solana Beach that night, on the sailboat with those surfers." Jody sees the recognition in Davey's eyes now. "Where'd you take those women and kids?"

"I don't know what you're talking—"

Jody interrupts him by pistol-whipping him in the face. He shoves the gun up against Davey's temple. "Where are they?"

Davey talks fast, sputtering. "C'mon, man, that was a few weeks ago. That wasn't even this batch. They're already gone. They're gone, man. They're gone."

"Gone where?"

"Overseas. Fishing boat."

No. The woman with the gap in her teeth. The boy with the harmonica. The girl with the Barcelona T-shirt. Jody tries to focus, but he keeps picturing their faces.

"Wait, you said that wasn't this batch. What does that mean? There are women and kids, what, here?"

"No."

"Don't lie to me."

"C'mon, man. I'm not lying."

"If there are no women and kids, you're no use to me. I'll just kill you now. Close your eyes."

"C'mon, man."

"Close your eyes. I can't do this with your eyes open."

"Hold on, hold on, hold on. I'll take you to them."

Jody cuts off the zip ties around his feet but leaves Davey's hands zip-tied behind his back. He follows Davey down the road as the pitched roof of a Victorian house comes into view.

They enter through the front door, head through the foyer toward the kitchen. Jody stops when he spots puddles next to a door. "Hold on."

Jody opens the closet. Inside, there are two twentysomething blond women, tied to a water pipe. In trying to escape, they must've cracked the pipe.

"Jesus Christ." Jody takes the tape off one of their mouths. "You're okay," Jody says. "I'm going to get you outta here."

"Get us out of here? Davey, get these ropes off me," says one of the two women.

"How long have you been a prisoner here?" Jody asks.

"I live here. Those thieves tied us up."

Jody puts the duct tape back over her mouth. "Sorry," he says before he closes the closet door.

He looks back to Davey. "Where are they?" Jody follows Davey out the back door. "They're on the property? Right now?"

"Yeah. I'm taking you there."

"You better not be lying."

"I'm not lying. It's a ten-to-fifteen-minute walk though."

"We can get to know each other," says Jody. They cross the backyard. "Tell me about Roller. The operation. Start at the beginning. How he got into trafficking people."

Davey hesitates but when Jody raises the gun, he starts talking. "In the nineties, early 2000s, he was a big deal in Humboldt County.

In the *green rush*, he got an edge 'cause he bought everyone's else's allotment. Word got around, if you didn't want to grow your own, sign up, Roller's guys would come in, grow it, pick it, kick back a portion of profit to you. Christmas present from him to everybody in Humboldt who didn't wanna be a farmer. I mean, yeah, he had illegal grow houses too, but it was getting the legit pot from a few hundred people that gave him an edge. Plus, Roller had the connections to Los Angeles. Other growers were trying to piecemeal it to buyers in towns in NorCal, Oregon, and Washington State. But Roller was selling in bulk. For years, he had the market. But then wholesale folks in LA started getting weed from the cartels. Even before it got legalized, the writing was on the wall. Roller knew his heyday had passed. After the LA market prices fell off, this was maybe seven, eight years ago, Roller started selling product to this guy in the Czech Republic. Went on a fishing vessel across the Pacific, through Asia. Long trek, but there was a growing demand in Eastern Europe. For a while anyway, but then they started getting it from Afghanistan. But he's still friendly with the guy over there, and he tells Roller what he really needs is *people*."

"To be trafficked?" Jody asks.

"Yeah. Roller constantly had these girls crashing in the house. Eureka? Humboldt County? This place is like a magnet for drifters. People from Oregon or California, Midwest, East Coast. Young types hear about a place in California where you could grow weed legally. Drifter folks, runaways, addicts, they flock here. Still do now. But before? When it was the only place to grow legally? Shit, they came in droves. Hippie girls with names like Dandelion who wanted to say *fuck the man*. No one knew or cared where they came from. People came and went like an amusement park. Like Vegas. So anyway, Roller hears from his guy in the Czech Republic about buying women. There are these two girls staying with him. He ships them to the CR and just tells everyone the girls went to Florida. Nobody even blinked. So that's what he did. A year of that. But occasionally you'd have the aunt from New Mexico, the best friend, the old lover who comes to town asking questions. So

Roller had to call it quits. Folks in Czech Republic think he's playing hardball, start offering twice the price per head. So Roller goes down to LA and meets with the guy who used to buy all his weed."

"Chester Montgomery."

"Yup."

They get to a tree line in the backyard. Davey motions toward a path into the woods, all still part of Roller's property. Black-capped chickadees fly between branches above them. They all seem to be calling out *sweetie, sweetie.*

"Chester . . . ," says Jody, urging him to keep going.

"Yeah, so Roller gets Chester to work essentially the same strategy in SoCal. Find the girls and kids nobody'd miss. Illegal immigrants. People who fled one place, just arrived to another. They worked that for two straight years. Truckloads of women and kids, up the 101, onto our fishing boat, and over to Asia and Europe. They had the operation down. But however in the cracks these people were, there was always somebody looking for them."

"Like Salvatore Jenkins."

"Yeah, exactly. So Chester and Roller were both getting worried they're playing with fire, gonna get burned. Chester had this friend in a cartel in Sinaloa from his weed-importing days. The cartel had a side gig. For a thousand bucks, they'd get you to the USA. Tunnels, boats, coyotes, however. So Chester cuts a deal with the cartel to bring him women and kids. The cartel didn't charge us much 'cause they were already getting paid by the women and kids. There was an endless supply. Trip after trip. All by boat, right to Solana Beach."

"And you picked them up in your cube truck."

Davey nods. And there's a cockiness to his swagger. Does he have an agenda? Jody grabs Davey, puts the gun to his temple. "If you're not taking me to the women . . ."

"I'm taking you there."

Jody shoves Davey forward and keeps following him. They get to a ravine. Jody follows Davey down the switchbacks. His knees and ribs ache from getting kicked and punched by the men from the cube truck, but he ignores the pain.

"The surfers, were they the only ones?" Jody asks.

"No. We have three or four crews working for us. Some fishermen. A couple other groups. A couple liberal hippies from New England. None of the crews knew about the other. The beauty of the whole operation was no one knew. The women and kids thought they were going across the border to live the American dream. And the crews sailing them up thought they were facilitating that."

"When's the current group going out on this fishing vessel?"

"Four days."

Jody assumes they're going to keep descending the switchbacks, but Davey leads him off the trail where there's a mine opening.

It's slow going because there's no light. Jody uses the flashlight on his phone when necessary, but he doesn't want to kill the battery. After ten minutes of making various turns down different tunnels, they come to a dead end.

"I made a wrong turn," Davey says.

"You're stalling."

"I'm not. I'm used to having more light."

They walk corridor after corridor. Jody recognizes a sharp left turn with a puddle. They've made a loop. He grabs Davey and digs the gun into his ribs. "You're taking me in circles."

"No, I'm not."

Jody punches Davey in the gut. "Last chance."

"C'mon, man, I'm taking you there." Davey leads Jody down another corridor. This time turning right into a chamber they must have missed—whether intentional or not—the last time.

There are metal boxes on the ground. A few cages. But too small for a human. "What are these for?"

"Roller used to collect exotic animals. He got 'em as gifts, sometimes gave 'em as gifts."

Jody is about to threaten Davey again when he hears rustling ahead. They enter another chamber. In front of him are four larger cages. Each cage contains ten to fifteen women and children, about fifty people in all.

"Jesus Christ," Jody mutters.

Jody shines the light from his phone up at the women and kids. The light blinds them. They look malnourished, terrified.

"I'm going to get you help," Jody says to them. No one responds.

Jody pulls out his phone. He'd been waiting for the right moment to bring in the authorities. He knew if Roller got wind of the cops looking into him, he would've gotten rid of these victims. The whole ring would have a chance to hide their tracks.

Now, Jody has the victims right here in front of him. He'll call the state police. Then the FBI. Local police. Press. He's not going to take any chances by having only one party show up.

He makes the first call, but it won't ring. No service. Not surprising, he's underground. "We're going back up to make the calls," he says to Davey. He shines the light from his phone onto Davey's face.

A face with a smile, a smile that gives him away. Jody's chest tightens up, acid coming up his esophagus. Fuck. Davey had come clean about Roller, about the whole operation, his part in it, not out of some guilt-ridden, conscience-relieving spill but because he knew it wouldn't matter. He was drawing Jody to the women and children, yes, but drawing him to an area where he knew his phone wouldn't work.

Jody shoves the gun under Davey's chin. "Is he coming?"

Davey's eyes dance.

"How do you know? Are there cameras down here?"

"You can't make it out in time. He's coming. He knows the mine. And he won't be alone. You're best to walk out of here and surrender. He might let you live."

"How do I know you're not lying?"

"The girls texted him when the thieves came for the art. He was only a couple hours away. There are motion sensor cameras at the opening of the mine. Footage goes right to his phone. He watched us walk in."

Fuck.

"C'mon, man, you going to kill three guys? What do you have in that round? Six? Nine? Do you know the weapons they'll be coming in here with?"

"Shut up."

"You'll die if you don't give up."

Jody hits him in the face with the gun again. Jody puts two layers of duct tape over Davey's mouth.

Jody knows he's fucked. If he dies, leaving aside his own misfortune, these women and children will be shipped off. The human trafficking ring will continue. Everything he's done up to this point will be moot. Everything Marty did will be moot. Everything Marty died for will be moot.

If he surrenders, he can't imagine a scenario where the kingpin of a human trafficking ring lets him walk.

It's settled. Can't die. Can't surrender.

He grabs Davey's right arm, keeping his gun in his shooting hand, and walks forward. Off to hunt the men who are hunting him.

He pauses when he gets out of the chamber. He doesn't know these mines. He'll be at a disadvantage if he goes and tries to find them. He should wait for them to come to him.

Jody turns his phone on and puts it on the ground on the far side of the chamber. The phone lights the chamber's entrance. Jody pulls Davey back behind a sheet of rock on the other side.

And waits.

Fifteen minutes later, he hears the sounds of footsteps.

He sees the gun first. A semiautomatic rifle. It rounds the corner, followed by the man carrying it. It's not Roller. Must be one of his guys. He has a circular barbell septum nose ring. The man spots the phone on the ground, guesses it's a diversion, and swings his head and gun around to the other side of the chamber, Jody's hiding spot. He fires.

Jody fires back. Hits him in the chest. The man falls, drops the weapon. He's still moving.

Jody steps out now. "How many more are there?"

The man ignores him and tries to roll on his side to reach his weapon.

"Don't reach for it. Don't do it, man."

The wounded man uses what seems like the last bit of energy in his life to pick up the gun. Jody aims, this time for the man's head, and fires. The man again drops the gun. Now motionless.

Jody needs the gun. It's fifteen feet away in the middle of the chamber. He's halfway to the weapon when he hears footsteps followed by gunfire. He gets a glimpse of another gunman, this one a tall bearded man holding a shotgun, as he turns and scrambles back to his safehold behind the sheet of rock.

The man unloads into the cave wall. Jody sneaks a glance. The guy is popping to his left, taking a shot, and returning for cover.

Jody has four bullets left. The next time he hears the shotgun blast, he sneaks a quick glance and pulls back in time to avoid getting shot in the face. The man is hiding behind a rock outcropping, but his left foot is exposed.

The shotgun blasts pick away at the sheet of rock offering Jody some semblance of cover. He can't last forever.

He picks his moment. Right after the guy fires, he pops out, aims at the man's left foot. The bullet hits his left shin and causes that leg to give out, and the man staggers to his left from behind the rock outcropping. Exposed. Jody fires the rest of his bullets, aiming for the man's center. One of them must have struck his heart. He falls.

Jody runs out from behind his crevice of cover and grabs both guns—the semiautomatic rifle and the shotgun—and runs back to cover. He catches his breath and waits. Ten minutes go by before he hears footsteps approaching.

"You in there? Quaker? Floyd?"

This must be Roller. When it came to the two other guys, Jody had little reason not to kill them. But he must keep Roller alive. As a captured prisoner, his arrest could lead to more arrests. Could lead to the dismantling of a global human trafficking ring that transcends his Northern California existence. Keeping Roller alive means a greater chance of rescuing the truckful of women and children that had gotten away from him in San Diego.

The footsteps draw closer. Roller doesn't ask again for Quaker or Floyd. The footsteps stop outside the chamber. Roller must see the two dead bodies.

"I got ten more guys coming in. I know you're here. Come on out."

If he had ten more guys coming, he'd've sent them in and waited outside the mine.

"All right. I'll come out."

"Drop the guns first."

"Okay."

Jody throws the shotgun and the semiautomatic rifle out into the middle of the dark chamber.

"I'm coming out," Jody says.

Jody pushes Davey forward. With his hands zip-tied behind his back, it looks like a man holding a gun behind his back. Bullets rip into Davey, and he falls to the ground. Jody stays hidden behind the sheet of rock.

Roller waits a moment, and when the body doesn't move, he emerges from behind the outcropping and inches toward "Jody's" dead body. Roller bends to make sure he's dead. And when he gets low enough and realizes it's not Jody, it's too late.

Jody stands over Roller, his empty pistol to the man's temple.

"Drop your gun."

Roller drops his automatic gun. Jody snatches the weapon and shoves his empty pistol in his waistband. Keeps the loaded gun on Roller.

"Who are you?" asks Roller.

"Jody."

Jody pulls zip ties from his backpack, binds Roller's hands.

"I was the one who ordered your brother's hit. So it was me. I killed Marty."

It's tempting to put a bullet in the man's head, to exercise vengeance. But Jody can sense Roller's desperation. His dread of going to prison. He's looking for a way out. Suicide by cop. Or in this case, suicide by amateur sleuth.

Jody won't give him a way out. But for good measure, he does pistol-whip Roller in the face. "Stop fucking talking. We're walking out of here."

As the women and children are loaded into ambulances, a new vehicle seems to arrive every minute. Police. FBI. DEA. Paramedics. Firefighters. Local police keep the news vans outside the perimeter. A news helicopter circles overhead. Amid the flashing lights of the jurisdictional nightmare, Jody's mind goes to Pen, how he couldn't have gotten here if her strange crusade hadn't intertwined with his own journey.

Jody approaches a couple of women who are being loaded into an ambulance. "Renata? Was there a Renata in the cell?"

An FBI Agent steps forward. "Jody, they'll be plenty of time to get answers."

"Please. Just ask."

The FBI agent talks to a few of the women before she returns to Jody. "There wasn't a Renata with them."

Jody figured. But he had to check.

Chapter Eighty-Five

Renata

Renata feels the shake of an earthquake, and she opens her eyes. Coral is shaking her.

"Food," says Coral. A man has arrived to the animal-cage-like cell where Renata and Coral have been imprisoned for a couple of weeks. He comes by most days and brings bread and juice. The rest of the group came across the border in an effort to immigrate to the United States. Several were brought by three American surfers in a boat. Others came in a tunnel. When they got across, they were all loaded in a box truck and told they were being taken to a bus station in San Diego. None had any idea they were being abducted. The others weren't blindfolded when they were brought in here. They tell Renata they're in a mine.

No food or water comes the next day. But the day after that, four men instead of one arrive. All holding guns. Renata, Coral, and the other women and children get escorted across a property and loaded in a box truck. From there, the truck drives out to a closed meditation retreat along the coast. The men take them in a rowboat out to an anchored fishing vessel.

Based on the forty-one days they're in a hidden crawlspace in the back of the cargo hold, Renata and Coral assume they're crossing the Pacific Ocean. The compartment is hot and crowded. Canned food and water gets dropped into the compartment a few times per week. When it rains, water leaks in through a crack from above. But the women figure out how to collect and store it, which allows them to bathe and store extra drinking water. During a three-day storm, they're sure the ship will capsize, but it doesn't.

On day forty-one, they're brought onto a dock by six Asian police officers. For a brief moment, Renata thinks they're being rescued, but when the officers separate the women from the children, it becomes clear these men are another rung of the criminal ladder. One mother and son cry and scream as they are dragged apart by the men with guns. Renata and Coral are placed with the other women.

The women are blindfolded and loaded in a cargo railcar. A few hours later, they're unloaded and escorted into a building where they're locked inside a former operating room that hasn't been used for at least a decade. There are sixteen young women in all being kept in the locked room.

They're given food most days, and mostly, they're left alone. A man starts bringing heroin. Many of the girls take the drugs. Renata doesn't know if they were already addicted or happy to escape into a new addiction. Coral is tempted to try it, but Renata talks her out of it.

Two days later, a bad batch of heroin kills four girls. The other twelve young women have to sit with the deceased girls for twenty-four hours. Finally two men wheel in a gurney. They've piled three of the dead girls up on the gurney, and they're about to lift the fourth when the smaller man's phone rings. The two guys jog out of the room, locking it on their way out.

For a moment, Renata stares at the four dead girls, wondering who their parents were and what their favorite flavor of ice cream was. She pictures herself and Coral as two of the dead girls stacked atop each other. The despairing image leads to a hopeful idea, and Renata reaches over and shakes Coral awake. "I have a plan. We gotta go fast though."

Coral follows Renata over to the gurney.

"One of us climbs in. Under her." Renata motions to a larger woman who's piled atop two of the other dead women.

"What?!" Coral asks.

"Regresáran. They'll come back. They will put the fourth girl on top, they'll put on the sheet, and then they'll take them out."

"Out *where?*"

"I don't know."

"It might work," says Coral. "We can't both fit in there."

"No. Only one of us. You go."

"Are you sure?"

"Yes."

"I'll come back for you."

"I know."

Renata made the offer to be nice. Because she cares about Coral. Because she wants Coral to survive. And because she's scared of doing it herself.

Coral looks over to see the women staring at them, wondering what they're going to do. "They won't say anything," says Renata.

Renata lifts up the top body, the flesh cold and heavy. The woman's eyes flutter open when she's moved. Renata thinks of Santa Muerte and looks away. Coral climbs in between the top two bodies. Renata lets go of the top woman. If they're looking for it, they'll notice there are four women already piled up instead of three.

"What do you think?" Coral asks, her voice lowered by the mass of the corpse on top of her.

Before Renata can answer, she hears a whistle from the far end of the room. Renata lies back down on her pillow as the two men return to the room, to the fourth dead girl. They *one-two-three* lift her up and pile her atop the other bodies. They wheel the gurney out of the room.

The woman who whistled stares at Renata, showing a little teeth. A little smile. A little bit of hope. Renata puts a palm to her heart and mouths, *Gracias*.

Renata struggles to sleep the next two days. When she does, she dreams of soldiers rescuing the women. In one dream, Coral is herself decked out in a lieutenant's uniform, leading the raid that rescues her.

But each day that passes, Renata loses hope Coral is coming back for her. Each day that passes, she loses hope Coral made it out alive.

Three weeks later, Renata and the other ten women are taken from the hospital room and loaded into the back of a shipping container sitting on a truck. The men angrily count and recount the women, each time landing at eleven. Renata knows this means they didn't catch Coral three weeks ago. But she doesn't know whether Coral got away. Maybe the bodies were incinerated, and Coral was burned to death.

After a couple days, the container gets moved from the truck—maybe to a boat or maybe to another truck. On some days, water and food get dropped down a hatch. At a certain point, Renata knows they're on a ship. Several women get seasick. Vomit joins the two-inch layer of sludge on the bottom of the container. Renata keeps her eyes closed, breathes through her mouth, meditating on the desire to no longer be alive.

The seasickness subsides, and they seem to be driving on a truck again. They're brought out by three guards who all look European. They're hosed off and given soup. They're given new clothes. Dresses and pairs of jeans and tank tops. Renata gets the sense the journey across the globe is over, but she still doesn't know what's next. So much of the world she might have seen if only she hadn't been inside a box. Four hours later, Renata hears gunfire. Several guards rush into the hallway outside the cell. They take cover and fire back.

The women all duck and crouch. Renata peeks out and sees men with guns storming the building. Are they cops, dirty cops, soldiers, mercenaries, Santa Muerte worshippers, wingless angels sent from God, or just a pack of thieves working for a rival outfit?

Chapter Eighty-Six

Jody

Jody sleeps for twelve hours the night he gets back to Los Angeles. When he wakes up in the morning, he stays in bed for another thirty minutes, lounging for the first time since he came home with a re-filled tank of gas for the grill and found his brother and father murdered.

After the authorities showed up at Roller's place, the FBI brought Jody to a field office in San Francisco. A newly assembled task force interviewed Jody for three days straight, asking about Chester, Roller, Marty, Penelope, and Renata. The information flowed down a one-way street; Jody asked questions but got few answers back. When he pressed them on Renata, they did tell him that according to Roller, Renata wasn't initially shipped because Marty was snooping around and asking questions. Their whole model had been selling women and children no one was looking for. Apparently they held Renata for several months in a cell with a woman who had a bunch of tattoos—if a woman or kid had recognizable birthmarks or tattoos, the ring waited to make sure a missing person report wasn't circulated that mentioned those identifying marks. But according to Roller, by way of the FBI, he was thinking of cashing out and moving to South America, so Renata got shipped off and sold overseas. When the FBI task force was done interviewing him on the third day, Jody asked what would happen next. The man running the task force said that was classified. Jody asked about the possibility of a mole in the FBI, and he said they were looking into it, but Jody suspects they'll never figure it out. One of the younger field agents escorted Jody down afterward.

In the elevator, she said, "Look, I get you feel like you're in the dark. I can't tell you exactly what's happening. But generally speaking, in an event like this, you lean into the arrested individual, get them talking, try to move up the chain as high as you can as fast as you can, ya know, crack as much of the ring as possible without giving too much time for the word to spread, and then you work with other governments and you try to do simultaneous raids across multiple continents, make as many arrests as possible, and hope to set free as many victims as possible."

After that, Jody had gone back to LA. And climbed into bed.

So many mornings over the last few months he'd woken up thinking about his murdered brother and father. This morning, he woke up thinking about Marty, about how proud he is of Marty. Even as he died, his brother wasn't asking Jody to help him; he was asking Jody to help Renata.

Jody finally gets out of bed at 10:45 a.m. He goes and eats a breakfast burrito and tries to think about what he'll do next. In his time in LA, he'd now been around enough actors, directors, producers, and executives to know the TV version of his life would mean this was just the beginning, his backstory of how he became a private investigator. And now he'd go on to solve hundreds of cases, around one per week, except over the summer, and occasionally the cases would tap into an element of his backstory, whether emotional or logistical. But in this world, the non-TV version of his life, Jody can't imagine what he'll do next. He takes a few days to think on it, resisting the urge to make a giant list of all the possibilities. He contemplates going back to Pennsylvania, but he knows he'll stay in California. On day two of contemplation, he lands on San Luis Obispo.

Jody tries to see a couple of people before he leaves LA. Nicole asks to borrow his truck for a couple of hours and doesn't come back. Jody assumes he'll get it at some point. He stops by Mount Washington and updates Travis. He reaches out to Pen, hoping to see her before he leaves. They exchanged a series of texts when she first got out of the hospital, but now her phone number is disconnected. He wishes he could see her one more time, thank her one more time. If she hadn't been sitting on his truck bed when he got back from that hike in Anza-Borrego, Jody might never have finished what his brother started.

And then there's Shiloh. He considers calling her. He considers stopping by her apartment. He thinks about the letters Marty wrote him all those years. And he decides to write a letter to Shiloh. Not an email, but a real, old-fashioned letter.

Dear Shiloh—

I hope this finds you doing okay. So many times, I've wanted to reach out to you, but I wanted to respect your wishes. I thought I should stay out of your life. I wanted you to have a normal life or whatever life that you want.

The me you knew was always trying to finish what my brother had started. But it's finished, Shiloh. It is. I'm glad we spent this time apart. There was always some fear I was latching on to you out of a desire to maintain a connection with Marty. But now I've found connections with Marty. A whole conspiracy. An investigation. A three-month tour of California. I've seen the whole state. I've seen the dream and the nightmare of it all. The beautiful and the dirty.

It had sort of become me, trying to crack this whole thing. And now that it's done, for the first time in a long time, I'm starting to think about what I want. When I was on that tour of California, I was out of sorts, but I saw a house in San Luis Obispo for sale. And something about San Luis Obispo made me think I could have another life there. SLO is what they call it. And it feels like what I need right now. The last year has been fast. And slow sounds good.

I don't know what this new life will be, but I'd like to try that life with you.

I could see you there with me. Us living in a house. Making meals. Walking. Raking leaves. And making each other laugh. I know you haven't seen *me laugh much. My dad used to make me laugh. I like laughing. I don't know what we'd do for work. But we'd figure it out. My dad's dad, my granddad, worked in a steel mill in Coatesville. He married my grandmother when he was twenty-two and she was nineteen, and they had exactly nineteen dollars. And they didn't know anything. They started a life and figured it out. I think about that sometimes.*

Maybe this is too much, going from not talking to seeing if you want to move to San Luis Obispo together. But the last time I saw you, you answered the door in that weird pajama onesie thing, and it made me think about you older and married, but not to me. I couldn't put myself in that scenario because I was so wrapped up in it all, so it was you and some other guy, just a silhouette of a guy. But when I picture it now, it's me who's with you.

I'm headed there in a week. On Friday. Taking the Surfliner up the coast. (Rory's never been on a train!) Meet me at Union Station if you'd like to come. It's the 3:55 Amtrak Surfliner to San Luis Obispo.

No pressure to join me if it's not what you want. No pressure to write back. I hope this finds you well. I love you. I know I do.

Sincerely,
Jody

Jody doesn't hear back from Shiloh. Had the old-fashioned letter gotten lost in the mail? Or maybe she hadn't checked the box? He resends it as an email. But he still doesn't hear from her.

Moving across the terra-cotta tiles of the train station, Jody remembers something Marty said in one of his videos. "Walking through Union Station, you get a little taste of everyone in California. The brown, the Black, the white, the yuppies, the hipsters, the tourists, the young, the old, the desperate, the employed, the hustlers, the homeless, and the dream seekers."

As he waits on the platform, Jody convinces himself maybe Shiloh's running late. Maybe she forgot something or got stuck in traffic. He waits an extra hour and forty-five minutes until the 5:35 train. At

5:32, he sends her a text message, double-checking she wasn't planning on meeting him. She doesn't text him back.

The Amtrak Surfliner snakes its way up the coast. The push-pull trainsets, diesel locomotive, and well-maintained tracks make for a smooth ride. Jody feels present in a way he hasn't in a long time. His feet feel hot, dank. The iced tea chills his throat. He notices himself noticing himself. As the train hugs the shore, cutting inland when necessary, he spots waves he'd like to ride and trails he'd like to hike. He pictures Shiloh, and a calm washes over him. His love for her holds pure—void of ego, narcissism, insecurities, jealousies, and *obsession*. At different times of his life, his OCPD had wreaked havoc on anything important to him because of his inclination to obsess. He's not obsessed with Shiloh; he loves her. He suspects she's happy, and that is calming.

Even though it'll be alone, he's ready for the next chapter in San Luis Obispo.

Chapter Eighty-Seven

Tiph

Tiph sits in the middle of the box truck's bench seat between the two guys as L-Chubbs drives the U-Haul truck south down the 101. It's the middle of the night. They drive with the windows down, the fresh ocean breeze keeping them awake.

She looks at the white stars and the white caps as they drive down the coast. And she thinks about Mike. And she smiles. *I did it. We did it.*

She thinks about all the struggles, the times she almost quit. The dead ends. Leaving behind that wine. That empty storage unit. It's like all those low points have stacked up to form a hill, and she's standing atop that hill, queen of the mountain.

No one has spoken for a few minutes. Tiph breaks the silence with a wild yell. Philly D and L-Chubbs echo her hoot with hollers, and now they're all three screaming into the salty night air as the box truck full of treasure flies down the 101.

And for the hundredth time in as many days, Tiph considers what she'll buy with all the money. Disneyland annual passports for her, Mike, and Gary. One of those virtual-reality videogame consoles for Mike. A new Huffy bike for Gary. A house in Baldwin Hills if only to stop the "Black Beverly Hills" from becoming white Beverly Hills II. A pool for their house. She'll buy dinners for her and Mike at all their favorite restaurants. They'll go out twice a week rather than once a month. She'll buy some nice lingerie since Mike's always asking her to buy *fancy panties*. And she'll let him buy the fancy weed to go along with them. She'll invest money in stocks she won't touch, stocks she'll eventually use to pay for Gary to go to college. And each year, the three of them will go on a family trip.

She pictures the moment she'll first have the cash, what it will feel like to have that money, to have the security of that much money. Which leads her to wonder how she'll move the art. She had spent so much time thinking about how to get this art, and she had spent so much time getting the art. She has the art now. But how the hell is she going to sell it?

Fuck it, she'll figure it out. And if she can't, Scheming Mike will come up with a plan.

Chapter Eighty-Eight

Pen

For the second day in a row, Pen approaches the teal house on Maricopa Drive. Yesterday, after she had found the stump and the ivy-covered stone lions, she knocked but no one answered. There were flyers from restaurants from weeks ago. The layer of dust caked on the front door suggested it hadn't been opened for months.

After leaving the house, Pen went to the Central Library downtown and researched the house on the computers. The owners disappeared three years ago and multiple parties have since claimed they own the property. The competing claims have resulted in a pending lawsuit. The house was built in the 1920s with permitted work being done every decade.

Today, Pen has returned, this time to enter. After making sure no one's around on the street, she heads into the backyard. A rotting back door has been boarded shut. But next to it, there's a window. Pen reaches up, and she tries sliding the window. It slides open. Pen cuts out the small screen with a pocketknife. She brings over a rusted folding chair she finds beneath a willow tree. She's able to pull herself up and into the house. She turns on her flashlight. It looks like someone might have been squatting here, perhaps before the back door was boarded up. In the bedroom, there's a mattress on the floor. A bureau with drawers and a mirror atop it. She checks the closet. Wallpaper and hangers. She searches the living room and the kitchen. It's not a large structure. Within seven or eight minutes, she's searched the whole house.

She had been sure this was Pandora's House. She keeps cycling through the rooms. Looking in every crevice. Under the couch. She shoves the fridge aside. But she finds no evidence there's any more to this house than meets the eye. Hours go by, Pen retracing every inch. Tears seep out as the doubt seeps in, as she thinks through the math. Of course if she looked at every house in Glassell Park, she was bound to find a house with stone lions. And maybe the stump was a California black walnut, but maybe it wasn't. And she had talked herself into teal being blue enough. All she can think about is a patient named Luther who she met in Norwalk who kept telling her the definition of insanity was doing the same thing over and over again but expecting a different result. Wasn't that what she'd been doing her whole life? One endless loop. She heads to the front door, wondering if Chelsea will take her back, but she stops.

Get back on the bike. One more time. She'll look through the house one more time.

She goes from kitchen to living room to back hallway. In the bedroom, she shines her light in the closet, sees it's empty. She's about to walk away when she sees the mushroom wallpaper design. *Mushrooms.* Fay had mentioned mushrooms. Pen shines her light on the wallpaper. She feels along the closet's back wall. She spots a metal sliding track at the base. She pushes left, and the whole back of the closet shifts as part of a sliding door. On the other side of the camouflaged sliding door is a hefty iron door. Pen pushes. The door opens outward, creaking with every inch, and beyond the door is a winding limestone stairwell. A hint of bluish light, a cerulean glow, comes from below. Pen pauses for a fraction of a second, long enough to think, *This is it.* She shines her light down and descends the stairwell.

Chapter Eighty-Nine

Renata

Renata watches the surfers at the Pismo Beach Pier for the second day in a row.

After being rescued in Prague, she was extradited back to the United States, where she was told she would be deported to Mexico. A day later, an FBI agent came to her and told her their department had intervened. They asked her to share her experiences with a human trafficking task force. They gave her hospital care and daily sessions with a psychologist to help Renata cope with the trauma she'd endured.

In her second week in the United States, she was given a laptop. She checked her old social media accounts and an email address. While poking around online for the first time since she left Mexico, she went to Instagram and typed in *Coral Anderson*. There were fourteen accounts. She clicked through them, hoping one would be her Coral. One was a young woman who said she lived in the Netherlands. Her profile picture was of a sunset. Renata was about to click off the profile, assuming it couldn't have been her Coral, when she saw a tagline beneath the profile picture. *Renata, if you're out there, message me.*

The next day, the two were on Skype. They stared into cameras and cried. Coral told Renata what happened. The day they smuggled her out in that pile of opioid tragedy, she was loaded in a truck and taken to a warehouse. She slipped out. She was chased and to escape, she jumped in a river. She was swept miles downriver and nearly drowned. An old woman took her in and nursed her back to health and got her over the border to Germany. From there, she traveled to Amsterdam, where she's been living. She and the woman who saved her reported the closed hospital to the police but they heard back that it was empty.

On their Skype call, Renata told Coral she could help get Coral back to the United States and similar treatment and payment through the FBI, but Coral told Renata she was happy, happy for the first time in her life and didn't want to jinx it.

After being granted citizenship, Renata moved to Los Angeles, where she got an apartment in Echo Park. She started working at Woodcat Coffee and taking classes at Los Angeles Trade-Tech College. She joined a coed soccer team. She met a group of friends, and they went to bars, played board games, and even went to Disneyland one weekend. The nightmares still haven't stopped, and she can't walk in a closet or small bathroom without having a panic attack, but Renata has crafted a version of life she thinks her parents wanted for her.

Before moving to LA, on her last day talking to the FBI task force, Renata asked to be put in touch with Jody so she could thank him. One FBI agent told her he couldn't give her Jody's contact info. Jody had started getting approached by journalists who were making a true-crime podcast called *My Dirty California*.

The agent added, "I can't tell you his exact address, but he lives in San Luis Obispo, and he often goes surfing at Pismo Beach."

After nearly two years of trying to forget the past, here she is, on a road trip, watching the surfers at Pismo Beach. She sits in the sand twenty yards from the pier, watching the men and women and children in wetsuits paddle and pop up, ride waves with varying levels of grace. A group of men calling it quits for the day pass by towing their boards.

"Excuse me. Do any of you know a man named Jody who surfs here?"

Two of the three men shake their heads and keep going. But the third stops. "I haven't seen him out here in a while. Think he might have moved. He had some of us over for a barbecue like a year ago. He lived in town. It was a little green house, on a corner, across from an elementary school, I think. Cazadero Street."

"Thanks," Renata says.

"But, like I said, I haven't seen him out here, and I heard he moved."

Renata drives the fifteen minutes from Pismo inland to San Luis Obispo. She drives along Cazadero Street. She finds a little green house on a corner. And there's the elementary school kitty-corner to it. She parks and approaches the green house on foot. But as she gets closer, she sees a woman sitting on the porch.

The surfer had said he thought Jody had moved, and it looks like he was right. Renata turns to walk away when the woman calls to her. "Can I help you?"

"No, sorry. I was looking for someone else."

"Who are you looking for?"

"This man named Jody."

The woman stares back with a blank face. Renata can't tell whether she's heard the name. But after a moment, the woman calls through the screen door. "Jody!"

"I'm doing the dishes!" says a male voice from inside, perturbed.

"Someone's asking for you," the woman calls back.

Renata sees a baby in the grass right next to the woman. The baby crawls through the grass, headed for a tire swing hanging from the branch of a coast live oak tree. "Mardi. Stop. C'm'here." The woman jogs over and scoops up the little girl. A brown mutt runs from the backyard into the front yard and stares at Renata.

"Did you say *Marty*?" Renata asks.

"Mardi, with a *d*," the woman says. Renata thinks about Marty. About that game of soccer played under the lights in Mar Vista Park. About the breakfast at the diner they never had. She thinks about a man who had looked for her and had died for it.

As Renata stares at Mardi, the girl's mother must take Renata's silence as confusion over the name. "She was born on a Tuesday's the simplest explanation," she adds. "Anyway, I'm Shiloh, by the way."

Renata is about to speak when a man with a clean-shaven face appears in the doorway. "I told you not to talk to those podcasters," Jody says to Shiloh as he steps out onto the porch.

He looks at Renata. Renata looks back at him.

"What's up?" Jody asks.

"Jody?" Renata asks.

"Yeah?"

"I'm Renata."

Jody puts a hand to his mouth, as if to smother his reaction. On the back of his hand, he has a tattoo that says the name Dori. Tears pool in his eyes.

And it causes tears to pool in her eyes.

She wants to say thank you. She wants to say thank you for what Marty did. She wants to say thank you to Jody for what he did. But she can't seem to say anything.

Acknowledgments

I pondered *My Dirty California* as a possible novel and television series for many years. Stuck inside, I started writing the manuscript in May 2020.

Thank you to my first reader, Josh. And thank you to Jake—our collaborations helped lead me to this novel.

Thanks to David Gernert for championing the book from sale through publication, as well as Ellen and Anna at the Gernert Company.

And to Marysue Rucci for believing in the book and guiding it. Thanks to Sean Manning for his instincts and dedication. Thanks to Erica Ferguson for her expertise and attention to detail. And to the rest of the team at Simon & Schuster, including Brittany Adames, Tzipora Baitch, Ryan Raphael, and Sara Kitchen. A special thanks to fellow Angeleno Hana Park for her ideas and support.

Thanks to Sylvie Rabineau for being patient and strategic.

And finally, thank you to all the Californians who I've met over the last eighteen years, many of whom inspired aspects of the novel.

Do ri.

About the Author

JASON MOSBERG lives in Los Angeles, California, where he works as a screenwriter and TV creator.